When **Kali Anthony** rea[...]
at fourteen she realised t[...]
never be too many happy [...] and that one
day she would write them herself. After marrying
her own tall, dark and handsome hero in a perfect
friends-to-lovers romance, Kali took the plunge
and penned her first story. Writing has been a
love affair ever since. If she isn't battling her
cat for access to the keyboard, you can find Kali
playing dress-up in vintage clothes, gardening or
bushwalking with her husband and three children
in the rainforests of South East Queensland.

Joss Wood loves books, coffee and travelling—
especially to the remote places of Southern Africa
and…well, anywhere. She's a wife, mom to two
young adults, and is bossed around by two cats
and a dog the size of a small cow. After a career
in local economic development and business, Joss
writes full-time from her home in KwaZulu-Natal,
South Africa.

DIAMONDS AND DECEPTIONS

KALI ANTHONY

JOSS WOOD

MILLS & BOON

First published in Great Britain 2026
by Mills & Boon, an imprint of HarperCollins*Publishers* Ltd,
1 London Bridge Street, London, SE1 9GF

www.harpercollins.co.uk

HarperCollins*Publishers*, Macken House, 39/40 Mayor Street Upper, Dublin 1, D01 C9W8, Ireland

ISBN: 978-0-263-41767-8

01/26

MIX
Paper | Supporting
responsible forestry
FSC
www.fsc.org
FSC™ C007454

This book contains FSC™ certified paper and other controlled sources to ensure responsible forest management.

For more information visit www.harpercollins.co.uk/green.

Printed and Bound in the UK using 100% Renewable Electricity at CPI Group (UK) Ltd, Croydon, CR0 4YY

VOWS TO
THE BOSS

KALI ANTHONY

MILLS & BOON

Naz, thank you for the conversations over our endless passion for Presents heroes, romance, these books that make us laugh and cry, and the stories that we're privileged to write. Thank you also for your advice when my characters aren't playing nicely, and helping me convince them to behave (or at least, misbehave in the best possible ways!). Here's to many more years of the magic that is writing these glorious books about love. There could be nothing more joyous than that.

CHAPTER ONE

LEO KNEW IT wasn't *who* you invited to your wedding that was important. It was those you *left off* the guest list that made your wedding an occasion to be talked about. He'd left plenty off his guest list for his wedding today. The writers of magazines and style blogs had estimated the number of guests would be in the many hundreds. They were wrong. Instead, those invited had been chosen strategically, with thought and care. Royalty mingled with commoners, select clients with trusted suppliers. Each invitation sending a message about where Leonardo Zanetti was now placed in the world, who had helped him to get there and where he wanted to be in the future. It was one of the things that made his wedding to Ms Simone Taylor the most talked about of the year.

Leo counted on the talk.

A crucial business deal relied on it. He *would* purchase the Tessitore textile company and in doing so cut the knees from Vito and Rocco Silvestri. Father and son. *His* father and his half-brother. Makers of world-renowned, bespoke furniture that was bought by princes, and coveted and poorly copied by paupers. They were the only ones who mattered to Leo and, when he had his way, they'd never use another metre of Tessitore fabric in their coveted designs, ever again.

A perfect means to avenge his mother's memory, using the father who'd stolen everything from them both. If Vito hadn't done so, Leo's mother would have still been alive.

A cold knife of guilt stabbed through him, lethal as the black ice that had stolen his mother's life all those cruel years earlier. Back then, he was an angry teenager, tired of being impoverished and living hand to mouth on his mother's meagre cleaning wage.

Instead of staying in Milan with her, he'd run to Rome to try and seek his fortune. There, he'd learned painful lessons about what poverty and hunger of the body and spirit *truly* meant.

How easy it was, when you were cold and famished in squalor on the streets and too full of pride to scuttle home with your tail between your legs, to fall in with people who made you feel you were someone else entirely. Powerful and important, when the ugly truth was, you were nothing but fodder for their illegal enterprises.

It turned out that, for a while, crime did pay. Yet not enough for the lifestyle he'd wanted to live. Leo's mother had paid the price of his failure to support her. Leaving a job one winter morning she slipped on the icy stairs. A simple fall, a mundane accident. Yet one with catastrophic consequences.

That was when life as he had known it had ended.

Since then he'd risen like a tainted phoenix from the ashes of his rage and grief.

'Everything okay?' Simone, his executive assistant and now wife, asked.

They'd been at a table mingling with guests who he considered to be some of his few allies in a world of old-money rivals. Amongst people who wanted to tear him down for the temerity of coming from nothing and making something of himself. This wedding was as much for work and shoring up alliances as it was for showing the world he'd put aside his playboy single days and 'settled down'. Still, Leo regretted that in his introspection he'd been ignoring Simone.

Whilst they both well knew the purpose of this marriage was business and not pleasure, now wasn't the time to be thinking all about himself. This was her day as much as his. More to the point, failing to focus on her wasn't a good look when they were supposed to be blissfully in love.

The mere thought churned acid in his gut. To Leo, love equalled being used, betrayed and abandoned. He'd learned that lesson well, taught by his father's neglect. Nothing he'd witnessed as an adult had convinced him differently.

'Everything's perfect,' he said. Aside from his dark thoughts that was, but Leo was sure he'd hidden them well enough. He was a master of disguise, after all. 'Why wouldn't it be?'

For good measure Leo threw out his trademark smile. The one that had earned him his first million-dollar pay check at the age of nineteen, after he'd been plucked from the Milan streets by a talent scout in the days after his mother's funeral.

He'd rocketed to the heights as a top model in a viral and now-famed aftershave commercial, which had earned him dizzying amounts of money. Then he walked away from it all and opened his style and design company, Circolo.

A role where he was feted by the rich and famous for his impeccable taste and advice on how they could achieve it for themselves. One which had made him his first billion dollars before he'd turned thirty.

The story told was an old and well-worn one. Seen as the ultimate fairytale every time the press dredged it up. But all Leo could think at the time was that his face and body were finally good for something more than picking up women or inflicting fear on Rome's small business owners.

Simone raised an arched brow and cocked her head. Her silvery gaze should have been cool and assessing. Yet the soft smokiness of her eyes and plush pout of her generous pink lips, so different from the barely-there makeup she usually wore, painted another picture entirely. Her intensity in this moment wouldn't have been out of place in their two-bedroom suite, alone, with both of them contemplating their approaching wedding night.

To hell with the separate bedrooms they'd agreed on…

A shocking heat ignited, settled in his gut, then scorched much lower. Leo schooled his face into neutrality. He was used to hiding his feelings. A skill learned in his modelling days pretending he was basking on a warm summery beach after a cooling swim, when in truth he was wet and freezing in a bitter winter's breeze.

'You have that look. Like something's on your mind,' she murmured.

There was a prickle of recognition. An uncomfortable sensation, like he was being exposed. Simone had an uncanny way of seeing right through him. It's what made her the finest executive assistant he'd ever worked with, being able to anticipate his needs before he even realised what he'd wanted himself. It was enough to give him pause. She didn't need to witness the errant and misplaced desire that suddenly seemed to have overtaken him. It was simply an adjustment period, that was all. Moving from the life of an avowed bachelor with any number of women similarly invested in fun-times-not-a-long-time, to one of a dutifully engaged and then married man, focused on one woman.

It didn't mean anything more. It never could.

'Business is on my mind.'

It wasn't exactly a lie. People believed his life had been charmed but recently, nothing had gone as planned. His efforts to atone for his youthful sins in Rome, finding the families he and the gang he'd run with had harmed, had run into some snags. Unnecessary questions were being asked when all he sought was to keep that part of his life his own, dark secret and repay what was owed to them through an impenetrable trust and charity. Then there was Tessitore, which he was intent on purchasing with single-minded focus. Especially after he'd discovered his father and half-brother were sniffing around, looking to purchase it too.

Simone placed her hand to her chest, her wedding and engagement rings sparkling in the soft candlelight.

'Always about business. On your wedding day too. Such a romantic, my husband.'

Husband. That word whispered through him. The real surprise was that if someone had told Leo a year ago that today he'd be married, he would have said they were deluded. Yet here he was, with a gold ring on his finger, sitting in the opulent ballroom of the finest hotel in New York, *The City That Never Slept.*

He flexed his hand. He'd always thought of a wedding ring as something akin to a noose, but this one sat comfortably snug, gleaming against his skin. To his relief, it was barely noticeable once Simone had slipped it on with cool yet unsteady fingers earlier in the day.

Their MC moved to the microphone. Given Leo had planned the running sheet for today to the last, obsessive detail, he knew this was the announcement of their first dance as husband and wife.

'Let me show you how romantic I can be,' he murmured.

People were listening, after all. Whilst everyone here were supporters, he still needed the talk about this wedding to be the right sort. How Leo Zanetti and Simone Taylor fit together perfectly, not that they presented as a discordant picture. It had been a whirlwind ever since their engagement only a few months before. There'd been no time to display themselves as a 'loving' couple, what with organising New York's wedding of the year, dealing with his concerns in Rome and the long hours trying to secure Tessitore.

The true illusion of their coupledom had meant to start today, and he was already failing. Their conversation seemed stilted, because people were watching and listening, and he was trying to play an unfamiliar part of the doting partner, rather than a casual lover. Leo stood and held out his hand palm up. Simone placed hers in his. Her flesh still cool, but solid and sure. No hint of a tremor now, which he took as a good sign. He led her towards the dance floor to scattered applause, as the band struck up a suitably romantic song.

Leo took Simone into his arms, trying to remember that he should hold her as if she was something precious. Then he gazed down at her as intently as he could and the pupils in her shale-grey eyes flared.

'You look beautiful,' he said. Finally, a truth he could admit. The vintage satin of her one-of-a-kind 1930's wedding gown, like warm liquid underneath his palms. Slipping over her body, slick as oil, teasing his fingertips. When he'd been sleeping rough on the streets of Rome in frigid winters, all he'd dreamt of was silk and softness. Of warm perfumed bodies that would chase away the cold, make him forget the scent of rot and rubbish in the alleyways he'd kept to. Leo pushed away the memory from that time long past. Focusing instead on Simone, because praising your bride's appearance and giving her your undivided attention was the sort of thing you *should* do on her wedding day.

'Thank you. You chose everything, after all.'

Her voice struck him, soft and low. A little more raw than normal. He'd heard her speak a thousand times and yet her tone in this moment shot right through his gut with the punch of an arrow.

From Cupid's bow, some might say.

Not him.

Cupid be damned. He'd seen what love had done to his mother. How she'd been *robbed*. First of her ideas, then of *everything* by his father who'd left them for a woman who could afford to fund him as he chased his stolen dreams. As he took Leo's mother's furniture designs and opened his own business selling her ideas as his own. As he'd cast off his old life like a worn coat and started afresh with a new, wealthier woman.

'I welcomed your involvement,' he said, as they executed a spiral turn. He reeled her back in as he continued. 'Some might even say, *encouraged* it.'

Simone's body pressed against him, even closer than before. They'd had some practice with a dance instructor to ensure they'd look seamless. In those few, short classes everything had felt stiff. Stilted. Yet something about today seemed to have transformed them both. Leo noticed for the first time how Simone fit into his arms like a puzzle piece. Her scent the citrus blossom of an Italian spring. Perhaps it was a leftover from her bouquet of the same flowers? Leo could almost close his eyes and imagine being immersed in it, so intoxicating and achingly familiar.

Instead he took a slight step back, to give them both distance.

'Welcomed? Really? Mr Zanetti giving up his famed control? I don't believe it for a second.' She laughed, yet the sound was a little sharp, tinged with cynicism. He knew that sentiment well, being one of the greatest cynics of them all.

'Surely marriage is all about compromise. My *famed control* wasn't so tight that I didn't offer you any choices.'

He'd been surprised at Simone's strange disinterest in her dress or in any of the plans for the wedding itself. She'd allowed him to have the final decision on everything, including the stylist who did her hair and makeup for the day because, in Simone's words, *that's what you do, Leo.*

'I'm sure each choice was offered through gritted teeth with a firm view on what you saw as the right one,' she said. 'Given that, it seemed easier to allow you to win from the beginning. I prefer to pick my battles. Because as you say, marriage is about compromise.'

There it was again, that spike of sensation at the realisation Simone could read him only too well. When his engagement had been announced, the rumour mill ran riot at his 'surprising' choice of bride. There'd been talk of him marrying just about every one of the many women who had graced his arm at one time or another in the past. Whether they'd been lovers or mere acquaintances, it didn't matter. Socialites, models, movie stars. All polished and perfect when they stepped out with him in public. Never once any mention of the person who was at his side in all ways.

Simone Taylor.

As he'd explained in the inevitable media storm that followed, the woman who he'd worked with closely for two years as his executive assistant, knew him better than any living human on earth. She was, therefore, a natural and inevitable choice. Throw out talk of Simone keeping him 'grounded' and the press lapped up the story of love blossoming in the heady environment of the boardroom like stray cats to milk.

That was the story they'd presented to the world and everyone had believed it, even staff at Circolo who'd been surprisingly happy about the news. The truth was far more practical.

'You *allowed* me? Did I get anything wrong?' he asked.

Most of the time he wouldn't have cared, because he *knew* his choices were right. Even when he offered options, to give the illusion of choice to some of the few clients he still dealt with personally, they always went with his first selection. As Simone had done. Yet with her, there was a strange sensation like a fishbone stuck in his gullet, that drove him to seek her answer.

'You know perfectly well you didn't. They don't call you the Sultan of Style for nothing.'

He'd been called something else, in his youth in Rome. The Handsome Viper. Sent in to 'encourage' small business owners to pay money for protection from imagined enemies, when the true enemy was him and those he worked with. If they didn't pay up? Then others in the gang would be unleashed. In the end, his looks, size and the gang's reputation got the job done and most capitulated.

Most…

He snorted. 'The Sultan of Style's a ridiculous title.'

There was that arched rise of her brow again. That intense look that speared right through him once more. Luckily he wasn't so transparent with Simone that he couldn't hide his greatest sins. She might know a lot about him, but she didn't know it all and he'd do everything in his power to keep it that way.

'But it's good for business and the press loves it. They love you.'

Her hand moved on his shoulder, almost a clench. Some quarters of the press had been unfair and unkind when he and Simone had become engaged in their reported whirlwind romance.

Plain Jane Marries Sultan of Style!

That's what one tabloid had printed and others soon followed. Unimaginative sheep, all of them.

It wasn't that Simone didn't have style. She had one which an uncharitable commentator he would never speak to again, had unfairly termed 'Funeral Director Chic'.

Leo preferred to say she was *businesslike, with a minimalist aesthetic*. Both were descriptions they'd tried seeding to the press but hadn't caught on.

Yet it rankled, a bitter pill he railed against swallowing, especially since she'd politely refused most of his efforts to gift her designer fashion. Though she had accepted a vintage item for their engagement dinner, when he'd told her it was a thrifty choice. Still Simone didn't seem to care about her appearance at all, or want to accept the offer of his credit card to facilitate some choices of her own.

What woman wouldn't want to spend his money? Most others of his acquaintance had and he'd enjoyed sharing it around. He'd never forgotten the cold, hard life he'd come from on the streets, when a little softness might have made a difference. And whilst he didn't care what was printed about him, leaving that to his PR department, he still couldn't help wondering whether Simone wasn't so circumspect about the criticism of her.

'I meant what I said.'

'You've said lots of things.'

'About you, being beautiful.'

Whilst they didn't have *that* sort of relationship, Leo was still driven to repeat his praise. Something about her seemed to light up then, in a way he'd never seen before. Her grey eyes widening a fraction. Her gloss slicked lips, parting. She didn't seem so disinterested now. His heart rate kicked a little higher, as if a world of possibilities had begun to crack open when there were really none, aside from a continuing professional relationship.

'Soon, everyone will see what I can,' Leo said.

It was a promise, and one he'd been working assiduously towards. The exclusive rights to their wedding had been sold to a popular lifestyle magazine with all proceeds donated to charity. They'd see what Simone usually hid. What he glimpsed in this moment. The way the ivory silk of her dress caressed her gentle curves. The fabric sinuous and almost alive as she moved. Her long golden hair not restrained in her usual bun or chignon, but swept back from her face by glittering combs. Tumbling over her shoulders in thick, glossy waves like a forties movie star. Add in the perfect lighting and a world-renowned photographer, and she'd finally be recognised for who she truly was.

Simone Zanetti. His *beautiful* wife.

She looked up at him, with a whisper of pink flushing her cheeks.

'I— Thank you, Leo.'

'My pleasure, *amore mio*.' Given a few guests had been invited to join them on the dance floor he'd tried the words of affection out for size, in the perfect timbre. Loud enough for the people dancing around them to hear. Soft enough to seem intimate.

They'd had no bridal party for their wedding. No one but each other. For him, because he had no family worth inviting. For Simone, it seemed her position was the same.

He was aware of her parents, as he had been with any employee who held a position of trust and importance in his company. She had a wealthy family in California. Her father was from the ivy league. Her mother, a famed socialite. Her brother was a corporate lawyer. She also had a younger sister, who hadn't yet made her way in the world.

When Leo had suggested inviting them all to the wedding she'd refused, for her mother, father and brother at least, saying they were estranged. Her sister, who she'd admitted to him when their arrangement was settled had needed her help, remained a mystery. Something about her health. That was all Simone would say on the subject. His interest had been piqued because there might have been a similarity between them he'd been unaware of before. Although for that very reason he'd let further discussion slide. Simone was entitled to her secrets. Hell knew, he was keeping enough secrets of his own.

No one knew he was the son of Vito Silvestri. Leo would never give his father the satisfaction of acknowledging him in any way.

'*Amore mio*? Isn't that a little…unnecessary,' Simone whispered, jolting him from his thoughts about the man who'd donated his genetic material to Leo's life and nothing else.

Leo leaned forwards, his lips at her ear. What would the guests think? That they were having a tender moment? He hoped so.

'Accept the endearment,' he murmured, his cheek against hers. Simone's breath hitched and something warm and potent slid in his belly like a shot of Grappa.

'What should I call you, then?'

For so long she'd called him Mr Zanetti or Sir. When she finally used his first name, he'd liked the sound of it on her lips. Leonardo. Leo. The way she said it, as if she was savouring each syllable.

'Whatever you want.'

There was a moment of hesitation, almost a misstep in their otherwise synchronous dance.

'What about… Pumpkin?'

Dio. With that one word she could destroy his reputation overnight. Yet the question carried a smile. He could hear it in the light, playful tone of her voice. Leo wished he'd seen it on her face, since her smiles were rare and fragile things more often granted to others, such as juniors in the office who needed encouragement. Most of the time she treated him with bland professionalism.

He chuckled and she pulled back from him grinning. Her eyes twinkled under the chandeliers adorning the room. Her look of mirth burst like a firework in his chest.

He leaned forwards again. His lips now barely touched her ear. The tease of them achingly close, the desire to connect and hear her sigh in pleasure, sang through him. This was not how things were supposed to be, his reactions unfamiliar after two years of them working together in a way that was entirely businesslike.

'Let's stick with *Leo*. Though I can teach you words of love in Italian should you so wish, *cara*.'

A tremor ran through her, like a fault line suddenly cracking. What was he thinking? Simone was a woman who'd been clear about what she'd wanted from him and what she didn't. It had aligned with his views *perfectly*.

He'd rejected any idea of marrying, until his reported playboy past became an impediment to the Tessitore family, whose heritage textile company had been family owned for hundreds of years. In all the wargaming over a possible buyout, it was the only sticking point he and his marketing department could see to him purchasing it. The Tessitores' increasingly concerned comments about his stability and Circolo's plans for succession. In truth, he had none. No desire for marriage or family, unlike his *father* whose own family seemed to be a small and perfect Italian success story. Yet what nobody knew was that the immensely successful Silvestri company had been started on the back of his mother's designs. Stolen when his father had left his mother and Leo behind.

'Leo, then,' she whispered, the brush of her breath caressing his cheek.

'*Perfetto.*'

He pulled back and looked down on her again. She'd picked up some Italian in their time together and this was another word she clearly understood, as a whisper of pink flushed her high cheekbones. He couldn't explain why witnessing her awareness of him appealed, because it shouldn't have. Their relationship wasn't one built on romance. Both had agreed on that.

Passion, however, was another matter entirely. Could still waters run deep?

What would it be like to dive in and find out?

'Nothing's ever perfect, *Leo*. Not even you.'

It was a salutary reminder of her opinion of him. So many executive assistants he'd employed had been…unsettled by him in some way. Female, male, younger, older. It made no difference. Except her. After her three-month probation had ended with a permanent contract, she'd stalked into his office with a spoken demand.

Stop dazzling the staff, Mr Zanetti.

It was rather like being attacked by a tiny kitten.

He enjoyed her claws.

Although *she* never appeared dazzled or affected by him at all. She seemed wholly unfazed. But as he'd told her, it was hard not to dazzle when you regularly hit the top ten world's best-looking men lists. It wasn't that he was vain; rather, Leo was pragmatic about the realities of his situation, as he'd told her.

It comes with the territory, Ms Taylor.

After that, he'd smiled and she'd turned on her practical heels and stalked right out again.

The mood had been set between them on that day and it hadn't changed much since.

'You're poor for my ego, Simone.'

Her face might have seemed impassive, but he glimpsed a silvery spark in her eyes. He didn't know why he thought so, but he almost *heard* her wanting to roll them.

'Stop. What I say has no impact on your rudely healthy ego. None. At. All.'

Funny that was exactly the same as he'd thought of her. His words were like rain from a roof, water off a duck's back.

'Does anything I say have an impact on yours?'

She cocked her head. 'You think I have an ego?'

He didn't doubt it, given how they'd become engaged. As his executive assistant, Simone had been fully aware of his efforts to find a wife, the reasons for his sudden quest for matrimony. She'd located a world-renowned matchmaker and worked with his lawyer to ensure his wishes were documented in an appropriate pre-nuptial agreement, in anticipation of a marriage. Yet he'd been overcome by frustration at the process, how the women he'd been matched with never seemed quite right. They'd been looking for love, or at least for something *more*. They weren't interested in his work, when his work was his *life* and what drove him.

The efforts to meet someone and engage in something with the hope of it being forever had become increasingly tedious, because his whole life so far had been about the temporary. The reset to permanence was an uncomfortable one. It didn't feel right, like wearing a poorly-made suit.

In a frustrated moment, after a failed lunch date with yet another beautiful woman who didn't *fit*, he'd returned to the office, glimpsed Simone and spat out the almost careless but perhaps his most insightful words he ever said.

Why can't I find someone like you?

She'd cocked her head at him, just like she'd done to-night, fixed him with her assessing gaze and then given the fateful reply.

Maybe you can.

What had started out as something entirely fanciful, sparked an idea that sunk its teeth into him and wouldn't let go. That in a world of people who wanted things he wouldn't give, here was a woman who only sought what he could.

In the beginning his negotiations were cautious because he valued Simone more as his executive assistant than any-thing else. His right hand in so many ways. Yet she'd been clear, harbouring no secret desires for love. She wanted her job, and money she couldn't raise even with her generous wage, to help her sister Holly.

Some tweaks to their pre-nuptial agreement and it was done. No need for any more dinners or painful 'getting-to-know-you' sessions, since both of them knew enough about the other to make the arrangement work.

And what they didn't know, wouldn't hurt them.

'You propositioned me, so you clearly believed you were worth it.'

The corner of her lips tilted in an enigmatic, Mona Lisa smile. Had Da Vinci ever sought to discover what was going through his subject's mind as he immortalised one of the most famous smiles in history? Because for Leo, what was going through his wife's mind had begun to intrigue him in ways he hadn't thought possible.

'You accepted, so you clearly understood I was.'

It was an enticing exchange. Their banter, such as it was when Simone was only his assistant, had always been professional. Now, with this woman in his arms, there was a whisper of something more. Yet she still regarded him with her wintry grey eyes, impassive and confounding.

'Once the seed was sown, Simone, I never had any doubt.'

A truth, in his carefully crafted life of lies.

The music began to slow, then stop. From the perfectly timed running sheet, Leo knew this was the end of the evening. He let Simone go and she moved away from him, stepping to his side. For a brief and unscripted moment he wanted to tell the band to start up again, so they could have one last dance, where he could hold her and they could continue this push and pull, and then he might find out what she truly thought of him. However, that would ruin the theatre of the evening, so he restrained himself as his guests clapped and they moved to what should have been the perfect send off. Except it wasn't perfect, when all he wished for was the impossible.

To have Simone in his arms again.

CHAPTER TWO

SIMONE LEANED AGAINST the rich wooden wall of the lift taking them both to the suite Leo had booked for their wedding night, to save on getting stuck in traffic. Really, it had seemed unnecessary when they could have simply returned to his townhouse. Her stomach swooped uncomfortably. This unsettling feeling didn't have anything to do with spending their first night living together. That couldn't be it at all.

As Leo's executive assistant, she'd spent two years in his proximity. They'd travelled together in his jet. She'd worked long nights and stayed in his brownstone, though admittedly in a suite designed exclusively for guests. She even kept spare clothes there, just in case. Being this close to him had never affected her before.

It had to be due to the speed with which the lift moved towards the top floor of the hotel. Nothing else.

Simone shook off the strange sensation, glancing at Leo's imposing profile as he stared ahead of him, seemingly lost in thought. A few bits of coloured confetti clung to his coal-dark hair and were sprinkled on the shoulders of his impeccable tuxedo made specially for their wedding. She *knew* he owned four other tuxedos already, so he could simply have taken one from his closet and been done. Why bother with the cost of another?

But that wasn't Leo Zanetti and never would be. He liked the excess of it. The admiring comments when he was seen in something new, even if it was a suit. No doubt the magazine that would write the article about their 'whirlwind romance' and show pictures of their wedding to the world, had already been given details of their wedding attire. Especially when Leo could make or break a tailor with a raised eyebrow when someone asked him about the fit of a suit. Or create a whole design trend just by saying he liked something.

It was so…frivolous. Like her own life had been before she'd smashed the mould made for her by her parents. Still, even with all of that, the night had caught her by surprise. Setting aside the breathless members of society gushing over the wedding, something about it had seemed unusually weighty. Their vows, all traditional. Promises made to one another, even if they were meaningless and only made to be broken.

It all sat heavily on her chest, pressing down on her. Making it hard to breathe…

Probably just a hangover from the realisation that the moment represented a final nail in the coffin of her childhood dreams. Of finding her prince, falling in love and marrying. Some things were clearly ingrained in her, even though life had taught Simone years ago that love wasn't to be trusted. She'd decided then to rely on herself and no one else.

The lift eased to a stop and Leo turned to her, their gazes clashing. His eyes a shade of blue so vibrant and shocking it always caught her by surprise. Like a jump-scare, except with a frisson not entirely unpleasant, the way those eyes of his pierced her very soul.

You look beautiful.

Her breath caught. The memory of those words still slipping seductively through her.

Simone knew she wasn't beautiful in any traditional sense. Her mother had told her that, often enough. That she had an *interesting face*. Eyes a touch too narrow, mouth a little too wide. Blessed with good hair, though, to her mother's relief. She'd spent her teens and early twenties trying to live up to the impossible expectations set for her by her family in her comportment and the way she'd dressed. Wearing couture and designer brands like others wore off the rack. It had all been so meaningless. Her true thoughts on anything had been irrelevant. All that was important was meeting her parents' exacting standards. Saving herself for marriage and marrying well, which meant marrying someone her parents chose for her.

Simone hadn't sought out praise for her appearance in years. Didn't need to. She'd become tired of people trying to turn her into something *they* wanted her to be and so she'd left that life behind. She was who she was, now. So why did Leo's comment twine its way round her like giftwrapping ribbon? Silver and sparkly. It must have been the champagne at the wedding reception, making her a little fuzzy, even though she hadn't drunk that much…

'Would you like a nightcap?' Leo asked as the doors slid open to their suite, all warm neutrals and impeccable styling. The lights of her adopted home city like a kaleidoscope beyond the floor to ceiling windows. Central Park a dark, velvety patch, hemmed by the twinkling cityscape surrounding it.

Simone wanted to take the jewelled combs from her hair, wash off her makeup and process the day. Remove her wedding dress, the bias-cut moulding to her, draping her body like liquid embodied in fabric. She hadn't worn anything like it for years, her life more about practicality now than being a hated mannequin on display for her family. The heavy satin slipped seductively across her skin, so smooth and silky it almost felt like a negligee rather than a wedding dress. A mix of feelings swirled in her belly at the memories of the evening they'd just left. How Leo had held her on the dance floor as if she was in some way precious to him. How he'd looked at her as if he'd *seen* her for the first time.

'Sure,' she said. Perhaps against her better judgement, but a final drink would be a reasonable full stop to what had otherwise been a long day. She hadn't really had one like it, with all the plucking, primping and pampering, since her Debutante Ball nine years earlier, when she'd been another woman altogether. 'But before we do, you have…'

She reached out and brushed his suit, scattering some of the coloured paper onto the carpet. His shoulders were broad and strong under the fine wool, as she'd known intellectually but discovered for real, when they'd danced for the first time. The strength in those shoulders might carry the weight of the world if you allowed them to.

Leo's eyebrows rose and she pulled back as if burned. What was she doing? She just knew Leo would hate to know that he still had confetti sprinkled on him. The man was impeccable in all things. Nothing out of place unless he'd styled it that way, or it had been styled for him.

'Any more?' he asked. His voice deep and a little rougher than usual.

There was some in his hair. For a fleeting moment she imagined brushing her hand through the strands to scatter the confetti to the floor. Simone's fingers prickled as she wondered what all that dark hair would feel like. Thick, no doubt, but soft? Wiry? No… *Impossible*.

Simone waved her hand about the general direction of his head, and his eyes widened.

'In your hair.'

He raked his fingers through his hair and the confetti fluttered to the floor, just as she imagined it would. His hair was now perfectly dishevelled in a way Leo was an expert at mastering. '*Grazie*. You're similarly afflicted.'

He didn't try to touch her and she didn't know why it stung. Simone moved to a mirror, barely recognising the woman who looked back at her like a ghost. A reflection of who she'd once been, not who she'd become. With soft, smoky eyes. Blushing pink lips. Hair gleaming and curled, tumbling over her shoulders. The hours it had taken to achieve this look.

In the reflection stood Leo, a little off to the side. His gaze on her in the mirror was intent. Though it always tended to be, his focus taking some getting used to, until you realised that it infiltrated every part of his life. From how he dressed, to how he worked, to how he exercised. Perhaps even to how he loved, if the string of women who'd constantly graced his arm on any given month was anything to go by. She wondered how it was possible for him to maintain that level of intensity. Their eyes met in the mirror. His gaze held hers with a hint of awareness.

He thought she was beautiful.

High praise, coming from a person often voted the most beautiful man on the planet.

She dismissed the moment, focusing instead on the confetti that adorned her as well. She couldn't brush her hands through her hair because that was likely impossible. A wedding hairstyle like hers wasn't held together by hope and good wishes, but by hairspray. She picked out some errant coloured paper that had clung tenaciously to her, dropping it on the sideboard.

'I'm surprised that you opted for confetti,' she said.

'Why?'

'It's messy.'

'I don't mind messy, in its place. Life's messy.'

There seemed to be weight to his words, but what was your wedding day if not a momentous occasion? Even though theirs was strictly business, it still carried a certain gravitas. That sensation pressed down upon her again, but she wouldn't dwell on it. Instead, Simone thought about the money in her bank account. Seven figures settled on her the moment she said *I do*. That amount would allow her to protect her sister Holly, who'd been abandoned by her parents because, like Simone, she hadn't fitted into the mould they'd tried to create for her.

Today ensured that the medical bills for Holly's increasingly complicated pregnancy, that she'd hidden till she couldn't any longer, were paid. That was all that mattered.

'I don't believe you've had a messy day in your life. You're all about the perfection. *Leo Zanetti never misses*. Isn't that what everyone says about you? And never forget, I hear the complaints your suppliers and others have about you. Your exacting standards. As your EA, I hear it *all*.'

A look flashed across his face, almost like a wince, then it was gone.

'Then you've discovered my secret. The real reason for handing out confetti.'

'What?'

'It allowed people to throw things at me. Make them feel better about the *exacting standards* I impose upon them. Think of it as relationship building.'

The comment was so startlingly ridiculous a laugh simply burst from her, as she thought of their leaving the reception in an entirely different light. People hurling confetti whilst muttering, *take that, Leo Zanetti, for the time you told me I had the colour wrong, and it should have been Pantone*

*654 instead of Pantone 655, so you demanded we repaint
twenty walls...*

Her eyes burned and blurred but at least her mascara was
waterproof so she wouldn't end up looking like a Panda. Leo
grinned. She could barely see it through her tears of mirth,
but she could now tell the difference between the smile he
flashed to his adoring public and the one he kept for private. The genuine smile. Relaxed, not studied.

This one was of the second sort. The private smile. She
knew because it met his eyes and because of her reaction
to it. Seeing that smile was like walking into the sunshine
on a fine spring day, warm and satisfying.

'I'm pleased I could entertain you at my expense.'

'What good would you be as an employer if you couldn't
entertain me? Though admittedly that usually happens when
you're not looking,' she said.

He raised a strong, inky eyebrow. 'Aren't I giving you
enough work? When do you have time to appreciate this
entertainment? I'm imagining it now. A cabal of executive
assistants all mocking their employers behind their backs.'

'That's secret EA business and I'll never tell.' Simone
tapped the side of her nose, her finger coming away damp
from her tears of laughter. The truth was that she kept everything about Leo's business entirely confidential, as he
well knew given her employment contract with its compre-
hensive confidentiality clauses.

His eyes narrowed, attempting to look stern but failing
because the quirk at the corners of his perfect mouth remained. 'What would you all talk about?'

'I don't know. About the time you told a supplier you
needed *a slightly warmer shade of black*?'

That conversation had involved a lengthy exchange of

warmer, cooler, getting closer like some game of Hot and Cold hide and seek. She started giggling even harder.

'They weren't listening and were wasting my time. That job won *awards* because we got it right. I'm beginning to think you're unserious about Circolo's reputation. That's troubling. Why did I marry you again?'

'I don't know, Mr Zanetti. Perhaps you should read one of your press releases or interviews on the subject. Or would you prefer I do that for you and give you a precis, so that you're not wasting your time?'

Leo muttered something that sounded a lot like *incorrigible*. She was about to retort, *you love it* but held back because that would be a weird thing to say.

Whilst she'd always stood up for herself, stood up to him, their conversation had never been quite like this. So…familiar. Instead, Simone wiped at her eyes. When had she last laughed so hard that she cried? She couldn't remember, meaning it had to have been years. A thought that struck her as almost sad.

Leo reached his hand into the inner pocket of his tux, removed something with a flourish and held it out to her. She took it. It was a warm, pristine, white square of folded fabric.

'A handkerchief? How old school of you.' Simone dabbed at her eyes. Closed them, took a deep breath. The fabric smelled like him. His aftershave. Like spices and vanilla with a hint of rum. An intoxicating scent invoking memories of wintry Christmases and hot desserts. The excitement of unwrapping gifts. Something so nostalgic and familiar a yawning chasm just opened in her belly and she *yearned*.

'Someone needed to be prepared,' he said, breaking the spell that seemed to have been cast over her. 'Little did I understand the tears today wouldn't be about our getting married, but at my expense.'

'What good's a wife if not to tease her husband? I've heard we're all doing it and I'm trying really hard for authenticity here.'

'Clearly you're succeeding. Your act's entirely believable. The Tessitores will never think otherwise.'

She'd needed to get away from all the weird feelings that seemed to have overtaken her and hadn't known how. Thankfully, Leo had done it for her. Reminding them both of the truth of this arrangement. To help him win a business deal from people who didn't seem to understand or appreciate him. Apparently concerned about the number of women he'd been seen with in the press and what that meant for his stability, when Simone had little doubt that most women on the planet would want to be seen on his arm.

Plus, he *made* careers. Leo would date a model and then she'd be booked for months. Be seen having dinner with an up-and-coming designer of any sort? Their catalogue would be sold out overnight.

Really, Simone wondered why Leo was so intent on acquiring this company whose owners didn't seem to recognise his worth, even though he'd told her it was a heritage firm and part of the cultural fabric of the Lombardy region of Italy, which he wished to preserve. Of course, what Leonardo Zanetti wanted he got. She guessed this was just more of the same.

She balled up his handkerchief and held it out to him. 'Thank you. I'm fine now. My composure's firmly back in place.'

He waved her away. 'Keep it. In case there are any other moments where you lose your composure because of me. As your dutiful husband, I want to ensure I look after you.

And on that point, whilst I offered you a drink I still haven't made you one.'

Simone hadn't had anyone looking after her since she'd walked away from her family seven years ago, at age twenty. At least she had her freedom now. She looked down at her wedding and engagement rings, glittering in the soft light of the room. When Leo had asked what style of ring she'd like and if she had a preferred colour of gem, she'd told him it didn't matter. Her only stipulation had been that she didn't want anything too ostentatious. He didn't plant a country-sized boulder on her finger as she'd feared he might want to do. What he'd delivered was a round, two-carat diamond set in a platinum band. Not too big, as she'd asked. However, the diamond was an uncommon gem, internally flawless. And bisecting the band sat a fine channel lined with a circle of tiny, sparkling pastel gemstones that made a watercolour rainbow round her finger. Her wedding ring matched. She hadn't picked a single colour, so he gave her every one of them.

Simone wasn't sure why something in her chest ached as she looked at it. She shook it off. In the end, Simone guessed her rings were symbols of the loss of freedom she'd so craved. But at least they were put there as a result of her own choosing, rather than her parents'.

'Nice that you finally remembered. I wondered why I was feeling thirsty. What do you have?' she said as she made her way to an oversized lounge suite. She sank down into the plush cushions and wiggled her toes in the shoes she'd worn, which had been handmade to match the era of her gown.

She loved shoes. They were her only weakness. She'd had an unreasonable collection in her other life, before she'd re-alised that none of it mattered and one pair might have kept a family's bills paid and food on the table for a month. But these shoes… Covered in satin to match her gown, with magnificent handmade, wax citrus flowers to match the real blossoms in her bouquet that had been gathered into a little cluster as an embellishment at the front of each shoe. Just like an original thirties pair of shoes might have had. Delicate and perfect.

'You can have whatever your heart desires. However, I asked for a hazelnut liqueur to be placed in the suite for you,' Leo said, making his way to a credenza and holding up a shapely bottle full of amber fluid.

Simone's traitorous heart skipped a little beat and she rubbed the centre of her chest, settling the flutter there, that had struck like moths to lamplight. Leo knew she adored hazelnuts. Once he'd found out just how much she loved them, for the past two Christmases he'd given her a box of exquisite, handmade Belgian chocolates with hazelnut praline as a gift, along with her generous bonus, and she'd savoured them.

'*Perfetto*,' she said and he stilled, cocking his head, those vivid eyes of his fixed on her with the intensity of a spotlight making her want to squirm in her seat. 'What are you having?'

He began to pour her drink first into a lowball glass with ice. He reached into the bar fridge for his own, pouring the straw-coloured liquid into a tulip-shaped glass.

'Grappa,' Leo said as he strolled towards her, with a lazy roll of his hips, drinks in hand. He held out hers and she reached out to take it, their fingers touching. The moment was unintentional, she was sure, but she still tingled at the brush of his warm, tanned skin on hers. The moment had become strangely electric. The grip on her glass was tenuous, so she held on more tightly.

She wanted to say thank you, but her voice had been stolen so she smiled at him instead. Their gazes held and his nostrils flared. The moment shockingly potent. Simone was transported back to their time on the dance floor. Their bodies close, moving as one in an intoxicating synchronicity. The way his thumb hypnotically stroked the gleaming satin of her dress at her side. Simone didn't want to think about it, or to dwell. It had to be the whirlwind engagement and getting swept up in the day. That was all it was. Clearly her romantic fantasies hadn't quite left her when faced with their current and strange reality of this marriage of convenience. Even if she'd learned from painful experience that love was meaningless and easily bought off. But today wasn't really for lingering on past hurts. It was all about navigating her future. She took a small sip of her drink, the sweet nutty flavour sliding over her tongue.

'Are you sure about the absence of your family today? Not even your sister?'

The words caught her mid swallow. She forced her drink down, her eyes watering, trying not to cough. 'Why ask the question now, when the day's over?'

He hadn't shown much interest before and had accepted without comment that she didn't have anyone she wanted to invite. His attention now was strange and unsettling.

Leo didn't answer her immediately. He placed his drink down on an occasional table beside him. He shrugged out of his jacket and draped it carefully over an armchair, then sat on the couch at the other end from her. He tugged his bowtie undone, unfastened the top two studs of his dress shirt, then simply sprawled in the chair. He looked magnificently indolent, though she knew him better than that.

'I'm curious now,' he said, retrieving and sipping his drink. He held his glass almost negligently in his elegant hand, whereas she now gripped hers so tightly she feared she might crack it.

Some people might have likened him to a housecat in that moment, the way he lounged with a lazy expression. His eyes hooded, almost sleepy. The corners of his generous lips quirked into a sardonic kind of smile that had been written about and dissected by too many fashion commentators to be at all sensible or logical. Yet she'd never make the mistake of thinking of him as anything other than a panther, waiting for the perfect moment to pounce.

The more casual Leo appeared, the more watchful you had to be.

Simone had seen him like this before, when a new subcontractor hadn't done their job, having been lulled into a false sense of security that he was so laid back they could get away with shortcuts, only to be trapped by the inevitable attack on their workmanship that they hadn't seen coming.

People soon learned he could ruin them with an offhand comment. That's when they all fell into line. It was an incredible power he held. Yet she wouldn't let him wield it over her. People, like her parents, had tried before. Everyone had failed.

She shrugged, trying to match his casual attitude whilst inside it felt as if she was tangled in complicated knots. 'I'm certain. My sister hasn't been well and as for the rest… You know what families are like.'

Hers had seen fit to pay off her boyfriend. She'd met Jace at college. He was someone she'd known that her parents wouldn't have approved of, but that hadn't mattered at the time. Who cared that he was a boy that people might have said was from the wrong side of the tracks? He'd made good and had been awarded entry on a partial scholarship. Simone had admired him for it. Jace had chased her. Courted her. Acted like he respected her. Showered her with attention that her emotion starved little heart had soaked up like parched earth on a rainy day. All her life she'd been taught to wait till she was married before sleeping with someone and, in her naivety, Simone believed that's what she'd wanted too. But on meeting Jace she'd questioned everything she'd once believed. Why would she have waited to sleep with him when he said he loved her? They'd planned a future together.

Even now, she didn't know what had been fake and what had been real. People claimed he'd been spreading stories about her. How simple it was to get her into bed. How he'd corrupted the poor little rich girl. Made jokes about it. And maybe that was true. Simone took a deep, slow breath. It might have been eight years ago, but it still ached like the wound was fresh. A knife to her tender heart that had never recovered. She blinked back the burn in her eyes because Leo would notice and he'd never get this part of her, that humiliation.

She'd learned a few things back then. How fickle her friends were. How they'd laughed behind her back for picking the poor kid to date. About how she'd *fallen*. Other boys in their group, sons of family friends she'd known since she'd been a child, had tried to come onto her because she'd apparently become fair game. A woman who could be fooled into bed. An easy mark.

The only thing she was sure about was how her parents had paid Jace off. Not for her own good, to save their beloved daughter, but to add to her humiliation. To show how easily they could wield their money to buy someone, especially when they threw it back in her face. Calling her home as if she was some kind of disgrace because she'd committed the sin of being talked about, rather than a heartbroken girl who needed their support. Showing her how little she was worth to the man she'd believed she'd marry one day, because they'd made promises to each other and she'd trusted them.

Simone realised then, that her relationship with her parents was entirely transactional. Her mom and dad cared more about their reputation than her. Even her brother had berated her, as if he was some scion of virtue when he'd slept his way through a swathe of girls, both in high school and in his own college years. It was then she'd decided to make her own way. The betrayal of her family was too great, their disdain of her impossible to bear. When she finally stood up for herself and said she didn't want what her parents demanded she accept as her life, they'd turned their backs. So, she'd walked away from it all, even Holly. Their relationship suffered because Holly was too young to understand why her big sister was leaving. That estrangement only really changed when her sister fell pregnant and recognised what Simone might have gone through. Getting in touch after eight long years of silence.

In all of this, the irony wasn't lost on Simone that she was now married to the kind of man her parents might have dreamed of for her. His wealth manifestly eclipsing theirs and all of their friends combined, even if he didn't have generations of illustrious family connections and old money behind him.

He was entirely self-made.

'Since I don't have a family, you might be surprised,' he said drawing her from a time she'd rather forget.

His past had been well ventilated in the press, though she was less interested in how Leo had been discovered by a modelling talent scout and more in how he'd survived when he'd been left with nothing. Born to a single mother, an artist and designer. Ending up on the streets as a teen, alone and hungry. His mother dying when he was barely an adult.

She hated thinking of that young man struggling to survive, which was why she was so determined for Holly to be protected. When she'd left home, she'd been lucky. Finding employment as an office junior. Working her way up in the company to become an executive assistant before leaving with an impeccable reference.

Not everyone had that kind of luck or those advantages.

'I didn't want what my parents wanted for me. They weren't happy about that. It's not an uncommon story,' she explained briefly. He didn't need any more of her sorry story.

'Then I'm surprised you didn't invite them to show them what you've achieved despite them.'

The only person she'd wanted here was Holly, but her doctors couldn't recommend she fly. Her placenta was low lying and she'd been bleeding. Holly also had higher than normal blood pressure. The constant threat of those complications meant it wasn't safe to travel and a lot of the time she needed bed rest.

'I have nothing to prove to people I'm wholly disinterested in. They don't need my emotional energy.'

'An admirable sentiment.'

Leo raised his glass to her. Like he'd raised it to her during his speech.

To my bride, who seems to have surprised everyone, but humbled me, by accepting my proposal.

There'd been chuckles in the crowd at that, even though Simone doubted Leo did much of anything, without knowing the answer first.

As for their engagement? There was no surprise about it at all. She'd been desperate to help Holly after they'd reconnected. Even with Simone's generous wage the medical bills were becoming crippling. She hadn't really thought about Leo's situation at all, given she never wanted to marry and Leo was her boss, until he'd uttered the fateful words in his office one day after yet another failed attempt at finding the right bride. After he asked why it couldn't be her, she'd immediately asked herself the same question.

Simone had known the eyewatering amount he was prepared to offer in his pre-nuptial agreement. It was enough to pay for an apartment in California for Holly. Her medical care. A nurse on call to visit whenever needed. Set things up for Holly and the baby. She could give her sister what Simone hadn't had for herself.

A soft place to land.

'Don't tell me you don't do the same to people who aren't important to you any more.'

The corner of his mouth kicked up. 'We're alike in that way, you and I. Were you at least happy with how it went today?'

Not so alike that their differences wouldn't keep pushing them apart like the same poles of a magnet. Yet if she was honest with herself, this had been the perfect wedding. Not for the teenage girl she once was, but the woman she'd become, even if she'd decided that love wasn't for her. From the intimate setting to the elegantly appointed room with whimsical floral centrepieces spilling from tall stands at each table's centre. The magnificent, tiered cake of different flavours, including chocolate hazelnut torte especially for her, decorated with cascades of blowsy sugar roses and tiny citrus blossoms that matched those in her bouquet. Leo's speech, which was strangely sentimental and delivered to warm applause.

The man knew how to please a crowd. It seemed like the whole day had been designed to make her happy.

'Yes, I was. Thank you. But with that, I'm going to turn in. It's been a long day.'

One she needed to process. Sift through. And she also needed to text Holly because Simone wanted to make sure her sister knew everything was okay. Wanted to send her photos of how beautiful everything had looked, since she'd expressed some suspicion as to what exactly was going on between Simone and Leo.

'Do you need any help with your dress?'

It was a benign kind of question and the look on his face seemed genuine enough, but something about today had been charged, a little electric. Hard to escape. The beautiful, silky dress that caressed her skin like a lover's touch. Leo, looking more handsome than any man had a right to be. The way he'd held her in his arms as they'd danced. She seemed to be enjoying the fantasy of the day a little too much.

But life wasn't a fantasy. She'd lived the end of hers. Jace's rejection. Taking money instead of a life with her. Her parents' disapproval. Her friends' disdain for and ridicule of her falling in love outside of her class.

Holly was living a kind of nightmare now too. Pregnant, unmarried. Once Simone had craved a loving family, one who accepted your failings. Embraced you and helped you through life. But that wasn't the world she'd come from and Leo represented everything that she'd left behind. A life she'd rejected because she'd realised it would never fit her. One where people cared more about how you appeared than who you really were and Leo was the *king* of appearances.

The Sultan of Style.

Simone stood and so did Leo. He was unfailingly polite that way. His manners impeccable. *Everything* about him impeccable when her life was really a bit of a mess. And whilst Leo claimed to like messy, she didn't believe him for a moment.

'No, thanks.'

'It has quite a few inconveniently placed buttons,' he pointed out.

A myriad of tiny satin covered ones down her side. It would be easier if someone undid them for her. She now had a sixth sense for bad intentions, having batted off a few CEOs who'd thought being their assistant at their beck and call meant in *every* way. Leo didn't give off those vibes. He never had. Their parameters were clear. For her, this was a job like any other. He'd promised her the same. Simone shook her head as he looked down on her with those famed eyes of his. Transfixed in a shade of blue the colour of a tropical sea.

'I got myself into this, I'll get myself out of it.'

CHAPTER THREE

IT HAD BEEN an eight-hour flight from New York to Milan on Leo's private jet. Simone had tried to sleep on the way in the stateroom at the back, given they'd left in the early evening and flown through the night, but all she'd done was toss and turn. Much like she had in New York. After she'd sent Holly some pictures hastily snapped of the venue, Simone had finally had time to replay the wedding and reception, recognising how much effort Leo had put into getting everything right. It was no less than she'd expected from him, but the day had been a whirlwind where she hadn't had time to think about the things that Leo had *no* control over. In bed on her own, on her wedding night in their suite, she finally had. How she'd felt like a different woman under the intensity of Leo's gaze. The sensation of being cradled in his arms on the dance floor, their bodies close, like she'd always imagined when she'd fantasised about being married for real.

A flush of heat washed over her.

When she'd agreed to this arrangement, Simone hadn't much thought about how it might affect her as she'd been in the midst of panic after finding out about Holly's situation. She'd been desperate to protect her sister, who by coincidence was the same age as Simone had been when her own life had imploded. The sheer relief of knowing she could pay all of Holly's outstanding medical bills and keep her safe had then obliterated the logistics of what it meant to be Leo Zanetti's wife. Because it wasn't like being his executive assistant, at all.

In the lead up to the wedding it had been easy enough to be all smiles. Playing the game she once knew intimately. She'd been happy that with each stage towards their wedding another payment mandated by their pre-nuptial agreement came through. That she could find Holly an apartment, make sure her high risk pregnancy was monitored by the best available team. That all her sister needed to do now was to sit back and relax while her baby grew.

The difficulty was maintaining the fakery to everyone else when Simone had fought to live her life true to herself, with authenticity. It didn't sit well. Yet she tried reminding herself that getting married to Leo was a means to an end, not the end itself.

'I've been advised there are photographers outside the house,' Leo said from where he sat in the back of the car as they travelled to his home in a fashionable part of the city.

'Photographers follow you wherever you go.'

'A teaser of one of our wedding photos for the magazine spread dropped today. It's not me they're interested in.'

He shot her an unreadable look. Simone was dressed as she always was for a flight like this, when they weren't going straight into the office or a business meeting afterwards. A white collared shirt with casual black trousers. Her uniform. Something she didn't have to think about. Yet she was thinking about it now. Was Leo judging her appearance? What might be written about her when the inevitable pictures hit the press?

In contrast, Leo looked stylish as ever with his casual elegance. *Sprezzatura* she'd heard it called, an almost careless perfection. Today he was dressed in buff tan chinos and similar toned loafers. A navy linen shirt with the sleeves rolled up. He'd strolled onto the tarmac after their flight carrying a worn and well-loved leather bag looking effortless and gloriously rumpled. If she didn't know better, she might have thought the flight attendant had fanned herself as they'd walked off the plane.

Simone almost did too.

'I see this as an opportunity,' Leo went on. 'Will that be a problem?'

'Depends on what opportunity you're talking about.'

'It'll be our first unofficial sighting in Italy, as husband and wife. I'll ask the driver to park out front rather than driving into the garage, so we can be seen walking into the home together.'

She understood what Leo meant now. Putting on a show. She sighed. They had a busy time in Italy. A few days in Milan where Leo had organised a mystery day out, then a dinner with the Tessitores to introduce Simone as his wife and hopefully discuss a possible purchase of their company. After that, they were heading off on a brief honeymoon in Verona, which she didn't need but realised was necessary to maintain the narrative their whole marriage was meant to portray. Then, they'd be going back to Milan, rounding off the Italy trip with a charity ball.

Simone rubbed her temple, the thought of it almost enough to give her a headache. They were supposed to present as a loved-up couple fresh from their wedding and she had little idea how to portray that. Her only experience had been with Jace and she *refused* to think about that relationship. How would she even behave now, if really in love? Simone had no idea.

'Are we talking about simply walking in here? Something

else?' Butterflies took wing in her belly, flapping about violently. Would he ask for a kiss? They didn't even kiss at the altar, he'd made her laugh instead… Her chest became tight and it was hard to—

'Breathe, Simone.'

She tried to relax. Took a breath as he'd asked. That almost made it worse because, as on the night of their wedding, Leo smelled *delicious*. She chanced a look at him. His lips quirked into a wry yet somewhat concerned smile. At her reaction no doubt. Leo wouldn't want his new wife swooning because she'd held her breath and fainted at the thought of getting up close and personal with him, even if it was only for show.

'As I said once before, you're bad for my ego.'

He'd completely misunderstood her inability to breathe and that was fine because she hardly understood it herself.

'All I'm asking is that we hold hands. Perhaps touch each other with affection till we get inside. I won't ever ask what you're not prepared to give.'

'So, we touch in a way that could potentially be judged as a breach of Circolo's *Working Together* policy but not in a way that mandates HR's immediate involvement.'

Leo laughed, his face lighting up with mirth and some element of self-deprecation.

'Since most women I've spent time with wish to touch me in a way that would flagrantly breach every HR policy available on Circolo's intranet, and even some decency laws, that'll do nicely.'

'Mr Zanetti, your ego clearly remains solidly intact. As I believe *I've* said once before.'

'Mrs Zanetti, my expectation is that you'll attempt to crush it with your ruthlessly efficient shoes at every given opportunity. It would worry me if you stopped trying.'

This would have been the perfect time for her to laugh too, to lighten the mood even further. Instead she glanced down at her black pumps. Boring. Practical. Ruthlessly efficient as he'd said. Simone wished she had another pair of shoes to wear. Like some towering, patent black heels because she loved patent leather, and they'd have added a bit of interest to her otherwise restrained, matte outfit…

'Are you happy with my suggestion?' Leo asked. What could she say? Simone nodded and he said something in Italian to the driver. The car changed course slightly, pulling into a side street. The street where his home was situated. Her heart jolted like a horse at a starting gate.

'Affectionate touching. Holding hands. Got it.'

The car slowed to a stop at the front of the house. A magnificent, semi-detached art deco villa. There wasn't far to go, a quick walk across the footpath to the front gate, then they'd be behind the vine-covered wall and away from prying eyes. Easy.

'The photographers are across the road. Wait till I open your door.'

Leo hopped out of the car and stood on the footpath waiting for her. The click of shutters sounded staccato to the left of their vehicle. Simone refused to look over towards them, even though they'd be unlikely to glimpse her through the tinted windows. She began to slide across the seat. Leo ducked his head to peer at her, then held out his hand as if to offer her some support. She took it, his grasp warm and strong as he helped her from the car.

Photographers called his name. *Leo! Mr Zanetti!* Then to her. *Simone, where's the honeymoon?* It was discombobulating, surreal, the world she'd been thrust into. Leo gathered her into him, against his hard body, ignoring the shouts from across the road. It was as if nothing else existed bar them. He leaned down so his lips were at her ear. His breath, a warm caress.

'Remember to breathe.'

Goosebumps shivered over her. Instead of pulling away, she melted in even further. Something about the role they'd slipped into suddenly became too easy. Seamless.

'Remember not to breach too many HR policies,' she whispered, a little breathless, despite his reminder. It was nerves, that was all. He was used to this. The man graced magazines covers, dated movie stars, walked red carpets. She was simply Simone Taylor.

Plain Jane.

Leo chuckled, throaty and deep. The sound rumbled right through her. 'I'd never dream of it.'

Leo threaded his fingers through hers and squeezed, then walked with her towards the tall, wrought iron gate that led to his property, ushering her through and locking it behind them. They crossed the small front garden and marbled terrace area with its potted olive trees, then through the front door and into the house.

That's where the closeness ended. He disentangled himself from her and she strangely mourned the loss of all his warmth and strength. It had felt good, having him talking her through, being able to rely on him.

Now, he was all business.

'I'm sure you'd like to see your room.'

She'd been in Leo's magnificent Milan property before. One of the few people privileged to see the living areas on the ground floor at least. Not many people had. Whilst style magazines gushed over his other residences that were dotted around the world, he'd never invited them into this one. The only photographs of it available online, were old real estate listings before he'd purchased it and done an extensive renovation. Whilst the palette of the villa was all warm neutrals, from the glorious, honeyed floorboards to the creamy walls, the spaces were punctuated with pops of colour. From the large antique rugs on the floor to the soft furnishings and art on the walls. It was a place that looked...inviting. Loved. Lived in. Unlike his more modern interiors, which struck her as showpieces, this one had history about it. It felt more like Leo than any other place she'd seen.

Like home.

Instead of heading into the lounge area Leo made his way up a flight of stairs to the upper floor, then up another flight to what appeared to be an attic area.

'I've given you the whole top floor. I thought you might appreciate the privacy. The main bedroom's below you.' He opened the door and walked in. She followed.

The space stole her breath. It was unlike any other part of the house she'd seen. Once Leo had asked Simone her favourite colour and she'd said she had none, probably more in a fit of rebellion than anything else. This room, *her* room, was entirely decorated in shades of white and cream. It should have looked cold, soulless, but the space was anything but that. The ceilings were ornately moulded plasterwork.

Against one wall was a four-poster bed in a pale, whitewashed wood. The covers were plush and soft and it was stacked with pillows that looked like you could sink into them and never want to leave. The canopy and drapes were filmy and light, tied back against the posts, giving the room an understated opulence. A velvet covered bench sat at the end of the bed.

Along a wall opposite to the bed sat a large couch in an off-white linen with matching cushions. It was a space designed for someone to inject their personality should they wish, yet still felt complete just as it was, an elegantly conceived blank canvas.

Designed by someone who'd listened to her.

'This is glorious,' she whispered, her eyes burning with emotion at Leo's thoughtfulness. Her own room in her old family home had been decorated by an interior designer. What Simone had wanted hadn't really factored into the plan at all. Her mother had demanded the space match the rest of the house and so Simone had always thought it was cold and soulless.

This room was none of those things.

'I hope you'll be comfortable here,' Leo said.

'I know I will.'

She couldn't look at him right now, because if she did, she might be totally overcome by it all. Instead, she moved to one of the windows set into the sloping ceiling and pulled back the filmy curtain. Below them sat a walled garden, a slice of green with lush plantings and what appeared to be a huge magnolia tree in the back corner, which would look magnificent when it flowered.

'Is there anything you need?' Leo asked.

All Simone needed was time to regroup. She shook her head. 'I think you've done more than enough.'

She turned and tried to smile but it felt weak and shaky. Leo didn't seem to notice. Nothing about his demeanour changed, apart from looking a little pleased with himself.

'As you've done for me. Don't think your efforts are unappreciated. For this morning, I have some work to do—'

'Can I help?' Work. That's what she needed to get back her equilibrium. It reminded her of what her role really was here, as his valued executive assistant.

Leo shook his head. 'It shouldn't take long. Something a little time sensitive is all.'

That of itself was strange. Disappointment settled like a stone in her stomach. Simone knew everything about his work and she'd seen nothing on her email indicating anything time sensitive had come in. There was also something a bit different about Leo in this moment. He appeared a little closed off. Though perhaps the 'work' had something to do with the 'surprise' he'd scheduled in for tomorrow.

'I also realise the only time you've seen Milan is for your job, so if you'd like me to take you sightseeing after I'm done...'

Simone didn't need more time in close proximity to Leo, not after this. And especially not with the risk of photographers following them to capture every glaring detail without the time to prepare herself. What she really needed was space and sleep. Perhaps if she was a little better rested her head would clear. At the moment, her thoughts and emotions were a complicated tangle she needed to undo.

'Maybe another time,' she said. 'I'd like to catch up with my sister this afternoon. Give her a call and see how she is.'

'Of course.' Leo hesitated. Slipped his phone from his pocket and checked it. Frowned. Tapped a quick message. Pressed send. Returned his gaze to hers with a tight smile. Clearly he wasn't happy about something. She might have asked what, but if he wanted to tell her he would. 'Your bags will be up soon. Remember our day trip tomorrow. Dress—'

'For a day on the water. I remember. I packed appropriately.'

'Of that, *cara*, I have no doubt. I'll let you get settled.' He gave her a sharp nod, then turned and left the room. Alone with her thoughts, doubting everything.

Leo motored the boat he'd hired across Lake Garda. The breeze cool and fresh over the vivid blue water. His mother had always spoken fondly of growing up around this place, before moving to Milan and meeting his father. An idyllic childhood in a little village, swimming on the lake, catering to tourists. They'd been back to Lake Garda a few times when he was a child, but then the family furniture business had taken over and consumed everything. He'd wondered whether his mother had felt landlocked, moving away from the water and a place she'd loved so much.

He'd always regretted that he'd never thought to ask.

Leo ignored the sensation, one that had plagued him unrelentingly in the years since his mother had died. Today wasn't about that past, but the present.

'You've been the international man of mystery today,' Simone said. 'Where are we going?'

'You'll see.'

'That's not helpful.'

Leo winked. 'I recommend living in the moment. Trust me.'

Simone's cheeks seemed to flush a gratifying shade of pink, a reaction he enjoyed a little too much. Of course, it could also have been the sun radiating warmth against her skin.

The purpose of today had been two-fold. He'd thought Simone might enjoy some time exploring one of the area's natural treasures. Then there was their impending dinner with the Tessitores. His marketing manager reported that the Silvestris had been wining and dining the family at some of Milan's finest venues. Acid burned in Leo's gut and he gritted his teeth. It was imperative their dinner tomorrow was successful and yet Simone remained a little reticent around him. Moments of trust and closeness like when the paparazzi had been photographing them and she'd sunk into his arms, then moments of pulling away. It was enough to fool the public in a photograph, likely not enough in a more intimate setting as the dinner would be. They needed something more. To cement an understanding between them that they hadn't truly achieved as employer and employee.

Today was meant to be fun, enjoyable. Reaching a kind of familiarity with one another, when to date they'd only ever been about work.

'Would it help if I told you we're visiting a place not open to the public, owned by one of my clients?'

'You mixing work with pleasure doesn't surprise me at all. That's who you are.'

The comment stung, even though it was fair. But in the end, it had been his desire never to be cold or hungry again that drove him to succeed where so many others had failed. Whilst there were a thousand things he needed to atone for, he wouldn't apologise for that.

Leo steered the vintage wooden motor launch towards a private jetty just visible in the distance. Simone matched the vibe of the day without even realising it. In white canvas shorts and a pretty blue and white polka-dot top. Her hair in a high ponytail, tied with a blue scarf. Wearing sneakers in a blue and white polka dot too, a hint of whimsy that surprised him given she always seemed buttoned up so tight. Add in some oversized sunglasses and a beachy looking wicker and leather bag and she looked like the perfect sixties starlet. He wondered what the fashion magazines might say about her today? They'd likely think the same as him in this moment.

She was perfect.

It shocked him that for two years he hadn't really noticed her appearance at all when now, he had trouble looking away. There was far more to Simone than she'd ever let on in the office. The woman had been as cool and opaque as the finest Carrara marble. Yet for him, he would only be able to admire from afar. Whilst Leo believed she enjoyed him telling her she was beautiful, their interactions would remain forever distant because that's what she wanted. So did he. Not to ruin a perfect working relationship or risk the deal with Tessitore he so fervently desired.

'Are you going to give me even a teensy hint of what's so special?'

'There,' he pointed as the historic villa came into view, rising above the treetops beside the lake. Its famed terraced gardens now obvious.

'Wow.'

That was a common reaction. The house was passed by most boating tours of the lake and was a favourite with its classical style of columns and arches. However, the true treasure of the place wasn't the house, as magnificent as it was, but the natural wonder the gardens held.

He pulled the launch up to the private jetty and jumped out, tying up the boat. Then he turned. Simone stood looking down at him as if getting ready to jump down herself.

'Let me help you,' he said.

'Oh. Sure.'

Leo reached up, his hands spanning her slender waist. Taking her weight as she hopped down. Their bodies close, closer. She didn't appear to be moving, like the day seemed to have paused on this moment. He should let her go, yet why didn't he want to?

'You okay?' he asked instead.

He was just steadying her, that was all. Her lips parted as if Simone was trying to take in more air. He wished he could see her eyes. How stormy grey they were in this moment, which seemed charged with something electric.

'Signor and Signora Zanetti. Welcome!'

The voice came from behind him. Leo released Simone and she swayed a little. He gently took her elbow and turned to see a man striding down the dock.

'My name's Guido and I'm the caretaker. I hope you both had a good journey?'

Leo shook the man's hand and Simone smiled. She made such a glorious picture against the vibrancy of the lake, her blonde hair gleaming like gold in the sunshine.

'I don't think I can imagine anywhere much more beautiful,' she said, looking around out over the water, up towards the house.

'Then it's my pleasure to welcome you here today. We have some refreshments, which will be served at the gazebo overlooking the lake. Would you like them now, or a little later?'

Leo looked over at Simone, his eyes raised, and she shook her head.

'*Grazie*, later,' he said. 'We'll explore some of the gardens first.'

'It's a good time to visit, we've had recent rains. The grounds are open to you for as long as you wish today. Should you need assistance, please ask one of the staff or come to my office. It's in an outbuilding near the house. I'll be here all day.'

The man waved and went on his way as they followed along the jetty till they reached a paved promenade stretching along the waterfront.

'Where to now?' she asked, the charged moment on the dock seemingly forgotten, by her at least.

'Pick a direction. There's no bad choice and we have plenty of time.'

Simone hesitated then turned left, the pathway taking them up through a series of garden rooms. From towering trees near the waterfront like some ancient forest, walking through to a riot of annual flowers, morphing into a wild looking meadow garden. Prizewinning and world-renowned, the only place most people other than a privileged few, would ever see all this beauty, was in photographs. As they moved further up the hillside the sound caught his ears. Rushing water. Although if you didn't know where the path led, you might mistake it for the sound of wind in the trees.

'What *is* this place?' Simone asked, stopping at a particularly beautiful view, framed by clipped olive trees and huge pots spilling over with red geraniums. Simone removed her sunglasses in the shade of the trees, took her phone out of her bag and snapped a photograph, slipping the phone into the pocket of her shorts.

'A privately owned residence. I helped the owner source some items for a renovation after he'd inherited it. Building a pavilion.'

'Are the owners here?'

'It's not the family's main residence. They spend most of the year out of Italy.'

'Why would you own this and not live here?'

'I have homes all over the world that I don't spend much time in.'

Though Leo was inclined to agree about this place. Its beauty needed to be experienced, not hidden away. When he'd come to know the place, he'd offered to buy it. The owner wouldn't sell, although they'd struck up a friendship and his client had said Leo could come back to visit. For Simone, Leo had called in the favour.

She rolled her eyes. No one else would have dared but he'd always enjoyed her sass. 'You forget. I know your property portfolio and you don't have *anything* like this.'

Simone was the only woman on the planet who might leave him feeling a little chastened.

'Are you trying to make me feel inadequate because of the size and breadth of my personal real estate?'

She cocked her head, her cool grey gaze almost assessing. The slightest wash of pink drifted across her cheeks again.

'I think you're doing just fine on the personal real estate front, Leo.'

The comment could have been innocent. It could also have meant something else entirely. The former was the safe conclusion. The latter, far more enticing.

Simone blew out a breath in a huff, lifting some stray hairs falling to her face. She brushed them out of the way, then she turned and kept walking like he'd been dismissed. It didn't matter. They were getting close to the place that held the real magic of the home. His heart beat a little faster. What would she think when she saw it?

She stopped at another beautiful view. Pink nerium vivid against the backdrop of the blue lake. Simone slipped her phone out of her pocket and took another photograph. There was something about her wanting memories that pleased him.

She turned to look at him, a slight frown creasing her brow. 'Do you want a selfie together? To show us in wedded bliss?'

He'd never taken a selfie in his life. 'Where would we post it? I don't do personal socials.'

There were enough fan sites extolling his imagined and not so imagined virtues. He didn't have the time or inclination to do anything more. His business sites were carefully managed by his marketing department. He supposed Simone could have posted something on hers, if she had any. Except when he and Simone had made the decision to marry, his marketing department suggested she make her own sites private. She'd told them she had none.

Simone Taylor was a ghost. A mystery.

She nibbled on her bottom lip. 'Send it to PR and see what they say.'

There was something about her, a little uncertain. He wondered whether it wasn't PR she was thinking of for the photograph, but herself. Once again, that pleased him in a way that was entirely foreign.

'Good idea. Then we'll let them decide.'

They positioned themselves with the magnificent view as a backdrop. Simone with her arm out, trying to catch the shot. It felt awkward, stilted like this. He guessed it would look even worse if it was ever shown to the public.

'My arms are longer, how about I take it?' he offered.

'Sure, why not.' She handed him her phone, warm from her touch. He purposely didn't think about how that warmth seeped into his palm as he held out the phone and they moved close. Her smile didn't seem genuine, her lips a little tight, which wouldn't do. He could give a winning smile, a money shot, on muscle memory alone.

'Say, Taleggio.'

'Why would I say that?'

'Taleggio's my favourite cheese.'

Her eyes widened and then she laughed. It was such a bright, joyful sound. Like birds waking at dawn. He smiled at the thought and took the photograph, then a few more for good measure.

The bare skin of her arm was soft against his own. She smelled like the citrus blossom that flowered everywhere at this time of the year. He didn't want to move, but they couldn't stand here like this any longer.

'I think that's enough to work with. Take a look.'

He handed back the phone. Simone scrolled through the pictures, looked up at him with a soft smile on her face.

'They're fantastic. Honestly, I don't think there could ever be a bad photograph of you.'

Leo rarely thought about his own looks, despite his stratospheric modelling career. His face was nothing more than an accident of DNA. However, Simone's simple comment sent a curl of pleasure through him.

'Why Mrs Zanetti, are you handing me a compliment?'

'It's my job as your wife to keep you grounded, so I'd never do that.' The corner of her lips tilted into a sly smile. 'You get far too many anyway. One more would be superfluous.'

'I don't like the way you keep imposing gravity upon me.'

'You're a highflyer. I'm just trying to keep your feet on the ground occasionally. Remind you what life's like, being a mere mortal like me.'

Her comment was an innocent one, said in a moment of fun, but it took him back to a time when he'd felt all too mortal. One he didn't want to remember, not today. The breeze changed and the sound from before became louder. Unmistakeable.

'What's that noise?' Simone asked, looking up the hill in its direction.

'The real wonder of this place,' he smiled, his heart rate picking up with anticipation. He wanted her to enjoy this, be struck by the wonder of it as he'd first been. 'Come on, this way takes us through the arid garden which is a bit rocky.'

He held out his hand to her and she slipped hers into it with no hesitation. They moved upwards, through the gravel paths and boulders, passing succulents and cactus, then onwards as the atmosphere began changing. Tree ferns dotted the space, the undergrowth lush. The air here cooler, more humid, almost like they'd been transported into a rainforest. The rush of water became even more pronounced as they rounded a corner.

Simone turned to him, her mouth open in wonder. 'Is that what I think it is?' Her voice was louder because the sound was now unmistakeable. The rush of water turning into a roar.

Ahead the hillside rose to their left and the path led through a grotto cut into the rock. But the wonder of it was that at the right time of the day, the mist that came from what was in the cave caught the light and a rainbow illuminated their way.

She let go of Leo's hand and hurried forwards, laughing as she took another photograph of the beauty and simplicity of white light shining through water droplets. He'd been all but forgotten, although that didn't matter. Her joy was all he'd craved to see and here he had it. He could take out his own phone and snap a picture of her smile, which would capture something more vibrant and beautiful than the misty rainbow ahead of him.

She disappeared into the dark fissure in the rock and he jogged to follow, not wanting to miss her reaction. He entered the space just behind her and she squealed. 'Oh my… look at this. Look. At. This.'

A waterfall cascaded through the rocks from above them, rushing under a stone bridge and away down the hillside to the lake. Simone stopped at the perfect vantage point, looking up from where the water roared over the hillside into the grotto where they stood, carefully placed artificial lighting accenting the space.

'It's so beautiful.' She shouted to be heard over the sound, far louder than when he'd been here before, clearly because of recent rains. 'I can't…'

Right now, with her smile as natural as the wonder surrounding him, she was the most beautiful thing here, without compare. She stood, gripping the railing. The mist from the waterfall drifted all round them and made their clothes damp the longer they stood here. Simone's pretty shirt began to cling to her body. Her nipples tight under the fine fabric. It was cooler here, that was all. Nothing more. His own polo was sticking to his body too. After a few more moments, Simone moved on, which was sensible because they were at risk of becoming drenched if they stood there too long.

'People should see this. People *need* to see this,' she said.

'Yet we're only two of the privileged few.'

'It pays to know you then, I guess.'

'I do come with some benefits.'

She caught him with her stormy gaze, her eyes flicking almost imperceptibly down his body then back up again. Most people wouldn't have noticed, but with her he saw everything.

Even in this cool hidden corner, heat speared through him potent and fiery. He craved to press her against the chill metal of the railings, kiss her. Hold her close. Hear her moan. There'd been no real kiss at the wedding. Only a peck on the cheek and whispered words in her ear to lighten the moment.

They believe we married for love, when I know you only married me for my choice of cake.

Her favourite flavour, one layer of chocolate hazelnut torte. That had made her laugh, which turned the moment from something that might have looked forced, to something warm and genuine.

Yet she'd made herself clear about not wanting anything further and in his vows he'd promised to honour her. Even if they were promises made in a fake marriage, he'd keep them. He'd spent his youth being dishonourable. He wanted to be honourable now, even though this seemed like a moment full of possibility and impossibility at the same time.

Leo clenched his hands, flexed his fingers. The urge to reach out, touch, hold. Seize the moment to see where it led, almost unbearable. He shut his eyes for a moment, took a deep breath. A reset.

'The property manager promised refreshments in the rotunda. It's a beautiful view there, one of the finest on the property.'

'Another beautiful view? How many can there be?'

Only one. Standing right in front of him, but that was something he couldn't admit.

'Countless,' he said to avoid the truth, in his own mind at least. 'If you'd like, we could go there, then walk the gardens some more?'

'Th-that would be lovely.'

'How about I lead the way?'

Simone nodded and he walked on ahead, the path curving down into the sunshine, to where a gazebo sat, overlooking the lake. There was jug of what appeared to be fresh lemonade, water condensing on the side. A platter of antipasto and *piadina* under an insect cover. They sat at opposite sides of the solid wooden table in the shade and he poured a drink for each of them as they nibbled on the delicious food.

The mascara below Simone's eyes had smudged from the dampness, making her look soft. Her eyes appeared smoky, as they did on their wedding day when he felt as though he'd seen her for the first time. She pulled out her phone and flicked through her photos. He took the moment to check his own phone and wished he hadn't. More problems in Rome. Reminders of the Tessitore dinner. His gut clenched, the food sitting like a rock. He took a sip of his cold, lemony drink.

'You happy with this one?' Simone asked and brought up a photo of them laughing. It was a good picture. Natural. Joyous. 'I wouldn't mind sending it to my sister and maybe Marchesa too.'

Marchesa was Simone's assistant, who was doing her job whilst they were away. Simone had been reluctant when he'd first suggested she have help, until he'd reminded her that as his wife, she'd be taking on additional roles so might need someone to relieve her of the administrative work that was now above her pay grade.

'She can pass it on to PR for us. Saves people wondering why you're thinking of work on what's supposed to be your honeymoon. How is Holly?'

'She's…okay. Thanks for asking.'

Simone's brow creased in a small frown, as if she was surprised he might have cared. Yet it was a salutary reminder of the whole purpose for this marriage. Business, not pleasure. He needed to make that his mantra.

'Our dinner with the Tessitores tomorrow…'

Their first public outing and a shot across the Silvestri family's bow. Once he'd started modelling, built his business, he'd vowed never to allow anyone to take anything from him again. Owning this famed, heritage brand would cement his reputation and mess with his father and half-brother's plans. *Nothing* was more important.

'Mmm?' Simone popped an olive into her mouth. Her glossy lips wrapping round her fingers, licking off the marinade oil. A dart of desire rocketed through him, spearing low.

Business, not pleasure. Business, not pleasure.

Leo cleared his throat.

'There's a fine personal shopper in Milan should you want something to wear.'

Simone's gaze shot up from her phone screen. 'I won't

embarrass you with my sartorial choices, if that's what you're worried about.'

'That's not what I—'

'Yes, you were. *Plain Jane*. That's what everyone calls me. Don't you like it, Leo? Do you think the title reflects badly on you, given everyone calls you the Sultan of Style? Because I'm not like them. I'm not obsessed with appearances instead of the person inside. I'm simply disinterested.'

She stood with her eyes narrowed. The cool grey burning hot with anger. He hadn't meant any of those things, yet this was like the rush of the waterfall, roaring over the rocks. He didn't know how to stop it.

'I'm aware—'

She glared at him, 'I'm not you, Leo. Don't try to turn me into someone I don't want to be. We had a deal. But if you're worried, I'm wearing the teal dress. The one you gave me.'

One he'd sourced with care when their engagement was announced. A dress he'd believed she'd find acceptable and, in her words, sustainable.

'The dress from our engagement's a nice touch,' he said, trying to repair what he'd clearly broken.

Simone crossed her arms, almost a protective move. 'I *know*. I thought it seemed sentimental. Now, I'm not so sure about anything. How about you stay here and eat so the effort the staff put in for us isn't wasted? I'm not hungry any more. I'm going to keep walking.'

Simone stalked off, taking a different path, rounding a corner and disappearing into the garden without looking back. Leo took a slow breath, trying to understand how quickly the moment had changed, from something wonderful, to this.

CHAPTER FOUR

SIMONE CHECKED HER PHONE. She'd finally sent Holly a picture of the villa she and Leo had visited the day before, their selfie, as reassurance that they were having a good time. Her sister's reply came quickly.

OMG amazing view followed by flame emojis.

She didn't think those flames were referring to the view in the background, admittedly amazing as it was.

Simone pulled up the photo again. Her, laughing. Leo's own grin, warm and generous. The corners of his eyes crinkling as if they'd just shared a secret joke. To someone who knew nothing about their relationship it would have told a story of a loving couple on their honeymoon. To her, it was a photo full of lies.

She put down her phone, satisfied that Holly was happy, and walked to the window of her room. Staring out onto the slice of garden lit up as night fell and then out to the city beyond. She mused about how life and moments could change in an instant, with only a word.

The day on Lake Garda and at the private waterfall had been a magical experience. Motoring at speed across the glorious water. The sun warm, the breeze cool. The planning it must have taken for Leo to arrange the day. Not somewhere people could sightsee, but a private residence because he believed she might like it.

It had shown thought and care. Or at least, she'd believed it had. That it was a result of someone considering her desires, what she might actually enjoy, rather than what they wanted with her as a peripheral consideration. It had been wondrous, beautiful. Looking up at that waterfall tumbling over the rocks and rushing away underneath them, gleaming with perfectly positioned lights. Surrounded by the rock walls, covered in mosses and little ferns, it could have been something out of a fairy tale. A portal to another world where she and Leo were different people and a realm of possibility was open to them.

But as she needed to remember, she and Leo weren't different people. He was Leo Zanetti, wanted all over the world for how he looked. To set trends. She was his reliable EA, Simone Taylor. It was good that he'd reminded her of that. Sure, he probably thought he was being kind when he talked about what she was going to wear tonight. Whilst she tried not to care because it was all so meaningless, Simone didn't want to be thought of as *Plain Jane* either, even though she knew that wasn't who she was deep down.

People had called her beautiful once, when she was younger, and wore the 'right' clothes. The designer ones, with the glam makeup and hair that had been styled for hours by a hairdresser. It's just that that wasn't what was important about a person. It was who they were inside that mattered. She'd met some of the most beautiful people on the planet in her time—at college, socialising with her parents, through her role as an EA and especially with Leo. Some naturally endowed, others surgically enhanced. She didn't judge. What she'd come to know was that beauty was subjective, but it was also a meaningless measure of someone's worth. Especially when some people were just plain ugly inside.

Well, if her outward appearance was what Leo was worried about, there wasn't much she could do about it. She'd made promises to herself about setting aside frivolous things like clothes and makeup and she was sticking to them. Simone checked the time. Tonight was their dinner with the Tessitores. What this whole marriage was about. Whilst all she wanted to do was stay in and eat a burger and a bowl of fries, Simone had a job to do. She'd never shirked before and she wouldn't now. But she wasn't interested in this game Leo was playing. Her illusions felt a little shattered, the ground beneath her somewhat unsteady. For one fleeting, ridiculous moment she'd believed Leo had been thinking about her when he'd arranged that boat trip, when most likely, all he was doing was buttering her up for the conversation he wanted to have about how she was going to look on his arm tonight.

It was like something inside her had been crushed and killed. What did that say about her? That she was so starved for attention she'd deluded herself into trying to find it in a relationship that was completely transactional? She shook her head. It didn't matter. Right now, her focus had to be on pretending to be an adoring wife. That was her job. What she'd been employed to do.

She walked over to the mirror, peering at her reflection. Her hair was done up but not in her usual, tight, shiny chignon. Instead, she was trialling a claw clip hack video Holly had sent her, which was meant to be quick and easy and without the need for so many hair pins. The problem was that her hair wasn't quite behaving. Not sleek like she preferred for business occasions as this was. Tonight, little pieces of it were falling about her face making the whole style a bit soft. A lot less like herself.

More like the girl she used to be.

Simone gave her makeup one last check, though why, she wasn't sure. It was the same as always. Natural, with her lips slicked with a little rosy gloss. She looked 'put together', as some people might have called it, though not high glamour, because that had never really been her, no matter the box her parents had tried to squeeze her into. And why she was thinking about them now, she didn't know. Her whole life seemed completely topsy-turvy. She needed to stop romanticising the trip on the boat, stop thinking about her parents, and remember who she was. Simone Taylor. A hard worker. A trustworthy and trusted employee. A good person who was more interested in internal substance than external appearances. And if people didn't like it, including Leo, then they could, to put it colloquially, take a hike.

Simone grabbed her clutch and left her room, standing at the top of the stairs leading down to the second level of the home where Leo's bedroom was. As she did, he walked through his own door, his timing impeccable, as always. Right now his head was down, checking his phone in one hand. In his other, holding something she couldn't really see. Seeing him, her breath caught. Her heart speeding to a thready rhythm as it fluttered against her ribs as if a kaleidoscope of butterflies had taken up residence there. He was wearing a suit, like so many men she'd worked with over the years, but Leonardo Zanetti wore a suit like nobody else. The way it hugged his broad shoulders, draped and shaped his body. His tie in a gorgeous check of teals and reds, complementing her dress to perfection. She squashed any lingering fantasy that his choice of tie showed he'd thought of her. Being who he was, she shouldn't have expected anything less.

Then he looked up at her and those piercing blue eyes of his stabbed right through Simone's chest. What did he see when he did that? It was impossible to tell, though his gaze did give her a kind of appraisal. A subtle up-and-down, with a slight smile teasing his perfect lips. She got the feeling he liked her wearing the things he'd bought for her and that did something weird to her insides. Like they'd taken a trip on a rollercoaster.

'The dress looks lovely,' he said as she made her way down to his level.

'You bought it, so you should know.'

The strange feelings of distance from yesterday still clung to her, even though they'd had a little reset today. A delicious coffee and pastry in a local café. A stroll through the cobbled streets where she'd picked up a few art prints as souvenirs.

'It's the wearer, not the clothing, that makes the outfit, *cara.*'

She tried to ignore the compliment, and the endearment, yet a flush of heat still crept to her cheeks. Leo had told her the dress wasn't modern couture like he'd tried to offer her before she'd put her foot down, but vintage. She'd wanted it the moment she'd set eyes on it. Glowing teal silk that had so much play of colour under the lights the dress looked alive. It was apparently from the fifties, a 'wiggle dress' the handwritten tag attached to it had said. The minute she'd slipped it on she'd fallen in love. The fit made her look like a bit of a fifties bombshell, the way it nipped in at the waist and hugged her hips.

He'd tried to imply in an offhand kind of way that being vintage, it was an economical choice and didn't offend her desire for more sustainable fashion. As if Leo didn't think she'd look up the brand on the tag. When she did, she discovered the designer was collectible and that this particular style and colour was rare, highly sought after and absurdly expensive. Yet the moment she'd placed it on her body she hadn't been able to give it up. It made her feel pretty, like she did tonight.

'You look good too. The tie's a nice touch.'

Simone wasn't unique in thinking that there was something about this man that would make even the coldest, most desiccated heart burst to life. Still, her own compliments were bland by comparison. If it bothered him, he didn't let on. All he did was stare at her. He opened his mouth and then closed it, almost hesitating. She'd never seen Leo hesitate at anything. Perhaps he thought there was something wrong with her appearance. She'd been used to criticism from her parents. Trying too hard to please them, yet never being enough.

'What?' she asked. 'Is it my hair?'

'Your hair looks effortlessly beautiful. It's perfect.'

Way to punch a woman in the solar plexus. It was like she couldn't breathe.

'I—I, thank you.'

Leo nodded. 'I have a gift for you.'

Simone clenched her jaw. Right, so that was what this was about. Would he ever stop? Each time he offered her something it was another reminder that he believed she was somehow lacking. What was it this time? Jewellery, because she didn't sparkle enough?

He'd married her, so he'd just need to get used to her as she was rather than keep trying to change her.

'We've been—'

'I know, but I thought of this dress immediately I saw them.'

He reached his hand out from behind his back and held up a pair of shoes.

They weren't just *any* shoes. These were teal patent

leather stilettos which matched the colour of the dress *perfectly*. Yet what made them more striking was the flash of a red sole, contrasting magnificently with the blue green of the leather and matching the hint of red in his tie.

Red is the colour of harlots, Simone.

Her mother's words shot into her consciousness. Even after all this time, those old censures returned like a tainted muscle memory. Worse now since she'd married Leo because everyone thought of him as a god who deserved a goddess, not a mere mortal like her.

'I have perfectly good shoes.' She looked down. Hers were nice. Elegant, neutral pumps that went with everything.

Leo followed her gaze, slowly, like he was taking her all in.

'You do. However, these…'

He held them up and wiggled his hand as if that would tempt her. Simone's eyes caught the pristine red of the sole again. The man was like the serpent dangling a shiny apple in front of her. Punishingly handsome and all temptation, just like she'd expect the devil to be.

Leo might be able to get away with pretending that the dress he'd given her was just some old thing that cost nothing, rather than a coveted collector's item. He couldn't with these shoes. She knew exactly how much they'd cost. Whilst they were a drop in Leo's ocean of money, they represented a life she didn't have or want any more.

And yet the way they gleamed under the lights. They'd look *gorgeous* with what she was wearing. Those towering heels would make her much taller…

'No.'

'If you're afraid of wearing heels this high, there's no need. I won't let you stumble.'

She'd been used to high heels once. They weren't prac-

tical to her life after she'd taken up the role as an executive
assistant, running around after billionaires who wanted her
at their beck and call. Yet his refusal to put those tempting, magnificent shoes away caused a swirl of irritation to
spark up inside.

'We've talked about this. I don't need expensive gifts.
Especially not clothes. I'm not you.'

'Thank God for that,' he said. 'Yet there's something I
know. You want them. I can see it in your eyes.'

She *hated* that he could and how right he was. She *did*
want them. Wanted to put them on with their gorgeous red
soles, slick on some red lipstick even though she didn't own
any and to hell with the words of her mother in her head,
even after all these years.

She loathed that conflict inside of her, sensations and
memories she'd thought were long buried. That fire of irritation lit to the hot burn of something a lot like anger.

Leo held out the shoes. 'It's not as if they're a choker of
diamonds. They're shoes. Why say no when you know you
want them?'

'Fine,' she said. He'd won. She placed her clutch on the
stairs behind her. Balancing against the handrail, taking
off one pump and dropping it with a thud, then another. He
didn't hand her the shoes, instead, Leo stepped forwards and
placed them on the floor in front of her. For a moment she
had the strange sensation he was bowing down to her and
the rush was intoxicating like a shot of the hazelnut liqueur
she enjoyed. It was sweet and went straight to her head.

She slipped her feet into the heels, took a moment to
adjust. The way they felt, her calves bunching. The height
they gave her. Red be damned. She didn't care. She wanted
them and she'd wear the hell out of them, even if it was only
for tonight.

Leo's vibrant, knowing eyes flared with something like satisfaction.

The heels brought her to the same level as his mouth. His lips were sculpted, with a perfectly defined cupid's bow. His lower lip slightly fuller, giving him a sensual, almost brooding expression that the world loved. Right now, they tilted at the corners, carrying the hint of a smug smile. That he'd won? That she'd capitulated? Probably. She hated how she'd given in, but even more, how much she loved how the shoes looked and felt. How Leo knew.

And even with that complex conglomerate of emotions swirling inside, she longed to grab him by the tie, kiss him and wipe that devastatingly handsome smirk from his face. She took the tiniest of steps back as her fingers itched to simply reach out and take.

'Great,' she said. 'Are you happy now?'

'Very. Do you need—?'

'I don't need help. It's not like I've never worn heels before. Let's go.'

She grabbed her bag then turned in a rush at the top of the stairs, wanting to escape the craving that had overtaken her, which was turning her into someone she didn't recognise any more. How Leo made her feel. How she felt like she'd sold out when Leo was right. They were only shoes, so why did it even matter?

Then her heel caught. She pitched forward. There was a shout, she flew, then…

Morbidity. Mortality. They were both words Leo had heard when Simone had been rushed by ambulance, unconscious, to Milan's top hospital two weeks earlier.

That moment where she'd pitched forwards, tumbled and all he'd been left with at the end was a body at the base of the stairs. The blood. Even now the vision, running through his head as if it were a horror movie, jolted him like a current of electricity. Making his heart race. Twisting his gut. He *saw* Simone but imagined at the same time, his mother on a dark set of stairs, alone.

In both cases, the fall had been his fault. With his mother, for not making sure she had enough money so she wouldn't have had to work nights, cleaning. She could have taken something easier, been safe at home instead of slipping on some stairs in the cold darkness. With Simone, giving her a wretched pair of shoes she hadn't wanted. In the end, the gift more for his sake than hers, because he'd wanted to show her off, crush the moniker of *Plain Jane* for ever. In the end, he hadn't done what he'd promised her he would. He hadn't protected her from stumbling.

Instead of a dinner he'd been looking forward to with a beautiful woman, wearing what he'd bought for her, he'd been plunged into a nightmare of his own making.

The memories were stark. Her lying in bed. Her eyes closed. The side of her face florid with dark bruising. And as he looked at her, willing her to keep breathing and begging her, *Open your eyes, Simone. Please…* The image was overlaid with one of his mother. Similarly unconscious, though with all the pleading in the world, she'd never opened her eyes again.

Fortunately, that hadn't been the case for Simone. When she'd finally woken in critical care, confused and disorientated, he'd thanked the heavens for what he saw as a second chance even as the terror had gripped him. At first, she'd not been able to remember much, till the pieces of her life seemed to fall back into place like a jigsaw. The only thing she couldn't recall was what had happened in the final moment at the top of the stairs, which he took as a blessing.

He wished he was similarly afflicted and could forget the vision of her stumbling, flailing, falling.

'Only a few more tests, Mrs Zanetti.'

'Thank you Doctor,' she murmured.

Leo leaned forwards in an armchair in Simone's hospital room, where he'd spent most hours every day since she'd been moved here from critical care after her fall. He checked his phone. His driver reported the paparazzi were still parked outside the hospital as they had been ever since news had broken of Simone's accident. The speculation about what had happened that night, salacious, until his lawyers had threated legal action and Simone had finally been able to issue a media statement. Or at least, his PR had issued the statement with her approval.

Thanking the hospital. Thanking Leo.

That last thanks was entirely undeserved.

He rubbed at the rough stubble on his chin, from going days without shaving, as the doctor asked her some more questions and performed yet more tests. Asked Simone to smell things, to look at charts. Neurological and other examinations all designed to test her mental status. The final steps before she was discharged.

'How is your dizziness? Photophobia?'

The blinds of her private room were closed, the lights dimmed, so Leo didn't need to hear her answer confirming she was still a little sensitive to light. He hadn't considered himself a religious man, yet the fact Simone was sitting upright in a chair and able to see at all was like every prayer he'd cast to the universe had been answered. She'd been given back to him, when his mother had been committed to a grave, in darkness for ever.

'Thank you for your care of my wife. Of us both.' His words choked in his throat. He breathed through the burn at the back of his nose. Staff had been immeasurably professional and kind, especially when for a while they'd feared her condition was critical, till scans had proved her head injury wasn't as serious as it might have been.

'You're doing well,' the specialist said. 'My star patient. We can discharge you today. I'll arrange for staff to bring the necessary paperwork and book a follow up appointment.'

As the doctor made to leave, Leo stood, held out his hand. She'd been recommended as one of Italy's finest neurosurgeons and nothing he could say to her would be enough to encompass how he felt in this moment.

'I'd like to make a donation,' he said. Money was all he had to atone for his sins. Just as it was for the people he'd harmed as a reckless teenager in Rome, it wasn't enough, but it would have to do. 'To the hospital foundation. Or is there a charity you'd prefer?'

'That's generous, Signor Zanetti. We have a foundation that evaluates novel brain injury treatment. However, there's never enough funding.'

'There will be now,' he vowed. 'I'll have my office contact you for details.'

'*Grazie*,' she said and left the room.

He walked towards Simone, sitting in a chair wearing a soft, casual black dress from her wardrobe, with gold sneakers. Items she'd asked him to bring for her. It had seemed strangely intrusive, searching through her clothes, yet as he did so, he'd gleaned a bit more about her style. How some of the things she owned that he'd never seen before, seemed a little whimsical. He wondered when she wore them. A soft and silky scarf in cornflower blue, black and orange. Earrings with little dangling enamel lemons. Things he'd never imagined she might wear yet once he'd seen them, he somehow couldn't imagine her not.

'How are you feeling?' he asked, touching Simone's hand, which was reassuringly alive with warmth. The last time he'd touched his mother her hand had begun to cool. He shuddered.

Simone looked down at his hand over hers. She shrugged. 'Fine, all things considered.'

Simone didn't look it. Her skin was pale and she had dark shadows under her eyes. She'd said that people kept waking her up through the night, every night, asking her questions and checking her vitals.

'Good. Photographers are still at the front door. Our car will be coming around back to avoid them.'

'Photographers? That's ridiculous.'

'I agree.' He knew what they wanted. To take photographs of any bruising that remained on her face and down her arm where she'd fallen. She was so lucky not to have broken anything. The marks were already fading and were at the stage of green and yellow now. They'd been gone within two weeks he'd been told. But it was still an awful reminder that things could have been so much worse. There'd been warnings about the effects of a head injury, given her period of unconsciousness and post traumatic confusion. Irritability, disinhibition, tiredness and so many more. Simone had seemed lucky to have been spared most of them. Not everyone would have been.

'Can you imagine what they'd say of me now? They wouldn't be as charitable as calling me Plain Jane.'

The heat that rose to his gut was instant and volcanic.

'Anything they say about your appearance, other than you are a beautiful woman still recovering from a serious injury, would be unwarranted and they will be punished.'

Her eyes widened. 'How would you punish them?'

It had been another failing of his. He'd believed that most

of the uncharitable commentary about Simone's appearance was an aberration that would die down if they simply ignored it long enough. No longer.

'I'll stop providing information or access to those who don't co-operate.'

His press releases were usually distributed equitably. Now, he'd cut off anyone who persisted in writing negatively about her. Circolo's media department wouldn't be happy, but he didn't give a damn.

A knock sounded at the door and it opened. An orderly walked in with a wheelchair.

'Is this necessary?' Simone asked. 'I *can* walk.'

A nurse followed behind carrying some papers. 'Since you've had dizziness, *si*. It's policy. Just to be sure.'

Simone nodded then stopped. Shut her eyes and pinched the bridge of her nose. She looked in pain and it was yet another reminder that he hadn't looked after her when he should have. When he'd promised to. After a few moments she raised her head.

'Did you manage to bring my sunglasses?'

He reached into the pocket of his jacket and pulled out a pair he'd found. He handed them to her and she slipped them on. They covered most of the visible bruising. She took a deep breath, as if steeling herself, then looked around the room.

'Okay,' she said. 'I'm ready. Let's get out of here.'

CHAPTER FIVE

THEY'D MANAGED TO avoid the photographers parked outside the hospital with a bit of subterfuge, for which Simone was thankful. She'd hated looking at herself in the mirror and at her bruises, which were still too tender to hide under makeup. There was no way she wanted photographs of herself plastered all over the press looking like this. Simone reached up and gingerly touched the back of her head. Apparently when she'd fallen, the claw clip had broken and cut into her. At the hospital they'd tried to wash the blood out as best they could, but she was told they'd had to cut away some of her hair to check her wounds. She almost didn't want to know how it looked. In the days after her injury she hadn't cared, because everything was fuzzy and terrifying when people kept asking her the year, who she was and what had happened to her. Especially that, because even now, the fall itself still remained a total blank in her memory.

'Are you all right?' Leo asked, frowning. 'Is your head sore?'

'I don't think I want to know what's happened to my hair. It feels like chunks are missing and I haven't really washed it in two weeks.'

'When you feel up to it, would you like me to organise a hairdresser to come and cut it for you?'

Something soft and warm lit in her chest. 'That'd be lovely.'

'I'll ask Marchesa to find someone suitable.'

Leo had been her only constant in the days after her fall. All she knew was that every time she woke from a sleep, Leo was reclining in a chair in her room, or sleeping on a trundle bed brought in for him because he refused to leave her side. Then the memories came back and the little bits she couldn't remember, he'd gently filled in for her. They'd been going out to dinner but she'd tripped in those beautiful high heels he'd gifted her and fallen down the stairs.

'I'm sorry about dinner with the Tessitores.'

He made a noise, an exhalation, almost like he'd been punched.

'You have nothing to be sorry for,' he said. The words spitting out of him with a surprising vehemence. 'My concerns were not about them. Only you.'

'Still—'

'There's nothing more to be said. They sent their regards and flowers, which I would have brought to you except they weren't allowed in critical care. By the time you were on the ward, they were past their best.'

A buzzing sound rang in her ears. She put her fingers to her temples. *Critical care…*

It was hard to believe how close she'd come to not being here at all.

The warmth of a hand settled on her knee, the weight of it giving her some comfort even if Leo had no idea what was troubling her.

'We're almost home.'

Their driver manoeuvred down a back street approaching a high stone wall. An automatic door opened to the underground garage of Leo's Milan residence and the car pulled to a stop. She took off her sunglasses and made a move to open the door.

'Wait here,' Leo said. He left the car and moved around to her side. He opened her door and held out his hand.

Simone shook her head. 'I'm fine, Leo. They wouldn't have released me if I wasn't.'

His expression appeared pained but he gave her what she could have described as an attempt at a warm and understanding smile. 'Humour me.'

She placed her hand in his. His touch solid. Safe. Yet nothing about Leo Zanetti was safe. The heat of that commonplace connection building through the act, simple yet powerful. She wanted to snatch her hand away but that would seem irrational, so she ignored the sensation and let him help her from the car.

'Thank you,' she said, expecting Leo to release her. He didn't and she found she didn't mind at all.

'I've cleared my study on the ground floor to make a bedroom for you there.'

'Why on earth did you do that? I don't want to move. I like the room you gave me.'

She loved the space. It was private and relaxing. One of the things she was most looking forward to after leaving the hospital was sleeping in her magnificent four poster bed, in the room Leo had designed especially for her.

He let out a slow, almost long-suffering breath.

'I thought you might say that.' Then in one swift moved he simply bent, lifted her into his arms and held her secure against his strong, hard body.

She squeaked. 'What do you think you're doing?'

He began to move, striding through the underground garage to a flight of stairs. 'I would have thought it self-evident. I'm carrying you inside the house.'

Simone wriggled in his arms. 'I don't need this. Put me down!'

Leo simply held on tighter. He made his way up the stairs as if carrying her was no effort at all. 'You've been dizzy. You left the hospital in a wheelchair. There are three flights of stairs to the upper floor where your room is. My aim is to get you there safely.'

'This is ridiculous. I was only in a wheelchair for the hospital's legal liability. I can walk on my own. I'm sure you won't let me stumble.'

Leo reached to top of the stairs, stopped. Stared at her intently. His eyes were so transfixing, hypnotically so. In this moment she developed an acute understanding of the idea that you could simply fall into a gaze and drown in it.

'Yet I didn't prevent you from stumbling and falling, and you were injured. That will *never* happen again.' His voice was deep and raw. It carried such gravitas behind it, a rough sound that seemed sincerely meant. This was important to him, her safety. Instead of feeling claustrophobic and strange as it did only minutes before, she relaxed into his embrace.

He was strong, solid. The intoxicating scent of his aftershave achingly familiar, carrying a mystery and depth that suited Leo to perfection. It was a smell she wanted to wrap herself in. To simply take whatever Leo was prepared to give.

For so long she'd been alone, with only herself to rely on. By design, because the people she was supposed to be able to trust the most, her friends, her family and the man she'd loved, had all abandoned her. This, someone wanting to look after her, seemed completely foreign. And right now she was tired of relying on herself. Tired of everything, really. She just wanted to settle in a comfortable bed of her own and sleep for a year, then wake up feeling like someone new.

After a third flight of stairs, where he didn't even break a sweat or get out of breath, Leo finally reached the door of her room. 'Are you okay for me to put you down?'

She nodded. This close it was clear how truly flawless he was. His warm, tanned skin without a single blemish. No part of him anything other than perfect. Then there was his strength. The way he moved, as if she weighed nothing at all. His hardness to her soft. He gently placed her feet on the ground and supported her, she assumed till he could make sure she was steady.

At least it didn't make her world spin, so maybe things would improve faster than she'd expected.

'Is there anything I can get you?'

'I'd love a coffee.'

'That can be arranged,' he said with a warm smile, opening the door of her room. 'You sit down. I'll be back soon.'

She walked inside the attic space and noticed immediately how much darker it was. The filmy sheers had been covered by thicker, blackout curtains. Tears prickled at her eyes and she wiped them away. He knew about her photophobia. Again, it was something Leo had done for her.

She put her sunglasses on a side table and flopped onto the soft, overstuffed couch. The neutrals of the room soothing on her overworked brain. She leaned her head back, and shut her eyes. Sifting through her memories of the wedding, Lake Garda, the waterfall, until she hit the blankness of the last few moments on the night she fell.

Nothing.

Or maybe something... There was a prickle of sensation. She opened her eyes. Leo stood at the door of her room with a tray, looking awfully domesticated.

'I thought you were asleep,' he said, walking in and setting the tray with two cups and a little bowl down on the occasional table in front of her. The rich, toasted aroma of coffee filled the room.

'Not yet. I'm trying memories out for size.'

Leo handed her a cup. Placed the little bowl in front of her, which she now saw contained some hazelnut pralines.

He sat down next to her and took a cup of his own. 'Did any fit?'

'No. My actual accident's still a blank.'

'Perhaps that's a good thing,' Leo said. 'It's not something you should want to remember.'

'I hate having moments of my life missing, even if it's only a few.' It reminded her of how fragile she was, how arbitrary life could be. 'Though I guess everyone has something they'd like to forget.'

'Indeed.'

The look on Leo's face seemed stark. Haunted. It suggested what he might have seen. From the moment she'd woken it appeared to her like he was looking at a woman returned from the dead. In the fortnight she'd been in hospital, once her shocked brain had started thinking a little more clearly, she'd begun to realise how close she might have come.

Simone didn't know what to say to make any of it better. Instead, she grabbed a chocolate and took a sip of her coffee.

'Thank you, Leo… I—'

He held up his hand in a stop motion. 'I don't want any thanks. There's nothing you have to say. If you need anything, call me and I'll come. But for now, rest. I'll see you later.'

He picked up his own coffee and stood. Striding out of the room as if being chased by a ghost, before closing the door gently behind him.

* * *

The next week passed in a blur. Given their honeymoon had been cancelled, Leo had started working again. Not going into the office but working from home. A somewhat remote yet powerful presence, as he gave Simone her space. Whilst recovering, she hadn't realised how much sleep she'd need, or how much even the little things took out of her. They'd taken a quiet walk to the local café since she was getting cabin fever and she'd slept for half a day afterwards. Her doctor had reassured her on the follow up visit that it was completely normal and she was doing remarkably well, even though her head felt like it was stuffed full of oatmeal when she woke up each morning.

All she wanted was to feel like herself again. At least her hair had been washed and styled, which helped. She was pleased with how it looked in a new below the shoulder bob. Quite a bit shorter because of how medical staff had cut into it but she could still wear it up if she wanted, which she took as a small win in what felt like weeks of losses.

She went to the bathroom and dabbed on some concealer, hiding the worst of her remaining bruises. She still looked pale and tired. Nothing a little cream blush wouldn't fix so she put some of that on too. After satisfying herself that she looked a bit more human again, Simone walked to her lounger and flopped into it, grabbing her phone. She hadn't had much communication with Circolo. Marchesa had sent her a text asking if she was okay and telling her everything was under control. Leo had shielded her from all talk of work, saying he didn't want her to worry about anything, which of course made her worry about *everything*.

Simone wanted to feel as though things were getting back to some kind of normalcy, so she opened her calendar. Checked on what she'd missed in those hazy few days when she'd woken, terrified, briefly not knowing where she was or even *who* she was till she heard Leo's voice and it came trickling back.

Her diary was absent any of Leo's appointments, which was strange because his diary was usually back-to-back. Had he cancelled everything because of her fall? It seemed shocking to her that he might have when in her experience, his business was *everything* to him. She went into his diary and it was all there. Meetings, the charity ball they were meant to attend. It must have been a glitch. Yet toggling back to hers…zero.

She flicked to her emails then, squinting and turning down the brightness of her phone's screen. Taking it slow as she scrolled because the movement of the screen still made her feel a bit woozy. Marchesa had done a great job of clearing out most of the admin emails. There wasn't much that hadn't already been read and attended to. She glimpsed an all-company email from Leo personally, about admin support. Opened and read it.

What. The. Hell.

She gripped her phone hard. He was excluding her? Marchesa was—

Simone stood in a rush. Probably too much of a rush, her head pounding. It didn't matter. She stormed to the door of her room and flung it back, marching down the stairs to Leo's level. Stalking to the top of the stairs that would take her down to the living area. As she reached the landing, a flash of something streaked through her, like a sense of déjà vu, her heart pounding against her ribcage. Simone stopped, took a deep breath. Grabbed the railing and as much as she wanted to run down the staircase in righteous anger, she composed herself and walked slowly, carefully, till she reached the bottom.

Even though she'd taken a moment, it didn't dampen the sensation scorching and furious, surging through her veins. He wouldn't be in his study. He'd turned that into a downstairs bedroom for her, which hadn't yet been changed back after she'd refused it. *Ha!* She'd thought his offer sweet but he was yet someone else in her life who was intent on making decisions for her with no consultation. The other place she knew he appeared to enjoy was a beautiful terrace off the lounge area that led to the garden, where you could sit at a large table under a pergola covered with grape vines.

'Leo!'

The sound of a chair scraping back on sandstone tiles grated through her head. The tap, tap, tap of leather soled shoes came closer as Leo jogged into view, his brow furrowed in worry.

Well, he *should* be concerned.

'*Cara*, there's a problem?'

She pinched the bridge of her nose, the pounding of her heart starting a corresponding pounding in her head.

'You need painkillers? A doctor?'

She looked up at him. 'No, Leo. I need you to tell me why you sent an all-company email telling everyone that Marchesa's now your EA.'

He cocked his head, but didn't look at all chastened. If anything, his frown deepened.

'What are you doing looking at your email? Your doctor said you shouldn't be working—'

'She said I could have a graduated return starting one day a week and increasing as I felt fit enough. I feel fit now. What I didn't expect, was that my employer would just... just...sack me!'

Leo held up his hands. 'Husband.'

'What? You're pulling the husband card *now?*'

'*Simone.*'

That tone in his voice. She was sure Leo meant it to sound placating but instead, he sounded so condescending it made her grind her teeth.

'There's no need for you to work. I can give you everything you need. You've trained Marchesa well and she'll be able to do the job admirably.'

'There's only one problem, *husband* dearest.' She lifted her hand, stabbing her fingers into her sternum as if punctuating every word. 'You. Didn't. Ask. *Me.*'

'I didn't want you to be concerned about anything. This seemed like a good solution—'

'As an interim measure. Nothing in our deal said I wouldn't continue in my role as your EA.'

'Circumstances change and I don't understand why—'

She began to pace, trying to expel the furious energy that had overtaken her. Leo could never understand what it was like, being subject to the whims of others. She'd *fought* to be able to make her own decisions and now he was intent on stealing everything away from her. She'd be entirely reliant on him. And when he decided he didn't want her any more… What then?

'We have an agreement, but I will not be kept. Since my twenties, I've been employed. I've *studied* to hone my skills as an EA and I'm damned good at my role. Now, you're taking it all away from me!'

She'd had enough people ruling her life, particularly her parents. Using their money as a weapon to be wielded. She'd left the family when she'd realised they'd never see her as autonomous, only as a chess piece to be moved. Where love was conditional, so long as you fit the family mould.

When she'd walked away Simone had made a promise to herself. She'd *never* go back to a situation where she wasn't in charge of her own destiny. Sure, she might be married to Leo, but she'd gone into that with her eyes *wide* open to help Holly. She'd been fooled into thinking that he'd begun to care about her, even if only a little, when what he really wanted, was to run her life how he saw fit.

'Come, sit down,' Leo said.

Her stomach twisted into agonizing knots. 'I don't need to sit down. I need you to *fix* this.'

'Simone, you look like if you don't sit down, you're going to fall down. Please.'

He moved towards her slowly as though he was approaching a wild animal. Leo touched her elbow gently. A sensation shivered through her, liquid and warm. Too pleasant and comforting. She hated that she felt like this. That he was *right*, because the emotion of it all had taken it out of her. She felt like she was wilting like a flower in baking sunshine. Knees a little unsteady. Exhausted, like all her batteries had run empty.

'Do I have to pick you up again and put you on the sofa?'

For a fleeting second a flare of heat rocketed right through her. The memory of how it felt to be in his arms. How solid. How safe. How cared for.

Yet he didn't care. If he had, he wouldn't have done this.

She needed to wrestle back the momentum. 'Fine, let's sit down then.'

Simone walked to the couch and lowered herself onto it. It was deep and as comfortable as the one in her bedroom. The moment she sank into it she decided she was never going to leave. She wanted to curl up and sleep the week away.

Leo sat next to her. Close enough, but the gulf between them seemed unbreachable.

'No one visited you at the hospital.'

Her heart rate spiked, sending another pounding into her head. She touched her temple. Why was he bringing that up?

'I asked for your emergency contacts from HR. Called Holly. She said she couldn't come because she's pregnant and doctors won't allow her to travel. Insisted I get in touch with your parents. Gave me their details. Your father emailed me in response to keep him appraised, *should I be so inclined*.'

Simone knew he'd been in touch with Holly. The moment Simone had been well enough she'd contacted her sister to reassure her that she was fine because she didn't want Holly to worry any more than she had already. It was bad for her blood pressure. They'd exchanged messages since, Simone downplaying the aftereffects of her fall.

Holly hadn't said anything about Leo contacting their parents.

'I told you I was estranged from them.'

Leo's eyes tightened. The expression was one that looked a lot like concern but she was used to that being wrapped up in a desire to control. She wasn't buying into it, not any more.

'You were injured. Seriously. If it weren't for me, who would have cared for you?'

It was as if the world stopped. She gripped onto the arm of the sofa because that terrible truth slammed into her so suddenly. She really had no one. Work was her life. She didn't have many close friends because those she'd thought she was close to once, had laughed at her behind her back. She was caring for Holly, not the other way round. Her throat tightened. What if she'd been alone, and fallen down a flight of stairs with no one to find her? She might not be here right now.

Simone shook her head. What was she thinking? Her New York studio had only been one level. There were no stairs to fall down there. She was jumping at shadows, at possibilities that would never have arisen.

It still didn't take away the creeping, terrifying thought that she could have died when she'd barely even lived. It was like a terrible weight of realisation pressing on her chest, making it hard to breathe.

'I take care of myself. That's what most people do. You don't get to make decisions for my life.'

Everything about this, how she'd thought he cared, seemed changed. Like when she'd arrived at this house and he'd shown her to her beautiful room. Or taken her to Lake Garda to see a magnificent waterfall and garden that few people ever would. Then when she'd woken in hospital to find him by her bedside. Those fond memories curdled in her stomach like sour milk.

'I was trying to help so you didn't need to worry.'

'And yet here I am, more worried than before.' She pinched the bridge of her nose. Trying to hold back the burn in her eyes.

Leo reached out and took her hand gently. Rubbed his thumb over the back of it. Anyone looking at them might see this as a tender moment.

Looks could be *so* deceiving.

'What do you need?' he asked.

She looked at him. His expression seemed so open, concerned. She wanted to believe what her brain told her she was seeing. That he really did care. That this was an aberration and he was just trying to do the right thing, not run her life. But trust was a hard-won thing and she'd been here before. People wanting to steer her life because they didn't like the way she drove it herself.

'My job back. To ease into things as I feel ready. But you can't exclude me from making decisions. Not ever again. I though you respected my autonomy.'

Now she was scared he didn't respect anything at all.

CHAPTER SIX

IN THE DAYS since their argument over Simone's work, they'd reached a form of truce. Leo was sensible enough to realise he'd overstepped, even though what he'd done was for Simone's benefit. He'd called Marchesa and apologised, saying that Simone would resume her role at her own pace, with as much or as little assistance as she chose.

All Simone's assistant had said was, *I knew she wouldn't let you go that easily.*

Simone had also demanded that he reinstate her attendance at the charity ball this evening. Whilst he'd said nothing to her, he was worried. He didn't want to stretch her too thin. Her photophobia had dissipated and she wasn't getting dizzy any more, but she still tired more easily than usual. Guilt plagued him about what he'd asked of her. It was unrelenting. The memory of Simone lying at the bottom of the stairs played over and over in his head. Yet she'd been firm, so he'd been sensible. Choosing not to pick a fight that didn't need to be fought, since clearly this was one he'd never win.

He adjusted his bow tie and checked his watch. An alert pinged on his phone, telling him their driver was on the way. He strolled from his room and waited outside. Not wanting to leave until he could safely escort Simone down the stairs.

She'd been somewhat elusive in the past week. Working with him on the days that she wanted to but otherwise taking herself into the city on her own. He'd resorted to asking Marchesa who claimed it was *secret women's business* and said nothing else. It piqued his interest but he didn't ask because he didn't want to interfere. He'd made too many mistakes already and he refused to make another, not where Simone was concerned.

She needed to understand that he valued her. To try to repair the damage he'd already inflicted.

The door of her room opened and she walked out, standing on the landing at the top of the stairs to her attic suite. At this first glimpse of her his heart simply tumbled from his chest and fell at his feet.

If there was ever a goddess embodied on earth, it was Simone in this moment. In a silk dress, encrusted with crystals, shimmering gold like sunlight at dusk. The front plunged in a vee, showing off her creamy cleavage. Draped over her shoulders and flowing down her back was a short cape, glittering with beading. The fabric clung to her curves, gleaming in the soft light.

He didn't know where to look or what to do. The heat of immediate and unrelenting desire scorched through him. Thank God his jacket was buttoned closed because her shocking effect on him would have been immediate otherwise. He'd been plunged into the ninth circle of unrequited hell.

She was so regal, like a queen greeting her subjects. Her lips the red of arterial blood. Her fingernails and toes a matching colour. On her feet she wore heels. Glittering sandals to match the dress. Tall. Spiked. He wanted to open his mouth and say something about her choice of footwear, but he gritted his teeth. She was a grown woman, as she'd already made clear. He had no right to butt into her life. That was not the relationship they had.

Yet for one brutal, blinding moment, he wished it was. He wanted to have it all.

'Exquisite,' he said. The word left his mouth before he could think. How dare anyone have ever called her plain? How could he have even dignified the idea with his own attempts at press releases to explain the way she looked when she was perfect, just the way she was?

She began to walk down the stairs. He held his breath, watching every step. Not relaxing until she was safely next to him.

'Our car's arrived,' he said hoarsely. 'Are you ready to leave?'

'Of course. I'm looking forward to it.'

Simone was a beauty with no compare. He'd known it to some extent before, but to his shame, it was as though tonight she'd been reborn and he was seeing her for the first time. He didn't know what had brought about this change but he liked it, far too much.

'Then let's go.' He held out his arm. She hesitated before slipping hers through it. They had another flight of stairs to navigate and he couldn't bear the vision now flickering through his head, of her pitching forward and falling.

She gripped the railing with one hand and lightly held his arm with the other. At the top of the stairs, his heart began to beat a rapid and thready rhythm. He made his way down slowly, one step, then another till they reached the bottom and he escorted her into the car. Safe.

'Where did you get the dress?' he asked. She glittered in the car, like the most precious of jewels he wanted to lock in a safety deposit and hide away. The sensation was overwhelming, irrational. 'I had no idea you were looking.'

She shrugged. 'It was time and Marchesa found the place for me.'

She'd put every other woman to shame tonight. There was no one who'd eclipse her. He wanted to cancel the evening. Tell the driver to turn the car around, take Simone home, carry her to the bedroom and make love to her for hours.

He hadn't been like this since he was eighteen and over-full with hormones. It had to stop. Simone had been clear about the parameters of their relationship. He was her employer. She was his executive assistant. Nothing had changed.

And until he could get himself under control, he needed distance.

'I have some people I need to speak with tonight,' he said. Business was something he could hide behind, something she'd understand. 'But I'll be claiming a dance.'

His mouth would *not* stay quiet but the temptation with her was too great. Later, after he'd taken some time, he'd be composed and back to his normal self. Then he'd dance with her, and not before.

'I'd like that,' she murmured. 'And I'll hold you to it.'

Leo was a man who kept his promises. This was one he might regret ever having made.

Their car slowed, pulling up along the red carpet of a charity ball to support homeless services. One of many similar charities that he backed after his time on the streets, in the hope of helping other young people stay out of trouble. Leo also knew that the night was a perfect one to show solidarity between Simone and himself. To put an end to whatever gossip remained in the aftermath of her fall. Still, he couldn't help thinking the night was centred on him, when all he wanted was for the focus to be on her.

The car door opened. He got out, waiting by the door as Simone left the vehicle, stepping out as if she was made of molten gold. The cries of photographers filled the night, calling their names to get their attention. He might have been used to this, ready to smile on cue, but Simone wasn't. Leo knew how intimidating a red carpet could be for the uninitiated.

He slipped his hand around her waist, almost expecting her to be stiff and uncomfortable, but she relaxed into him, as if this was where she was always meant to be. The perfect fit, just as on the night of their wedding. He leaned down, murmured in her ear.

'Just smile,' he said.

At every call of her name, Simone turned and beamed like the consummate professional she was. More beautiful than any human had a right to be. They passed through the gauntlet, talking to a few people on the way in till they got inside and he reluctantly relinquished her.

It was for the best, because whilst he wanted to keep her close, Leo knew in the end, he always had to let her go.

The ballroom was Italy at its most opulent. Frescoes adorned the ceiling. A beautiful blue sky filled with cherubs, angels and pastoral scenes. The walls gilded in an extravagant Rococo style. Chandeliers dripping from the ceiling. Huge urns of flowers filled niches along the walls. It felt as if Simone had stepped into another world, half-expecting Titania, Queen of the Fairies, to burst through a doorway at any moment.

It was glorious in its excess. Once she might have criticised it as unnecessary and frivolous but tonight, she leaned right in. The ball was for a good cause. One close to Leo's heart. She knew how much these kinds of functions could raise, when the wealthy opened their pockets. If it helped homeless teenagers like Leo had once been, all the better.

When they'd arrived, Leo had spoken to a number of

people who'd all sought him out. Spending so much time in his presence, she'd noticed that people flocked to him like moths to a bright light. He was blinding.

Yet whilst he might turn every head in a space, when she'd stood at the top of the stairs outside her bedroom he'd called her...

Exquisite.

She'd liked that that's what he thought of her, perhaps a little too much, even though she shouldn't. Especially since she'd gone out on an unfamiliar limb and opted for glamour, from a small local designer. To hell with thinking the glorious, golden dress she wore was frivolous. She loved it, the way it draped and glittered. She was tired of making herself small. It was like, after her fall, this was her second chance at life and she was taking it. She'd decided she could be true to herself and still show her feminine side.

The side that still loved beautiful things.

Leo had excused himself a little earlier. Business always came first for him and she assumed he was networking about the Tessitore deal. She picked her way through the crowd of people in dinner suits and gowns and sparkling jewellery, looking for him. Once, she'd thought she didn't fit in these spaces any more but now she realised her place was wherever she wanted it to be. She didn't know where Leo was in the throng of people but she didn't take long to find him, in amongst a small group of men. Hoteliers, property magnates. Potential clients no doubt. She realised then, that Leo was moving puzzle pieces around in a way that would advantage him. Making introductions. Helping others so that they might help him right back, when he called in the favour.

She felt a burn in her belly. Was she just another puzzle piece too? Although why should she care if she was? Did she even want the answers to those questions? Simone hesitated. Maybe she could come back later...

No.

If that's what this was, she refused to allow herself to be a part of Leo's complicated jigsaw, not any more. They were supposed to be a team. She began cutting through the crowd towards him. As she approached the group, he was engrossed in conversation but some others noticed her. She wasn't a fool, she knew those looks on their faces. Admiration, attraction. Maybe it made her throw her shoulders back a little more, put a smile on her face. It was the first time in such a long time she'd felt noticed.

Simone realised she liked it. A strange tightness gripped in her chest. She'd like it a lot more if it had come from Leo rather than some strangers. At that discovery, she almost turned around and left. But he must have seen their attention move to somewhere other than him. Noticed their appraising gazes. And he turned to face her, eyebrow raised.

What was he thinking in this moment? It was hard to tell. She realised he was a man who kept a great deal hidden and whilst she might have let that slide once, now she seemed to want all of the answers.

'*Tesoro*,' he said. The endearment washed over her. It was for show and perhaps to stake a claim of sorts. 'You need something?'

Dinner was over, the band had started in earnest. She knew what she wanted...

'I was going to claim the dance you promised.'

'I'm in the middle of something right now.' He nodded to the men with him. 'I'll find you shortly.'

Was he putting her in her place? She wasn't sure, though clearly he was signifying their importance over her, because where were all their wives? Were they off in some corner somewhere, all wondering whether their husbands would ever ask them to dance too?

'Of course,' she said, not wanting to rock the boat. She wasn't sure what this discussion was about, its importance, so she didn't want to crash some business deal by being difficult. 'I'll look forward to it.'

Simone was about to leave, when Leo smiled. It didn't reach his eyes. It was the smile she'd seen him give to countless numbers of people who he'd dismissed, who were unimportant to him. A smile that was a meaningless platitude. Something exploded inside of her, a volcanic type of sensation that burned from her solar plexus outwards. She gritted her teeth.

She was not going to keep herself in hiding, not any more.

She turned with as much composure as she could, then stalked off back through the crowd, not knowing where she was really headed. Her usually cool, calm demeanour shattered. There was a terrace she could go to, she supposed. Maybe she could grab a glass of champagne and cool off, when all she wanted to do was run raging into the night. Simone looked for a waiter as she neared the dance floor. The couples on it all swaying to the beat of a song designed for a slow dance.

'*Signora Zanetti.*'

The voice made her stop, a familiar one she'd heard before, once, when after a number of approaches from recruiters and third parties, he'd called her personally to offer her a job. She turned and looked up at the imposing form of Rocco Silvestri.

'Mr Silvestri.'

'Rocco, please.'

Rocco and his father's company made some of the finest and most sought-after designer furniture in the whole of

Italy. Yet Leo refused to use any of it in his work. Anyone who worked in Circolo knew of Leo's disdain, if not enmity, for the Silvestris. She'd never asked why as it hadn't been relevant to her role. She'd thought it might have been that Leo and Rocco were the same age and both were eligible, Italian bachelors. Perhaps natural rivalry had morphed into something more than mere competitiveness. Style magazines often compared the two men, even though there was no comparison to be had. In her opinion, Leo won in all ways. Though Leo didn't seem like the kind of person who'd hold a grudge for frivolous reasons. It had to be something more…

A question for another day.

'Let's not stand on formality. Call me Simone.'

The corner of Rocco's mouth kicked up. He wore a tuxedo like Leo, but was somehow stockier, brawnier. More like a fighter, as opposed to Leo's indefinable, almost aristocratic sophistication, which she realised now she preferred. Rocco was still a handsome man in his own right though, with his dark hair and dark eyes. Typical Italian good looks, she might have said. Simone could see why he always appeared to have a different woman on his arm. Although tonight he was without the usual female accompaniment.

'Your husband wouldn't like that.'

'My husband isn't here to express any thoughts on the subject.'

'Which makes me a lucky man. Where were you going in such a hurry?'

A loaded question, she was sure. Did it mean he'd been watching her? The burn might still be in her gut at Leo's rejection but she wasn't one to air her grievances in public. Especially not with someone who Leo viewed as a kind of enemy. She was angry, not petty.

'I was about to find myself a drink, whilst waiting for Leo to join me.'

'Why don't I find one for you?' Rocco made a minute gesture with his hand, and a waiter arrived like magic. She took a glass of champagne from the man's tray with thanks and sipped the chilled bubbles. Rocco took a dark, blood-coloured glass of red wine for himself.

'If I were your husband, I wouldn't be leaving you alone like this. You never know who you might run into.'

She laughed, seeing this for what it was, a kind of harmless flirtation. Probably begun by Rocco to annoy Leo.

'I'm sure I'm safe enough.'

'I'm gratified by your confidence. And why is Zanetti keeping you waiting?'

The hair prickled at the back of her neck in warning. 'Oh, you know. Business.'

Rocco lifted the glass of red to his lips, took a hefty swig. 'When there's so much pleasure to be had? What a waste.'

The band struck up another tune. This one jauntier, less romantic. She looked over at the couples there, smiling, having fun.

When was the last time she'd done the same? As Rocco had said, it seemed like such a waste. Especially this existence of work and little else. She could have fallen down a flight of stairs and never regained consciousness, and what would she have achieved out of life? Simone wasn't sure she liked the answer.

'You want to dance.'

It wasn't a question. She hated that she was so transparent.

'Yes. But I'm sure my husband will be along soon.'

Rocco snorted. Clearly not believing her. 'Why not dance with me?'

'You still have a glass of wine to drink.'

'What's a glass of wine when I can dance with a beautiful woman?'

'Now you're trying to flatter me.'

'I'm telling the truth. You'd know that if your husband told you often enough.'

If they had that sort of marriage, Rocco might be right. Still, they were admissions she couldn't make.

She raised her eyebrows. 'Perhaps it means more coming from him.'

Rocco smacked his palm to his chest as if she'd shot him through the heart. Then he started laughing. Warm, genuine and if she wasn't mistaken, a little chastened.

'I'm wounded, Signora Zanetti. And it's only a dance.'

She wasn't so sure about that, but right now, she didn't much care. Anyhow, she'd dealt with a hundred men like Rocco Silvestri before. She could do it again.

'Then it would be my pleasure.'

Rocco reached out and Simone handed him her glass. He found another waiter and deposited both on their tray and came back to her. Then he crooked his arm.

'Shall we?'

She slipped her arm through his as he led her to the dance floor. The couples there made way for them. Some looking on in interest. Most, absorbed only in each other. As they moved into the crowd, he eased one hand round her waist, took hers in the other. She placed her free hand on his shoulder, the fabric of his suit, cool under her palm. Rocco didn't try to pull her closer than he should for two strangers, keeping a respectable distance. The music's rhythm singing through her as they began to move, even though this didn't feel as seamless as it had with Leo on their wedding day. Like a shoe that was a bit too small. Like it wasn't quite the right fit.

But she wasn't looking for the right fit with Rocco Silvestri, she was just looking for fun. To find the woman she'd lost so long ago, through her family's rejection, the hard work she'd had to put in to break away, to earn her own money. She'd lost part of herself in trying to make something of her life so she could support herself, and now, support her sister. It was time to rediscover who Simone Taylor really was.

Except she wasn't Simone Taylor any more, she was Simone Zanetti. Her marriage yet another thing she'd done not for herself, but because of circumstance.

When would it ever be time just for her?

'I'm glad you appear well. Are you fully recovered from your accident?'

'I am, thank you.' Things were mostly back to normal. She still woke up a little fuzzy, and needed more sleep than normal, but she was almost back to her old self.

'Everyone appears to be watching us,' Rocco said, breaking Simone out of her reverie.

'Really?' After so long trying to fly under the radar she enjoyed hearing that perhaps, she might be creating a bit of a stir. Sure, marrying Leo had done that too, but the aftermath had been so tightly controlled by marketing, she'd felt like a chess piece being pushed around rather than a person in charge of their own destiny. Rocco guided her as they executed a seamless turn and Simone smiled. 'Surely they have enough to do rather than to worry about us?'

'The Zanetti and Silvestri rivalry is renowned.'

'And why is that?'

It seemed as reasonable to ask one of the participants in that rivalry now, as anyone else. A look passed across Rocco's face, something intense, although she saw him pull it back in. Try to hide it.

'Zanetti's a pretender. Pushing in where he wasn't invited and isn't wanted.'

Simone stiffened and the burn of indignation rose inside her. Leo might have been relatively new to the game of design after exploding onto the scene when he'd left modelling, but he'd been phenomenally successful. Nobody could deny that.

'Please don't forget, Mr Silvestri, that you're talking about my husband.'

'Your husband… *Mi dispiace.*' Whilst he might have said it, Rocco didn't seem sorry at all. 'Then why isn't he here dancing with you, instead of me?'

She opened her mouth to say something else in Leo's defence, but no words came out. She'd spent most of her life trying to fit in with what other people had wanted of her. Even when she'd broken free, her role as an executive assistant had her taking charge of other people's lives, making them easier, sometimes at the expense of her own. Then in choosing to marry Leo, it was to help Holly, not because she'd wanted it for herself.

When would *she* start to matter to others, even a little?

'So, Simone. When are you coming to work for me?' Rocco asked with a sly kind of grin teasing the corner of his lips.

She wasn't unhappy about the change of subject.

'Is that what this is about? Some kind of job interview? Why didn't you just pick up the phone?'

'I tried that once and you rejected me.'

She cocked her head. She'd told him before she was under a restraint of trade. Seemed he wasn't keen on listening. 'So you thought you'd dazzle me with your winning personality by insulting my husband?'

Rocco laughed without affectation. Like the one before, it was warm and sounded like he was genuinely amused.

'I like you, Simone. You're wasted where you are.'

She didn't have time to disagree.

Over his shoulder, into her startled vision, came Leo. Stalking through the dancers like a shark parting a school of fish. Leo's vibrant eyes fixed on her with the cool intensity of a predator watching its prey. Goosebumps showered over her skin as he approached and clapped a hand on Rocco's shoulder. Not hard enough to start a fight, but firm enough to send a message. Simone had only accepted that people were watching her and Rocco dance before. Now, she sensed the attention of the crowd shift onto the three of them.

'I'm cutting in, Silvestri.'

Rocco shrugged Leo off and turned.

'The music's not finished.'

'But your dance is.'

Rocco's grip didn't tighten, but he didn't relinquish her either.

Leo's jaw was clenched hard, his nostrils flaring. His anger appeared barely reined in. Simone wasn't sure what the issue was between them, but she wasn't about to let them have a fight over her, as perplexing and in so many ways, thrilling as that might have seemed.

No one had ever fought over her before. People were generally only too happy to give her away.

'You haven't asked the lady what she wants,' Rocco said coolly. She supposed she should have liked that he was giving the choice entirely to her but she realised it was less about her as a woman and more about needling Leo. Intimating that Rocco cared what she thought and Leo didn't.

'*Tesoro*?'

Leo held out his hand. She took it. If there was a side to be taken here, Leo would always win.

'It seems my husband's finished what he was doing, Mr Silvestri. Thank you for the dance.'

The corner of Rocco's mouth curled in a sardonic kind of smile. 'You're not someone who required babysitting. *Alla prossima,* Simone.'

He nodded and then disappeared into the crowd without looking back.

Leo bundled her into his arms and held her close against him. Not the distance of strangers but of intimates, even though there hadn't been any intimacy between them. Every part of him seemed tight, barely leashed. Part of her liked to believe that it might have been jealousy but that would have required a certain level of emotion between them, when she knew there was none.

'There will be no *next time* with him. There shouldn't have been a *this time,*' he hissed into her ear.

The music took on an intensity. More of a tango type of beat. Leo led the dance in a way that left Simone in no doubt as to who he thought was in charge. Well, as they said, it took two to tango and she wasn't about to play whatever game he'd started. She refused to be scolded like some errant schoolgirl.

'Don't pull the jealous husband act, Leo.' He'd danced them deeper into the crowd of people on the floor, out of the way of those who'd witnessed the exchange between the two men and towards the opposite edge of the dance floor near a set of doors. Then he pushed one open and led her from the room into a darkened corridor, wheeling round to face her. Toe to toe. She didn't care. She wouldn't back down.

'If anyone could be said to have an enemy, Silvestri is mine. How do you think it looks if my *wife's* dancing with him?'

'Perhaps it looks like there's a *détente* between you.'

'*Never*. He's after my secrets. He's after my wife. What a coup that would be.'

'A coup?' she snorted. 'I wonder what the press would say about your Plain Jane wife then?'

Leo snaked his arm round her. He was so strong, so hard and uncompromising. The planes of him pressing into her, leaving no space between them, just their bodies flush against each other. Still, she had no doubt that if she demanded distance he'd give it to her.

She didn't want any distance.

'Silvestri can see what you can't. A beautiful woman,' Leo bit out. 'And you'll never have anything more to do with him.'

Simone ran hot and cold, a mix of anger and something far more potent coursing through her.

'You're not the boss of me, Leonardo Zanetti.'

His hand flexed on the small of her back, burning and possessive. 'I believe you'll find I am. You, in fact, demanded to remain in your role.'

'And what are you going to do? Terminate my services like you tried to do earlier? Be careful what you wish for. I've had more than one job offer whilst working for you. It wouldn't be hard to find another.'

'*Silvestri*,' he said, jaw clenched, clearly guessing at least some of what she and Rocco had been discussing on the dance floor. 'There's no world in which I'd ever permit you to work for him, as your employment contract clearly sets out.'

'And that ends if you sack me rather than me leaving of my own accord. You promised me a dance, then dismissed me like I was nobody when to the world, I'm your *wife*. Well, I discovered almost dying has a way of changing your perspective on everything. I want to dance the dance.

I want to live my life. *Mine*, not someone else's. I'm tired of waiting. For you, for anyone and I'm not going to do it any more. I'm done.'

She placed her hands on his chest intent on pushing him away yet instead her hands simply rested there, relishing the feel of his sculpted muscles under the fine cotton of his shirt far too much.

'You don't want to dance.'

'Oh really?' Simone asked, her heart punching at her ribs. 'Then what do I want, Leo?'

'*This.*'

His lips crashed to hers and he groaned. His mouth hard, uncompromising. The music in the background faded to nothing but white noise roaring in her ears. This was a possession, him staking a claim, and she claimed him right back.

His arms wrapped round her as a cool wall hit her back. She curled her fingers against his chest, not caring that her fingernails pricked his flesh through the fabric of his shirt. He groaned, his hands flexing and gripping her body, as if he was warring with himself when there was nothing to win here. She was already lost to him. His body pressed hard into hers. The scent of him overwhelming her, a rich, heady spice, like she'd been transported to another place. He invaded every part of her. Their mouths clashed, fused together. His tongue conquering hers, only urging her to take more, kiss harder. She was nothing but passion and flames. Perfect heat. Desire and wanting. It was dizzying. If Leo hadn't been holding her up she'd have dissolved, slipping through his grip and pooling at his feet.

He tore his mouth away, his chest heaving. The front of his shirt impossibly crushed. Now it was her turn to groan, though hers wasn't a sound of passion, but protest.

She didn't want him to stop. She wanted this to never end. He took her hand in his uncompromising grip and began walking. She followed, not caring where he was leading her. He tested one door, then another, till he found one unlocked. A room in darkness, only the lights of the city illuminating it through the plate glass window. A smaller ballroom? A meeting room perhaps?

It didn't matter where, it just mattered that they were alone. He backed her into a table. His eyes glittering in the reflected city light, as he lifted her onto the surface. She wanted to be closer, melded to him. Her legs parted to accommodate his hips, and his mouth dropped to hers once more. Capturing her lips with his own. Their tongues duelling as if neither could get enough. She *burned* for him. Every part of her pure fire. The need like a living thing, ravaging through her. He rucked up her dress, his hands hot and fevered against her skin. She moaned at the feel of his palms, stroking her thighs. Then Leo placed his hands on her backside and pulled her towards him, the table height perfect. The centre of her against his hardness. He reached to her left breast, stroked a thumb over her nipple and it was like shooting stars streaking through the night sky in her head.

'What you do to me,' he murmured and flexed his hips. Simone moaned again. Wrapping her legs round his, as an ache bloomed deep inside. An empty sensation that only he could sate.

'Shhh. I told you I knew what you needed. I'll give it to you.'

He held her close, continuing to flex in a slow, steady rhythm as she rubbed herself against him, his arousal. The sleek, fine wool of his dinner suit almost rough against the over sensitised skin of her inner thighs. She craved having nothing between them. No underwear, no clothes. A bed and the two of them together naked and entwined. Yet at the same time she wouldn't give up this moment, here, in a darkened room, if someone had offered her millions.

Their breaths came in pants, like a love song to the darkness. He pulled back a little and she clutched onto his jacket, to stop him. 'More,' she said. Unable to express how much she needed him in this moment.

'It's what I'm about to give you, *cara*.'

He gently pressed his thumb against her lips and she opened as he slid it into her mouth. She sucked, running her tongue over the rough, warm flesh. Now it was his turn to moan and the power of that sound, of what she was doing to him, coursed through her like a shot of spirits.

'Minx,' he murmured, as he slipped his thumb out, tracing his hand down the front of her body, to her underwear, moving it aside and easing his thumb through her folds. She gasped, the consuming pleasure of it blooming inside her as he touched and teased. She *knew* he was toying with her, never going quite where she needed him. Perhaps he wanted her to beg him and she knew that she would, if he'd just tip her over the knife edge she skated. Then his thumb gave the merest of brushes over her clitoris, and that light touch almost caused her to burst with the force of an explosion.

'Oh, God,' she whispered. Wanting, needing.

'You called?' Leo chuckled, a dark, satisfied sound. Yet he didn't withhold much longer. Moving his thumb to the perfect spot. The centre of sensation. Stroking and circling as she was lost to him. Inside of her coiling tighter and tighter till she cracked in two. Leo captured her cries with his lips as she exploded into a million pieces, which seemed to hang and float in the room before those parts reshaped and reformed. Whole again, yet totally changed. She rested her cheek against his chest as he held her there, like she was something precious.

'We're getting a room. I want to spend the night making you scream.'

'Yes.' One word was all she was capable of uttering.

'Stay here.' Leo eased himself away for her, cupping her cheek. Gently kissing her lips. Then he buttoned his jacket and turned, stalking to the door of the room. As he opened the door, backlit against the soft light outside, he made an imposing and impressive silhouette. Looking up and down the corridor, for what, she wasn't sure. Then someone in uniform, a staff member, approached him.

'Tell your concierge it's Leonardo Zanetti,' he said, his voice deep and dark like black velvet. 'I want a room for the night. My wife's unwell.'

'Of course sir, would you also like us to call a doctor?'

'No, a room will do. We'll be waiting here.'

There was a little more hushed conversation and Leo returned. Wrapping his arms round her once more. Kissing her soft and deep. She placed her hands on his chest. The strong, solid muscles there keeping her grounded as the rest of her trembled with wanting.

'You'll be the death of me,' he murmured.

'I hope not before the night is over,' she said, running her fingers over the studs of Leo's dress shirt in an attempt at a tease. 'You have promises to keep.'

'And I will.' His voice was almost a growl. A warning. Her experience was so limited. What would it be like to be with a man like Leo? All confidence and power. Well placed arrogance and ego.

Another wave of heat flooded over her. She wanted to simply melt onto the tabletop and slide to the floor. It was as if every bone in her body, every muscle and sinew, had forgotten how to hold her up.

Within minutes, another staff member arrived. A man in a suit. The concierge she presumed.

'Signor and Signora Zanetti? I have a suite organised for you if you'd like to come with me. We can take the staff lift for privacy.'

'Thank you,' she said. Feeling a little guilty at the deception and the work it must have taken to organise a room so quickly.

They headed out and then down another corridor. Leo kept his arm possessively round her waist. The effects of her orgasm still singing through her veins, making her weak at the knees, her bones like rubber. They approached a lift at the end. The concierge activated it with a keycard and then handed something similar to Leo.

'This will take you direct to your floor. Your room's the only suite on it. You have late checkout.'

The door slid open and the man activated the button for the top floor.

'Please call us if there's anything we can do. I hope you're feeling better soon, Signora Zanetti.'

He nodded as the doors closed. Leo turned to face her, pressing her back against the lift's cool, metal wall. He cupped his hands to her jaw, thumbs gently stroking her cheek as he kissed her. Simone's lips opening under the tease of his tongue against her own. The heat. The need. All the seductive slickness of it, twisting and tightening the desire inside of her. Ramping up the sensation till she became a bright, pinpoint of wanting. In what seemed like seconds, the doors opened on their floor. Leo pulled away, cheeks slashed with a flush of colour under the burnished gold of his skin. He took her hand, led her to the door, unlocked it, then swung her as if weightless into his arms. Pushing through the door, he entered the room. A few lamps were illuminated in the opulent space but it wasn't the décor that interested her. She couldn't take her eyes from Leo's face. How intent he was. Driven. All because of her.

Goosebumps flowered over her skin, the ache deep inside intensifying again. It had been so many years since she'd made love to anyone and that was really only youthful fumbling when she'd kidded herself she was in love. Right now, she might as well have been a virgin. This was different. Leo was a man, one with a reputation and who routinely topped the best of everything lists.

It hit her with a flash of realisation. She deserved nothing less.

He strode through the space with purpose till he found the bedroom. The bed turned down for them already. He gently placed her on the carpet and held her steady when she swayed into him, a look of smug satisfaction on his face. She couldn't blame him. It was well deserved.

'Turn,' he said. His voice low and rough. She shivered at the erotic promise of the sound as she turned her back to him. An indefinable sensation like water trickling down her spine told her he was close. Then his breath caressed the back of her neck in warm gusts. After a few moments there was a touch at the base of her neck, gently stroking down to her zip. A slight tug and the cool air of the room eased the burn of her overheated flesh. After the zip was undone, Leo traced his finger gently up her spine, then swept her dress from her shoulders, as it slid down her body in a silky rush and pooled on the floor at her feet.

CHAPTER SEVEN

LEO ROCKED BACK on his heels. It was as if time had suddenly stopped. Simone stood before him in her underwear of sleek coffee-coloured satin and lace. A vision before him. The swell of her backside, the tempting nip of her waist. Her skin like rich cream. Needing to stay away but wanting to get closer.

He knew he'd put her off on the pretext of business when she'd come to find him. When she'd asked him to dance, what he wouldn't have given to simply take her hand and lead her to the dance floor. Yet he'd been trying to wrestle his aching need for her under control. This magnificent, confounding woman. That was until he'd overheard someone saying gleefully, *Silvestri's dancing with Zanetti's wife...*

Feeling stabbed in the gut at the thought, he'd left to find her immediately.

'Face me,' he ground out, words almost impossible. She inflamed him. Undid him. He wasn't a violent man though some from his past might beg to differ, yet seeing her dancing with his half-brother made him want to roar and tear apart the world. How he'd maintained any semblance of self-control in that moment, was beyond him. Leo knew why Silvestri had done it. Just another game, trying to steal something from a Zanetti that wasn't his. Leo wouldn't allow it. A Silvestri would never steal something from a Zanetti, ever again.

For as long as his ring was on her finger, Simone was *his*.

Simone turned, slowly. An attempt at a tease or shyness, he couldn't tell. It could well have been both. He knew nothing about her past and whilst she'd been working for him she hadn't dated as far as he knew. She'd been focused entirely on the job and catering to his needs. The sharp, potent stab of jealousy hit him in the gut again. No matter, tonight he'd ruin her for any other man or die trying.

What a way to go.

Finally, she faced him. Simone was glorious partly dressed. A magnificent body only hinted at under her clothes. Flesh and curves. Breasts, a perfect handful. Was she a goddess sent to tempt him? Or a siren luring him to his doom? It was hard to tell. Right now, his thoughts scattered. Leo craved to kiss and taste every part of her. Whatever she was it didn't matter. He'd be worshipping her either way.

She raised her eyes to his, almost hesitant. He wanted to leave her in no doubt how beautiful she was. He unbuttoned his jacket and her gaze dropped to his groin. With that one glance an arrow of heat shot direct to the heart of him. Tearing the jacket off, he tossed the handmade garment to the floor.

He couldn't take the distance any longer. Leo stepped forwards and took her into his arms. She was still shorter than him in her heels but tall enough to be level with his mouth. The perfect position.

'*Sei bellissima.*'

Yet she was more than merely beautiful. Something about her struck a chord deep inside. The scent of her like citrus blossom. Fresh and sweet, with a bite. Full of spring promise. He tightened his grip on her and she dissolved into his embrace as he brushed her hair over her shoulder and pursed his lips, wondering where to start. With his tongue at the centre of her, his fingers embraced by her slick heat, or simply plunging himself deep inside? All of him so greedy for her, it was difficult to decide. Yet one thing kept pounding like a drumbeat in his head. Words said over and over.

Make. Her. Yours.

He raked his teeth gently over the tender flesh at the juncture of her shoulder. She trembled in his embrace. He'd promised to make her scream and she told him she'd hold him to that.

Her cries would be the sweetest of sounds.

He opened the clasp of her bra in one practiced flick of his fingers. Drawing it from her shoulders and throwing it to the floor. Her dusky nipples tightening in the cool air of the room. He stroked her left nipple with his thumb and she moaned. When she was almost mindless, writhing against him, he pinched the tight peak and she threw her head back. Crying out in pained ecstasy.

Her last orgasm had been in the dark. Now, he'd watch as the pleasure overtook her. She wasn't there yet, but her gaze was glassy, unfocused, as if she'd retreated deep inside herself. Swept away with the pleasure of his touch and nothing else.

Something darkly possessive overtook him, a pounding drumbeat deep inside. After tonight, any other man would be swept away from her memory, for ever. Replaced only by him. His lips, his hands, the memories of him inside her.

He ceased his ministrations at her breast and slipped his hands into her underwear, gripping her bottom. Stroking. Inflaming and soothing all at once. Drawing her close. Letting her know how much she affected him. She rubbed herself against his arousal as he gritted his teeth, exercising patience and restraint because he knew this wasn't enough for her and that her frustration would only ramp up her desire.

He was right. The noises she made, of pleasure, of need, were sweet music. He hooked his fingers into her panties and began to draw them down as he followed, till he was on his knees as if in worship. Leo pressed his mouth to the golden curls at the centre of her. Slipped his tongue through her folds, then slid his hands to her hips, holding her close. Gently teasing her clitoris. She speared her fingers through his hair as shudders wracked her, but if she thought he was going to let her tip over the edge this soon, she was wrong. Tonight, she'd been playing a game with him of sorts and he aimed to return the favour before giving her what she so desperately desired. Teasing and toying as she tried to press his head closer to where she needed him most, as he enjoyed the salt sweet taste of her on his tongue.

When her moans turned into sobs, he pulled away and she swayed. He stood, picked her up in his arms again and placed her on the bed where she splayed, her body flushed pink with arousal. He slid off her shoes and dropped them behind him, then he kicked off his own and removed his socks. He tore off his shirt, his trousers, till he stood there. Flagrantly aroused. Simone licked her lips. She could use that mouth with devastating effect on him later, if that was something she enjoyed. He prayed it was. Yet for now, he needed protection before he lost himself like a teenager before he was even inside of her.

Leo strode to his jacket and bent down. Reaching into the inner pocket to a card wallet, which held two precious condoms. They'd need more but in his experience a suite like this often came prepared with whatever those who booked it might require, and he suspected this was no exception. He tossed one on the bedside table, opened another and then made a show, rolling it down himself slowly whilst she watched, her pupils huge and dark. Breath coming in fevered pants.

Whilst he would have liked to continue standing there, letting her take her fill of him, he'd reached the end of his endurance. Leo crawled over her. Buried his tongue at the centre of her once more then licked up her body. The taste of her overheated skin like the finest of wines to his senses. He took one nipple in his mouth. Sucked. Laved his tongue over till it peaked, then moved to the other. Slipped a hand between her legs to test her. So slick and wet and hot it almost undid him.

'I want you, *tesoro*. I wish you knew how much.'

She arched her hips to him. 'You couldn't want me more than I want you.'

'Let's see then.'

Leo positioned himself. Notched at the centre of her, entering slowly as she moved underneath him, then with one swift thrust, buried himself deep. The pleasure of it so fast and sharp it was as if the world exploded in a shower of stars. Simone's hands gripped his shoulders, her fingernails digging into his flesh as he began to thrust. Hard, uncompromising, yet she was there with him stroke for stroke, moving her hips in time to his relentless rhythm. There was just her and him, the soft bed and sensation. He was a captive of it. Of her. Pumping his hips and driving them both on to their ultimate pleasure. He ground into her as she pressed up into him. Both of them working as one to chase each other up to a cliff edge hanging just out of reach. Then, Simone stiffened and cried out. Her body spasming around him. That's all it took to throw him over the edge too. Falling and spinning into an abyss that seemed to have no end.

Instead, it felt more like a beginning.

* * *

Simone woke to soft light filtering through the windows of the room. The heat of a body at her back. The weight of an arm round her waist. She shut her eyes again, relishing the sensation, letting the memories flood back to a night where she'd felt truly wanted. In a way, she realised now, that she'd never experienced before. Desire washed over her like a rush of hot water. Leo had made love to her for most of the night with a ferocity and need like he was on a mission to imprint himself onto her. If he'd wanted to ruin her for anyone else, she was pretty sure he had but she didn't know why that left her both elated and untroubled. In the end, she'd been reduced to a begging mess of sensation, before they'd both crashed into a dreamless sleep.

She wasn't sorry about any of it, although she couldn't help wondering… Had he not seen her dancing with Rocco, would it have been the same? Did Leo do it just because he really wanted her, or, like Jace, because he felt he had something to prove?

Leo's hand flexed over her belly and pulled her close. Hard against him, her back to his chest.

'I can hear you thinking,' he murmured into her hair. His voice was rough with sleep. 'If you can string together any thoughts this early in the morning, I must not have done my job well enough last night.'

And there it was, like walking from central heating into a frigid winter's wind. Because that's what this was, a job. Did Leo believe he'd done his job well? Was he congratulating himself?

'Hey, hey,' he said, releasing his hold on her and easing her onto her back. He propped himself onto his elbow and looked down at her, his eyebrows raised. 'Any regrets?'

No regrets for the passion. It wasn't like she was an innocent girl. She was an adult, making her own choices. Her regrets were for the fears.

'Why would you say that?' she asked, trying to sound nonchalant.

'Your whole body was tense and when you worry you have this little crease…' he held out his finger and stroked it gently between her eyebrows, '…right here.'

Of all the things he could have said, this was the evidence he was trying to understand her. It was an insignificant thing about her and yet he'd still noticed it.

Her mother's voice immediately rang through her head. *Stop frowning, Simone. You don't want lines that injectables won't take away. Perhaps we should end that line before it really begins?*

She'd tried to book Simone an appointment with her own plastic surgeon the next day.

Simone had been eighteen.

More power to anyone to whom that appealed. Simone didn't judge. It was every woman's right to feel good about themselves, however they wanted to. But at a time when she was still trying to find herself, growing into her gawky limbs and foreign curves, it had made her feel insecure about everything. It had taken another few years for her to stop caring, once she'd realised that how she looked and presented herself wouldn't make anyone love her any more than they were ever going to. And love could be bought, anyhow.

It was all meaningless.

'No regrets,' she said.

'Then what's troubling you?'

'Do you really care?'

The words simply blurted from her mouth, all too needy. Yet she was lying naked here, both physically and emotionally, and part of her, the one that still carried her wounds, needed to know.

Leo's eyebrows shot up. 'Why would you even think to ask that question? Of course I care.'

Simone believed him. Now, questions churned inside her. So many. Leo appeared to be an open book because there'd been so much written about him. But he'd mastered the art of disclosing only what was on the surface, whilst making people believe he'd let them into a deeper part of his soul. She saw it now. Whilst she couldn't say why, she wanted to unlock that part of him that he held on to so tightly. She asked the first thing that came into her head.

'Why the rivalry with the Silvestri family?'

It was Leo's turn to frown. She reached up her own hand and stroked at the line with her forefinger, like he'd done to her. His eyes drifted shut for a moment, then he rolled over onto his back, carrying her with him. She lay, her head on his chest, palm splayed on one of his pectoral muscles dusted with dark hair, as he held her tight. Like he was a man lost at sea, holding onto her as a life preserver.

'That's a long story.'

'We have late checkout.'

He chuckled but there was nothing happy about the sound.

'We do.' Leo's chest expanded as he took in a deep breath, blew it out. His body tensed.

'Rocco Silvestri...' Leo almost spat out the name like it was poison on his lips, '...is my half-brother.'

Simone sat up, almost wrenching from his grasp in her rush to do so. Heart pounding.

'What? But I thought you didn't know who your father was?'

'I've *always* known who my father was. I simply never acknowledged him as such and nobody ever asked.'

'And does he know who y—'

'Whilst I took my mother's name, he knows *exactly* who I am.'

She had trouble believing what she'd just heard. Everything written about Leo's life…where did the fiction end and the truth begin?

'But the story of you on the streets…'

'All true. My mother and I weren't wanted. He started another family and left my mother destitute. Vito Silvestri is a liar, a cheat and a thief.'

Simone couldn't comprehend what she was hearing and yet she was sure Leo spoke the truth. All of him was so tense. His lips a thin, hard line. He wouldn't look at her, his gaze somehow distant, lost in a past where the memories were clearly unhappy ones. This was a secret that he'd carried, clearly weighing on him. She wanted to purge him of it, ease that burden somehow, if she could.

Heaven knew how her own had weighed on her.

'Does Rocco know?'

A dark look cast over Leo's face, like a thundercloud passing over the sun.

'That name is *never* to enter our bedroom again.'

The words were a growl and she shivered at the possession threaded through them. At the suggestion that *they* had a bedroom, and they'd be in it together once more.

'Of course he knows. He *must*.'

Simone guessed what Leo said made sense, even though she wasn't so sure what with the conversation she'd had with the man last night. But she wasn't on the Silvestri side, she was all on Leo's. Simone reached out her hand, stroking the soft whorls of dark hair on his chest.

'You want to know the story,' Leo said. It wasn't a question. The words were almost a capitulation, although uttered with a hardness that coloured them with a hint of defiance. She glimpsed in that moment what a proud man he really was.

'If you want to tell it…' She didn't say she believed he needed someone to hear it, even though that's exactly what she thought.

He turned to look at her, his gaze boring deep. Almost to her soul.

'I'll have questions of my own for you.'

Simone had little doubt but if he was giving her some of his truths, then Leo deserved some of hers, no matter how little she might want to tell them.

'Sounds fair.'

'So magnanimous,' he said, his voice droll. 'Yet it's a simple enough story. My mother and father were furniture makers and designers. They were in business together. They weren't married, something I didn't know till much later. I believed that we were a family. That's how it seemed to me, as a child.'

'Did you get your interest in design from them?'

'From my mother.' Leo's jaw clenched. 'I liked seeing how something plain, with what appeared to have little potential, could be turned into something beautiful.'

'What happened?'

'A tale as old as time. My father had an affair with a client who was, by all accounts beautiful, but also extremely wealthy. She convinced him, or perhaps he convinced her, that he'd be better in business on his own and that she could fund it. One day, he packed up and left. Took everything. Left us destitute.'

'How old were you?'

'Seven.'

She imagined him as a little boy. Whilst no photographs existed online of him from that time, she had no doubt he would have been a beautiful child. What would it have been like for him to have had a happy life, then have it ripped away from him, without warning? For his father to simply give him up. Then she considered the mathematics of it all.

'You're thirty-five.'

'Mmm.'

'A-and...' she wouldn't mention the name, '...*he's* not that much younger.'

'The affair had been going on for some time. My father led two lives. Apparently, it took time for his lover to reach an age where money held in trust for her became unencumbered. When it did, he left.'

'I don't know what to say. He just...abandoned you.'

'I accepted that my father didn't want us.' Leo laughed darkly, a bitter sound. 'But it's worse than you could imagine. I was just seventeen and I left my mother to seek my fortune in Rome. What a fool. I was young and angry but I saw and learned a lot in my two years on the streets. Everyone there had a story. Broken families, alcohol, drugs, infidelity. It was my life and that of so many other wandering souls. Then, when I was nineteen, my mother died and I had to go back to Milan and clean out her flat. And I found...'

He turned his face away from her and she knew that this hurt him. That this was where his pain lay. Something deep and ingrained like an abscess poisoning him from the inside out.

She simply sat with him, stroking his chest, saying nothing and waiting.

'... I found furniture designs, sketches. All in my mother's hand. My father wasn't the genius behind what they made. He might have been the craftsman, but the designs themselves...' Leo turned to look at her, his gaze bleak, 'He stole them from my mother.'

* * *

The acid burned in Leo's gut. His mother had never said anything to him about his father taking her designs as his own. However, the evidence was clear. He knew his mother's writing, how she drew when she'd do little sketches for him occasionally. It was her work. He was sure of it. All the pictures of furniture, the designs his father had taken and turned into his own, had been stolen.

'Did she ever try to get them back?'

Leo shook his head. 'He left her with nothing but a child to feed.'

All he could remember was her trying to keep a roof over their heads and something on the table, meagre though it was. She'd worked herself to the bone doing so. There was no time for anything else.

'With the drawings, could you prove this?' Simone asked.

At the time he was simply a young man, angry and grieving and a solicitor had said he couldn't help, not without more proof. By then, the designs had already been trademarked and registered by his father. Later, even with all his resources, there was still nothing he could do. He'd been advised that the sketches would prove nothing in a court of law.

'Not with my mother dead. Perhaps if she'd been alive, with her word against my father's and the drawings, then maybe. But with her gone and all the money behind him, there is no proof conclusive enough. Though *I* know. He became famous by building his wealth from lies and theft.'

'And that's why you hate him,' Simone said. 'For leaving your mother. Stealing from her and leaving you.'

Leo closed his eyes not wanting to see the look of pity on Simone's face. This was the part of his story he'd divulged to no one.

'Your mom must have still been young when she passed away.'

'She was in her forties.'

'I'm sorry,' Simone said, leaning over and kissing the centre of his chest, right where his aching heart lay.

'She gave up all her dreams to keep me fed, to look after me as a child and then I left, searching for my own dreams. I should have been there for her. I should have sent more money home, so she didn't have to work so hard. Then one night when coming back to her apartment from a cleaning job in winter she slipped on ice on some stairs and she died.'

He shut his eyes, fighting the burn of tears he refused to shed. He wasn't worthy of the grief. When he'd seen Simone lying broken at the bottom of those stairs, it was like his life had flashed before his eyes. History repeating itself because he'd been thinking about himself and what he'd wanted, instead of her.

'Oh, Leo,' Simone said. 'You've carried so much grief on your own.'

'Yet here I am.'

'Here you are.'

Still, he'd carried on. For so long he'd been so angry about everything. In his teens, before he'd left for Rome, it had been because he'd wanted more than the threadbare life they'd led, the constant struggle. Then trying to assuage that anger on the streets and ending up getting involved in organised crime, which was another secret he'd managed to keep hidden from the world. He'd been trying for years to help the families he'd once hurt, although it never felt like it was enough. He had to atone for his mistakes.

Simone cupped his cheek, her expression soft and full of care. 'Are you going to do anything more with what you know?'

He didn't want to talk any more. Right now, it was as if Simone had cracked open his chest and asked him to show her his heart. Although he had to admit something about the weight of all he'd been carrying, had lifted a fraction.

He didn't deserve the respite, the relief, but he'd take it, nonetheless. Take whatever else she might offer him. Herself included. But for now, he was going to share the reason for their marriage. It wasn't merely that Tessitore was a heritage brand he wanted for himself. It was so much more.

'I'm going to buy Tessitore. The Silvestris want it, badly, and they will never get it. I'm going to take the company right from underneath them.'

CHAPTER EIGHT

SIMONE SAT ON the stone terrace at the rear of the home, shaded by grape vines, overlooking the garden. She'd wandered through the space a few times since she'd been here, through the olive and fig trees. Hidden away from the bustle of Milan. A little oasis. This morning, she sipped a coffee. The silence only punctuated by the twitter of birds. It had been two days since the charity ball and they'd barely left the bedroom since arriving home. Simone rolled her shoulders, stretched her neck, enjoying the subtle aches from their lovemaking.

Simone had known Leo was a perfectionist when she'd begun working for him. He was driven, a workaholic. Everything she'd expected from a man who'd come from nothing to own an empire. She'd just never really thought what it would be like to have all that drive and perfectionism turned onto her. A wicked slide of heat journeyed through her veins. Yes, the man was a perfectionist in the bedroom too and she'd reaped all those delicious rewards. Making love through the night, into the early morning. They'd been insatiable and perfectly attuned to each other's needs, their desires. It consumed her. And Leo too, his well-earned ego seemed to be overfed by making her scream.

It's better than music, he'd murmured into her ear the night before.

It was better than just about *anything.*

'Why are you not still in bed?'

Simone shut her eyes at the deep lilt of his voice. Right now she wanted to ditch her coffee and do just that, run to the bedroom and make love all morning, but she'd come out here for a reason and Leo had a business to run. He'd left her dozing to go and work and she'd felt guilty lying there whilst there were things plaguing him, like the so-far failed attempts to purchase the Tessitore family's textile company.

She realised now what it meant to him to acquire it, as a way of avenging his mother. And whilst she didn't really think revenge was the healthiest coping strategy, she understood him better than she ever had before. For that reason, she wanted to help.

'You were working and so was I.'

He leaned over and kissed the side of her neck. She angled her head sideways allowing him more access as he drifted her lips over her sensitive skin. Goosebumps fizzed over her, making her shiver, even in the warmth of this perfect morning. Leo stroked his hand over her arm. 'Are you cold, *tesoro*? Should I take you back to bed and warm you up?'

'*Yes*, I mean, no! You make it impossible for me to think.'

'I don't want you thinking. I want you *feeling.*'

'Leave feeling till later.' She waved at the table. 'Sit down, I have some ideas.'

Leo grinned, the look one of pure wickedness. 'So do I. Since you're not cold, did you know that ice applied in the right way can be extremely pleasurable?'

The whole of her flushed hot. She was sure she'd gone as red as if she'd suffered a bad case of sunburn.

'Leo! Take a seat. I'm *serious.*'

'So am I,' he murmured into her ear, his breath warm as it feathered against her overheated flesh.

She sighed. 'Later then.'

He gave her neck a final kiss then drew out a seat next to her and sat. Whilst he said he'd been working, he wasn't dressed for it. All he wore were a pair of black, silk pyjama bottoms, slung low on his hips. His skin a rich gold in the morning light. The man wasn't shy in showing off his body, for good reason. She knew exactly why the talent scout had taken one look at him and contracted him almost immediately.

'You said you were working and yet here you are, feasting on me with your eyes. Maybe you could feast on me for real instead?'

She only noticed then that he had his own cup of coffee in front of him. The man was a menace to her concentration and clearly an excellent multi-tasker.

'You're still not gaining any headway with the Tessitore family?' Simone asked.

Leo raked his hand through his thick, dark hair, leaving him looking gorgeously dishevelled. 'No. They blow hot, they blow cold. Right now, they're cold.'

'Are you sure they want to sell?' Simone asked.

Leo frowned. 'That's what they claim.'

'And you've tried phone calls and meetings?'

'Every approach. Direct and indirect.'

Then there was the dinner they'd meant to go to before her fall, but neither of them would mention that. She didn't want to think about it, even though she still couldn't remember the fall itself. Yet she could see it in Leo's eyes, a distant expression. He seemed to remember it all too well. What must it have been like, to see her lying there? Especially after his mother had died after an accident like hers?

Simone couldn't imagine. Maybe that's why he'd reacted like he had. Clearing her diary and giving Marchesa her job, albeit fleetingly. He'd been trying to *protect* her, not control her.

'What are you thinking of?' Leo asked.

That she'd had a stunning realisation, but there was no time to dwell on it now.

'They're a family,' she said. 'That's why you married me. Because they had trouble with you and your playboy lifestyle.'

'Yes. They're a deeply traditional Lombardi family, who've been textile makers for centuries. Where are we going with this?'

'Then that's what you have to show them,' Simone said patiently. 'You might have married me, but that didn't really mean anything to them. With you, it's been all about the business. You need to make it about family instead. Show them who you really are.'

Leo cocked his head. 'I'm not sure how to do that.'

She understood him a little better now. Leo held back, always kept something in reserve. He was well-liked and on the surface seemed to connect with people, but deep down, there was something about himself he protected. Spaces he kept his own. Things locked deep inside he wouldn't divulge. He was known as a consummate businessman, warm and generous with charities. Yet at their wedding, were there any real friends of his there? Allies, yes. But did they go any deeper? She wondered if he ever let anyone get close to him, at all. And that's what he needed to do to gain Tessitore, if only Leo could let it happen.

'Invite them here for dinner. To your home, not your office, not a fine restaurant. Here, where you can host them. It's a place you've always kept private, so why don't you show it to the Tessitores?'

She stood with her cup of coffee in hand and began walking around the terraced area, envisaging what she had in mind.

'It can still be a business dinner, but something a little more casual. Maybe out here with a long table under the vines. It's a beautiful space if the weather's good. Maybe I could cook something?'

Leo raised his eyebrows. 'My wife does not need to cook. I have a personal chef.'

'Yes, yes…and he's brilliant.' Each meal magnificent, a refrigerator always full on the days he didn't work. Details of each meal left behind, what was in it, how to heat it up. She felt spoiled, but having a chef wasn't the same. 'But there's a soft power in real hospitality.'

At the back of the property was a vibrant kitchen garden with eggplant, tomatoes, radicchio, rucola and other vegetables and herbs. Had Leo's chef and gardener not protected that patch of the home as their own domain, she would have made something with it all. Maybe in time…

She wasn't sure where that random thought was headed.

'We can use vegetables from the kitchen garden.' She waved to the back of the property. 'Eat—I don't know—not fine food, but something a little more homely. Traditional from the region. I could make something, but maybe not so traditionally Italian, if you think they'd like that? It can still be about business, but with a more personal touch. You've been showing them Leonardo Zanetti, the empire builder. Maybe you need to let them get a peek of Leo Zanetti, the man behind it all.'

Leo cocked his head. He was thinking about it. Simone was pretty sure that it would work. 'What would you cook?'

She thought back to her training in hospitality as a young

woman and what made a good wife for a wealthy man. Whilst her parents had had a chef too, and her mother was renowned for her parties, she'd always said to Simone…

A woman should know how to mix one good cocktail, make one great hors d'oeuvre and have a signature dessert.

So Simone had learned to make a martini and smoked salmon canapes. As for dessert…

'I make a mean caramel apple pie,' she said. 'I think I'd cook one of those. That's my favourite.'

'I enjoy sweet things.'

The way Leo looked at her in this moment, with such intensity. The vivid blue of his eyes, which should seem so cold, piercing through her like a hot poker. The man could inflame with a single glance.

'So, what do you think?'

He downed the last of his coffee and stood, as if charged with a kind of fresh energy. The consummate businessman, hard, driven. Leonardo Zanetti at his best.

'Nothing I've tried has made any real headway. I'll get in touch with them. Arrange something and we'll see.' Then he looked down at her and smiled, something rare, precious and real. The type of smile Leo granted to only a privileged few. She finally felt like one of them.

'You're inspired, Simone. And I believe it might just work.'

It was an uncomfortable sensation inviting people into his Milan home, the one place in the world that he'd kept apart from everything else. Let lifestyle magazines and style bloggers wax lyrical over his other properties dotted for convenience throughout the world, the showcases to display his 'expansive vision and impeccable eye' as they liked to say. But this was the one place few strangers ever glimpsed. A private space where he could hide away and lick wounds he allowed no one else to see.

The first home he'd ever bought for himself.

Yet here, he'd shown Simone those wounds. Let her in. And now, watching her with the chef, his housekeeper, planning for this dinner, setting the table, dotting fresh flowers in empty corners, he realised that here, she *fit*. It left him feeling discombobulated, how seamlessly she had taken over his life.

Perhaps that's the way it had always been. How she'd managed his workload, suppliers, clients. Made his life simpler in every way as his executive assistant and yet he'd never truly recognised it before.

Now, the time had ticked over to eight and the doorbell rang. Simone smiled.

'I guess it's showtime,' she said, looking magnificent. Her hair in a messy updo. Wearing flared black trousers that fitted her to perfection. A white halter neck top in a silky kind of fabric, with a tracery of black and silver flowers. A bow at the back of the neck with ties trailing down her spine that his fingers itched to undo. She was the picture of sophistication, the consummate hostess. He'd underestimated her, when he should have expected nothing less.

Tonight, they had minimal staff in the home. The chef, some servers to help, but he and Simone had agreed this was to feel like a family dinner. Something more intimate, even if vitally important. They greeted the Tessitore family at the door. Patriarch, Gino and his wife, Fia, daughter, Rita, and her husband, Enzo. It seemed warm enough. Kisses for Simone, handshakes for him. Firm but not crushing in an attempt at some futile power play.

'Please,' Simone said as she led the delegation through the

house. 'Come through. I thought we could have some drinks and canapes before the final touches are put to the meal.'

They entered the lounge, one of his favourite spaces here. Overlooking the garden outside, still light out being summer. The bell-shaped flowers of his mother's favourite, a Madonna Lily, nodding in the breeze.

Simone invited everyone to sit, but Rita stood in the doorway, looking at an armchair in the corner. A minimalist design of sleek, honeyed wood burnished with age. Covered with a worn and well-loved fabric he'd never changed, in a bold floral style of red, blue and gold. He'd modelled the whole room around it.

The one piece he had left from his childhood, designed by his mother. They'd had a house full once, but he suspected she'd sold it all when his father had left. Leo should hate it, because it was likely crafted by the man, but all he saw when he looked at the piece was the beauty of its timeless design. His *mother's* design.

'Vintage Tessitore fabric,' Rita said, with a slight frown. He'd never thought to check, because he'd never recover the piece. He wondered if they thought the moment contrived, when it turned out to be a strange coincidence. Simone moved close, placing her hand on his back. He welcomed the silent support.

'I was unaware of that. It was my mother's chair. She designed furniture. That's the original fabric I recall from my childhood. I never wanted to recover it.'

'Our daughter maintains our archive,' Gino said, as he took his place next to Fia. 'We've tried to keep a sample of most fabrics the family have designed, in modern times at least. I didn't know your mother designed furniture. It looks a little like a Silvestri piece.'

Leo clenched his jaw, breathed through the heat like lava rising through his gut.

Simone rubbed her thumb over his spine, grounding him. 'My husband holds a great deal close to his chest. Family most of all. Now, would you all like a drink and some hors d'oeuvres?'

He looked down at her and smiled at the perfect save before getting the drinks as Simone offered a tray of delicacies to their guests, and sat.

'These are delicious,' Rita said.

'They're my favourite. Smoked salmon canapes. My mother always said a woman should know how to mix one good cocktail, make a great hors d'oeuvre and have a signature dessert. The hors d'oeuvres and dessert tonight, are mine.'

It was strange, her mention of family, when he knew so little of her past apart from the estrangement. He'd never asked why. That seemed like a critical failing that he needed to rectify.

'If the dessert is as good as the canape, I can't wait. I love sweet things.'

'So does my husband.' Simone laughed, casting him a knowing look that was like a punch of heat arrowing to his groin. The woman could invoke incinerating desire with a glance.

'It's comforting to see that you're recovered after your fall,' Fia said. 'We were shocked to hear the news.'

'And thank you for the flowers you sent me. It was so thoughtful. It's been difficult at times, but I'm mostly recovered. The care I received was excellent.' She looked up at Leo and smiled. 'Both from the medical professionals and from my husband.'

Gino took a sip from his drink, fixed Leo with his dark,

assessing gaze. 'It must have been difficult, so soon after you were married.'

Leo knew that this night was a set of crossroads where he faced a choice, to open up to these people who were strangers to him, or remain firmly closed. Over the years many had tried to take from him, bring him down. Saying he was too much, or not enough. A pretender to the role he'd claimed and made his own, as the arbiter of all things stylish, whether they be a person or a piece of furniture. For that reason, he didn't give readily of himself about anything that would impact the image he'd spent years cultivating. The one that hid the worst side of himself. Being closed was easy.

Yet tonight was about building relationships. Showing his true self when some days, he wasn't sure who that was any more.

He glanced at Simone. She kept things hidden too and yet in so many ways, she brought out in him what was most authentic. He'd told her more about himself than he'd revealed to anyone. Not everything, that was true. There were some things in his past no one needed to know. However, it was enough to allow himself to feel a little less…constrained.

'Few know that in my late teens my mother fell after work one night and died from her injuries. Simone's fall…it brought back some terrible memories, but at least this time I was there. If I hadn't been, it could have been so much worse.'

Simone reached out her hand, placed it over his and squeezed. It was more comfort than he deserved.

'It was a silly accident, really. I put on a new pair of heels Leo had gifted me and tripped. But I'm here and everything's fine.'

Everything might not have been and that still haunted him.

'I can't imagine what that must have been like,' Rita said, looking lovingly at Enzo.

'No, yet my wife continues to wear heels,' Leo said dryly.

'I *love* heels.' Simone gave a wry laugh. 'Just not around stairs.'

His guests laughed a little too, the mood lighter. Simone turned to him with a soft smile. What she was trying to convey, he wasn't sure. The emotions inside of him too tangled to properly interpret the meaning. She knew the story of his mother, so he hadn't said anything that would have come as a surprise.

Out of the corner of his eye he glimpsed movement. One of his household staff. They discreetly signalled to Simone.

'Ah,' she said. 'Dinner's ready. Would you like to join us outside? We thought it was a beautiful night so we could eat on the patio under the vines.'

Simone joined the rest of the guests, leading them through the home. Only Gino held back to walk with Leo, looking on as his wife, daughter and son-in-law, chatted to her.

'We're alike, you and I,' Gino said. 'Lucky men. Our women are too good for us.'

Simone laughed at something said, warm and gracious.

Leo couldn't help but agree.

CHAPTER NINE

IF EMPTY PLATES were anything to go by, then Simone judged that the dinner had been a huge success. It had been a simple enough yet traditional Milanese meal. Osso Bucco, risotto, some salads made from greens grown in the garden. She'd wanted it to feel like something homely, rather than a business meal and it had worked. The patio, where they sat, was lit up with fairy lights. The vibe elegantly casual. Simone was sure that all of this was something Leo wouldn't have agreed to if asked, but she hadn't asked and he'd let her organise everything.

Considering the man controlled every facet of his life and his image, it had come as a surprise. She'd expected him to have asked the chef about the menu, or say something about the flurry of activity around the house in preparation, but he hadn't even offered any advice. It was so unlike their wedding, when he'd planned the whole thing down to the last second. Even when he'd offered her a choice, she *knew* it was under sufferance and he'd had a firm view of what he wanted.

This? It made her feel trusted. Valued. Like she had an opinion and a place in his life. It meant something.

'Your apple pie was magnificent,' Rita said. She was about Leo's age, with short black hair and dark, expressive eyes.

'Thank you. I worried it might be a bit heavy after the meal we just had but...'

'I know. Dessert. How can you go wrong?' Rita smiled. 'It reminds me of my time studying in the US. I must have the recipe.'

'Of course. Before you go give me your email. I'll send it to you.'

There'd been some talk of business tonight. How to grow and evolve a brand. Meatier topics such as the challenges of managing a business that relied on a discretionary spend, in a downturn. Leo was less affected, the Tessitores a little more so. Is that why they'd talked of selling their business? What should have been a purely financial transaction seemed so much more. She'd always suspected that it was personal for them. She began to believe it more strongly, but there was something else. Simone wondered if they wanted to sell at all. These were questions everyone seemed to be skirting round. Something almost...personal. She guessed that it would have to be a very personal decision to divest yourself of a company that had been in your family for generations...

'May I ask...' She directed her question to Fia, who she'd discovered had been Tessitore's designer for a number of years. It was how she and Gino had met, a workplace romance. 'I understand you're looking to sell Tessitore Fabrics. But why, since you so clearly love the company? It's been in the family for generations. You're still the principal designer.'

It was like a stylus scratching across a record, as if she'd said something discordant and the sound simply stopped. If there'd been an elephant in the room, it had just stomped into plain sight. Fia gave a sad smile.

'My health.'

Gino reached out and placed his hand over his wife's, just like she'd done for Leo.

'I'm sorry for raising it,' Simone said.

Fia sighed. 'No, no. It's been a long time coming. It was a flaw that we relied too much on me and my designs. And as for our children, it's not where their talents and interests lie. Rita is an archivist. My son, a textile chemist. My granddaughter, my son's eldest, is artistic and we've encouraged her to try fabric design. She shows immense promise, but she's only fifteen and who knows what she'll want to do when she's older.'

'So there's currently no one you trust but yourself?'

Fia shook her head. 'No, we have some designers.'

'But they're not Fia,' Gino said.

Leo had sat back, watching. Not really contributing, until this moment. 'How much time are you looking at, before your health intervenes and divesting becomes a necessity?'

Fia shrugged. 'It's my eyes, a rare condition. I require surgery, though not immediately. Whilst I can still design, it's sometimes harder to do what I used to. Surgery carries risks. If it's unsuccessful my sight will deteriorate. If the risks eventuate, I'll be left unable to see. So perhaps it's time to move on, spend it with grandchildren and family and work less. You believe you're invincible, until suddenly you find out you're not. Then you have to think about life and what you need to do.'

It was all so familiar to Simone. How she still felt about grasping what was offered to you and not letting it simply slide by. Life was for living, not merely existing.

She should know. She'd existed for long enough.

'I know that feeling, even though it's for different reasons. Life can be short. One day everything's fine. The next, everything can change in an instant.'

Everyone around the table looked sombre, nodding.

'I'm only sorry for dampening the mood of a lovely evening by asking,' Simone said.

'No.' Leo turned to her. There was something in his gaze, an intensity, like he'd been lit from within. It *burned*. Then he focussed on the Tessitores once more. 'This is an important discussion. I'm coming to understand that you're under pressure to do something. Would I be right in saying that if things were different, you wouldn't be looking to sell the company at all?'

The family members looked at each other. Gino shook his head.

'Fia is the soul of the designs. If we had more time, other plans could be put in place. If it happened in ten years, our granddaughter might have been old enough and interested enough to join the company. For now, nothing's clear and our only interest is in seeing Tessitore survive. We'd prefer to plan, than to sell when the news is out and the vultures have started circling.'

Leo lounged back in his dining chair. The space was lit up by candles and the glittering lights above them. People might like to believe he was relaxed. However, Simone knew him far better. She could see it, the way he was thinking. The merest furrow on his brow when he turned and the light catching his face the right way. Appearing relaxed yet really, just all power sheathed. Like she'd thought once before. A panther waiting to spring onto its prey. A liquid kind of heat flooded through Simone. Pooling, settling low. There was a reason no one should ever underestimate Leo Zanetti and she was witnessing it right now.

'What if I proposed not a sale or takeover, but a partnership? Circolo has the financial capacity to support the business if it needs to transition. That could give Tessitore time and space. The family wouldn't have to forgo all their shares. Should Fia have the capacity or desire, she could still design. Should your granddaughter decide her future lies with the business, and she has the talent, the opportunity to continue the family tradition wouldn't be lost to her. Then, hasty decisions wouldn't need to be made. We could invite guest designers to create fabrics whilst Fia's getting treatment. It might be a better solution for you.'

Fia and Rita's eyes widened. They smiled. Gino cocked his head and fixed Leo with a dark, assessing gaze.

'What do you get from the deal?'

Leo laughed. 'Don't worry. I'm no charity and I'll take my fair share but I understand the importance of tradition. Circolo would be partnering with the oldest and finest textile maker in Italy. That would give us significant cultural and design capital. I'd expect exclusivity on certain fabric patterns, which only Circolo branded or approved products would carry. I might ask for a veto on who the fabrics can be sold to. I can draw up terms, then we can talk more, should you be interested in my offer.'

Simone sat back in her chair. Simply marvelling as Leo had pivoted so effortlessly. But even more, he'd taken the realisation that the family didn't want to sell and offered something which let them keep at least part of the company in the family. They didn't have to let it go. The offer was stunning. Generous.

It showed a new side to him she hadn't known existed.

Gino looked at his family. Fia and Rita nodded. 'Then we might be able to make a deal.'

There seemed to be a lightness that came over the table. A sense of hope. They drank wine, talked some more. A friendly getting-to-know-you, till it was time for them to leave. It was like the edge had been burnished from the evening, sharp sides sanded smooth. Leo and Simone walked them to the front door and said their warm goodbyes. After closing the door, he turned. The look on his face intent. He stalked towards her, backing her towards the wall. Pressed her up against it, a hand above her head.

'You are an inspiration.'

So was he, but she didn't have time to say so before his mouth crashed onto hers. A kiss hard and fierce, tasting like the after-dinner espresso they'd consumed. Leo devoured her. She kissed him back, her body going up in flames. She didn't know how she survived him without perpetually crumbling to ashes at his feet. His tongue danced with hers, inflaming, enticing. Whilst kissing him was one of her life's greatest pleasures, it wasn't enough. She needed more. She needed *everything*. She grabbed his shirt and pulled him even closer as he groaned. Their bodies melded together. He could take her right here and it wouldn't matter but instead he pulled away, his lips gleaming in the soft light, breaths coming in heavy pants.

'I want you.'

'I need you,' she said.

The feelings he ignited inside, consumed her. A complex mix of passion, possession and completion. Feeling settled and unsettled, all at the same time.

He swooped her into his arms and captured her lips again before striding through the house and up the stairs to the main bedroom. Crossing the threshold, the only light in the room came from the ensuite, casting the space in a contrast of golden glow and shadow. For all the aggressive passion, Leo let her go gently. Placing her carefully on her feet. It was such a small thing and it still meant the world that he could think about her, when she knew he was as desperate as she was for them to be naked together. But whilst she wanted to be selfish and take, tonight she also wanted to give. He'd shared his past with people and it had been no small thing, given how deep she knew his wounds ran. How her own fall had re-opened them.

Leo toed out of his shoes, stripped off his belt as Simone began unbuttoning his shirt, tugging it from his trousers then tossing it to the floor. He undid the bow at her neck, the halter neck top falling free to her waist, exposing her breasts. He grunted as her nipples tightened in the cool air of the room. Leo cupped them with his hands, stroked his thumbs over the hard peaks.

'*Perfetto*,' he murmured. '*Amore mio, sei una bellezza*.'

Whilst she could listen to him for hours, Simone was too desperate. She wiggled away, undid her own pants, threw off her top. Stood in front of him in nothing but the fine lace and silk panties she'd chosen because she knew he loved them.

'On the bed,' she said, injecting as much dominance into her voice as she could muster. Trying to wrestle control of the evening for herself.

He cocked an eyebrow, his eyes glittering like sapphires in the light. 'Really?'

His voice was as rich and rough as coffee grounds. His fingers flexed and released as if he wanted to touch her, but she was sure that he'd like this game. Being with Leo gave her a new kind of confidence and she wanted to give him the same pleasure that he always seemed to give her.

'Yes, really. I intend to have my wicked way with you. Or doesn't the great Leo Zanetti want to listen to what he might find is actually good for him?'

Leo chuckled. '*Tesoro*, I'm happy for you to do whatever you want to me. I'm looking forward to it.'

He moved onto the bed, flopping onto the mattress in a way that suggested he was being imposed upon. Yet she knew it was an act. Leo lay there, arms behind his head, a smug smile on his face. He'd ceded control to her but she knew that he wasn't giving it away completely. She wanted to break him apart like he routinely did to her, break herself and then let them be stitched back together. Entwined, knitted. Two cracked halves making the other whole.

She eased off her panties in a slow tease, then undid his trousers and slid them from his body. Hooked her fingers into his black briefs, dragging them away and tossing them over her shoulder. A liquid heat pooled low in her belly as his impressive erection sprung free. She loved the sight of him, potent, aroused, intoxicating. Simone licked her lips.

'Want a taste of what I have?' he asked hoarsely.

'I'm hungry for you, Leo. You'd better hang on.'

He chuckled but when she took him in hand the sound was rapidly cut off. She smiled, then lowered her head and wrapped her mouth round his smooth, silk-steel length. He was salt and sweet and everything she could have desired in this moment. Simone relished teasing him with her tongue as he gripped the covers of the bed. She *ached* for him. He'd barely touched her yet and already she needed to clamp her legs together against the burn that built at her core. Could she come like this, with not a hand of his on her? Feasting on him? After so many years of feeling nothing, no desire, like walking through a kind of haze, this was a revelation.

Simone looked up at him, as his head arched back. The sounds he made, not so elegant and restrained now, but feral and out of control. She knew he was close, as his body quaked, but she didn't want the moment to end yet. Perhaps she was still allowed a little selfishness, but she wanted him inside her. She eased away from him and he groaned, his eyes glassy and distant with arousal. She crawled over his body, sliding the centre of herself over his length, relishing in his hardness, how slick they both were. Him from her mouth and her because of how Leo always affected her.

The burn built between her legs as she rubbed herself back and forth, his hands on her backside, encouraging her. She was panting now, close. So close. Simone sat up.

'Condom,' she whispered. She reached over to his bedside drawer and grabbed a foil packet. Her fingers were trembling and she fumbled so Leo took it gently from her, tore it open and slid it down his length in one practiced move. Simone leaned forwards and kissed him again, their mouths clinging to each other as she lifted herself and positioned him at her entrance. Lowering herself onto him, relishing the sensation of being filled. The relief of it so intense it was all she could do not to orgasm in that moment. He groaned and gripped his hands tight to her thighs as she took all of him in. Rising and falling as she toyed with her nipples because she knew he'd love to see her doing that. Arrows of pleasure spearing between her legs whilst she rode him. He released one of her thighs, easing his thumb between her folds to her clitoris, circling and stroking.

It was like a competition now, as to who would win and come last. The pleasure burning through her. She clenched her body around him and his breaths became shuddering gasps as he stopped lying there taking what she gave and began to thrust up into her. Simone was lost to the sensation. It was all heat and need until Leo's movements became uncoordinated and he threw his head back, shouting her name.

Words toyed at the edges of her consciousness about what this meant, what *he* meant, although they were elusive, formless things. More feeling than reality. Then the conflagration of ecstasy roared over her, burning her to the quick. Simone fell to his chest. He took her in his arms and the world became soft and hazy as Leo's coiled body relaxed and she drifted into an intoxicated sleep.

CHAPTER TEN

THE SOFT MORNING light bled through the room's curtains as Leo woke to the chirping of birds. He checked the time. Still early after their late night. Yet he didn't feel tired, he felt invigorated. A deal with the Tessitores was close. He wouldn't relax till it was final; however a partnership would be a masterstroke. He had little doubt it would be marvelled over, considered a coup of sorts. Together, he was sure they could do great things and he'd ensure that the Silvestri family never got their hands on Tessitore fabrics for their furniture, ever again. They'd have to find another supplier, someone inferior, because there was no company quite like Tessitore Textiles.

All of that had been made possible by the woman lying next to him. He propped himself up on his elbow and looked down on her sleeping form. Her hair a golden tangle on the pristine cream cotton of the pillow. Sheet round her waist. She looked peaceful in slumber, that slight line he sometimes saw between her brows when she concentrated, smoothed away. A warmth lit inside of him, a sensation intensely satisfying, like in those days on the streets when he'd been bone-numbingly hungry and had managed to make enough money for a fulfilling meal. He realised his whole adult life had been about searching for something more, interspersed with only brief moments like now, when he felt he had *enough*.

This morning, it was as if he was finally sated.

Of course, it could have simply been a hangover of their lovemaking the night before. Her lips were a revelation. Then the vision of her looking like a goddess, over him. Taking her own pleasure from his body. Giving him pleasure in return, an experience so mind blowing, it had been a struggle to hold onto consciousness long enough to scoop her into his arms before he'd tumbled into a deep, dreamless sleep.

Those memories were enough to have him hard, aching and wanting again, but there was something more. Simone was a mystery. She remained an enigma. Intelligent, beautiful, but in many ways as far away from him as the day he'd employed her. It was like a tiny splinter digging into him, an irritation.

He'd given her some of himself and yet she'd shared nothing of herself at all. He'd told her once that he'd have questions and that time was now. To him, his failure to ask anything of her now seemed like a personal one. He wanted to know what she liked, disliked. What kind of life she'd come from, why she was estranged from most of her family.

Simone was a puzzle he wanted to solve. He had questions. He could think of no better time than today for her to answer them.

As if some sense in her knew, Simone stirred. Her eyes fluttering open. At first her gaze was unfocused but then she fixed her cool grey eyes on him and the most beatific smile broke over her face, like a shaft of sunshine through a crack in the curtains. It was as if that beautiful light in her smile settled smack in the middle of his chest. An unfamiliar warmth, soft and bright. He rubbed at the spot with the heel of his palm.

'Good morning,' she said, her voice a little husky from sleep.

'It's an excellent morning.'

Simone lifted her hand and traced one gentle finger from the base of his throat to where that warmth in his chest had begun to ignite and burn. She placed her own palm over it as if somehow, deeply and intuitively, she knew it was there. Did she feel the same when she looked at him, when he smiled at her? It was yet another question in the long list he had for her.

'Last night went well I think.'

'Thanks to you.'

'All I did was to ask a question everybody seemed to want to avoid.'

'I was planning to address the issue over drinks at the end of the meal.'

A little crease formed in the centre of her brow again. He wanted to reach out and stroke it away.

'Sorry to change your game plan.'

He shook his head. 'It was perfect. *You* were perfect. From me, there would have been no way for the question not to sound forced. From you, it was organic, curious. Thank you. For that, and for your food. It made the evening far easier. I don't believe I'd have achieved the result as quickly, on my own. I've been dancing around Gino for months. I believe even had I asked outright, he would never have told me about Fia's illness.'

A flush bled across her cheeks. Simone gave a self-satisfied, and well deserved, smile.

'You're a revelation, *tesoro*.'

'I'm just me. What you see is what you get.'

'You're an enigma and a mystery. You know about me and yet I know so little about you.'

Her soft grey gaze left him, to where her left hand toyed with the sheet as if wanting to wrap it more tightly round herself. She shrugged.

'You're the interesting one. The one whose story regularly makes the press.'

'Yes, I'm a legend in my own lifetime,' he said. 'Such an achievement. Whereas you… I said that one day I'd ask questions. Today is that day.'

'So early in the morning when there are more interesting things we could be doing…'

She arched her back. Simone was in avoidance but her display wasn't contrived. Her nipples peaked in perfect, dusky points. Tight with desire. She was temptation incarnate. He could immerse himself in the pleasure of her body for hours on end and never be sated.

Yet, that didn't seem like enough. Not now. He wanted to *know* her. Not simply as his efficient, insightful personal assistant, convenient wife and now, lover. He wanted to share thoughts, *feelings*.

'Questions now, distractions later,' he said.

She pouted, but he could see the skin puckering at the side of her mouth where she was worrying the flesh with her teeth.

'Then I need coffee.'

'I'm happy to oblige you.'

Leo left the bed and as he did so he could almost feel Simone's eyes on him, as palpable as her fingers digging into skin. There were no staff in the house this early and the grounds were private so there was no need for him to dress. Leo strolled to the door of their room. If she liked what she saw, then he'd give her a show. He walked to the kitchens and set about what he'd always found to be the relaxing routine of making coffee. Espresso for him, caffè latte for her. Since she believed she needed a little fortifying he hunted through the cupboards and found some hazelnut syrup, adding a dash to her drink. He placed both cups on a tray and then carried them back to their room.

Leo couldn't imagine what Simone might have to tell him. Did she believe he'd judge her? After his own past, he was in no position to condemn anyone else, although she didn't know that. Some things, about himself at least, there was no need to disclose. Nothing she'd done would have been worse than his own youthful actions, of that he could be assured. As he walked back into the room Simone was sitting up in bed. Her hair was neater, as if she'd brushed it. She was wearing his shirt, the one torn away and discarded in passion the night before. A rush of heat flooded over him, possession, at the sight of her in a piece of his clothing. The way it swamped her. Made her look somehow small, fragile. In that moment, he didn't want to talk. He wanted to scoop her into his arms and hold her. Tell her it would all be okay, even if he didn't know what the problem was. As he came into the room her grey eyes became stormy, darkened. Not too fragile for desire then, which was good. He could work with that.

'Like what you see?'

Her gaze drifting over his naked body, fixing at his groin. In a moment he was half hard. Simone did that to him. If he didn't constantly wrestle his own desire under control when she was around, he'd never get any work done.

'A tray of coffee? Yes.'

He chuckled. If he was another kind of man, that comment might have cut him off at the knees, the way she said it. Dry as ancient dust.

'Don't prefer the look of anything else?'

'Mr Zanetti, I do believe you're fishing for compliments.'

The corners of her mouth quirked as if she was trying very hard to suppress a smile.

'I don't need any, given you orgasmed into near unconsciousness last night. I feel none are required.'

She raised a slender, pale brow. 'I might suggest that you were similarly affected, but unlike you, I wouldn't like to brag.'

He chuckled, loving how Simone tried to put him in his place, even if right now it was only for show. She'd always had a way of keeping him grounded, reminding him that he was simply a man and not the ridiculously titled Sultan of Style as the press proclaimed. He placed the tray of coffee on his bedside table and propped up his own pillows. Slid under the covers and then handed Simone her coffee, taking his own and finishing it in a few short mouthfuls.

Simone looked to be savouring hers, eyes fluttering shut at the taste. Her throat dipped softly in a swallow and she took another almost as if fortifying herself. Her chest rose and fell in a deep breath, then she opened her eyes, her jaw seeming hard, as if she was somehow resolved. She placed her cup down.

'Thank you. The hazelnut was a lovely touch.'

'*Prego*. This isn't your last meal, Simone.'

She snorted. 'There are things I don't talk about much.'

'Like why nobody visited you at the hospital after your accident.'

'Holly can't travel right now, which she told you. And you know the rest of my family and I are estranged. You of all people should understand what that's like.'

'Yet I told you why. Now I'm asking the same of you.'

Simone let out a slow, pained breath. 'Let's just say there were expectations placed on me as a child and a young woman. I was supposed to look and act a certain way, to prepare myself for finding a husband my parents approved of, or even better, marrying a person they chose for me, who might help my father's business. I always guessed the idea of choice was really an illusion.'

'What sort of husband were they looking for?'

'Funnily enough, probably someone a lot like you, although not Italian. An American would have been preferred.'

'And you didn't want that.'

'No, yet here I am. The delicious irony of my situation.'

'All to help your sister.'

Simone nodded. 'You know she's pregnant. Holly hid it, till she couldn't any more. And for good reason. My parents didn't react well and threw her out of their home. Holly needed a place to live, medical care. The pregnancy's complicated and once she has the baby he'll need a stable life, a good education. I could do a lot on what I'm paid, but it didn't cover everything she needed. Now, she can have whatever she wants.'

'What about you? Your wants?'

'I wasn't looking for love. You agreed. And I was confident you wouldn't ask anything of me that I wasn't prepared to give.'

In truth, she'd given him almost everything. At least he could be confident that she'd come to his bed out of desire rather than any sense of obligation. Yet he *had* taken from her and she'd almost lost her life in the process. She'd been clear when they'd signed the pre-nuptial agreement that love wasn't on the table. In his extensive experience, most women he'd known had wanted love in the end. He'd had to be quite clear with anyone he'd spent consistent time with that whilst he'd be generous financially, and in the bedroom, love and permanence would never be on the cards. He'd been wedded to his business and that was all he'd needed.

What was her reason?

'What happened to you, *cara*? What really made you leave?'

Simone took another long sip of coffee. Sat staring at the wall ahead of her, not at him.

'When you're young, it's easy to believe a lot of things. Mine's an old, well-worn story. I was at college. I met a boy. I thought I'd fallen in love.'

She seemed to somehow shrink into herself, become smaller. He wanted to take her into his arms but she seemed so distant right now. He feared that if he did, he wouldn't get the story or the insights that he needed, to try to understand her. Maybe that was selfish of him, but Leo was also driven to find out more about her.

'He was on a partial scholarship and wasn't the sort of person that my parents would have approved of. I didn't care. He said he loved me and I thought I loved him. I had all these dreams, you know? Saving myself for marriage. Just being with one man, in love, for ever. My friends seemed supportive but really, they thought I'd lowered myself. Word got back to my parents who paid him off and the relationship ended. His professed love for me was worth a surprisingly paltry sum, in the end. I suppose he could have finished college debt free. Anyhow, he'd seen me as a conquest, a challenge, nothing more.'

She placed her coffee cup down on the bedside table and wrapped her arms round her waist in a protective move.

'My parents claimed to love me, but it was transactional. They loved us only as long as we did what they wanted. Look at me. Look at my sister. Then Jace. He said he loved me. We had dreams and promises and he didn't love me at all. Money was worth more than I ever was.'

As she spoke, Leo's heart felt like it was being crushed inside of him. Sure, he'd seen the damage misplaced romantic love could do to a person. Yet, in the end, he'd always been sure of his mother's love of him. It was one of the things that drove him, what he was doing in her name. Whilst he'd been alone for a long time, the desire to avenge what had happened to them always carried him forwards. For Simone, what did she have? Only herself. In that way she was a thousand times stronger than he was.

'You're worth—'

'I know *exactly* how much I'm worth.'

He wasn't sure whether she was talking about her intrinsic value as a person or their pre-nuptial agreement. He hated to think that all she saw her worth coming down to was a financial value of some sort. Leo cupped her cheek. She leaned her face into it, the warm weight of her in his palm. Her eyes glittering as if with unshed tears. Perhaps she wasn't as immune to it all as she pretended to be.

Even touching her, the distance between them seemed too far. He needed to close it, to comfort her in the only way he knew how.

'Come here,' he said, opening his arms. She shuffled over and into his embrace as he held her against his chest. His lips to her hair. Breathing her in.

'I'm sorry for what happened to you.'

'It was clear that the universe was teaching me some powerful lessons and I learned them well.'

Leo wrapped his arms tighter round her, to try as much as he could to let her know that she had his support, for as long as she needed it. Because whilst Simone might have believed the universe had taught her powerful lessons, he wasn't sure that what she'd learned were the right ones.

They'd had a slow start to the morning, drinking coffee together. Eating a quiet breakfast on the terrace. Something about purging herself to him, telling Leo about her past as he'd done with her, was freeing. It was like a weight lifted, one person to share her past with because even Holly hadn't really known what went on and Simone hadn't wanted to burden her. She would have been happy for a quiet day round the house, easing back into a little work except Leo had suggested he take her sightseeing and then out to dinner. Turning off their phones and forgetting about work for a while. Now, they sat in the back of a taxi, travelling to the centre of the city.

'Are you ever going to give me any hints about where we're going, other than what I should be wearing?'

Leo grinned, his eyes hidden behind dark sunglasses. He'd told her to wear clothes to cover her knees and her shoulders, and also put on comfortable shoes.

'I like surprising you,' he said. 'Although, you always seem so resistant.'

'*I* like to be prepared.'

'And yet each time we've gone out, you have been. Have I ever let you down?'

She sat with that for a while and of course the answer was clear. No, he hadn't.

'Anyway, as much as I'd like to spend every day locked in the bedroom making love to you, we had to cancel our honeymoon. I thought you might like to play tourist instead.'

Spending days in bed with him sounded like a *perfect* honeymoon. Still, Leo's suggestion was kind. Thoughtful. Something unfamiliar to her when she spent so much time thinking of others. On previous times she'd been to Milan they'd worked. One night she'd managed to get to La Scala, but that was all. It was nice to take the time to look around, especially with her own personal tour guide. The most handsome tour guide in the whole of Italy, if not the world.

'I always wondered about your choice of Verona. I thought the whole point of getting married was a happily ever after. Romeo and Juliet didn't achieve that.'

'I thought Verona was romantic.'

That gave her pause. Nothing about their marriage was romantic and yet that's what he'd wanted for their honeymoon? She shouldn't read too much into it. A romantic honeymoon was good for PR. That had been the reason behind it, she was sure.

'It's a town famous for two hormonal kids who thought they were in love coming to a sticky end because of a family feud.'

'And yet, people find it compelling. I can't remember you being this cynical before, Mrs Zanetti.'

She hadn't been, once. Simone had been too trusting, too naïve. Believing that her life would work out well, because why shouldn't it? She'd only really recognised the privilege of the position she'd once held, when that position was taken away from her. It had taught her that in her world, people only cared about how you looked and how you dressed. That you behaved yourself and didn't create a scandal. Love was transactional. So long as you toed the line it was fine, but heaven help you wanting a little something for yourself, or trying to break out of the mould created for you, because then people didn't want you at all.

'What is it they say? *Marry in haste, repent at leisure*? Are you repenting, Leo?'

A look passed over his face. Not exactly a frown, more like a moment of something that looked like pain. Though it had disappeared so quickly she could have imagined it.

'I may have many things to repent for. Marrying you is not on the list. This will never be something I regret.'

The vehemence of his words. She didn't know what to

say because the truth was, she couldn't regret this either. She was saved from having to respond as their cab pulled up at the side of a street. Leo paid with a generous tip and they both hopped out.

'It's not far,' Leo said, holding out his hand. She took it, threading her fingers through his as they began to walk. 'In fact, there it is.'

Rising above the cityscape were the spires of Milan's magnificent Duomo cathedral.

'I thought you might like to see the terraces. If there's one thing you should do in Milan, it's this.'

The plain marble square in front showed off the elaborate gothic architecture to perfection. People milled around, taking photos. A few children chased pigeons which took flight, flapping only a small distance away to land, before being chased again. They walked up to the door, avoiding the queue. Someone met them and handed Leo two tickets.

'So, we don't have to line up?'

He took off his sunglasses and winked. 'No. I have a few friends in high places. It pays to know me.'

She placed her hand on his chest. 'Why, Mr Zanetti, you do come with some benefits.'

His pupils flared dark in the languid blue of his eyes. 'Later I'll show you just how many, but for now, come explore.'

They walked inside the vast space. The floors, beautifully patterned marble. The plain walls spliced with jewel coloured stained glass windows. The vaulted ceiling, soaring above them. The cathedral's magnificence gave her a new perspective on her own existence. It made many of her all too human problems seem small, insignificant.

'We should see the terraces first, then we can explore the rest of the building, if you wish. I might light a candle…after.'

To honour his mother. She reached out and squeezed his hand. He squeezed back.

'How do we get up top?' she asked.

'There's an elevator for which we have tickets, or we can climb over two hundred stairs. Your preference?'

It sounded like the decision was hers to make and whatever she chose didn't matter, but there was a tightness around his eyes that told another story.

'Let's do the elevator.'

It was almost like he let out a long breath. 'Good choice.'

Even with their express tickets, there was a small queue. When they finally got into the lift Leo seemed bristling with what she guessed was excitement.

'This is the best view of the city. Even with all the tourists it's one of my favourite places in Milan.'

The doors opened, and they walked out through a plain, stone-walled corridor, then up a few more stairs and onto a rooftop.

Simone gasped.

Above them towered the Gothic spires of the cathedral, like a forest of stone intent on piercing the heavens. Each spire topped with a figure, like sentinels watching over the city. Everywhere she turned there was another intricate carving. Gargoyles, animals, people. The flying buttresses a marvel in themselves, richly decorated with their own architectural carvings.

'This…' Words were stolen from her. It was overwhelming, surrounded by all the glorious excess.

'Now you understand why it's my favourite place in the city,' he said pointing. 'Look. It's clear enough. Today you can see the Alps.'

The mountains rose above the horizon, capped in snow.

'It's so beautiful.'

He smiled, but Leo's gaze wasn't on the view, but on her. 'I know.'

The moment seemed to slow, like a pause in the world turning. Then he blinked and focused on the city ahead of them.

'Would you like a photograph to send to Holly?'

'That'd be great,' she said pulling her phone out of her bag, setting up the camera and handing it to him. She stood with the spires and buttresses behind her, smiling as he took pictures.

'That should do for now.' He handed the phone back to her. She opened her gallery and flicked through. She almost couldn't recognise herself because she looked...

Happy.

As she was about to slip her phone back into her bag a text notification popped up on the screen. Whilst they were having downtime, it was from Circolo's accountant. She opened the message in case it was important.

Leo hasn't picked up.
Pls ask him to call re the charity for Roma.

Strange, she didn't know anything about Rome, or a charity.

'I have a message from Roberto. Something about Rome? He wants you to call. It sounds urgent.'

Leo's mouth tightened almost imperceptibly. 'I'll deal with it later. We're sightseeing, remember?'

'Are you sure? Is there anything—'

'No. Nothing.'

She frowned. Leo walked up to her, reached out and stroked his finger gently down the middle of her forehead, as if smoothing out the crease there.

'Allow us to have this time. If there's anything I need your help with, I'll ask. I recognise your value to me, in all things.'

He pressed her against the marble balustrade, slid his arms round her waist, dropped his head and captured her lips in a gentle, passionate kiss.

It was like she was standing on a precipice of choices and in this moment she simply let herself fall into it, above this beautiful city, like she was standing in the heavens. It overwhelmed her, the sensation.

She felt valued. She felt seen.

She felt loved.

The kisses slowed to a stop, and Leo pulled back. She looked up at him—so solid, tall, those shoulders broad enough to carry the weight of a world. To carry hers. He had a soft, knowing smile on his face. It was on the tip of her tongue, to say three words that might change them both for ever. But now wasn't the right time—not when everything was so new. Like a butterfly just hatched from its chrysalis, its wings fragile and fresh.

It needed some more time, till those wings became solid and it could take flight. So that's what she'd give it, since time was what she'd been granted. Because whilst she'd almost died, Leo had shown her a life she wanted to live.

CHAPTER ELEVEN

SIMONE WALKED INTO Leo's Milan office. They'd returned to work and she joined him a few days a week, working the rest from home. She always enjoyed coming back here. In New York, his office was high in the sky, the view an imposing one. It was as if Leo wanted to look over the city he now ruled, because he'd brought his business to the US and become an overnight sensation, rather like he had when he'd been plucked from the streets here. Yet Milan was different. The ground floor in the more historical part of town, with large plate glass windows overlooking a lush green garden accessible to staff. A lot like his Milan home, she realised. It seemed in this city, Leo was more himself than anywhere else.

Yet today, there was something edgy about him. There had been for a few weeks now, ever since their visit to the Duomo. At night, things hadn't changed. He still held her. Made love to her. Told her she was worth more than she knew and then showed her with his lips and hands. His whole body. Yet something was off. It made her ache inside, like he seemed to be drawing away when she wanted to hold onto him even tighter. To tell him that this no longer felt like a business deal. It felt real.

'I have a jet on standby for Rome, if you need it.'

He looked up at her. Distracted. Gave her a tight smile.

It could be the Tessitore deal. Things had moved frighteningly fast since that dinner with the family. Long hours worked to put together something everyone was happy with. They'd sent the contract off a week earlier, which Leo had already signed, so confident he'd been that what he'd proposed would win them over. They were still waiting for an official response...

'Thank you,' he said, his eyes flicking back to his phone almost like she was an afterthought. Her stomach clenched. She couldn't help feeling as if something was wrong yet how could it be when the passion between them was undiminished? Like he could never get enough of her. It had to be Tessitore, they were so close but still so far. And yet...

'Are you sure you don't want me to come with you?'

He'd been cryptic about the possible trip to Rome but then he'd promised that if he needed her, he'd ask and she trusted him to do so. Leo frowned, and shook his head. 'No. You stay here and wait for the Tessitore contract to come through.'

It made sense on an intellectual level, but her waiting behind wasn't necessary. Someone else could open the envelope if it arrived and if there was a problem, the Tessitores or their lawyer would call. That could be done anywhere in the world. The thought of him simply going without her... they hadn't been apart since they'd been married.

Since when had she become so needy? She was a grown woman. She could spend a night away from her husband—

Except nothing was certain, nothing was real. Her desires unvoiced. She looked at the rings on her finger. How they glittered under the lights. Still new, and beautiful. Thoughtful, and personally designed by Leo for her. Their marriage might not have started out being real but it felt that way now. Her suite in Milan, a beautiful testament to his thoughtfulness, now only a place that she kept her clothes, having moved permanently into his bedroom.

'I just thought…'

He raised an eyebrow, his blue eyes blindingly bright and his expression unfathomable. She didn't know what she really thought, or how to voice this complex mess of feelings that seemed to overtake her. Admiration, desire, something all-encompassing and endless.

'I won't be gone long. If I need to stay it'll only be a day or two at most.'

She opened her mouth to say something, to argue but she wasn't sure why. Why this trip didn't feel normal, but like distance was growing between them. There was a quiet rap at the door. A welcome break from the tension. Simone went to see who it was and one of the staff stood there.

'A delivery's just come through.'

The staff member handed over a large envelope. She took it, turned it over. Saw where it had come from, her heart skipping a beat. She held it out to Leo.

'From the Tessitores. Do you think…?'

Leo stood, his nostrils flaring. Any distance she'd perceived, disappeared. It was replaced by bristling expectation.

'You open it. The success is as much yours as it is mine.'

Simone carefully opened the envelope. Slid the sheaves of paper from it. A letter she didn't read being in Italian, which she was trying to learn, and the contract Circolo had returned. She flicked over to the last page.

It was signed.

She carefully placed it on the desk in front of him. This business deal had meant so much to Leo, and it had begun to take on the same importance to her as well. A spike of adrenaline coursed through her. It was done, the reason for their marriage, fulfilled…

Was that why he was pulling away, because her usefulness had ended? It wouldn't be the first time that had happened to her… No, that's not what was happening here. This was more. She knew it. Whilst it should be an ending she couldn't help but think of it as a beginning. She smiled as Leo looked at the page, traced his finger over the Tessitore signature as if he didn't quite believe it, then looked up at her. The expression on his face, fierce. He stalked out from behind the desk towards her.

'I couldn't have done this without you.'

Leo took her into his arms and her body instantly relaxed. All her worries and fears gone as he held her, then his lips crashed on to hers. She kissed him with all the emotion she'd held within herself. Thrusting her hands into his hair, gripping tight, not wanting to let him go. They were a team. Unstoppable. It was like together, anything was possible. He pressed her back against the desk and lifted her up onto it, pushing up the skirt of her dress. Stepping into her, pulling her forwards. His hardness against her core. She burned for him. It was the same as the night of the ball when he'd taken her into a darkened room and their passion had exploded for the first time. This was madness. The office door was unlocked, anyone could walk in, and yet she didn't care. He eased one hand up, toying with her nipple through her bra and she moaned softly, gripping the front of his shirt, not wanting to let go. He pulled away from the kiss, trailing his lips up her neck to her ear. Whispering words in Italian she couldn't grasp. Endearments, encouragement, thanks? She couldn't be sure and she didn't care. Then he eased his hand to her centre, teasing her body through her panties. Capturing her lips again as she moaned louder this time. So much inside wanting to simply take flight. Things that she never expected to voice again, emotions that she couldn't deny or hold in any longer as he stroked her and wound her higher and tighter. Then the orgasm simply exploded through her. Searing and hot, rolling on and on like there'd never be an end. Just like she wanted for them. But like all good things, it did end, easing, stuttering, then finally stopping. Leaving her floating in a haze of bliss and what she knew was inescapable.

They were good together. A team. Professionally, but more important, personally. Simone was certain that they were better as one than apart. And then the words she'd tried to hold in simply came out on a sigh.

'I love you, Leo.'

He was hard, aching. Wanting release. Wanting to forget. Rome had become a problem. A place he needed to travel to in order to continue to try to put to bed the sins of his past by helping the families he'd hurt. Then the Tessitore contract had arrived and he'd lost his head completely. Simone had wrecked him and remade him. But her words…

I love you, Leo.

No. That had never been part of the deal. It was based on a lie. She claimed to love him but he was a man who'd been created by the media, hiding his sins. Carefully curating his life so that he could atone for his crimes in peace.

Her words had just shattered everything he knew or wanted. He couldn't be trusted with love. He couldn't be trusted with her.

She'd slumped against him, replete, and part of him ached to simply ignore what she'd said and make love to her, here, on his desktop. But in doing that he'd be cementing the fantasy she'd wrapped herself in. One where she could truly love him for who he was, and he was actually deserving of that love.

He pushed away from her and she looked up at him, her glassy grey eyes confused.

'Do you…?' Her cheeks flushed pink. He adjusted himself, uncomfortable but that was his problem. This, between them, needed to be dealt with.

'I'm perfectly fine.'

Her face crumpled a little, before she put on what he saw now was her own carefully crafted mask. He rounded his desk and gathered up the precious contract. Read the attached letter. Soon he'd be informing the Silvestris that once their existing agreements with Tessitore had expired, they wouldn't be renewed.

It should have been a triumph. He didn't know why it suddenly felt so meaningless.

'Okay then,' Simone said, though the words were only a whisper. She began straightening her clothes. 'I might just go—'

'You can't love me.'

She turned back to him, eyes wide, skin pale, like all the life had been drained from her. A lot like when he'd first seen her lying in her hospital bed. All his fault. But he wouldn't think of that. He couldn't…

'Isn't that for me to decide?'

'That wasn't the deal.'

'Deals can change.'

'This one never will.'

He'd taken enough from her. Over the past two weeks he'd realised that's what everyone did. Her parents, her ex, even her sister Holly. She had so much to offer and now he'd done the same. Married her because she'd been perfect for his plans, not thinking how it might affect her. Making love to her when he should have known better. He'd thought only of himself and she'd almost died because of it. Simone didn't need someone like him who could never give her what she truly deserved. Who had *taken* from her without any thought. She needed someone whose heart was open. To free herself from the self-imposed shackles of her own hurt and pain and to live. To *love*.

It felt as if a switchblade had speared through his ribs.

He could never be that man, when all he'd done was take from her.

'You're a businessman. You know that's not true.'

She was so beautiful, standing there wanting and hoping. Her cheeks still flushed from the orgasm he'd given her. That she hoped for more at all, let him know he was right to push her away. He was not the man for her. In truth, he never was and never could be. Releasing her from this arrangement was a kindness, even if doing so required some cruelty.

To show her the man he really was.

'There, you're wrong. Since my teens, I've only ever cared for myself. Me and *my* needs were what was important. That's never changed.'

She shook her head. Whilst she said she'd learned lessons in life it was so like her to try to see the best, even if she was looking at the worst.

'That's not true.'

'This man you see here? He's concocted from lies. You're only seeing who you want to, Simone. Not who *I am*.'

'Then who are you? You keep yourself so closed off. If you'd just let me in—'

'You want to know me?' Leo strolled forward with the swagger he'd used in the old days when he was full of bravado and out to extort money from some small business owner. Not surprising how it came back so easily, like another part of him. An evil twin. Two sides to one coin. 'Then you need to know about Rome.'

Her eyes widened and she chewed on her bottom lip like she was afraid of what he might say. Good. Leo knew she'd wanted to come with him to that cursed city and he'd refused. He hadn't wanted her tainted by what he'd done, or finding out because he'd feared what she might think of him. Now, he wanted her to think the worst because in the end, that's all that would save her from him.

'I want to know *you*.'

He held out his arms, 'Well, here I am *cara*, ready to tell it all. I told you I'd left home when I was barely seventeen, travelling to make my fortune. Tired of my mother and my life. Nothing was enough. I wanted *more*.'

His mother had cried when he'd left but in his bravado he hadn't really cared. He'd promised to send back money. But there wasn't much he could do as a teenager with no skills or education past high school. He'd been impoverished and homeless when the gang had found him and made him feel as though, finally, he had some worth.

'I was cold and hungry, on the streets. Too proud to return to Milan. But I found an underbelly and embraced it. A gang, who needed the type of services I could provide because I was tall and strong. But I could also be very convincing, so they hired me for a very specific task.'

Whilst he didn't want to look at Simone, to see her disgust, he couldn't help himself. Yet all he saw was her eyes filled with tears. A look of sympathy. It was wholly undeserved.

'Who you see here is a man who was happy to stand over people for money. Extorting small business owners. Feared on the streets, not caring who I ruined. I even had a nickname. One I was proud of. The Handsome Viper.'

In truth, he'd loathed the title but he'd owned it at the time because he was playing a part and instilling fear got the job done, without blood being spilled. If everyone thought him beautiful but deadly, then all the better for them. It was survival in a vicious world. He'd played a role and played it well. Just like he had when modelling. Just like he was doing now.

'I don't believe you.'

As much as Leo didn't want to, here he knew he needed to sink the knife deep.

'Then you're fooling yourself. I'm still the Handsome Viper if I want to be. I used people for my own ends, because it suited me. Just like I used you, although I admit you were paid handsomely for it. That's certainly new for me, paying money instead of taking it. Now the Tessitore deal's done, there's no need for this charade to continue any longer.'

The tears in Simone's eyes spilled over onto her cheeks. 'Don't do this to us.'

'There is no 'us', there never was. One day you'll see that I…how did you put it…*dazzled* you, just like you accused me of doing to other staff.'

She shook her head, her spine stiffening. 'No, you never fooled me. I walked into this marriage with my eyes open. I won't have you treating me like some innocent with no clue.'

'For someone who claims they weren't fooled, you're certainly acting like one, so let me be clear. By the time I get back from Rome, I want you gone. You can be out of Milan and in the US in a matter of hours. I'm sure you'd like to see your sister again.'

'So, I'm being dismissed.'

He shrugged, taking his fill of her because he knew she was about to leave. Simone's eyes were as cold and hard as flint. She'd told him she understood her worth and she wasn't going to take this lying down.

'I don't much care. There'll be a role in the company if you want it. If you choose to resign, you'll receive excellent references. You were, after all, an exceptional and most attentive executive assistant. I couldn't ask for better.'

'Thank you for making things so crystal clear. But I refuse to stay where I'm not wanted.'

She turned and strode to the door, placed her hand on the handle. Hesitated. He knew he needed to make sure she walked away with no shred of hope or love left in her.

'Oh, Simone.' He'd pitched his voice softer, ready for the final strike. She whipped round, eyes a little wide. Still looking for the best in him.

'Yes, Leo.'

'I'd like your resignation in writing, to make sure it's official. Don't forget the NDA. Or the restraint of trade that prohibits you from ever working for Rocco Silvestri. I'll enforce both to the full extent of my abilities should you choose to breach either.'

She reared back like she'd taken a direct hit. He knew they were the words that ended any chance of reconciliation. Exactly what he wanted.

'Don't worry, Mr Zanetti. I wouldn't want to experience any more of your venom.'

No matter how much of what he'd said had cut him to the marrow, it was for the best. He hoped she now hated him as much as he hated himself. It was better for her in every way.

Far better than loving him.

CHAPTER TWELVE

LEO SAT IN the bar, a bustling place, but not one of the popular tourist traps. It was a hole in the wall, frequented by locals or those in the know. He couldn't be alone, yet he didn't want to speak to anybody. Here, in the noise, surrounded by people, he could lose himself.

He took out his phone and checked Circolo's intranet for a photograph that had been posted by the team. The one of him and Simone, from Lake Garda. A moment frozen in time when he'd had something good within his grasp and simply didn't hold on tight enough. He'd let it go.

Right now, Leo had everything he believed he'd wanted and yet he had nothing at all. The Tessitore deal had been signed, sealed and delivered. Within days, a message would be sent to the Silvestri company that after their current orders had been fulfilled, they would never use Tessitore textiles again. It should have made him feel like a victor, yet he felt like a loser in all ways.

He took another slug of his drink, not caring about its quality. Cheap Grappa, because he was punishing himself with firewater. After his mother had died, he'd had so many regrets. But most of all, he wished he could have had the time back to say all the things he'd left unsaid. Now, he wished he could have had the time over not to say some words, but to keep his mouth shut.

He'd hurt Simone. Callously. Deliberately. Leo deeply regretted the way he'd ended things, even though it had been better for her, to cut things off with no hope of reconciliation. Whilst he might always look back, he wanted her to look forwards to a life without him. To find someone to love who was good. Whose background wasn't tainted by sins of the past. She'd almost died because of him and he hadn't let her go, even then. Because he was a selfish man, who only ever thought about his own needs, and people suffered as a consequence. If Simone had stayed with him any longer, she would have suffered too.

She'd lived enough of her life for others. Running round after him as his executive assistant, marrying for Holly's sake. It was time for her to live for herself. She had money. Their agreement also stipulated a generous settlement on their divorce, so she'd never have to worry, about herself or her sister again.

It was done. She hadn't resigned yet, but it was only a matter of time before the official letter hit his inbox.

So, why did he feel so empty? He downed another mouthful of his drink, continuing the punishment he'd started an hour ago. Drowning his sorrows, yet they weren't drowning fast enough.

'You look like a man who's lost something valuable. Or someone.'

Rocco Silvestri.

Leo gripped his glass so hard he thought it might crack, but that didn't matter. The pain of broken glass might assuage his guilt.

Leo said nothing. Took another sip. The fluid burned in his gut. Or was that anger? Perhaps the night was getting hazy, as he'd wanted it to.

'Leave now, Silvestri,' he hissed, slamming his glass on the counter.

Rocco picked it up and sniffed. 'Cheap booze. You might pretend to have left the streets but you never actually did.'

Leo turned on his seat and stood slowly. Maybe a little unsteadily. 'This boy from the streets has just bested you.'

He was sure Rocco was goading him and that no one knew what he'd done. How he'd threatened people, stood over them, destroyed livelihoods that he was still trying to rectify.

Rocco snorted. 'Bested me? You wish.'

'I have a deal with Tessitore.'

Leo should have felt satisfied at Rocco's frown, but it was like he was dead inside. Whereas once he might have taken pleasure in what was to come, there was no pleasure to be had any more. Numbness was all he sought.

'You're speaking rubbish.'

'You wish,' Leo echoed because he could be petty too. 'I now have an exclusive partnership with them. As long as that exists, your furniture will never use another metre of Tessitore fabric in any design.'

'I see you're trying to bring them down to your level rather than elevate them.' Rocco said with a sneer. 'Since you seem to be making new acquisitions, maybe I'll make some of my own.'

'I don't care what you acquire. You're wasting your time.'

'Word on the street says your EA might be looking for a new job. Or a new husband. Or both. She was wasted on you. The woman needs a real challenge.'

Never.

Over his dead body.

The rage boiled and spilled over. He moved from his chair, the legs scraping back, grabbing his nemesis by the shirt. 'Leave her alone. If I ever hear you've been bothering Simone—'

'Then what? You'll try and destroy me? You've been trying in your own way for as long as you've been in business and yet I'm still here. It's like you want everything I have,' Rocco taunted. 'And why? I'll tell you. You're just a pretty boy, a pretender with no substance. All envy, when the truth is, I've done *nothing* to you.'

'Done nothing? Ask our father what was done to me. Ask him about—' Leo's voice broke on the thought of his mother's name. Rocco didn't deserve to hear it. 'Ask him about his designs. Remind him that he's a thief who stole them.'

'*Our* father?'

Rocco's eyes widened at those words, a look Leo recognised—shock. Leo released Rocco's shirt and pushed him away. Rocco stumbled back.

'Vito Silvestri. My father. Who had an affair with *your* mother while he was still living with mine.'

Now it was Rocco's turn to grab Leo by the shirt, twisting the neck tight. '*Liar.*'

Leo laughed, but it was a mirthless, mocking sound. 'They were in business together. He stole my mother's furniture designs and then left us destitute. Ask him. Take my DNA, I don't care. It'll prove I'm telling the truth, *brother.*'

He wrenched from Rocco's grasp, a few buttons on his shirt tearing off, scattering on the floor. Then Leo threw some money on the bar—too much for the alcohol that had rotted his gut. But he didn't care. Leo needed to go. He turned and stalked into the night. After all these years of believing Rocco Silvestri knew everything, it might be that he was as much a victim of their father's sins as Leo was.

And knowing that didn't make Leo feel any better at all.

* * *

Simone sat in the back of the taxi, caught in Milan's notorious traffic. She tapped her fingers restlessly on her hand-
bag, her stomach knotting painfully. Wanting to get to her
destination faster, whilst at the same time wanting to ask
the driver to turn round and take her back to her hotel. She
reached inside her bag and took out a bottle of water, un-
capped it and sipped. It didn't help, just churning in her
stomach together with the meagre breakfast she'd picked
at, leaving her feeling ill. Because today was important.
Today was *everything*.

Like an interview for the most important job of her life.

She took a slow breath, looking out the window at the
city that had felt more like home in what had only been a
few short months, than New York had in years. Because
home wasn't about the place, it was about the people you
were with. Or in her case, a person.

Leo. Who'd hurt her more than she'd believed any living
human could have.

The man she still loved, with all of her heart.

Others might say she was the fool Leo had accused her
of being, given the things he'd said to her. After leaving the
Milan office, it's what she'd believed, at first. That she'd
been chasing a fantasy cooked up in her own head, and not
reality. That he was yet another person who wanted her only
for what she could do for him in some material way, rather
than wanting her for the woman she was.

Yet she'd come to the belief, slow at first then with a
shocking rush, that what Leo had done wasn't because he
felt too little.

It's that he felt far too much.

The taxi moved forwards a few feet, stopped. Horns in the

distance blared, the energy here still frenetic even though it appeared everything was at a standstill. A lot like her life.

Since leaving the Milan office what seemed like years ago but in what could be measured only in weeks, she'd been busy. First, nursing her crippling heartbreak. She'd flown straight to California to see Holly, to make sure her now heavily pregnant sister was really okay. There, she'd cried on Holly's shoulder as her sister had held her. It was the first time in years Simone had accepted the support of another person without a fight. It was there those old insecurities had roared back—echoes from her parents, from her ex, from every voice that had ever whispered she wasn't worth it.

Leo's own words too—that he didn't want her. She'd believed him. At first.

Until she'd turned to her phone, ready to delete every photograph of their time together and that's when she'd stopped. Took a giant pause, as if the universe had come to a loud and screeching halt and screamed.

Use your eyes and your heart.

She didn't much trust her heart at that moment, but her eyes? She'd scrolled back through her photographs and in her pain and through her tears she *saw*. Lake Garda and then Milan. Their selfie, where he'd smiled. Not the professional smile that could make him millions but one that was deep and warm and true.

And then she began to really *think*. Not about his words, but his actions. How he'd considered what she might enjoy. How he liked surprising her. How he hadn't left her bedside whilst she'd been in hospital. They were all the actions of a person who genuinely cared.

That's when she'd stopped crying and got busy.

The taxi started moving again. Whatever had been holding them up had cleared. She'd be at Leo's Milan home, *their*

Milan home, soon. There she'd fight for him, fight for *them*. Simone had come to realise that while she'd spent her whole life believing she wasn't enough, she strongly suspected Leo felt the same. And wasn't that the trap? Two hurt and broken people believing the one they wanted could never want them in return? In the last few weeks she'd discovered so much more about the man Leonardo Zanetti truly was. Especially since she'd called the company accountant and learned what she could about Rome.

Because, whilst the press liked to write about Milan, Rome was where Leo's real story began.

The taxi finally pulled up outside his house, and she paid, her heart beating a frantic rhythm in her chest. Taking out the keys he'd given her and hoping that he hadn't changed the locks. Trying them.

They still fit.

Just like her and Leo, if only he'd recognise it.

Simone made her way quietly through the house finding him on the back terrace. He sat at the table, laptop open. Working on something because he consumed himself, both personally and privately. She relished the view of him against the backdrop of their home's beautiful garden. His broad shoulders—the ones that had carried so many of her burdens and the burdens of others. Those burdens that he'd kept secret because he'd thought what he was doing showed the worst of him, when really, it showed the *best*.

As she eased closer, it was like he *knew*. Leo stiffened and turned.

The moment those vibrant ocean-blue eyes fixed on Simone, twin aches of love and pain crashed over her like a wave onto the shore. Then she caught his expression—surprise and need, before it hardened and he hid behind the veneer he so often presented to the world.

Leo seemed to unfold from the chair, lifting himself up.

It was then she noticed other things. How he wasn't as put together as normal. Stubble on his jaw, like she'd witnessed in the days after her accident. His hair was a little longer than she'd ever seen him with before, and messy. Like he'd run his hands through it too many times. His shirt, usually pressed and perfect, a bit wrinkled.

He looked like he'd just come home from some corporate battle.

Well, she was here to start an emotional war.

'Simone.'

One word, but it was *full* of meaning. A rough sound, like it hurt him to say the syllables. Then he frowned.

'What are you doing here? Have you forgotten something?'

There were so many answers open to her, but she told him the truth.

'I left because you said you were a bad man. That you didn't want me. I came back because I discovered—you're a liar.'

His eyes widened.

'You're not a bad man. Even though you think you are. And I'm here to remind you of that.' She took a step closer. 'Because I know all about Rome.'

Leo hadn't seen her in over a month and, whilst it might have been a cliché, she was like an oasis in the desert. A cool drink to a parched man.

She stood before him, looking more like herself than he'd ever seen. In a beautiful denim dress, no sleeves. Espadrilles that made her look summery, as if she was about to go to the beach or for a stroll by a lake. Embodied with a casual elegance he'd always known lay inside her. It struck him then, how she'd grown without him. Morphed, like a chrysalis turned into a vibrant butterfly. It ached, seeing her. Knowing without a doubt that she'd moved on without him…

And yet, Rome?

'You've heard the story about Rome. I told you myself.'

'You told me the lies you tell yourself. When are you going to see the truth for what it is?'

He didn't understand. He'd laid out the truths of his past. The things he'd done. Whilst he might pretend he was a better man now, the reality was harsh and incontrovertible. He hadn't looked after his mother and he hadn't looked after Simone. He was, in all ways, a selfish man.

A good man wouldn't have entered into an arranged marriage with his executive assistant to secure a business deal, no matter the merits and knowing what he could do for the company in the partnership. A good man would have been there for his mother. Wouldn't have tried to change the woman now standing before him.

She'd fallen and almost died because she was trying to please him. Just like his mother had fallen because she was trying to ensure she earned enough money for him.

He always hurt those he loved the most…

Loved? No. He loved no one. If he did, he wouldn't have done the things he had. Yet why did it feel something inside him had torn in two and was bleeding in torrents?

'*Morzone.*'

It was as if a shock of electricity jolted through him. A name from a past he wished was more distant. Or wished he'd never heard at all.

'I don't know what you're—'

'*Bazzoni, Antonelli, Riccardo…*'

She kept going. The list went on and on. Names of the

families he'd helped extort. Families he'd tried to ruin. Each sin he was required to atone for.

'I know about them, Leo. I know about them all.'

It should have been impossible. 'How?'

'Circolo's accountant. It seems you haven't told anyone you'd asked me to leave and since I'm still your wife and EA…'

He hadn't wanted to admit to anyone that he'd pushed her away, most of all himself. He'd been waiting for the inevitable resignation letter when it would have been impossible to deny the rumours currently swirling round, that all wasn't sunny in the Zanetti household.

'All these people, they show the best of you, not the worst,' she said.

Leo shook his head. 'You know nothing.'

She didn't. Repaying debts owed was meaningless. It was the *least* he could do. Giving back money didn't make the taking of it any better. Because he couldn't give them back the time they'd lost, and money didn't heal all wounds—as he well knew.

There were some people who would never recover from what he'd done. The trauma he'd inflicted.

'I know a lot, because I've spoken to some of the families. They've told me how their lives have been changed, even though they never knew who their benefactor was.'

His blood turned icy. He'd buried that part of his life so well by creating a charitable foundation that gave back to the families he'd once helped to ruin. His greatest shame and yet the heart of all he was. He never wanted it revisited. No one was ever meant to find out.

'Did you tell them who I am?'

'No. That's your story to tell, not mine. What I asked,

was whether they'd like to say anything to the person who'd helped them.'

She reached into her bag and pulled out a folder with sheaves of paper in it.

'I have these. Letters to the charity. Thanking you for what you've done. How you've saved each of them. Changed their lives for the better. Look.'

She thrust the folder into his face. He shook his head. He didn't want to look at the words when all he could see was her.

'You think this is the worst of you?' Simone asked, 'The worst was doing nothing. This is the best. It's not who you were once, Leo, but how a person changes that makes the difference. You rose from your earlier life like a phoenix. You became someone better.'

'Money doesn't change anything, it just papers over wounds.'

'Here's the thing. You have all these people believing you're good. You're the only one who thinks you're bad. Have you ever thought that might mean the problem's not with all of us? It's with how you're thinking about yourself.'

'All I ever do is hurt people. These families. My mother. You.'

Simone cocked her head, frowned. He wanted to smooth that troubled crease away. He clenched his fists instead.

'What do you mean, *me*?'

'You fell because of me. Because of my vanity.'

'You wanted to give me a beautiful gift of that pair of shoes and I wanted to accept them, so I did. My fall was an accident. Just like your mother's. Do you think either of us would want you carrying misplaced guilt for ever? These things aren't your burden to bear. When I was in the hospital…' Simone's voice trailed off, Cracked. She took a deep breath, gave a shaky smile.

Would his mother have wanted this for him? She'd worked hard, long hours, to make his life better. But in the end, he didn't know, because he couldn't ask her. As for Simone…

'You stayed by my side in hospital,' she said. 'Looked after me at home. Those weren't the actions of a bad man, but a good one.'

She walked towards him slowly, almost as if she was scared he'd try to get away.

'I love you. Despite everything. I wasn't looking for it. I wasn't expecting it, but it hit me all the same. You care about your staff. You cared about me. Around you, I began to like who I was again. And I hope, that if I love you, then maybe you can love yourself.'

For so long, he'd been dead inside. Rejected by his father. A petty criminal. Believing himself selfish. Vacuous. Good only for his looks and what he could sell. Yet, it was as if an ember had burst to life inside of him, bright and blazing.

Simone, believing in him. Loving him.

Everything seemed suddenly clearer, like a blindfold being torn from his eyes and he could see for the first time. Those moments when all he wanted to do was please her. To make her smile. Now, Leo didn't think about what he'd done, but how those things had made him feel. Like a good man, a man who was worthy. A man who could make Simone happy.

'Do you love me?' she asked. 'Because I think the man who showed me a waterfall on Lake Garda. Who sat by me every night when I was in hospital. Who created a beautiful room for me in his home that showed he knew who I was. The man who didn't want me to fall again… I think that's a man who loves.'

* * *

It was as if every part of Simone had been holding its breath and now, she'd allowed herself the briefest of moments to exhale. He hadn't asked her to leave. He was listening and maybe it meant he might also *hear*. She stepped towards him again, reached out her hand tentatively and placed it in the middle of his chest, the muscles firm and solid underneath.

'This is where I feel it, in my heart. Maybe, if you let go of the things your head's telling you, you might feel something in your heart too.'

She'd almost expected him to step back but he didn't. Instead, he leaned into her touch. His chest rose under her hand, then he shut his eyes. The slightest of frowns on his forehead. She didn't know what he was thinking. All she could do was stand there and hope, as the heat of him burned into her palm. Then his lips parted and he let out an exhale, opened his eyes and stared at her. The deep blue of his intense gaze burning like a pilot light, pointed in her direction.

'I have no idea what I'm doing,' he admitted.

She gave a shaky laugh. 'Neither do I. All I know is how it feels. Like I'm too big for my skin. Like I want to burst from myself.'

'The only way it's any better, that it feels like you finally fit, is if you're with the other person,' he said.

'It's too big to hide or run away from.'

'Because it's all-encompassing.' He placed his hand over hers. 'It takes over your life. It takes over your soul.'

Simone was certain in that moment, that he understood. Her eyes stung with tears and she took a breath of relief.

'It's so easy not to listen, when you don't trust yourself,' she said.

'This marriage was a means to an end. It should never have been that way and you deserve something more.'

'And yet in the end, we still chose each other.'

'Why can't I find someone like you?' he asked, with a smile.

'Maybe you can,' she replied.

'Maybe we always knew we were meant for each other.' Leo laughed and wrapped her in his arms. 'I love you, *cuore mio*.'

My heart. Her home.

'So, what now?'

'Our honeymoon was rudely cut short by an accident. I'm thinking we should arrange another. Verona perhaps?' Leo winked.

She answered with a smile. 'Are you being a romantic, Mr Zanetti?'

'Around you, always, Mrs Zanetti.'

'Then how about Lake Garda? That's a place I'd like to get to know better.'

'*Perfetto*,' he said. 'But right now?'

Leo dropped his head and she rose to meet him. Their mouths capturing each other's. The kiss unlike any that had come before it because this one was full of love acknowledged, not suppressed. After a few breathless minutes of searching lips and hands, of recognition and reconnection, Leo eased himself away, though he didn't let her go. His talented mouth curling into a slow and wicked smile. 'I think we should start the honeymoon here, *tesoro*.'

Simone laughed as Leo swung her into his arms.

'It's the perfect place to begin our lives again.'

* * * * *

FAST-TRACK DATING DECEPTION

JOSS WOOD

MILLS & BOON

CHAPTER ONE

Shanghai

'HE'S LATE. WHY is he late?'

In the luxurious De Rossi hospitality suite above the pit lane at the Shanghai International Track, Millie James swallowed the urge to sarcastically ask Sylvie whether she'd *met* Taz De Rossi. Since starting work as Taz's press officer at the beginning of the Formula One season six weeks ago, he'd never been on time for anything PR-related. As the person responsible for managing his media requests and his public relations commitments, she spent a great deal of time apologising for him being late or for being a no-show. She didn't know why Sylvie expected Taz to attend this PR briefing for the De Rossi team; he hadn't attended any others so far this season.

The owner and principal driver of the famous F1 team never did anything he didn't want to do. And why should he? He came from a famous racing family and was on track to beat his older brother's record of three consecutive Formula One championship wins.

He was also, by far, the most difficult—if sexiest—client she'd ever worked with.

Arrogant, assured and annoying, but still *so* attractive.

Like her parents, he was one of life's golden people. Counting back, she realised she hadn't heard from them in many months. It was a measure of her discomfort that she found it easier thinking about her dysfunctional family than her very inconvenient attraction to her brusque boss.

Millie sighed. Her family…

It was impossible to think of her parents without thinking of her aunt and uncle—her mum and aunt were twins and lived two doors apart—as the quartet of semi-famous actors operated as an elegantly vicious pack. She and her cousin Ben, both only children, had been raised as siblings and had been extremely close, their bond fuelled by parental criticism, benign neglect and apathy. Ben often joked that they were shockingly well-adjusted considering they'd been raised by the four most self-involved people on planet Earth. To be fair, Ben had been less affected than Millie by their collective crazy.

It was true that the good died young…

Millie looked at the silver racing-car charm dangling from her heavy link silver bracelet. Over the past few months, as she inched closer to the tenth anniversary of Ben's death, she'd started questioning her life: who she was, what she wanted and where she was going. Ben's voice had been loud lately—*You're overqualified for your position as junior publicist, You should not have been passed over for that promotion, You're treading water.* He'd been the one person in her life who believed she was smart, capable and interesting.

In her late teens and early twenties, she'd ignored his offers to spend the weekend watching him race in glamorous cities and rejected his offers of free VIP race tickets. Her shyness and lack of confidence stopped her from visiting his sophisticated world. She'd been so convinced they had all the time in the world and would toast each other at their weddings and on milestone birthdays…until Ben had died in a horrific crash, and for years Millie ignored anything to do with Formula One racing.

Then she'd seen the press liaison position advertisement for De Rossi Racing, Ben's old Formula One team, and felt compelled to apply. Two months ago, she traded in her secure job as a junior accounts manager within a PR firm to take a ten-month contract with De Rossi Racing for the F1 season.

Despite hating the uncertainty of what she'd do after her contract ended, Millie never once second-guessed her decision. She needed to be here, in the world Ben loved, where his voice was loudest in her head, to make some hard decisions, including whether she saw herself as Ben did—capable, smart, interesting—or, as her parents did, boring and unadventurous. They were bold and beautiful, outrageously at ease standing in the spotlight. They craved attention and saw Millie's shyness and reserve as serious character flaws. In their eyes she was inadequate. *How did we create something so banal?* were their exact words.

Since Ben's death, she'd avoided them and her aunt and uncle as much as possible as she adjusted to the Ben-shaped hole in her life. Through avoidance, sheer grit and emotional distancing, she'd just managed to keep her head above choppy emotional waters. But the opportunity to be Taz De Rossi's press officer seemed to be a sign to stop treading water and start swimming. To move on, to change…to *live* by stepping into the world Ben—her best friend, her brother—had adored.

Mika, the team's senior public relations officer groaned and banged her phone against her forehead, jolting Millie out of her reverie. Millie recognised Mika's exasperation, as did Sylvie, who beat her to the punch. 'What has he done now?' she demanded.

Mika lifted her phone, and she and Sylvie took turns peering at the photographs on the screen. She recognised the club, Lily's, in London. In the photos, Taz was exiting the upmarket venue, a common occurrence. What made these photos newsworthy was that instead of walking out of the club with the always-volatile Phoebe, his on-off ex-model/influencer girlfriend, Taz held the hand of a stunning blonde.

Meredith, Taz's dead brother's fiancée, held her other hand up to her face, trying to shield her eyes from the blinding camera flashes. Taz looked like he wanted to hurt someone.

To be fair, he often looked like that. Unlike his brother Alex, who'd been charming, outgoing and gregarious, Taz's default expression was one of two: intimidating or brooding. And he had the face to pull it off: dark brown, almost black hair, laser-focused grey eyes, a long nose and high cheekbones. While Alex had been poster-boy pretty, Taz's face, with its severe angles, was harder, rougher and a great deal more masculine. Like a good painting, it was a face you could look at for a lifetime and still find it compelling.

But everyone knew Taz would never settle down. The notion was incomprehensible. He was the world's most eligible—and determined-to-remain-so—bachelor. He was selfish, a tad narcissistic and ruthlessly ambitious. Demanding, dismissive and difficult, he was very like Millie's parents. There had been many times since starting work six weeks ago when she felt tongue-tied and uncertain in his presence. She'd reminded herself she was an adult and not the scared, shy and shunned child standing in her parents' too-bright shadow.

In her personal life, she avoided Taz and people of his ilk, bright and bold, effortlessly and innately confident. Unfortunately, avoiding her employer wasn't an option. Professionally, in PR terms, Taz was *messy*—and he was *her* mess. 'What *does* Taz think he's doing?' Mika demanded. 'He knows Meredith is off-limits.'

'Do you think they went to the club together?' Sylvie asked, frowning.

'Well, they certainly left it together,' Mika snapped back. 'And according to gossip online, they spent most of the evening snuggled up together in a booth.'

Millie took another look at the photograph. The six-foot-two Taz, dressed in a white button-down with the sleeves rolled up and dark blue jeans, towered over the slim ex-model. His honed physique, wide shoulders, thick arms and muscled legs made Meredith look even more petite than she was. He was unquestionably attractive, and he exuded an attitude of not caring what the world thought about him.

She was the daughter of narcissistic, vain parents. She wasted so much time wishing she could be the child they wanted her to be, to reach what she now realised were unrealistic expectations of her. She admired Taz's rebellious, devil-may-care attitude. How nice it would be not to care what people—including the semi-famous Quartet—thought.

Millie squinted at the picture… Something was off. She wasn't getting the vibe that there was anything sexual about this encounter with the woman who'd been poised to be his sister-in-law. While she wasn't Taz's biggest fan, and he often made her job fifty times harder than it needed to be, she wasn't sure all was as it seemed.

'I'll show Taz the photo and ask for a comment,' Millie said. She wouldn't get one, but she'd ask.

Mika grimaced. 'I suggest you tiptoe through that minefield. Taz once threatened to fire me for asking about his love life. And Alex is never to be mentioned or discussed, *ever*.'

Alex had been racing royalty, Ben's best friend and racing teammate, but he'd died in a fluke accident seven years ago after slipping and smacking the back of his head on the corner of a marble kitchen counter. In internet chat rooms, fierce conspiracy theories raged over whether it was really an accident. Imagination, but no proof, was the only requirement needed to be a part of those discussions.

Two young men from the same racing team, both charismatic and confident, both top Formula One drivers, dead before their thirtieth birthdays. Life could be incomprehensibly awful on occasion.

Millie squinted. Something about the photo of Taz and Meredith still bothered her. Should she say anything? Did she have the right to comment? Would they listen? 'I...' she said.

Mika looked impatient at her hesitation. 'What?'

'I don't think they are dating,' Millie stated. 'Their fingers aren't interlocked. That's not how lovers hold hands. And he looks...worried.'

Sylvie sent her a thin-lipped smile. 'I think we know him better than you, Millie. We've been working with Taz for more than a decade.'

It had been stupid to say anything, foolish to think they'd listen. They had known him longer, and she had only been working here a short time. But perhaps they also saw what they expected to see. He was the quintessential bad boy, and they expected bad-boy behaviour from him.

Millie looked down at her iPad as Mika and Sylvie stepped into the conference room. While she waited for Taz in the passage, she'd read through the briefing report and Taz's schedule on her tablet—not that he'd follow it. He had a press interview with an influential sports journalist at one thirty—he shouldn't miss that—and he needed to attend the FIA press conference. He had the sponsors' dinner at eight...

'How did you know that it wasn't a date?'

Taz's low, deep voice reached her ears, and Millie shuddered at the huff of his warm breath on her cheek. Shock kept her standing still; she hadn't heard him come up behind her. Heat rolled off him, along with his gorgeous cologne, something summer-fresh and sexy. She turned her head and noticed his bloodshot eyes and drawn face. It was obvious he'd had no sleep, and she wondered what or who had kept him up last night.

She hated the way he made her feel, shivery and shaky. Taz De Rossi made the world shift below her feet. Around him, she felt off balance, and it took all her mental energy not to let him see how much he affected her. His ego was big enough already.

And she had no experience in dealing with men who walked through the world with complete ease and confidence. The last man she dated—if two dinners could be called a date—was in his early forties, lived with his mum and was obsessed with video games. While she wasn't a virgin, she wasn't experienced.

Did experience matter? For her, marriage wasn't a long-term goal. Having grown up with the Quartet, she'd witnessed two highly dysfunctional, manipulative marriages, and she wasn't a fan. Besides, she still needed to unpack her emotional baggage and didn't have the mental fortitude to deal with someone else's.

Before she had the chance to answer, Taz jerked his head towards the hallway. 'Follow me.'

Yes, sir. Right away, sir. Millie cradled her iPad to her chest while Taz closed the door to the hospitality suite behind her. He moved further down the hallway, stopped and widened his stance. He crossed his arms across his wide chest, and Millie had to tip her head back to look into his harsh face. She wondered how he'd look with a smile on his face. She'd yet to see one.

'Good morning, Mr De Rossi,' she said, determined to be polite. Maybe one day he'd catch the hint and be polite back. But she wouldn't hold her breath. He didn't have anyone in his life brave enough, or important enough, to challenge him to change.

His eyes narrowed, his jaw tightened, and his lips thinned. Maybe she shouldn't poke the bear. She looked down at her screen. 'Can I run through today's schedule with you? The track walk is at ten, and the final seat fitting is at eleven. Then you have a *Fan Zone* appearance before lunch. You have an interview with—'

'Cancel it.'

His instruction wasn't unexpected, but it did make her cross. He'd been messing the sports journalist around for weeks now, and she was losing patience. Millie didn't blame her. 'I don't think that's a good idea. She has a massive social media presence and is more influential than you probably realise.'

'A million followers across her platforms, with a demographic of twenty to thirty-five-year-olds,' Taz snapped back.

So he did listen to her. 'Then, why are you refusing to do the interview?'

His grey eyes burned into hers, and his mouth tightened, but he didn't answer. Not unexpected.

She'd try once more. Because getting him to do positive PR was her *job*. 'She told me that if you don't meet with her this time, she is going to run her story without your input.'

He lifted one broad shoulder. 'Let her.'

Millie sighed. Taz De Rossi didn't give a flying fig what people thought or wrote about him. He didn't only march to the beat of his own drum, he composed its music as well. Millie wanted to tell him he was being inconsiderate, disrespectful and rude. But, like her parents, Taz didn't care what she thought or felt. She was his employee, and he was her arrogant, egotistical and imperious boss, a man determined to make her job a thousand times harder than it needed to be.

And she'd never told anyone off in her life.

Thankfully, she wasn't as shy as she'd been as a teenager, and leaving home to go to university had helped her gain a little self-assurance. But she still tended to retreat into her shell when she felt uncomfortable, and Taz De Rossi made her feel very uncomfortable indeed. He was dauntless, so certain of his place in the world. In the face of people like him, she felt her self-confidence drain away. She straightened her shoulders and reminded herself that she'd taken this job, joined the De Rossi team, to do something different, to *be* different. She wanted to change her outlook and her life because she was tired of coasting, wondering whether there was more to life, more to *her*. To push, as Ben had always wanted her to, through her cocoon of self-doubt. Ben had been so convinced that she was bolder, braver and more self-assured than she believed herself to be. Millie's way of honouring him, ten years later, was to find out whether he was right or not.

It was proving to be a one-step-forward-three-steps-back situation, but six weeks in, she was still working for Taz De Rossi. She'd count that as a win. 'Cancel the interview,' Taz reiterated. 'I'm not in the mood to make nice with journalists.'

To be fair, he never was. Millie sighed and nodded, hoping the journalist wouldn't shoot the messenger. 'I'll walk the track, and I'll do the seat fitting,' Taz's words shot out, bullet-fast.

Of course he would. Despite being at the top of his game and being familiar with the track, Taz would still inspect it with his race and performance engineers and his race strategist. Winning his fourth consecutive championship was all that mattered, and he was on record as saying he'd do anything and everything to make that happen. Interviews, PR and making nice with the sponsors and his brand partners were way down on his list of priorities.

Now for the hard bit… 'There's a lot of buzz about you and Meredith. How would you like us to handle it?'

His gaze pinned her feet to the ground. 'How do you think I want you to handle it?' he asked, his tone silky with disdain.

'By not responding to it?'

'So why did you bother to ask?' His voice remained low but edged in steel.

It was a good question. Millie looked around for an answer, but the empty corridor, uninteresting and silent with its polished floors and stark lighting, held no answers. She swallowed, conscious of Taz's cool confidence, so sure the world would accommodate itself to his will. He didn't move or speak, but he didn't need to. Wherever he went, his sheer presence demanded complete attention, and Millie wasn't immune. She remained immobile, her composure wavering under the intensity of his stare.

Why was he looking at her like that?

He was, she frantically reminded herself, a Formula One legend.

Untouchable. Ruthless. Relentless.

His eyes remained locked on her face, her body still tightened beneath his scrutiny, and baby fireworks erupted over her skin. Electricity ran through her, down her spine and out of her toes. Her heart flip-flopped around her ribcage, and her stomach vibrated. And where had all the moisture in her mouth gone? Did he have to stand so close? And why was her stomach suddenly doing somersaults?

Judging by his narrowed eyes and the infinitesimal hint of a smug smile from lips perpetually set in either a smirk or a scowl, he was very aware of his effect on her. She cursed her treacherous body for liking his and him for knowing that it did. After another tense few seconds, Millie wrenched her eyes away and stared down again at her tablet.

She was, she reminded herself, here to figure out her life, not to date. She did not need the complication of having any kind of feelings for her boss.

It galled her to admit that whenever she thought of dating, Taz's tough face flashed before her eyes. Something beyond his good looks and aura of capability and confidence intrigued her. He was the human version of the Chinese nesting boxes she'd seen sightseeing yesterday. Which box held the authentic version of Taz De Rossi? No one knew, certainly not her. And it didn't matter because he was…

Out. Of. Her. League.

He would never ask her out; she would never accept. But it was a universal law of life that people like him, people like her parents, didn't look down, they looked up or around. Like, after all, attracted like. The reality was that in today's world, there was an unspoken status system, a psychological way of pushing people into their lane. The rich and beautiful occupied one top echelon, and so it went down in layers of beauty, charm and wealth. It was how the world worked, and anyone who thought being rich and beautiful didn't put you in a position of power was naive. Of course it did.

Millie pushed her thoughts away: It was time for her to

get back to work. But more than anything, she needed distance from Taz. When she wasn't around him, she was sane and rational. When she was within twenty yards of him, lust-coated stupidity lived in her head rent free alongside questions like why he acted the way he did and why he, on some level, intrigued her. Why did she keep hoping for more beyond his haughty attitude and stop-the-traffic looks? Why was she hunting for a hint of authenticity?

Enough, Millie. He's a lost cause.

She turned to walk away, but his hand shot out, gripped her elbow and stopped her in her tracks. She turned to face him and raised her eyebrows. 'You didn't answer my question.'

Her pulse quickened. 'Which one?' she said, pretending she didn't understand.

He stared at her, calling her bluff. Millie rubbed the back of her neck. He wasn't going to let her walk away until she gave him an answer to his original question about Meredith. 'Uh, you looked protective, not…um…turned-on. I saw it in the way you held Meredith's hand.'

Confusion raced across his face. 'The way I held her hand?'

Millie locked her fingers together. 'Lovers hold their hands linked this,' she said as she demonstrated. 'You held her hand like you would hold the hand of a daughter or sister.'

'Pretty observant,' he stated.

She tipped her head to the side and noticed curiosity in his eyes.

No, she *had* to be imagining it.

'It's my job to analyse the way the media covers you, just like it's my job to keep you on message.' She kept her tone crisp and professional, ignoring the way her body tightened beneath his scrutiny.

He didn't move a muscle, but it felt like he'd leaned in, closer than he was before. 'So how's that working out for you?' he asked, his voice husky, the tiniest glint of humour in his pewter-coloured eyes.

They both knew the answer to his question was *Badly*. Millie released a heavy sigh, and beneath the dark scruff edging his lips his mouth curved into a super-swift, able-to-melt-glass smile. So that was what it felt like to touch a lightning bolt.

Millie suppressed the urge to check whether anyone was standing behind her. This was the first time he'd said anything even vaguely personal to her, had instigated conversation. Was he toying with her? She wrinkled her nose and rocked on her heels, uncomfortable. Was she judging him harshly because his confidence, charisma and success triggered the same feelings of inadequacy as her parents' did? Was it easier to think poorly of him?

Millie looked past Taz to the door to the hospitality suite. 'I should get back in there.'

When he didn't say anything, she skirted his big frame and put her hand on the door-handle. As she started to open the door, Taz spoke. 'It's not your job to defend me, and I don't appreciate you gossiping about my private life.'

Millie stiffened, and heat climbed up her neck and into her face.

'Do it again and you will be fired.'

Yes, there was the demanding ass who paid her salary.

CHAPTER TWO

ON SUNDAY, RACE-DAY, Millie stood at the back of the De Rossi hospitality suite, her eyes on the huge screen in front of her. She could've gone down to the paddock to watch the race, but, like most sports, you got better coverage by watching and listening to the race on the TV.

She pulled her De Rossi–branded black-and-pink polo shirt off her clammy body. She'd tucked the shirt into her favourite black skinny jeans and wore high-top black trainers because being on her feet for long stretches made her feet ache. She'd pulled her mass of curls into a haphazard bun on the top of her head and had bitten off all her lipstick long ago.

Watching a race wasn't her favourite thing to do—a result of Ben's deadly crash at the Imola Circuit—but she didn't usually have such a tight knot in her stomach or a lump in her throat. Why did she feel like she was waiting for an axe to fall? Sure, Taz had been in a filthy mood since Thursday, biting off heads and stripping skin, but that wasn't unusual. He wasn't a sunshine-and-roses guy, and she'd learned not to take his moods personally. How could she when she spent minimal time with him? So why was she feeling so uptight, so incredibly tense? What was wrong with her?

Millie kept her eyes fixed on the TV screen, which showed Taz had an extensive lead over the rest of the field.

She continued to be impressed at his total control of a projectile speeding down the track at three hundred-plus miles per hour. It took intelligence, guts and incredible reflexes to handle the multimillion-dollar car. Racers required a warrior-like attitude, lots of verve and a certain amount of arrogance to be world champions.

Taz roared up to a slower car, one he was lapping and veered right to overtake. The driver of the other car, a rookie driver according to the race announcer, tried to tuck himself in behind Taz as they approached a sharp corner, and he touched his brakes a millisecond too late. His front fender clipped the back of Taz's car and sent both cars spinning across the track. Millie lifted her clenched fists to her mouth, praying neither car would hit a barrier. Eventually both cars stopped, and everyone in the room, in the pit, on the stands and watching around the world on millions of screens let out a collective sigh of relief. Because the drivers reached impossible speeds, safety was paramount in Formula One. Everyone knew serious injury or death was a possibility.

But not today, not with Taz. But there was no chance of him winning the Shanghai race now. It was okay: He could afford to lose a race or two. But she knew that wouldn't matter to him. Winning was everything.

Millie slumped, tuning out the curses at the rookie driver, the aspersions cast on his driving and his team. Closing her eyes, she hauled in a couple of deep breaths, grateful Taz wasn't hurt. Was she shaking because his crash reminded her of the deadly injuries Ben sustained when he went careening off the track? Maybe.

The sport was exciting, but it was also exceedingly dangerous.

The volume of noise rose. Millie opened her eyes and, on the screen, saw Taz's car limping into the pits below them.

The car door opened, and Taz climbed out and ripped off his helmet. The camera zoomed in on his face, and Millie caught his deep frown and bright eyes. Fury rolled off him in waves.

Ignoring his mechanics, he stomped out of the pit and half jogged down the concourse, the cameras following his progress to the rookie driver's pit. The race announcer's voice sped up, his words nearly indistinguishable as Taz stormed up to the driver. There was no doubt he knew his mistake had cost Taz the race.

Taz called his name, and the rookie winced, panic evident on his face. The next few seconds were a blur as Taz lifted the rookie to his toes and backed him into the wall. Millie watched, stunned, as Taz yelled at him. Taz ignored the hands pulling him away, but when a burly mechanic wrapped his beefy arm around Taz's waist and hauled him off, Taz finally backed down. The cameras panned in, and Millie caught his ultra-brief what-the-hell-am-I-doing expression before his frown returned. He batted away the mechanic and, as if making a point, punched the wall next to the rookie's shoulder. Dropping his hand, he stalked away, his head held high and his eyes blazing.

Millie rubbed the back of her neck and grimaced. Well, if he was in a bad mood before, he was going to be in a worse one now.

Coming down from a massive adrenaline spike, Taz left the pit and stalked into his driver's room, slamming the door behind him. To make sure he wasn't disturbed, he twisted the lock and headed to the small bar fridge behind a cupboard door. He pulled out a bottle of water, cracked it open and drank it down. Tossing the empty bottle into a trash can, he drained another before reaching for the bottle of

Macallan he'd stashed away in another cupboard. He removed the lid and took a hefty swig straight from the bottle before pouring three fingers into a glass. Sure, whisky wasn't on the dietician's list of approved food and drinks, but right now, he didn't give a damn. His arms ached from steering, and his neck was tense from holding his head upright in the corners.

He was exhausted. And he'd messed up. Badly.

Taz sat on his leather couch and rested his forearms on his knees, the whisky bottle dangling from his hand. He'd allowed his temper to override good sense today, and he would have a price to pay for his loss of control. He would, at the very least, face censure from the officials, maybe even a race ban.

He pushed his finger and thumb into his eye sockets and cursed. He had a good lead over his arch-rival, but it would quickly be erased if he wasn't allowed to compete. When he returned, he'd have to fight for the title, harder than he'd expected to. He'd put blood in the water, and the sharks were swirling.

Losing his temper had been moronic, and at thirty-five, he knew better. Was better. Even if the rest of the world didn't see it. Even if he didn't let them see it.

Taz took another sip of whisky, recapped the bottle and placed it on the floor. He'd had a couple of awful days, but today's crash was a highlight. He should've accelerated faster and made allowances for the rookie's inexperience. But, because he'd allowed his attention to drift, he hadn't.

When his two main rivals had retired earlier in the race, one with an engine failure and one after a crash at the start, he'd gone on autopilot, doing what he did best while allowing his brain to wander into territory it shouldn't have while guiding a bullet around a twisty track. He'd been driving from muscle memory and experience, with thoughts of his press officer drifting in and out. He didn't give anyone that privilege, that mental space, not when he was racing. So why Millie?

She wasn't glamorous, nothing like the sophisticated women he slept with. A spray of freckles covered her nose and cheeks, and in the sunlight her honey-coloured curls held hints of strawberry. Her mouth was full and wide, her chin stubborn and her body curvy. The slight rasp in her voice set his nerve endings alight.

But her far-too-beguiling looks weren't his only distraction. He'd remembered how she defended him the other day, for standing up for him when everyone else assumed he was dating Meredith. When was the last time someone had spoken up on his behalf? His mum, maybe? Sometime before her death shortly after he turned five? He genuinely couldn't remember and didn't think his father or brother ever did that for him. He was, after all, the family afterthought, the spare to the heir, ignored and neglected. He was the owner of this team, and the principal driver, only through death and fate.

If Alex hadn't died, sending their father into a spiral of despair that had led to a series of strokes, he might still be the De Rossi family outcast. Not worthy enough to take a seat at the table.

On the track, while overtaking the rookie, he'd been thinking of how nice it was to have someone standing in his corner, if only for a minute, imagining how it would feel to have someone like Millie, someone genuine, standing by his side supporting him. A second later he heard the thud and started to spin.

He'd risked everything, put his all-consuming goal of winning his fourth championship in jeopardy because he'd lost focus, because Millie hadn't, like everyone else, jumped to conclusions about him. Because she'd looked deeper beyond the image the world had of him. Not that he'd done anything to challenge the public's perception of him... If anything he'd gone out of his way to perpetuate the myth of being unapologetically confident, brazenly selfish and boldly carefree. He'd rather be hated than pitied, loathed than looked down on.

Nothing came between him and what he needed to do on the track, and he was mortified, furious that he'd let a woman—his press liaison officer, for God's sake—get under his skin. What was wrong with him?

He didn't need her or anyone's validation. He was Tazio De Rossi, and nobody warranted an explanation of his behaviour. Besides, would anyone believe that his running into Meredith at the club had been a coincidence? Probably not, but he would never have *chosen* to spend four hours listening to her talk about Alex. Seven years had passed, but to Meredith his death had happened yesterday.

And that was why he normally avoided her, and why he never displayed any pictures of Alex, not here or at any of his houses. He couldn't stand reminders of the brother his father loved so much. All his life he'd been compared to Alex, with his father telling him he wasn't as smart, as nice, as charming or as good-looking. That he would never be as good a driver...

When he died, Alex was feted as the darling of the racing world, a devoted fiancé, a super-involved philanthropist and a regular on talk shows where he was renowned for his wit and charm. Taz wondered what his legions of fans would think if they knew the truth...

On the surface, it was simple: a horrible, tragic accident, something no one could've predicted. The press had recounted the events accurately: During the F1 summer break, Alex flew to New York City for a long weekend, while his long-time fiancée Meredith attended a bachelorette party in Rome. While staying at the family's brownstone mansion Alex, wearing socks, rushed to answer his ringing phone and slipped. On his way down, he cracked his head on the sharp corner of the Italian marble slab covering the island in the gourmet kitchen. He died on impact.

Everyone, F1 fans or not, agreed Alex's death had been heartbreaking.

Later that night, Matteo De Rossi had suffered the first of a series of strokes. The last one would take his life just two years later.

When Taz visited his father in hospital the day after Alex's death, Matteo's high-priced lawyer briefed him. There had been a breakdown of communication between Matteo and Alex: Both had thought the house would be unoccupied that weekend. Matteo heard a woman screaming and came downstairs to find a half-dressed teenager on her knees next to Alex, her hand on his chest. He'd seen rows of cocaine on the island counter and liquor bottles on the coffee table in the lounge area adjacent to the kitchen. The girl—still a month short of eighteen—was Mount Everest–high. Knowing Alex was dead, Matteo called his lawyer instead of 911 and the police. The lawyer arrived and removed the girl, the drugs and all traces of their private party.

Only when the brownstone was clean and empty, the threat to Alex's reputation neutralised, were the police called. The story Matteo told was simple: He'd come downstairs for a drink, saw Alex and called 911. He held himself together, and at three in the morning he collapsed while talking to his lawyer and was rushed to hospital.

When he regained consciousness days later, his first and

only demand was that Alex's *indiscretions* had to remain a family secret. And so it did. Five years had passed since Matteo's death, but only he and the lawyer knew the truth about that night. After going through Alex's phone and laptop, they discovered that drug-fuelled orgies with under-age girls was a favourite pastime. Given his high profile, how he'd never been outed was a complete mystery.

Was Taz's anger and bitterness compounded by the fact that his father, even after Alex's death, continued to denigrate and dismiss him, while extolling Alex's virtues in public and in private? Alex, a larger-than-life figure before his untimely death, became almost godlike in death. Taz often fought the urge to scream the truth, to tell the world that the perfect Alex was anything but. But he kept quiet and remained in the shadows cast by his brilliant brother.

Taz scrubbed his hands over his face. Something had shut down in him the night of Alex's death. Years had passed, yet he still felt like he was encased in ice, watching the world from a distance and unable to break free. And the only way he could step into the light was to beat Alex's record of three driver championships in a row. He knew he'd never be as popular, as universally adored, as his brother. He didn't need to be. But if he beat Alex's record, the world would see him as the better F1 driver. In the competition between him and Alex, it was the only prize up for grabs.

But he'd torpedoed that goal by losing his temper with the rookie driver. What the *hell* had he been thinking? He knew better than that! He *was* better than that. But he'd been caught in a storm of resentment, fear and fury. The kid had been a handy target...

His actions in the pit were wholly unacceptable. Not only was he one of the senior drivers on the circuit but he was also a role model to the younger drivers. And the owner of a team. He was, not for the first time, ashamed of his actions. He needed to apologise privately to his colleague and publicly to the racing world and his fans.

He'd messed up before, but nothing as serious as this. And it had happened because he'd allowed his attention to wander to his press liaison officer.

Taz shoved his fingers into his hair. He'd put his championship in jeopardy, and he'd risked everything he was working for.

It was completely and wholly unacceptable. And it stopped right now.

He put his hand on the arm of the chair and tried to push himself up but nearly fainted as hot, searing pain rolled from the tips of his fingers, down the back of his hand and into his wrist. He sat again, and when the black dots disappeared from behind his eyes, he lifted his injured hand and noticed his swollen blue-black fingers and bloody knuckles. The bruise extended down his hand and covered his wrist. He'd broken a finger, maybe cracked his hand, his wrist. *Shit.* He was in a world of trouble here.

Pushing himself to his feet, hissing from the pain, he walked over to the door, flipped the lock and eyed the group waiting in the hallway. His CEO, his technical director, the team's long-time race engineer and, behind them, his PR team. Including Millie.

He gripped the door-frame and caught the sympathy in her purple-blue eyes, along with a healthy dose of exasperation. He could brush off his team's frustration and anger—he didn't care about their approval or disapproval—but for some reason, he cared what his press liaison officer thought about him. It was not an emotion he liked or was familiar with.

He kept his expression cold. 'I take it my actions made the news?' he asked sarcastically.

His race engineer was the first to speak. 'Alex would never—'

No, he couldn't deal with any references to Alex right now.

'Not now, Len,' he snapped. No matter what he did or how long he lived, he'd never manage to live up to Saint Alex's legacy.

He looked at his CEO. 'Any word from the disciplinary committee?'

'Nothing official, but it's not going to be good.'

Taz looked down at his rapidly swelling hand.

'You do realise that you have wiped out any advantage you had, don't you?' Len persisted. 'You will have to win most of the races going forward and hope your competitors mess up.'

Yes, he'd already run the scenarios and reached that conclusion. He rubbed his uninjured hand over his face, met Millie's eyes and saw the worry in hers and the way they kept darting to his swollen hand. He considered his predicament. Not least how he was going to navigate the next few weeks of his life one-handed—without allowing anyone into his inner sanctum. He would never do that. Even when he slept with a woman, he always went to her place, and his driver room and hotel suite were solidly off-limits to everyone, his safe spaces. That was why he was holding this meeting in a hallway.

But he needed professional help to navigate the bad press heading his way. This wasn't a situation he could fix on his own. The thought settled like a wet, heavy blanket, unfamiliar and deeply uncomfortable. Relying on others wasn't in his nature. He thrived on self-sufficiency, answered to no one and carved his own path. That's what happened when your father and brother thought of you as surplus to requirements. He was perfectly content in his emotional isolation.

But this situation needed PR expertise and someone he could trust. He recalled the way Millie had considered the photo of him and Meredith. Instead of jumping to conclusions, she'd looked deeper. Given him the benefit of the doubt. He couldn't remember the last time anyone had done that. He needed someone in his life who could look past his reputation and his brother's achievements, someone who saw *him*. Someone he could work with…

From somewhere he also recalled hearing that Millie had left her job at a PR firm in London to work as his press liaison officer. So she clearly knew her stuff.

Decision made.

'I'm promoting Millie from being my press liaison officer to being my PR officer. You need to speak to me, go through her.'

Millie's mouth fell open as a chorus of disapprovals rose in the hallway. She looked as shocked as everyone else. Tough.

'Millie, get the team doctor up here.'

'Um… I think we need to discuss this,' Millie said, with more than a little panic in her voice.

He was tired, he felt like he'd been hit by a truck, and his hand was on fire. 'Doctor, *now*.' Then he stepped back into his room and slammed the door, welcoming the silence.

He walked over to the couch and lay down on it, gently resting his injured hand on his flat stomach and placing his other forearm over his eyes.

How was he going to dig himself out of this hole?

CHAPTER THREE

MUCH LATER THAT NIGHT, Millie slipped inside Taz's private hospital room, wincing at the plaster encasing his hand from the tips of his fingers to an inch below his elbow. A few hours after the team doctor looked at the X-ray of his hand, he was wheeled into a state-of-the-art theatre and had the best orthopaedic surgeon in China operating on his hand. Now his cast lay next to him on the bed and his other hand cupped the back of his head. His eyes were closed and he didn't look like he was in pain.

Millie hesitated. She didn't know Taz well enough to visit him in the hospital, to be in his room so late at night, but she needed to ask how he wanted her to respond to the incessant demands from reporters desperate for a comment, update or interview. If he'd threatened to fire her for sharing her thoughts on a photo, taking the initiative and putting out a press release without Taz's approval was surely a fireable offence.

But as much as she wished she could say that she was here solely as his press officer, she couldn't. Since their conversation in the corridor, she'd felt unsettled and unsure why. Working for Taz had always been a challenge—demanding, relentless—but manageable. Her attraction to him had been little more than a quiet hum beneath the surface. That vague hum was now a strong current—sharp and impossible to ignore. Why did she suddenly feel super aware around him? What had changed between them? Was she being overly imaginative? Highly possible.

During the race, she'd been on edge, hyper aware, waiting for something—anything—to happen. And it had. He crashed, lost his temper and then, out of nowhere, announced her promotion. It floored her, and she didn't understand it. Neither did anyone else. But as she stood in the doorway, she froze. His closed eyes and pale face suggested this wasn't the time. He was injured, and she and everyone else could wait.

She turned to tiptoe out, but then Taz's deep voice floated across the room. 'Millie.'

She wrinkled her nose. *Busted.* Millie looked down, but instead of sporting glassy eyes and a loopy smile he looked fully alert. 'How long have you been out of the theatre?' she asked.

'Two or so hours,' he replied. 'What are you doing here?'

Millie jammed her hands into the back pockets of her jeans and rocked from side to side. 'The press is all over you for pushing the rookie driver, and they are not being kind. I need to know how you want me to mitigate any possible damage to your brand. And I really need to talk to you about my unexpected promotion.'

He looked at the cast on his hand. 'And this couldn't wait until morning?'

'Well, the sooner I start spinning the story, the sooner this will blow over.'

'Again, it could've waited.'

Millie shuffled on her feet. She couldn't tell him the third and last reason she was here. It was super simple: She wanted to see how he was and felt compelled to visit him because she didn't think any of his staff would bother. Taz was their boss, and they respected him, but she knew they didn't particularly like him. But nobody should be alone after an operation. Not even the incredibly self-sufficient Taz De Rossi.

'Are you in any pain?' she asked, walking over to stand next to his bed.

'Despite the anaesthetic and the drugs, I feel remarkably clear-headed.' His lips curved into a disarming smile. He looked so much younger when he smiled. 'And pain-free.'

When the meds wore off, his injured hand would let itself be known. 'What did they do?' she asked, nodding to his hand.

'Put in a pin to stabilise my middle finger,' he replied. 'I also have a minor crack in my wrist. I punched that wall pretty hard, but they both should heal within four to six weeks. It wasn't my finest hour.'

Millie lifted her eyebrows at his self-criticism. It had been a foolish thing to do, but she'd never expected Taz to admit it. It was late, the hospital ward was quiet, his private room felt like a cocoon, and Millie felt like they were the only two people around. His navy T-shirt—no hospital gown for Taz De Rossi—covered his broad chest and hugged his muscular shoulders, and his cast was blindingly white against his tanned upper arm. His stubble was thicker, his grey eyes tired but still sharp. Assessing. It would take more than a high-speed crash, a media PR disaster and an operation to make Taz De Rossi break out in a sweat.

'How bad is the fallout? On a scale of one to ten?'

She considered lying but lifted one shoulder instead. 'Twelve?'

He cursed. 'And what have the stewards decided?'

'They are still discussing it and said they'd send an email first thing in the morning.'

He pulled a face. 'If it needs that much discussion, then I'm in trouble.'

Frankly, he was. His actions had been broadcast to millions of people around the world. At best he'd lost his temper and was a bully, at worst he'd resorted to violence. Either way, team owner or not, high profile or not, he wasn't the poster boy for good sportsmanship.

'It's been a rough day,' Taz murmured, the king of the understatement

She agreed. He was difficult and reticent and frequently rude, but his day had gone from bad to worse to edging into catastrophic.

'And unfortunately the next few days will be as bad, if not worse. If the stewards came back with a rest-of-the-season ban, that's it for the season. And there will be no way I can beat—'

He stopped speaking and turned his head away, but not before Millie caught the apprehension in his eyes and the panic on his face. It was the first time she'd seen his I've-got-everything-control façade slip. Seeing that chink in his armour made him seem more attractive—if that was even possible.

And dangerous. So dangerous. She needed to keep *not* liking him so she didn't do anything rash like make her attraction to him known. She felt like she'd already lost ground to him; she couldn't surrender anymore.

She looked at the door and tried to smile. 'I'm going to go. I'll be back in the morning. As I said, there are things we need to discuss, including this promotion you dropped in my lap—'

'Most people would be happy to be promoted.'

If they thought they could handle the job, sure, then happiness was warranted. But Millie had her doubts. She'd only ever handled small accounts, and Taz had the eyes of the world on him. This was a job for the best in the business, not for an inexperienced woman working out who she was, what she wanted and how she should walk through the world.

'As I said, we need to discuss it.' She shouldn't be here: It was inappropriate, and he looked tired. 'But it can wait until morning.' She looked at the closed door. 'I should go.'

'Wait,' Taz replied. He lifted his free hand to grip her upper arm. He tugged her down so that her mouth was an inch away from his, and his breath warmed her lips. 'You don't like me very much, do you?'

Up until Thursday, she hadn't. Or not much. Like her parents, he was ridiculously arrogant and entirely too used to getting his way. But something had shifted, leaving her disoriented and off balance.

It was as if she'd slipped on a new pair of glasses and suddenly, the world—*he*—had come into sharper focus. Maybe it was the lines of pain etched into his face, his tired eyes or the white cast, but his hard edges now seemed less jagged, the aloofness less tangible, his loneliness palpable. She felt rattled: She wasn't ready for anything to change between them.

Like him, she was weary. It had been a long day, and she was emotionally and physically drained. It was natural to overthink *everything*…

'Are those drugs finally kicking in?' she asked, changing the subject.

'I'm fine.' The side of his mouth lifted in a half smile. 'You don't need to answer, I can see it in your eyes. Few people like me, and I can live with that.'

She wanted to deny his words, but a sense of self-preservation held her back. What was the point of admitting that he fascinated her? There could never be anything between them. He was a shooting star, and she was…*not*.

Taz had made being emotionally unavailable into an art

form. 'I don't think you let people close enough to decide whether they like you or not.'

His eyebrows rose at that assessment, but instead of responding he tipped his head to the side, his hand still on her arm. 'But you do want me to kiss you. You're attracted to me.'

His words were softly uttered but no less powerful than a shout. He was an experienced guy, and she'd been foolish to think he hadn't picked up on her attraction, wouldn't be surprised to hear that, whenever he was close or within twenty feet of her, she felt like she'd been struck by lightning. Thoughts of how it would feel to have her lips under his, to skim his hard, muscled body with her hands, consumed her.

Attracted was too tame a word to describe her reaction to him. The truth was, in this moment, she'd never wanted anyone more. She burned for him, and she wasn't a woman who liked playing with fire. *Why did he make her feel like this?*

Millie held her breath as Taz's hand moved up her arm and slid around the back of her neck. He tunnelled his long fingers into her hair. She knew she should be sensible and pull back and put some distance between them. But she was so tired of being sensible, of doing what was expected. She wanted to step into the fire and feel the flames lick her face. Kissing him was a very bad idea, but she was, strangely and uncharacteristically, going to do it anyway.

Taz lifted his mouth and pulled her head down, and their lips met in a kiss that was as soft as it was sexy. She placed her fingers on his jaw, surprised at the softness of the stubble on his jaw and cheek. It tickled her lips as he explored her mouth, his tongue pressing the seam of her lips, demanding entrance.

She shouldn't—he was her boss, for God's sake! He

paid her salary. She shouldn't even be here, in this hospital room, with him. But her body, more specifically her mouth, failed to decode her brain's frantic messages. Her lips parted, partly from shock, partly from need, and he slipped inside her mouth, setting off a chain reaction of baby fireworks on her skin. His tongue tangled with hers, and she heard his rumble of appreciation and felt his hand tightening on her head. Her blood heated, her eyes closed, and she never wanted him to stop. This was, bar none, the best kiss of her life...

His soft grumble, deep in his throat released the last string holding her control together, and the fingers of her hand speared into his hair, and her other hand pulled his soft T-shirt up his stomach to find warm male skin. All she wanted to do was to straddle him, rock herself against his hard length. Why was she reacting like this? Who *was* she? Why did he make her feel so reckless?

And breathless.

His hand ran up and down her back, over her hip, up her ribcage. It wasn't nearly enough. Nothing but being naked and having him inside her would be enough. Millie didn't recognise herself: She never responded like this, was never needy and...*wanton.*

Men never made her feel wild and out of control. Taz, through some dark magic, did.

And boy, did he know how to use his lips. Was he as good at making love as he was at kissing? Of course he would be: He'd had lots of practice with a steady stream of women. But knowing what type of woman he usually went for—slim, sophisticated, *famous*—why was he kissing her?

Except that he wasn't. Kissing her. Not anymore. His lips weren't moving, and his hand fell from her head to his side. Millie pulled back. His eyes slammed into hers, and she thought she caught shock in his, echoed by his bobbing Adam's apple. She straightened, and Taz rested his head on his pillow and pushed his hand through his messy hair.

If he was anyone but Taz De Rossi, she would suspect he was a little off balance and that he'd been caught off guard by the heat of their kiss. But that wasn't feasible. He closed his eyes, and his thick lashes lay against his pale skin. The lines of pain were deeper now, and he pressed his lips together.

'Are your pain meds wearing off?' she asked. She had to say something, the silence between them excruciating.

'Yeah,' he replied, his voice a little rough.

It was a perfectly reasonable explanation: He'd had a high-speed crash and an operation. But Millie wasn't buying it. She was starting to read his body language, and his tight lips and the muscle jumping in his jaw suggested something was bubbling under the surface. She was tempted to push but decided not to. Did she want to know? Could she handle it if she did?

It was late and so much had happened, there was no need to toss an accelerant on a runaway fire.

Maybe their kiss was simply an unusual end to an unusual day. She shouldn't read anything into it. He might not even remember it in the morning. And if he did, he would probably, hopefully, write it off as a spur-of-the-moment thing.

God, she hoped so. Millie left his room, shut the door behind her, plopped down in the nearest chair in the hallway and rested her forehead on her fist.

A normal Sunday night back in London meant a curry in front of the TV, maybe folding some laundry, vacuuming her flat if she felt energetic. But here she was sitting in a hospital in Shanghai, newly promoted to a job she didn't think she could do, reliving a kiss with her boss.

Who *was* she?

And that was the issue, wasn't it? That was why she was here. Because she didn't want to be who she was, but didn't know who she wanted to be. Or who she could be. She needed a new version of herself, a Millie 2.0, but had no idea what that person looked like or what she believed. About the world or herself.

When she was younger, she'd been intimidated by the sophisticated and wealthy world of F1 racing, by the sophisticated girls Ben dated, the circles he socialised in, and the wealth and the luxury surrounding him. Both her and Ben's parents glittered and glowed, and they'd easily slid into Ben's world and navigated it with ease. Unlike the rest of her family, she didn't like the spotlight.

Her parents had only ever planned on having one child. Another child would've demanded more—time, money and input—than they were prepared to offer, but they'd been vastly disappointed in the child they got. They'd told her, quite often, that they felt cheated she wasn't confident, charming or talented enough to share their limelight, to be loved.

It had been the same for Ben until his racing career took off and he started building a reputation at De Rossi Racing. His friendship with Alex De Rossi hadn't hurt and had boosted his profile further. His parents and hers had welcomed him back into the family like the prodigal son. Was her refusal to join Ben at his races, to step into his glamorous and sophisticated world, motivated by her anger and resentment that he was successful and popular and therefore acceptable and valuable to his parents and hers?

Maybe? Her insecure behaviour aside, Ben always reminded her that she was strong, lovely and smart and could hold her head up wherever she went, with whoever she met. He was the only one who saw her doing and being more...

Weirdly, in some strange and expected way, Taz promoting her and then kissing her made her feel the same way. That maybe she could do hard or unexpected things, handle more responsibility and...

And that she was more attractive than she believed herself to be. That she mattered.

No, she was being naive and making unfounded assumptions. The world didn't work that way. Her promotion was likely to be rescinded in the morning when Taz had some time to review his impulsive decision. He'd only kissed her because he'd been half-asleep and was a little woozy from the anaesthetic. It meant nothing: He'd been acting on instinct.

'Is everything all right?'

Millie jumped at the sound of a nurse's voice, and jerked her head up, her hand on her heart. 'Sorry, you frightened me.'

'You look tired.'

Millie *was* emotionally and physically exhausted. It had been a day.

'Maybe you should go now.'

Millie nodded, picked up her bag, slung it crossways across her chest and looked at Taz's closed door. She thought she should say something, ask the nurse to keep an eye on him, but that was stupid and unnecessary. She was his *employee*, not his girlfriend.

She needed to remember that. She had things to do, and falling for her attractive boss wasn't on the agenda.

Taz heard the door snick shut and lifted his good arm and placed it across his eyes. Spikes of pain ran up his other arm and into his shoulder, and all he wanted was the oblivion of drug-induced sleep. Or Millie's lips back on his.

While he'd kissed her, he'd forgotten everything in his life, totally lost in her heat and her mouth. The agony of his injury faded, humiliation lessened, and his anxiety about the championship dissipated. He'd been utterly, wholly into her: her light, feminine perfume, the softness of her hair, her glorious mouth.

His harsh F-bomb shattered the silence of his private room. Maybe the drugs and anaesthetic had affected him more than he realised. Because women, especially a woman like Millie—a little unsure, not-so-sophisticated, very real—didn't make him feel like this. Off-kilter. Out of control.

He liked being alone. He'd embraced self-sufficiency because it was easier to stand by himself than to be disappointed and abandoned, to be shunned as he had by his own father and brother. They had been a team, and he'd been squeezed out.

He'd had a choice: to curl up into a ball, to fade away or to make them notice him. He'd chosen the latter. When he was sixteen, he'd begged his father to send him to the right racing academies, and his persistence eventually paid off. Luckily, he was talented, and when his father didn't give him a position on the De Rossi F3 racing team, he was quickly snapped up by another team. It didn't take him long before he'd made his way to F1, joined another racing team, and when the press questioned why he wasn't on the family team, his father smoothly replied that he didn't believe in nepotism. Taz had to earn his spot on the De Rossi team. It couldn't have been further from the truth. His father hadn't wanted him on the team full stop.

That had only fuelled the fire of his ambition. While driving for a rival team, he became a top driver, a contender and

Alex's rival. Then Ben was killed at Imola, and his father, hampered by his words about only employing the best, reluctantly offered Taz a place next to Alex. He nearly refused, but the De Rossi team was the pinnacle of racing. And like his father, he never settled for second best.

Nothing about their family dynamics changed, and he kept his distance, never reacting to his father's and brother's gaslighting, understanding that they needed to find a chink in his armour to exploit. He became…stoic. Unimpressed. Unemotional.

Appearing impassive and detached became a habit, and eventually, after years of training, he became the way he acted.

Until tonight when he kissed Millie. Maybe it had started on Thursday when he realised she could see past his cold façade to the storm brewing under his layer of ice. Or maybe it started weeks ago when he'd first looked into her purple-blue eyes and felt himself tumbling.

Bottom line, he'd boxed himself into a corner. He didn't like the way she made him feel, and his first impulse, and the easiest option, was to be shot of her. But if he demoted her back to being his press liaison officer, he'd still have to work with her, which defeated the objective. And he didn't have any cause to fire her. Either action would make him look like indecisive.

Besides, firing Millie a day after promoting her would also be grossly unfair. He'd raised her expectations by telling her she was promoted, and ripping the opportunity away would be a cheap shot. Or was he grabbing onto any excuse to keep her around? He shoved the idea away, uncomfortable with its many implications. He'd promoted her: He would stick by his decision and make it work. And pray that in the morning, everything would be back under control.

CHAPTER FOUR

LATER THE NEXT MORNING, Millie walked into the penthouse suite of the team's hotel, her eyes widening as she took in the skyline views of the Pudong district, Shanghai's Bund and Huangpu River, and the Oriental Pearl Tower from Taz's high-in-the-sky hotel suite. It wasn't just the views outside, it was the suite itself too, the luxurious furniture, the baby grand piano and the bank of floor-to-ceiling windows. The white, black and grey colour scheme was interrupted by splashes of tangerine. The décor was stark, hard, severe... just like her boss.

Talking of, where was he? He'd been discharged from the hospital earlier this morning, and he knew she was here to see him. The only place he could be was the suite's bedroom. After their kiss last night, she wasn't going anywhere near where he slept, so she dropped her bag onto the couch and walked over to the telescope standing in the corner of the room.

She'd lain awake for most of the night, her thoughts bouncing around her brain. Ben's death, Taz's kiss, how she viewed herself, how her parents viewed her. Why she was here, how she was going to save Taz's reputation, if that was even possible. Why had he kissed her? Promoted her? What did it all mean? And why was life getting *more* complicated, not less?

'Millie.'

Millie turned, and Taz stepped into the room to her right. Behind him, she saw a brief glimpse of a massive free-standing bed in the middle of a huge room. But it was Taz's appearance that caught her off guard. He was a stylish dresser and usually favoured designer suits with open-neck shirts and expensive shoes, or business casual outfits that screamed *style and sophistication*. Today he wore a loose T-shirt over straight-legged track pants, his big feet bare. His hair was unbrushed and his scruff was thicker than before. He looked disreputable and dangerous and so, so sexy.

She dropped her head and cleared her throat, cursing her attraction. Maybe it was because he was the polar opposite of the men she'd dated over the past few years. They'd been bland, uninspiring and so very uninteresting, all the things her parents accused her of being. When she finally took time to work out why she sat through the interminable meals and boring weekends, why she tolerated bad or mediocre sex, she realised it was because she believed she didn't deserve any better. Tired of wasting her time, she'd distanced herself from men completely.

Sabotaging herself had to stop, and she decided she needed to find a new way to navigate life, to figure out how to view herself going forward. That was why she'd up-ended her life to join the F1 circus, to take on a new challenge. And if part of her life lesson was dealing with her attraction to this charismatic man, then so be it.

Had life thrown Taz into her path to challenge her habit of second-guessing herself?

Millie cleared her throat and nodded to his cast. 'How are you feeling?' she asked, sitting on one of the two bucket chairs opposite the enormous boxy couch.

'Like they shoved a pin into my finger to stabilise the

bone,' he retorted. Sarcastic as always. Millie watched him, but nothing in his eyes or his expression suggested he was going to mention what had transpired between them last night.

He was back to being her grumpy, detached, frequently annoying boss. This was what she wanted, right? For them to go back to normal, and Taz being sarcastic and difficult was normal.

Taz dragged his free hand down his face. 'Sorry.'

Damn, just when the earth had stopped moving under her feet. Taz apologising was *not* common, but Millie didn't know how to handle him doing it, so she ignored his snappy, one-word apology.

'Being indisposed makes me tetchy. Showering was a bitch, dressing wasn't easy. I've been in a foul mood all morning,' he added.

She could imagine his frustration at only having one working hand. Millie waved her phone at him. 'I got your message to meet you here, and here I am. Can we talk about you promoting me now?'

He frowned at her. 'Why is that such an issue? Most people would have thanked me a thousand times over by now.'

God, he was arrogant.

'Because I'm not sure I want the promotion, and more importantly, I don't know if I can do it!' she half shouted, surprised she'd raised her voice. She'd trained herself not to react emotionally. In her family, it wasn't safe to lose her grip on her emotions, to let them see that what they said bothered her. It only made it worse. Why was she losing that tight grip now? What was it about Taz that pushed her to the limit?

He brushed her words aside with the swipe of his hand, unfazed by her reaction. 'Of course you can.'

His conviction was contagious, and for a few seconds, she believed him. Then reality strolled back in, and she shook her head. 'You don't understand. I haven't worked on a big campaign.'

'It's the same principle, isn't it? To build and maintain a positive image, right?'

Essentially. 'Well, yes, at the most basic level,' she admitted.

Taz's shrug suggested their discussion was over. But she still had questions. 'I don't think—'

'It's done. Moving on.' Just like that.

'The F1 stewards doled out community service as a punishment for me pushing the rookie,' he informed her, sitting down on the couch and casually placing his bare feet on the glass coffee table. He looked at her and grimaced. 'In a meeting late last night, they agreed that I'd punished myself enough by punching the wall and putting myself out of commission, but they still had to censure me.'

Millie had to think fast to keep up with him. She'd come back to her promotion and her worries around it later. 'Community service isn't so bad,' she said, linking her hands around her knee. 'How much do you have to do and by when?'

'The only proviso was that I had to make an impact, so it's up to me.'

Millie mentally ran through some options. 'You could do what your brother did and visit a children's hospital or an orphanage, speak at high schools, do a shift at a community kitchen feeding the homeless.'

An emotion she couldn't pinpoint flickered in his eyes before they turned flat and unreadable. Was it frustration, annoyance or anguish? She wasn't sure. 'No. I don't want to be seen to be taking the easy way out by doing what he did,' he replied. But something in his tone suggested it was a pat answer, one he trotted out to get over what he thought was a bump in the conversation.

'Your brother got a lot of good press doing those appearances,' Millie pointed out. But doing community work had reportedly been part of Alex's personality, fed by his deep desire to help people less fortunate than himself. Alex was as lauded as much for his philanthropic endeavours as he was for his racing. Losing him was a tragedy. It must still be deeply painful for Taz.

Yet, how could two brothers grow up in the same house, under, as she believed, the same set of circumstances and turn out so different? She'd often wondered if she'd had a sibling whether they would have been like her, quiet and withdrawn, or more like her parents, a sunflower constantly turning its head to the light, happy to bloom?

Ben was raised in much the same way as her, but he'd been happier, sunnier, more confident. Was it a male thing or was it because he discovered his passion for racing young and was able to pour all his energies into his sport? The sport that he lived—and died—for.

'Why do the good ones always die young?' she murmured.

'You assume Alex was good?' Taz asked, dropping his feet and leaning forward, his eyes blazing with an emotion she couldn't identify. Millie frowned, confounded by his fierce expression. In reality, she'd been thinking about Ben but wasn't about to reveal that. She rarely told anyone about her semi-famous parents, and she'd yet to tell anyone, including Taz, that she was related to Ben, partly because talking about him was still hard and partly because she wanted to avoid comparisons between her and her gregarious and popular cousin.

Still, his reaction was…confusing to say the least. Almost as if he was daring her to contradict the narrative.

'Um…he was well-known for giving his time and attention to causes he cared for, always visiting sick kids in the hospital or making guest appearances to help charities,' Millie stated, confused.

'He was a saint.' Taz's tone was so bland she wasn't sure if he was being sarcastic or not. Then as quickly as it had come up, he moved on.

'I haven't had a moment to read Mika's reports on the PR my crash and fracas caused. Update me.'

'It's a train wreck,' she warned him.

'Not unexpected,' Taz murmured. 'Give it to me straight.'

Millie took a deep breath and told him how he was being called *temperamental* and an *uncontrollable, spoilt, overprivileged hothead*. How he was risking his title and his brand, and when was he going to grow up?

'That reporter I wanted you to meet on Thursday? She's now one of your harshest critics. Her podcast, the one where she discusses how different you are to Alex, has shot up the popularity charts.'

Taz narrowed his eyes at her. 'If you tell me I shouldn't have blown her off on Thursday, I will fire you.'

Chance would be a fine thing. Millie gritted her teeth. She'd almost let that phrase slip. She could handle managing his press—press releases, interviews, the usual chaos—but being responsible for his *image*? Spinning it, rehabilitating it? That terrified her. Taz didn't need a PR manager, he required a miracle worker. Someone with the nerves of a pro gambler and the skills of an acrobat juggling ten balls on a unicycle. Someone who exuded confidence, who could command the narrative with unquestioned charm.

How could she possibly reshape his image when she barely understood her own? Sure, she could write a flawless press release or schedule his interviews down to the second. But transforming the world's perception of him? That required unshakeable confidence and bold, unapologetic chutzpah—qualities she didn't possess.

'Why isn't your PR team here?' she demanded, still looking for an out and hating herself for not throwing herself into this new challenge like she knew she should after all the promises she'd made to herself and Ben. 'They have far more experience than me.'

'They are also set in their ways and have a narrow way of thinking,' Taz replied. 'Why are you still trying to talk yourself out of this promotion?'

'Because you need someone more qualified!'

'We're done talking about this, Millie,' Taz retorted. 'You're bright, observant and clear-thinking. Stop putting yourself down, and get on board.'

Millie's mouth opened and closed in shock. It was an unexpected compliment, and she didn't know how to respond to it.

'Tell me about the press coverage.'

His sharp order made her pull her thoughts together. 'You're getting annihilated. And the sponsors aren't happy.'

'Because any impact on my brand is an impact on theirs. And if they are complaining, then I'm in bigger trouble than I thought.'

His main sponsors were an energy drink company whose advertising was risqué and always controversial and a worldwide travel company whose tag line was that *If it wasn't naughty, it wasn't nice.*

'It's a perfect storm,' Millie admitted. 'People aren't happy you went on a date with Meredith—'

'That's not what happened, and you know it.'

'The truth doesn't matter, perception does. After the press implied you are sleeping with your brother's fiancée,' Millie countered, 'you crashed, putting your championship in jeopardy. Then you pushed a rookie driver, one of the nicest around, and you punched a wall, putting yourself out of commission. The press and public hate unforced errors, Taz.'

'I don't need you to rehash my mistakes,' he said, black ice frosting his voice and eyes. 'And regret doesn't change a damn thing.' He raked his hands through his hair and linked his fingers behind his neck. 'I need to move forward, and that requires solutions and strategies, and I need them *right now*.'

A discreet knock on the door interrupted their conversation, and Millie let out a long, unsteady breath, grateful for the reprieve. She might see herself as underqualified, acutely inexperienced, but for some inexplicable reason Taz seemed to believe she could cope with the pressure. He was putting his faith, and more importantly his reputation, in her hands.

He was Taz De Rossi, famous for hiring the best and firing them when they didn't live up to his exceedingly high expectations, but… She rubbed her hands over her face.

But if he believed in her, perhaps it was time she stopped doubting her capabilities. At the very least, she owed it to herself, and to Ben, to try.

Taz greeted the room service waiter and walked over to the floor-to-ceiling window. The waiter poured coffee and left, as quiet on exit as he was on his entrance.

Millie joined Taz at the window, handed him a cup of black coffee and folded her arms. 'So I've been thinking…'

'Is that dangerous?' he asked, but Millie caught the delicious, but very unexpected, glimmer of amusement in his eyes. So Taz had a dry sense of humour. Good to know.

'Look, I think you're unwise to promote me, but it's obvious that you need to rehabilitate your reputation.'

'I am *not* doing hospital visits or visiting youth groups.'

'If you did, you would be compared to Alex,' Millie mused. 'The public would accuse you of being inauthentic, of trying to ride the coat-tails of your brother's sterling reputation to restore yours. It would be a disaster.'

His expression hardened, and Millie wondered if she'd hurt his feelings. No, that wasn't possible. Nobody was sure Taz *had* feelings. Though his kiss last night suggested otherwise. *Don't think about how his mouth felt on yours, Millie...*

'Please, don't hold back,' Taz murmured.

Sarcasm, or not? She didn't have time to try and figure it, or him, out. Millie put down her cup and paced the area in front of the window, flicking her thumbnail against her front tooth, thinking hard.

'Apart from racing, what do you do well?' she asked. Before he could speak, she answered her question. 'According to the internet, you are a fantastic skier, a better polo player and a golfer with a plus-one handicap. It's been said that if you didn't go into driving, you could've made a living in pro polo or golf.'

Millie couldn't see Taz doing either: Both were far too tame for a man who lived life at a thousand miles per hour. And drove cars at a third of that speed.

He collected wine and owned a holding company that owned and operated the De Rossi team and its many subsidiaries. He had a vineyard in France and a villa in Tuscany. A brownstone in New York—not the same one where his brother died—and a flat in London. No doubt he had an English country house too. Then it hit her.

'I have an idea...'

'Should I be scared?'

Millie narrowed her eyes at him. Please, the man didn't *do* scared. 'Why don't you do what you do best?' she asked.

He lifted his cast. 'Because my hand is out of action,' he replied at his mocking best.

'You're a *socialite*, an A-list celeb, someone who is as at home at parties and functions as you are on the track. We can use that to rehab your rep.'

Taz closed his eyes. 'I haven't even heard your proposal yet, and I know I'm going to hate it.' He sighed and gestured for her to continue.

'I think you should offer yourself as a drawcard, for charities to raise money from your presence at their functions. We can contact charities and ask them how they could use you. Maybe it's to co-host a ball, be the VIP guest at a cocktail party, attend a golf tournament or offer meet-and-greet sessions. It would qualify as community service, and it'll help rehab your appalling reputation.'

'I'm no Boy Scout, but I don't quite have a foot in hell,' he protested.

Millie started ticking off points on her fingers. 'You and Phoebe have had a tumultuous on-off relationship for years—'

'I think calling it a *relationship* is stretching the truth,' Taz interjected.

'Noted. You're rude, impatient and, frankly, uncontrollable.'

'Who is supposed to be in control of me?' he shot back. 'I own my team, I call the shots, I make every decision.'

Good point. 'You never push back on bad publicity.'

He shrugged. 'People can write what they like, believe what they want.'

So confident. 'Up until this point your saving grace, from a PR point of view, has been your exemplary behaviour on and off the track. Journalists have often commended you for not carrying your bad-boy antics onto the track and into your professional life… Until now,' she concluded.

He tensed, and Millie knew she'd made her point. 'They—the press and the fans—are asking whether your personal life has spilt over into your professional life. People might excuse your antics off the track, but they won't stand for it on it.'

He nodded. Was he taking her comments on board? 'You're not offended?' she asked.

'I'd much rather be hurt by the truth than comforted with a lie,' Taz replied, lifting his shoulders in a quick shrug. 'So you think lending my pulling power to charities will redeem me?'

'Along with an apology to the rookie? Yes. Well, it certainly won't hurt.'

'I intended to make my apology to him in private. I think it means more that way.'

Millie agreed. 'A public statement is also necessary, Taz. A photo of the two of you shaking hands would be even better.' He was unlikely to agree, but what was the worst he could say? No?

'I wanted to catch him before he left for the two-week break before Miami, but,' he said as he held up his cast, 'the operation delayed me.'

Throughout the F1 season, everything the team needed at a race—from invaluable cars and the team's headquarters to tyres, fuel and Taz's preferred brand of coffee— was transported to every location the sport visited around the world. Their next stop would be Florida, for the Miami Grand Prix. Formula One was one big moving circus: Set things up, race, take them down. Rinse and repeat.

'Can you apologise to the rookie by video call? That way we can get a statement out to the press quicker.'

Taz didn't look happy at the suggestion but finally nodded. Millie did a mental fist pump and, because her luck was holding, pushed for more. 'And will you consider collaborating with charities?'

His eyes connected with hers, and Millie felt the pop of a champagne cork in her stomach, the fizz of bubbles. 'Draw up a list of twenty charities, a mixture of established and new, and let them make a one-page pitch or short video message as to how best they could use me. I'll decide who to support.'

Excellent. That was a solid win. Except there was one little fly in the ointment. Phoebe. Who tended to resurface in Taz's life whenever there was an excellent promo opportunity. She couldn't let their turbulent relationship spoil his PR rehabilitation. 'I can explain you meeting Meredith, as she was Alex's fiancée. But Phoebe is a troublemaker, and she has to stay away from this, Taz.'

The woman in her, the one who'd kissed Taz last night, would prefer Phoebe to drop out of Taz's life entirely. Millie told her to be quiet. She wasn't allowed an opinion.

His eyebrow lifted at the use of his first name, but she didn't break eye contact. He needed to know how deadly serious she was on this point. Millie gathered her courage. 'Her reputation is worse than yours, and the charities don't deserve to be caught up in any drama. If she's going to be around, then tell me and I'll find another way to rehab your rep.'

'I like your idea,' Taz replied, his agreement shocking her. 'And Phoebe and I are done. Permanently.'

Really? Millie hoped Phoebe had got that message. 'I track the press releases mentioning your name, and she's been giving interviews left and right, saying that you'll be back together soon. That you will be heading to the Caribbean to recoup and reset your relationship.'

He scoffed. 'There is *nothing* to reset. I made it clear to her a few days ago, before I left London, that we are over.'

He sounded like he meant it, but Phoebe was a bad penny who kept showing up. But Millie saw the warning light in his eyes and decided to heed his silent admonition. The subject was closed.

She looked down at her iPad, reflecting that she'd made more progress than she'd expected.

It was time to go. 'I'll get working on the press statement and researching charities.'

'Link the charities to where we are racing next. A Miami charity for Miami, an Italian charity for Imola.' Millie swallowed. She'd been trying to forget they were heading to the racetrack where Ben lost his life. She didn't know if she could do it. But the Imola race was still a month away, and she'd worry about the emotional impact of being at the crash site later. She had bigger problems right now.

'I'll see what I can do.'

She stood and picked up her bag and pulled it over her shoulder. She shouldn't ask but she couldn't help herself. 'Are you going back to London or New York?'

'Not that it's got anything to do with you, but I'm not sure yet.'

Just when she'd thought he might be evolving into a halfway decent conversationalist and boss, he'd proved her wrong—yet again. The memory of their kiss still lingered, but she was determined to be professional and courteous.

Taz was a master at being difficult. He was also exceptionally good at testing her patience. *Deep breath, Millie.*

'Have a good flight. I hope your recovery goes well.'

She smiled, and when he didn't say anything she turned

her back to him and walked to the hallway and the front door of his palatial suite.

'Millie...'

She slowly turned. He sat on the arm of the couch, and she could feel the intensity of his stare. 'That kiss...'

She thought they'd dodged that landmine, that his silence on the subject was his way of telling her that it meant nothing. Heat crept up her face. She had no idea what to say or what he wanted from her, so she hugged her iPad to her chest as a bead of sweat ran down her spine.

He kept looking at her, and it took all her willpower to keep her from bolting out of the door. When the tension became too much, the silence too weighty, she spoke. 'I work for you, *Mr De Rossi*. What happened was against company rules.'

'I know. It's *my* company. But it was a truly excellent kiss.'

She wanted to grab his shirt and shake him, not that she'd be able to make his muscular frame budge an inch. This man, she was convinced, was born to drive her mad. 'I think you enjoyed it as much as I did,' he stated, his tone silky and deliberately provocative. Was he trying to get a rise out of her?

Be sensible, Millie. Do not let him goad you into being reckless or admitting to your attraction. 'I don't get involved with people I work for, Mr De Rossi. It would be highly unprofessional. Besides, you have a girlfriend, and she would scratch my eyes out if she found out.'

'I thought I explained that Phoebe is no longer in my life. I dislike repeating myself.' Should she ask whether he was certain Phoebe had received the message? No. He'd already clocked her interest; she didn't need him to know that he *fascinated* her.

Millie lifted her chin and gathered her courage. 'Apart from not dating bosses, I don't date bad boys. I don't date *at all*.' Well, not anymore.

'Pity,' Taz drawled.

Millie gripped the door-handle and twisted it with more force than necessary. She needed to get away from Taz before she did something really stupid. Like dropping her possessions and walking into his arms. Hauling that T-shirt up his chest, kissing his neck...

Leading him into his bedroom. She shook her head at her lust-coated thoughts, not recognising herself. She wasn't a lose-her-clothes, roll-around-the-bed-with-a-billionaire woman.

Besides, there was too much at stake for her to risk making such a mistake. Taz had the power, wealth and influence to recover from his mistakes...

But she did not.

CHAPTER FIVE

Miami

IT WAS A beautiful spring day in Florida, hot and blue, and when the stewardess opened the jet's door, a stream of hot air rushed into the air-conditioned plane. Taz unclipped his seat belt and stretched, wishing he'd slept for more than a few hours last night.

He shouldn't have accepted an invitation to meet some friends at Lily's last night. But after reports started surfacing that he was hiding away because he couldn't handle criticism and was sulking, social media influencers started echoing the nonsense. Millie sent him a message telling him to get out and about and to look cheerful while doing it. He'd thought about ignoring her directive—he wasn't the kind of man who let anyone, least of all inconsequential voices online, dictate how he lived. He did what he wanted when he wanted. Always had. But then he remembered how hard Millie was working—some of her emails were time-stamped after midnight her time—to salvage his tarnished reputation. He rubbed the back of his neck, slightly concerned, and feeling a little guilty that he might've handed her a poisoned chalice.

After Shanghai, he'd needed to retreat, to nurse his self-inflicted wounds, to mentally beat himself up in private. He'd put everything he and his team had been working for in jeopardy and had torpedoed his personal, private goal of being a better racer than Alex, the only competition he could win against his dead, seemingly perfect brother.

But the longer he was alone, the louder whispers of past failures, the brutal echoes of his father's harsh words and Alex's casual dismissal of his talent became. Sometimes solitude wasn't peace, and sometimes the only way to evade the past was to drown it in bars and clubs, pumping with too-loud music and shouted conversations.

So he'd gone to Lily's in London, and naturally he'd run into the press.

And Phoebe, who'd tried to renegotiate her way back into his bed. He'd sharply and succinctly shut her down. He'd told her when they first started sleeping together that he didn't make long-term connections, but she thought she could change his mind and that she would, eventually, take his name.

Not happening. Besides, being a De Rossi wasn't as marvellous as the world thought it was.

All his life, he'd been looked at through the Alex lens and been found lacking. As a result, he'd gone out of his way to be as different from his brother as he could be. And if you were always acting, then how could anyone get to know the real you? Any personal connections were false because nobody knew him.

On the surface, he had everything anyone could want: the houses, the money, the cars, the clothes…but no one to share them with. And that was how he liked it. He'd been his mum's kid, and after her death, neither his father nor his brother knew how to, or wanted to, handle a grieving child. They'd pushed him away, and he'd spent the rest of his childhood and teens desperately trying to catch up, to reach the ever-increasing bar they set for him. His only hope of beating his brother at anything was on the racetrack. Once he won his fourth championship, the world would have to admit that he was a better driver than Alex. In their eyes he'd never be as good a man. He'd never taint the De Rossi brand by telling the world who Alex really was, but he'd revel in being known as the better driver.

But he'd put that in jeopardy by losing his temper in Shanghai. He'd apologised and approved a short press statement publicly apologising to the rookie, the FIA and his fans. Millie's statement made him sound authentic without being obsequious. She'd also talked him into a press conference in—he glanced at his watch—an hour. The first since his crash and where he'd announce his community service plans and put forward the charities he'd be supporting.

He should be practising, talking, *breathing* cars. But he was now sitting on the sidelines.

Taz pulled his aviator sunglasses onto his face and jogged down the plane's steps to the waiting SUV. The driver opened the door, and he pulled back on seeing Millie sitting in the far corner, her face pale. She wore a brightly coloured patterned sleeveless sundress that hugged her curves. Her hair, as usual, was piled up on her head, and she'd smudged her eyeliner and mascara. She looked…beautiful.

And therein lay his other problem. For the last two weeks, he hadn't been able to stop thinking about their kiss, wishing that it had lasted longer, that he'd pushed for more. Her mouth had been sweet, her hair soft. Her perfume was light, and her fingers on his jaw and her hands on his body had felt so damn right.

He rubbed his hand over his jaw, thinking that recently Millie had come into proper focus for him. Oh, he'd been attracted to her from the moment he met her—he was a sucker for the combination of blue eyes and reddish-gold hair—but because of that and because she worked for him, he'd thrown up more shields than he usually did.

With Millie, lust and work collided, and it was as frustrating as hell. He wanted her, and that night, after one of the worst days in a long, long time, he'd lowered his control and given in to the temptation of kissing her. It had been better than he'd imagined, and he had a damn good imagination. He shook his head at his wayward thoughts as he climbed into the car. She worked for him and was off-limits.

'Millie? I didn't expect to see you here,' he said, shutting the door. He wondered when last she'd had a decent night's sleep. She looked…stressed. 'Everything okay?'

'Oh, I'm peachy,' she muttered. She glared at him. 'Could you not have stayed out of trouble for a couple of weeks, Taz?'

He was a grown man, someone who owned and operated a racing team and all its subsidiaries, a company worth billions. Nobody told him what to do or how to act. Especially someone whose salary he covered. Despite that, he enjoyed her annoyance, liked the way it pushed colour into her cheeks and the light of battle in her eyes. He knew she preferred negotiating to arguing, so he admired her attempt to venture out of her comfort zone.

'Lie low, I said. It wasn't that big an ask!'

Right, she'd run out of rope.

'Check your tone, Millie,' he suggested, keeping his voice low. He raised the privacy screen between them and the driver. 'Would you like to tell me—*calmly*—why you are angry?'

'You went to Lily's last night.' She pushed her iPad into his hands.

He didn't bother to look down. 'So?'

'The bad press was finally beginning to die down, but

your partying at Lily's last night has the press once again questioning your sincerity. There are over a dozen stories today, all insinuating that you aren't sorry, that having a good time is more important to you than racing and that you're not taking your career seriously.'

Racing was the only thing that meant anything to him. Taz ran his hand through his hair, his back teeth grinding. He wanted to justify his actions, something he never did. 'You told me to go out!'

'I meant for you to go for coffee or visit a friend! I did not say that you should go to Gossip Central!'

He struggled to hold on to his temper, knowing he wouldn't bother if this was anyone other than Millie. What was it about this woman that had him checking his words and reining in his temper? Why her? And why, for God's sake, now?

'I got to Lily's shortly after eleven. I'd been working, and I couldn't sleep. So I went out. I went into the VIP section where I had two whiskies and then left.'

'Phoebe was there.'

Taz clenched his uninjured hand.

'She's quoted as saying that you've lost your interest in racing and that you have a temper. And she's seen you lose it. She tossed gas on the already-fiery press reports.'

Taz gripped the bridge of his nose and closed his eyes. He could *not* catch a break. After last night's hopefully final last rejection, he could see Phoebe lashing out. But insinuating he'd lost his temper with her? That was low.

Would this drama ever end? And why did he feel so unbalanced? Was it because he wanted Millie to believe he was better than he was portrayed? And why was he worried about what she thought?

She was nothing like his usual women; she was grounded

and down to earth. Impatient with nonsense. He liked her. More than he liked most people. But this conversation proved that she, like everyone else, couldn't see him clearly. Perhaps her astute observation back in China that there was nothing between him and Meredith had been a fluke.

He felt irrationally disappointed.

'Look, I know it's nonsense, but the world doesn't.'

Her words doused the fire under his temper, and a measure of calm returned.

'I'll admit I'm impatient when things don't go my way or when my orders are not followed. But I have never, ever lost my temper with a woman.' He never cared enough to expend that amount of energy. He nodded at her iPad, resentful at having to explain. 'I ended it, permanently, at the beginning of the season. She's now stirring the pot, unhappy because I rejected her again last night.'

'She wants you back?'

He lifted one shoulder and shrugged. 'Phoebe doesn't take no for an answer. Last night's *no* was final and emphatic. She understood that, was angry and wanted her revenge.' Last night he couldn't help comparing Phoebe to Millie, and the ex-model came up very short. How? He didn't know. He couldn't define his attraction to Millie, but it didn't make it less potent.

'By calling tabloid journalists at midnight?'

Calling? He smiled at her naïveté. 'She just needed to walk outside the club, a bunch of them were outside. They shouted questions at me, but I ignored them. They would've asked her about me, and angry because I rejected her, she probably vented to them.'

Millie looked out of the window as they travelled down the highway to the purpose-built temporary circuit around the Hard Rock Stadium in Miami Gardens.

'I've never worked for anyone standing in such a bright spotlight,' she murmured. She looked at him, and he caught the confusion in her eyes. 'Being your press liaison officer was easy, but this is a high-profile campaign.'

Great, now he was a campaign. 'Maybe you should hire someone with more experience,' she said, biting her sexy bottom lip.

This again? How many more times would he have to explain? 'Millie, I could hire anyone I wanted, the best PR company in the world. I do not want them, I want *you*.'

He couldn't move past the thought that no one would do a better job than her. It was a gut reaction, and his intuition had yet to steer him wrong.

Their eyes clashed and held, and awareness slid into all her purple-blue gaze. Intuition and work aside, did she know how much he craved her? In his bed, under him, in the most primal way possible. Her curly hair spread over his pillow, hearing her pants as he pleasured her, lathing her pale skin with his tongue, tracing the contours of her curves with his teeth. Her eyes widened, and she touched her top lip with the tip of her tongue, a wholly subconscious reaction. He was experienced enough to know she was as attracted to him as he was to her, but she needed to make sense of what she was feeling.

Lust was lust, a basic diving force. It didn't have to mean anything. A clash of pheromones and chemistry, it frequently didn't. There was no need to make it more than it was. But Millie, he suspected, was someone who dissected it from every angle, to make sense of what she was feeling. Her brain would make her body-related decisions. And that meant he wouldn't see her naked anytime soon.

Dammit.

He shoved away his lusty thoughts and told himself to

concentrate on business. He'd promoted her because she saw *him*, not the owner or the driver but the man he was, more clearly than anyone had before. That was worth *everything*.

'You were my press liaison officer and now you're my PR person,' he told her, getting back to the subject. 'I expect you to do your job.'

She released a long sigh. Millie chose her battles, which suited him fine. He didn't like people arguing with him; he preferred they did it his way the first time he asked. 'It would be helpful if your ex would stop stirring the pot,' she muttered. 'Would you consider—'

No. There was no chance he'd ask Phoebe to shut up. He wasn't going to open a shut door. 'People will think what they think, and I don't care. I only care what they think about my team and my racing, my abilities as a driver. Everything else is superfluous.'

Focusing on his racing was how he managed to stumble through those years after Alex's death and then his father's. Sorting through the legalities and establishing his right to the De Rossi assets had taken some time and a chunk of money. His dad's will stated that Alex was to inherit *everything*, and because he hadn't made a new will yet in anticipation of his marriage, Alex had left everything to him. If had Alex had died after their father's death, it would've been a simple process, but it happened the other way around. It took the hiring of expensive lawyers to establish he was the rightful heir to the De Rossi assets. Knowing Matteo hadn't wanted him to have even the smallest slice of the De Rossi empire had been, and still was, acid in an open wound.

When he won a fourth championship, the world would see him as successful in his own right. It was, after all, something neither his father nor his brother had managed to achieve. He'd be seen as himself, and not a reflection of his brother and father. It would be *his* achievement, untainted by the old resentments and harsh memories.

He'd vowed to himself that this season would be drama-free. He'd all but stopped bar-hopping and partying, and it was bad luck that on two of the few occasions he'd been out at clubs, he'd met up with Meredith and Phoebe. Did the gods of good PR have it in for him?

'Tell me about the charities you've short-listed for me to support,' he asked, placing his ankle on his knee. Millie ran through the charities and gave a brief explanation of what they did. Within ten minutes, they'd decided on him lending his support to five organisations: attending a polo cross tournament this weekend, a golf tournament, a ball, a garden party and a cocktail party. Five charities over six weeks.

Millie tapped her pen against her lips, lips he desperately wanted to kiss. 'It's a pity you don't have a decent, nice girlfriend, someone who can accompany you to these events.'

'I've been doing solo events for years now,' he pointed out.

'But a pretty girl in a pretty dress, someone who isn't known for getting into arguments and being confrontational, would be helpful.' She nodded at his phone. 'Do you know any women like that?'

It was true that he preferred women who were a little edgy.

Millie was anything but edgy. But something about her called to him, and if the chemistry crackling between them translated to the sheets, sex would be explosive.

She works for you, De Rossi. That would be a stupid move.

'Well?' Right, she'd asked him a question. What was it again? Did he know any nice women? Of course he did: the wives or girlfriends of fellow drivers, and his senior staff.

It was true, men liked to party with bad girls, but they invariably married good girls. Not that marriage was something he'd consider. The De Rossi brand was his wife and mistress and took up all his time. And best of all, it didn't talk back or act out. And he didn't have to consider its feelings or opinions.

'I know *you*.'

Their eyes collided, but Millie waved his words away. 'Anyone else but me? Anyone you can ask to be your plus-one?'

As the person responsible for rehabilitating his image, she was going to be accompanying him everywhere he went for the next six weeks anyway. Why deal with the hassle of having to make nice with someone else when she could do the job? '*You* can be my date.'

She stared at him, then laughed. 'Yeah, right,' she scoffed.

Annoyance spiked. Was she denigrating him or herself? Both rankled. 'And why not?'

'Firstly, because I am the last woman in the world you would date,' she told him. 'I'm not your *type*.'

There was a note of desperation in her voice, tinged by resignation. And she wasn't being coy.

'But you are, on the surface, nice and normal, and you are pretty,' he countered, using her words against her.

She frowned. '*On the surface?* What does that mean?'

He narrowed his eyes, intrigued by the glimpse of deeper layers beneath the surface. She had secrets, and he wanted to know what they were. Surprising, since he normally never cared. Neither could he tell her that when he got her naked, he simply knew she'd turn wild in his arms. He chose to ignore her question, knowing she wasn't ready to hear what he wanted to do to her in bed.

You have enough problems without adding bedding Millie to the long list, De Rossi. Get your head in the game.

'You are going to be everywhere I am,' he stated. 'It would be far easier if you acted as my date.' If he asked anyone else to be his date, there'd be complications, expectations he wasn't willing to meet. He'd have to entertain her beyond the events and navigate a minefield of raised hopes and assumptions. But Millie? Millie was easy. As long as he kept everything surface-level—and he would—she could play the role of his date, then slip back into her role as his PR person when the event was over. No drama, no fuss, no strings.

Having Millie as his date wasn't just convenient, it was safe. Predictable. And Taz needed a little predictable. And some easy. 'Millie, it makes sense.'

'To you, maybe,' Millie retorted. 'I stay in the background, Taz. It's what I do. I don't make headlines, I *spin* them. I couldn't think of anything worse than standing in the limelight next to you.'

Her words made a sharper cut than expected, and he mentally flinched. He knew too well how it felt to stand in someone else's shadow. He'd spent a lifetime trying—and failing—to be worthy of his father's praise, and as much time coming to terms with the con job Alex had pulled on the world.

Or maybe somewhere deep inside him, in those places he rarely visited and never acknowledged, he wanted her or someone like her to be proud to stand next to him, proud to be with him, to think that the sun and moon rose with him.

Not because he was Taz De Rossi, Formula One driver and team owner, not for the fame and wealth that came as effortlessly as some of his track wins. But for the man he wanted to be. The man beneath the façade.

But it was senseless, and pointless, to think that way, and he wasn't a stupid man. The world didn't work that way. It ran on transactions, and he was a brilliant negotiator. 'How much?' he bluntly asked.

'How much for what?' she asked, confused.

He snapped his fingers, impatient. 'For you to act as my girlfriend,' he clarified.

'You're offering to *pay* me to date you?'

Why not? He had an obscene amount of money and could afford it. And she was right, having a sensible girlfriend would look good as he stepped into his temporary role as a brand ambassador, as someone there to attract interest in the charity.

'If I invited someone else, I'd have to pay for her flights, her hotel room, her food and probably her clothes. I'm already paying those costs for you. You'd need clothes, cocktail dresses and some ball gowns, some designer outfits... Stop frowning, I'll pay for the clothes you'd wear while acting as my date.'

'I'm not going to *be* your date!' Millie's voice rose as they turned into the business entrance to the track.

'Five hundred thousand pounds.'

Her mouth dropped open, and she shook her head. 'Seven fifty?' he offered. He could carry on inching his way upwards. He was still in petty cash territory.

Millie stared out the window, her shoulders up to her ears and her cheeks cherry red. 'It was your idea,' he pointed out.

'I never thought *I* would be the star of the show,' she shot back.

'You won't be,' he told her, fighting his amusement. 'That's my job. You would be there to provide a little additional sensible sparkle.'

'You're off your head,' Millie told him as the car pulled

to a stop in front of the area allocated to the De Rossi entourage.

Maybe. 'Well, it's you or nobody,' he told her, reaching for the door-handle. He'd learned how to negotiate when he was a kid with his taciturn, ungenerous father, and he'd honed his skills since then. Everyone had a number, and he'd find Millie's. Florida heat and humidity rolled into the car. 'Seven hundred and fifty thousand pounds for acting as my girlfriend at five events isn't a bad deal, Millie.'

'I think your Shanghai crash addled your brain,' Millie told him, shoving her iPad and phone into her enormous tote bag.

'Is that a *yes*?' he asked, looking back at her from outside the car.

She pushed her hand through her wayward curls. 'It's an *I'll think about it.*'

Taz swallowed his grin, knowing he had her. Nobody *thought* about such a big offer. She'd say yes because it would be the easiest money she'd ever make. And the best he'd ever spend.

Because Millie, for some reason that eluded him, was the only person he could see himself spending any time with. She was smart, down to earth and surprisingly sassy.

But she was also dangerous.

He hauled in a deep breath, reminding himself that he was Taz De Rossi and that he could easily resist her. He'd walked away from princesses and principal dancers, actors and models without a backward glance, and he wouldn't allow himself to fall under the spell of his down to earth press officer.

And even on the off-chance he did, he was an F1 driver, the best around, and he regularly danced with danger. He knew exactly how to exit any situation unscathed.

CHAPTER SIX

THE DRIVER PULLED into the parking area close to the entrance for VIP passes and pulled to a stop, letting the car idle. Millie gathered her possessions along with her thoughts and prepared to exit the car. Three-quarters of a million pounds? Had she heard him correctly? Just for acting as his girlfriend? That was…

Madness. He was joking…right?

Instead of climbing out of his side of the vehicle, which was on the right side of the entrance, Taz followed her out of her door, took her laptop bag out of her hand and slung it over his shoulder. She heard the roar of the fans gathered outside as they recognised Taz.

Millie looked over to the crowds and the waiting press, cameras in hand. She tipped her head in their direction. 'You've got fans watching you and cameras pointed your way. Try to smile.'

She wanted to discuss his wild offer, but there were too many ears around, too many eyes on them. When she was next alone with him, she'd sit and explain why she couldn't do it, why that wasn't possible.

There were seven hundred and fifty thousand reasons why it could be possible. The money aside—she could donate it to the trust she'd set up in Ben's name—*why wasn't it possible?* And why did the voice asking sound like Ben?

You crashed out of my life. You don't have an opinion anymore, she crossly told him.

You keep saying you want to figure out who you are, where you fit...

I don't fit in, Ben.

Millie scrunched up her nose and shuffled on her feet. That was what she told herself when Ben invited her to join him at Monaco or Silverstone. Not fitting in and knowing how to handle their rich world was also how her parents justified leaving her alone when they jetted off on holidays to places like Monte Carlo and Ibiza, Jamaica and Rio.

That was then, this is now. How do you know if you don't fit if you don't try?

What if I embarrass him?

Dead Ben actually scoffed. *Taz isn't easily embarrassed, and do you think he'd ask you if that was a concern? When it comes to women, Taz is a picky bastard.*

And yes, her ego just doubled at the idea of playing Taz's girlfriend. Millie placed a hand on her jittery stomach and reminded herself of what was important. She was trying to figure out who she was and where she was going, how she was going to navigate the rest of her life, but she wouldn't be able to do that standing on the sidelines. Taz was offering her a way to step into Ben's world, her parents' world.

Of all the ways she imagined coming to terms with her past, with Ben's death, with her parents and her lack of confidence, she never thought she'd be acting as Taz's girlfriend when she did it. Her parents had practiced smiles and knew how to stand, when to answer press questions and when to appear mysterious. Taz played by a different set of rules, mostly because he was rich and powerful enough to make them up as he went along. But she was just an ordinary woman living an ordinary life; she wasn't rich, famous, important or charismatic. She far preferred to stay away from the lenses of any cameras, to live a quiet life.

If she took Taz up on his offer, she'd be thrust into the spotlight and would have the eyes of the world on her. She was, as she'd been told a million times, not cut out to stand in the limelight. She wasn't even sure she was cut out to do PR. Sometimes her insecurities, fed by a lifetime of her parents' criticism, threatened to overwhelm her.

Also, accepting his offer was tantamount to inviting her family back into her life. They would barrel back in, blithely ignoring the past and their inattention and neglect. They'd insert themselves into her life, playing at being one big happy family, all the while desperately hoping her relationship with Taz would raise their own public profile. Her parents were publicity parasites.

No, she couldn't risk that happening...

Millie frowned, annoyed by her reaction. Why was she allowing her parents to influence her decision? Wasn't she trying to break that habit? Taz was offering her a way to explore whether the messages she received and believed as a child and teenager, that she wasn't good enough or that she was an embarrassment and didn't fit in, were true. If she managed to navigate the wealthy, sophisticated world that Taz was so comfortable in, she could rewrite the criticisms she'd been fed and swallowed. Believed. And if her parents swooped in? What would she do then? Millie released a long breath, feeling overwhelmed. She could cross that bridge if and when it came to that. First, she needed to decide whether posing as Taz's girlfriend was something she wanted to do.

It was a lot of money to turn down. With three-quarters of a million, she could make a difference in many people's lives and do it in Ben's name. How could she pass that opportunity up? She couldn't, could she?

But this wasn't the time to make rash decisions. She'd consider his offer later; right now she needed to work. She hurried to catch up with Taz's long-legged stride to the entrance to the track. 'Your press conference will take place in the press room shortly. The journalists will quiz you on your actions in Shanghai and will have questions about your injuries. And I can carry my laptop bag.'

'I've got it, and you sent me an email briefing me about today's press conference. It's fine.'

She braked, not sure she'd heard him correctly. She'd expected him to moan and complain about sitting down for a Q and A. 'Right, good.' She squinted at him. 'Did you hear what I said?'

He gave her a quick eye-roll. 'I'm not deaf. And if we don't keep moving, we are going to be swarmed.'

Fans and members of the press corps started drifting in their direction, and Millie started to walk, battling to keep up with Taz's pace. The noise level intensified as they approached the crowd that stood between them and the turnstiles that would allow them access to the paddock. Millie glanced up at Taz, whose sunglasses covered his startling eyes. A fan asked him to pose for a photograph, and Taz—notorious for ploughing his way through crowds—stopped to take the selfie, then another one. What was happening here? Then, to make things even stranger, he grabbed her hand and threaded his fingers through hers.

She tried to tug her hand away: He was going to give everyone the wrong impression, and that was a headache neither of them needed. If he'd let go of her hand, she could slip behind the crowd, swipe her pass and wait on the other side of the paddock.

A journalist pointed his camera at their linked hands. 'Are you in a relationship with your press liaison officer, Taz?' he demanded, his eyebrows raised.

Taz looked down at their hands but didn't release the clasp. 'You know I never answer questions about my personal relationships.'

Millie tugged her hand out of his, and when he looked at her, she motioned to the turnstile. 'I need my hand to get my pass out of my bag,' she hissed.

Taz pushed his sunglasses into his hair and caught the eye of one of the security guards manning the turnstiles. 'Can you let us through, Juan?'

The turnstiles clicked open, and Millie stumbled into the paddock, still feeling the heat of Taz's palm on hers. She watched as he casually pushed his hands into the pockets of his pants, and she caught the corners of his mouth lifting.

'You did that on purpose!' she shout-whispered, as they walked to the De Rossi section of the paddock.

Taz greeted a driver and shook hands with another. After answering a question about his hand from another team owner, he looked down at Millie. 'I didn't want to lose you in the crowd,' he told her.

What nonsense! There weren't that many people on this side of the fence, and she could've easily dodged them if he'd let her go. No, he was trying to manipulate her into acting as his girlfriend and thought by creating the perception, she'd bend.

It was something her parents would do, had done. Like Taz, they never took no for an answer. 'I won't be pressurised into acting as your girlfriend, Tazio De Rossi' she told him, surprised at her vehemence. And, maybe, a little proud of herself. It was about time she was able to stick up for herself.

He stopped, pulled her out of the way and folded his arms. 'What do you have to lose?' he asked, keeping his voice low, intimate, a hint of a challenge in it. 'You're going to be spending the next six weeks with me anyway. Why not get an extra million for holding my hand and looking at me in a somewhat adoring manner?'

He'd increased his offer again. The mind boggled at what he was offering, thinking of all the things she could do with that kind of money, like how she could fund Ben's dream of training talented underprivileged teen racers. But she needed to keep thinking clearly. 'Everyone will think I am unprofessional mixing business and pleasure,' Millie shot back.

'Everyone knows I am difficult to work with. They are already impressed you've stuck it out this long,' Taz responded wryly. 'Most of my press liaison officers barely last the week, never mind two months. They certainly don't get promoted.'

He wasn't wrong that this could help people see he wasn't the man they thought he was. She was also trying to step out of her comfort zone, to do things that challenged her, be less like her ultra-cautious self. *You're mad if you don't take him up on his offer, squirt.*

Ben's voice was so clear, she could swear that if she turned she would see him standing there.

Be brave, take a chance.

She stomped her foot and released a low hiss of frustration. She had Ben's voice in her ear, and if she said no, she felt she'd be letting him, as well as herself, down.

'Is that a *yes*?' Taz asked.

Millie scowled at him. 'A million. A third now, a third in three weeks, the balance at the end of six weeks.'

Taz dared to grin at her. The blasted man never doubted

the outcome of his proposal. What was it like being so certain all the time, so convinced that the dominoes of life would fall in line for you?

'Deal.'

Millie thrust her hand at him, expecting him to shake it and was caught off guard when Taz clasped her fingers and lifted them to his lips. She shivered, and ribbons of heat and light darted down her fingers and up her arm. Damn the man for being so sexy, and relentlessly charming. 'Excellent.'

He wrapped his uninjured hand around hers and tugged her toward the De Rossi section of the paddock. 'I'm expecting a decent turnout for the press conference,' Millie said.

'I'm Taz De Rossi, and they've been baying for one. They'll be there,' Taz stated with complete conviction. 'They wouldn't miss it.'

Oh, to be so self-assured. But he was right, as they'd been flooding her email and phone requesting interviews or asking for a comment. 'I have a draft statement I'm still working on. I'll get it to you within thirty minutes,' she told him, very conscious of her hand in his. People started noticing, their eyes darting to their linked hands and their eyebrows rising. Five minutes in and she already felt like a goldfish in a too-small bowl.

'I'll look at it, but expect changes,' Taz stated, pushing her ahead of him as they walked into the area allocated to the De Rossi Racing team. Of course he would change what she wrote, because Taz never did what was expected of him. Millie watched as members of his technical team approached him.

Taz squeezed her hand before letting it go. 'Text me when you've finished with my statement, and we can go over it. If I'm not in the pit, find me.'

Millie nodded and watched him walk away, surrounded by his people, everyone wanting something from him. She'd been swept up into Taz's world, into the maelstrom he created. He was taking her acceptance to be his fake girlfriend as a given.

And she was, probably, going to let him.

And if she found herself floundering in choppy, unfamiliar waters, she had no one to blame but herself.

Taz, sitting alone at the long table, a raft of microphones in front of him, tapped his finger on the white linen tablecloth and schooled his expression into what he hoped would pass for pleasantness. He was a pro at press conferences; they were a necessary evil, but there were better ways to spend his time.

Taz sneaked a look at his watch and sighed. They were running ten minutes late, mostly because members of the press were still trying to get into the now-packed room. Millie stood in the corner to the right of him, her iPad clutched, as it frequently was, to her chest.

Unfazed by the eyes on him, he saw Millie staring at a spot on the floor, the corner of her lip caught between her teeth. Her shoulders were an inch from her ears, and he knew she was second-guessing herself and him. He lounged in his chair, wearing his usual mask of detachment, pretending to scroll through his phone.

He had a girlfriend. He grimaced at the childish term; it didn't suit him, a man who'd spent his life avoiding emotional entanglements. His career was his greatest love, the only mistress he ever needed. He was doing this to benefit his company, to bolster his brand. Dating Millie was a strategic move to repair his image, to keep his fans, sponsors and the media focused on what mattered: his path to his fourth championship. After a few weeks, everything would go back to normal. Or whatever passed for normal in his world.

Tension crawled up his spine, and he told himself to relax. This wasn't a big deal. But it was, because this was Millie. The same Millie he kept imagining naked beneath him—or on top of him because, honestly, he wasn't picky—her skin flushed with pleasure, her breathless moans in his ear.

He wanted Millie almost as much as he wanted that fourth consecutive championship. A sliver of self-doubt slid under his skin. What had he gotten himself into? And why did the thought of being with her thrill him? Racing was his world. Winning his satisfaction. Yet here he was, his thoughts on a woman he employed. A woman he was paying an obscene amount of money to hold his hand and play a part.

Maybe if he banged his head against the table hard enough, he'd knock some sense into himself. But then again, maybe not.

'Ladies and gentlemen, Taz De Rossi will now read a statement, after which we will take a set number of questions.'

Right, he was up. After pushing his hand through his hair, he looked down at the statement Millie had carefully prepared. *Off his game, irritable, the rookie should've slowed down while navigating the corner. The strain of driving and owning a team had caught up with him...*

It was a raft of excuses for his questionable behaviour, and he knew the press corps would lap it up. It was also all BS. He picked up the statement and scrunched it into a ball. Noticing the surprise on the faces of the journalists directly in front of him, he almost smiled.

'I could sit here and give you a dozen excuses about my behaviour in Shanghai, tell you how stressed I am, how the demands of owning a team and being its number one driver got to me last Saturday. I could tell you that...' He looked at Millie amused by her shocked expression. But was that horror or approval he saw in her eyes? A mixture of both? 'But I'm not going to. The truth is that I lost focus on that race, my mind wasn't completely on my driving. Jackson did nothing wrong, the blame for what happened in Shanghai should be placed on me.'

Oh, well, he'd stepped into the hurricane, so he might as well see if he could ride his way out of it.

'I have apologised to Jackson personally. I'd also like to apologise to the sponsors and my fans.' He lifted his cast-covered arm. 'I am paying for my stupidity, as I should.'

The silence in the room was absolute, and all he could hear was the scratching of pens on paper and the occasional cough from a reporter at the back of the room. The rebel in him enjoyed their shocked silence.

'You know I was given the punishment of community service by the FIA stewards,' he said. Should he mention Alex's philanthropic efforts? No, he was not going to invite them to make comparisons between his brother and himself. They would do that anyway, without his help. And, as always, he'd probably come up short.

'I intend to complete that service by working with five charities until my injuries are healed, hoping to shine a spotlight on what they do.' He went on to name the charities, giving a brief description of the organisations' work. 'You can find links to all the charities on the De Rossi website, and if you can, please donate. Any amount is helpful and would be gratefully received.'

'I will be at all the races, supporting my team and, hopefully, not driving them too crazy.'

That statement elicited a laugh. 'I'll take a few questions now.'

A wave of questions rolled over him as the journalists shouted over each other.

He glanced over at Millie, and she gave him an encouraging smile. Surprisingly, it instantly dropped his irritation levels. Strange, because no one ever made him feel like that before.

'Can you tell us how you felt when Jackson nudged you in Shanghai?'

God give him strength. This? Again? 'As I've said, twice now, my behaviour was unacceptable. I'm not going to rehash it again.' He couldn't keep the annoyance out of his voice.

How much longer was he supposed to endure this? He glanced at his watch. He'd give them a few more minutes, and then he'd leave.

'Are you worried about losing championship points?'

Of course he was; he wasn't an idiot. If his nearest rival won all the races he'd miss, they'd be level on the board. It made him furious to think that he'd wasted that lead because he'd lost his temper. That he was the disappointment his father believed him to be. Had called him such to his face on numerous occasions.

Thinking back, he preferred his father insulting him than ignoring him: At least he could be bothered to interact with him. But those stretches when he was consistently disregarded or dismissed were worse. They were right. Bad attention was better than no attention at all. Being made to feel insignificant and unimportant was far more dangerous to the psyche than being told you were bad.

In his father's eyes, the world's eyes, Alex had been as perfect as a human could be. Handsome, intelligent, charming, nice…he had it all so Matteo hadn't hedged his bets or spread his attention. Everything he wanted in a son he had in Alex.

'You seemed quite chummy with your press liaison. Something happening between you?'

It took Taz a moment to make sense of the question. When he did, he leaned back in his chair and placed his hands on his thighs, his fingertips digging into the fabric of his pants. He made sure his expression remained unruffled. 'You know I never answer questions about my personal life.'

'Is Phoebe still on the scene?' the reporter persisted. 'Are you going to the Caribbean with her?'

Damn, the urge to launch himself across the table and punch the smirking journalist was strong. But he hauled in a breath—he'd done enough damage lately. This line of questioning grated more than usual. Normally he shrugged such queries off and gave them no more thought.

It was because the journalist had mentioned Millie. His instinct to protect her left him reeling. When she appeared with him at the polo tournament on Saturday, she would be on everyone's radar, something he wanted, *needed* if he was going to ride out this media storm. The press would focus on them and would blow the smallest interaction into a drama. It was part of dating a celebrity, of being seen with him.

Taz pushed a hand into his hair. What would it be like to have someone standing in his corner, providing support for no extraneous reason?

He brushed his thoughts away. He wouldn't know what to do with a serious girlfriend—or how to handle her. It wasn't for him, never had been. Trust wasn't something he could do on a long-term basis.

Millie was different—interesting and funny—but she

was his employee and would be playing a part while she handled his PR. This was a business deal.

And because it was business, he had to stop thinking of her as a potential lover, someone he wanted in his bed. He was aware of the power imbalance: He held it all, and he had to tread carefully through this minefield. Had to play the game, get this deception underway—and draw on every bit of his willpower to keep his hands to himself.

'Taz? *Taz?*'

He jerked, his attention returning to the curious faces in front of him. He turned up his cuffs, pushed back his hair again and cleared his throat 'I didn't hear your question. Would you mind repeating it?' he asked, thinking that he was being a great deal more polite than he wanted to be.

'Are you and Phoebe still on track for that Caribbean getaway?'

He let out a slow breath, and turned toward Millie, pulling up a smile he hoped was both affectionate and intimate. His gaze locked onto hers, and he caught the flicker of panic she couldn't quite hide.

Better to rip the bandage off. Brutal, clean. Yes, this was an ambush, but this way he could take control of the narrative. Control was everything. Besides, it was time for her to start earning her million pounds.

'Ladies and gentlemen,' he began, keeping his tone smooth, 'allow me to introduce Millie James. Not only does she manage my PR, but she's also my significant other.' He let that land, enjoying the shocked gasps followed by stunned silence. 'Our relationship is still new, but we both agree it holds a lot of promise.'

The crowd in front of him gaped, and he handed them a wry smile. 'I'd ask you to respect our privacy, but let's be honest—that's not going to happen, is it?'

He rose to his feet, the scrape of the chair on the floor the only sound in the room. Then, taking his time, keeping it casual, he crossed the room to Millie. He cupped her cheek with one hand and brushed his mouth over hers—keeping the kiss soft, but deliberately possessive. He swallowed her shocked gasp, and her fingers trembled as he laced their fingers together.

'Let's go,' he murmured against her ear before pulling her toward the exit. The room behind them erupted with shouted questions, some laughter and the general chaos that followed the detonation of a conversational landmine. He didn't care.

As always, he'd accomplished exactly what he'd set out to do.

CHAPTER SEVEN

LATER THAT NIGHT, Millie left the second bedroom in the hotel suite—apparently sharing a suite was part of the devil's deal she'd agreed to—and crossed the lounge area to the streamlined galley kitchen, hoping to find some hot chocolate. If she could find whisky, she'd add a slug, hoping the liquor would help her get a few hours of sleep.

She'd been prepared to return to her own hotel room, but Taz had other ideas. When he'd ordered her to move into his suite, she'd protested—loudly and quite vehemently—but he wouldn't budge.

'Are you looking to give the press a story?' he'd demanded. 'The world expects us to share a suite. *I* expect us to share the suite.'

He ended their discussion by calling an intern to arrange the collection of her belongings and move them to this suite twenty floors up.

This was the first time she'd shared a living space with a man, and Millie would've felt uncomfortable with a non-celebrity, someone normal. Sharing a fantastically expensive suite with Taz, incredibly famous and ridiculously good-looking, felt surreal.

How was she supposed to handle this? Handle him?

Dressed in loose and comfortable pink-striped pyjamas,

she heated some milk and tried to loosen the tension in her shoulders and neck.

It had been a long day, and she'd have a longer one tomorrow...or was that later today? Either way, she had a raft of meetings, including an appointment with the stylist Taz kept on retainer. He was flying in from New York courtesy of Taz's private jet, with a vast range of clothes, shoes and accessories in her size. She and Taz had agreed that, while she was on the track, she'd stick to black jeans, her hightops and De Rossi–branded shirts, but when she accompanied Taz to his charity appearances, she needed to look like someone he'd date.

Sophisticated, cool, at ease.

Everything she was not.

Millie dashed a shot of expensive whisky into her drink and walked back into the lounge area, dropping to sit on a too-low backless couch in front of the floor-to-ceiling windows. The lights of Miami spread out before her, and she wished she could head down to South Beach, take in the Art Deco buildings, and experience some street food.

As Taz's press liaison, she'd been able to fade into the background, slipping around the press coterie with nobody noticing. But as Taz De Rossi's *girlfriend*—his brand new, unexpected and highly scrutinised girlfriend—she couldn't take a step without having a press pack on her heels. They were a bunch of hyenas, looking for an angle, hoping for a soundbite as they shoved microphones in her face. They made her feel disoriented and exposed.

She'd seen the pictures from the press conference earlier, which were now online, and she barely recognised herself. Wide-eyed and pale, she looked like a terrified deer frozen in the headlights of a sixteen-wheeler truck. Young. Vulnerable. Out of her depth.

Being with Taz wasn't for the faint-hearted. But she wasn't a child anymore, and if she was going to survive this, she had to find some courage and learn how to play the game. And she didn't have any time to waste.

Taz's reputation and a million pounds were at stake...

It was so much money. While he was alive, Ben quietly sponsored up-and-coming racers, and after his death Millie had established a charity in his name to continue that tradition. After the courts had told Ben's parents that she was his legitimate heir, Millie moved the many millions she inherited from Ben to the charity's account. Eight or so years later, she still got a kick knowing there were drivers on the F3 circuit who wouldn't be there had the charity not stepped in to help. Ben, she knew, would approve. After all, it had been his dream. She'd also inherited his London flat and a car, so she didn't need the money that Taz was paying her. She planned to donate that to Ben's charity as well.

It seemed the right thing to do.

And for a million pounds she could and would fake confidence, channel sophistication and play the part of Taz's perfect girlfriend.

But with publicity came the risk of her parents sliding back into her life to take advantage of her and her newly acquired fame. How long would it take for her parents to hear about her dating Taz? Not long, she decided. They'd quickly find a way to leverage her connection to Taz. What form would that take? Would they fly into Miami? Start dropping his name everywhere they went? Sell their story to a tabloid on the flimsiest of pretexts? When it came to her parents, truth never stood in the way of good publicity. That was part of the reason she'd stayed away all these years. She didn't want that life. It had damaged her already.

A part of her wanted to call it quits, to retreat, but then

she'd lose the chance to find herself in this world that Ben
had been such a huge part of.

And wasn't she done, or trying to be done, with allowing her parents to influence how she lived her life? Millie
heard the snick of an opening door. She turned, sucking in a
sharp breath when she saw Taz step into the lounge, nude but
for the cast of his wrist and a pair of black sleeping shorts.

His chest was incredible—broad, lightly dusted with dark
hair, and tapering to a stomach showcasing his defined six-
pack. Every inch of him, from his thickly muscled shoulders
to his strong, sinewy arms and long, sculpted legs, screamed
raw, masculine power. He was, quite frankly, a work of art
wrapped in impossibly tempting packaging.

Her mouth went dry looking at him, so she took a hurried sip of her hot chocolate, hoping it might restore a little
moisture and distract her from the bedroom-based thoughts
racing through her mind.

The expensive whisky made her catch her breath, and
she spluttered.

'Millie?' he asked, in a rough-with-sleep voice. 'It's after
two. What are you doing up?'

She lifted her cup. 'I couldn't sleep so I made myself
something to drink. I hope you don't mind.'

He ran a hand through his messy hair. 'That's fine.'

She grimaced. 'I also helped myself to what I think is
very good whisky. Whisky that isn't meant to be added to
hot chocolate.'

He walked over to her, taking the mug from her hands.
He sipped and grimaced. 'I'll have a whisky without the
hot chocolate.'

'Want me to get it for you?' she asked. They might both
be in their sleepwear, but she did work for him.

'I've got it.'

Millie tried not to react when Taz sat next to her, heat rolling off his body. She thought about asking him to put on a T-shirt, but then he'd know she'd noticed his body. No, it was better to keep her eyes on the lights of this amazing city spread out in front of them.

'Are you in pain?' she asked, wondering why he was awake.

Out of the corner of her eye, she saw his shoulder lift and fall. 'It's more annoying than uncomfortable.'

'Why can't you sleep?' he asked, lifting the heavy crystal tumbler to his lips.

It was her turn to shrug. 'I've got a lot on my mind.' She was still trying to wrap her head around everything that had happened today.

'Maybe we should talk about how we are going to act when we are together at these charity events,' she said, placing her mug on the floor at her feet. Along with backless couches, the decorators responsible for these expensive suites didn't like side tables either.

Sometimes less was less. And impractical.

'I'm not a fan of standing in the spotlight. I don't enjoy having eyes on me,' Millie said, biting the inside of her cheek.

Taz leaned back on his elbows and looked at her. It took all her willpower to keep her eyes on his gorgeous face and not take a lazy stroll down his fantastic body. *He's your boss, Millie. Half-dressed boss and a short-term fake boyfriend, but you can't forget that he is your boss.*

'How do you think we should act, Millie?'

She didn't know. That was why she was asking him. She threw her hands up in the air. 'Are you going to hold my hand, put your arm around me…?' She wanted to ask him whether he'd kiss her too, but her tongue wouldn't form the words.

He looked at his glass, frowning when he saw it was empty. Grateful for the reprieve, Millie snatched it from his hand, walked over to the small bar and poured him another two-fingered shot. 'Should you be drinking this with painkillers?' she asked him, handing it over. Their fingers brushed and electricity erupted on her skin. Dammit. With everything else that was happening in her life, why did she have to be so attracted to the man as well?

'Well?'

She frowned at Taz. 'Well, what?'

'How do you know what standing in the spotlight feels like? Are you an influencer or the aristocratic daughter of an earl? The girlfriend of someone famous?'

'Ha, no. As if.' But he wasn't too far from the bull's-eye. Should she tell him who her parents were? It hadn't occurred to her before, but perhaps he deserved to know who he was getting involved with.

He leaned forward, rested his arms on his thighs and dangled his hand holding his glass between his legs. 'How do you *know*?'

He wasn't going to drop the subject. If nothing else, she should tell him about Ben, before he found out via someone else. Secrets were difficult to keep in any workplace. 'I'm the daughter and niece of pretty famous actors.' She gave him their stage names and recited some of their popular roles.

Taz frowned, his razor-sharp mind making connections. 'I met them, years ago. Through Ben Brennan.'

It didn't take long for him to connect the dots to Ben. Would the final piece slot into place? His gaze sharpened. 'You're related to Ben, aren't you?'

'He was my cousin and, in many ways, my protector and my best friend growing up.' Millie sighed. 'Our parents, both sets, love attention. If there's a camera, they want to be in the shot. I was dragged to art galleries and show openings and premières and made to pose. I never could, not in the flattering way they wanted me to, and the photos with me in them always bombed. They eventually decided it was easier to leave me and Ben at home with our nanny. My mum and his mother are twins and share *everything*.'

'That sounds ominous.'

He had no idea. 'Ben and I had four parents, all equally demanding, equally narcissistic, equally uninterested in anything but themselves. Ben and I became a team to keep them at bay.'

'Sounds like a nightmare,' he commented. 'But why keep your connection to Ben under wraps?'

A good question. How to explain? She stared at the floor. 'Ben asked me, probably every week, to come see him race, but I was in my late teens and early twenties when his career took off, and I wasn't particularly interested in cars.' She saw him wince and smiled. 'I found every excuse to dodge a visit.'

'Why? It's such a dynamic, exciting place.'

It was one thing to feel insecure and another to admit it. She looked away, looking for the answer in the view. He, surprisingly, didn't push her for an answer. 'Ben was, genuinely, one of the best people I knew. I was gutted by what happened to him,' Taz said, sounding sincere. 'Was he the reason you joined De Rossi Racing as a press officer?'

Taz could be, occasionally, incredibly perceptive. And there was something about the way he looked right now. Less like a racing team owner or arrogant driver and just like a man who made her feel that she could open up to him.

'Next month will be the tenth anniversary of Ben's death.

I don't expect you to understand, but I joined this world, his world, as a tribute to him.' And as a means to find, within herself, the confidant, secure woman Ben believed her to be. 'But it's turned out to be more complicated than I expected,' she added, linking her hands around her knee.

'Because of me?' He was quiet for a few seconds. 'Are you wanting to bail on being my fake girlfriend?'

'Yes. But I can't.'

'Because of the money,' he stated, his voice flat and his expression unreadable.

She nodded. 'Yes, because of the money. I can't afford to pass up the opportunity to raise a million quid for his charity. It would normally take us years to raise so much money.'

'You're donating the money I'm paying you to a *charity*?'

It was wonderful to see him caught off guard for a change. 'I would *never* fake-or real-date you, or anyone, for personal gain,' Millie told him.

'I think you'd better explain,' Taz told her, his voice brusque.

Millie quickly told him about her inheritance from Ben and about the charity she'd established in his name. Taz kept his eyes on her face, his expression stoic, but she knew he was taking in every word. At the end of her two-minute-long ramble, he nodded but didn't comment.

Millie hated herself for wanting his praise. She shook off her disappointment and pushed back her shoulders. 'Coming back to my original question… How are we going to act when we are out and about?'

He looked at her, his expression still serious. 'How do you want me to act, Millie? It's your call.'

'I don't know. That's why I asked.'

He took her hand and linked his fingers in hers, his thumb stroking the top of her hand. 'We'll have to hold hands.'

When his hand swallowed hers, she felt grounded and safe. But the action itself was innocuous, so she nodded. Taz moved closer, his thigh against hers, and dropped his head to lay his lips on her temple. 'A couple of light kisses?'

Another nod, and her eyes went to his lips, soft in contrast to his heavy stubble. His face came closer, as his hand ran down her shoulder to her hand and back up again. He swiped his lips across hers, in a kiss that was as hot as it was brief.

'That's as far as I will go,' he told her. 'In public. And in public is where our bargain ends.'

She frowned, suddenly confused. 'You've lost me,' she admitted.

'I'm paying you to act as my girlfriend, but everything that happens privately has nothing to do with our bargain,' he told her, his voice harsh.

'What's going to happen privately?' she asked, her heart stuttering when he smiled.

'God, you're sweet. And a little naive.'

He wasn't mocking her. He seemed in awe of her. He brushed the pad of his thumb over her lower lip and leaned in close so that his words brushed her lips. 'In private, I'm going to seduce the hell out of you, Millie.'

Taz looked into her lovely face, his thumb still on her lips. He should get off this couch and go back to his room, but there was more chance of an asteroid striking this penthouse suite. He wanted Millie. It was as simple and as complicated as that. And he always got what he wanted.

And now that he knew where his million pounds would land, a massive barrier to seducing her had crashed and shattered. He wasn't paying *her* but a charity. And yes, she was still his employee, but he now felt the pendulum of power had swung back to the middle, levelling the playing field. If they kept work and play separate, if they played by the rules—*his rules*—they could explore their intense attraction.

But the rules had to be explained. There was no room for misunderstandings.

'Millie, I want you, I'm not going to deny that. I would love to take you to my bed, strip you down and make you mine.' Her eyes widened, as he'd expected them to. She clearly wasn't used to men being direct, telling her what they wanted and how they wanted it. But being direct was the only way he knew how to be. 'I can't wait to have you under me. I want to be inside you, giving you the best orgasm of your life.'

It wasn't a boast; he knew he was an exceptional lover. He made it a point of being good at everything, and a long time ago he'd decided that if a woman was gracious enough to let him love her, then he was obligated to make her see not only stars but also a meteor shower or two.

'But what we do when we are naked has no bearing on you being my fake girlfriend, the money I am paying you or your work as my press or PR person. When the world goes away, you and I are equals, and there's no power imbalance in bed.' There was zero fun in coercion. 'Nothing you do or say will have any bearing on what happens in the outside world.'

He saw her swallow. 'I want to take you to bed. But you should know that all we'll ever be is lovers. I don't fall in love. I *won't* fall in love. I'm not interested in a relationship or commitment. The only thing that's important to me is my team and winning a fourth championship.'

Millie touched her top lip with the tip of her tongue, and he wished she wouldn't. He was already steel-hard, and when she made those unconsciously sexy actions, it took all he had not to lay her back against the cushions and ravage her mouth, slowly making his way down her body.

'Uh…'

Great, he'd rendered her mute. He lifted his eyebrows and waited for her to gather her thoughts. But instead of speaking or retreating, she surprised him by sliding her cool hand around the back of his neck and lifting her mouth, a silent invitation to kiss her.

Taz obliged. Her lips on his were soft and feminine, and when his tongue slipped between her teeth, he tasted chocolate and whisky. And Millie. His tongue swirled lazily around hers.

'This isn't like me,' she murmured, as she pulled away and moved onto her knees, trying to get closer to him, and lust, hot and electric, shot down his spine and straight to his groin.

He lifted his mouth from hers to respond. 'It is when you're with me. I need you to touch me, Millie. *Everywhere.*'

His words, as he intended them to, granted her permission to explore, to stop thinking and start doing. Who'd made her question herself, made her so skittish? Her small hands raced over his shoulders and down his back, and she slid her finger under the elasticised waistband of his shorts while she moved the other hand to cup his butt. As he suspected, beneath her layers of doubt was a sexy, sensuous woman. He responded by dialling up their kiss, turning it hotter, *raunchier.*

Fuelled by her impatience, his hand moved from her hip and moved up and under her pyjama top, massaging her breasts, his fingers exploring her already-tight nipples. She straddled his thighs, the inside of her knees pushing into his hips and she scooted forward, rocking herself into him. Through their clothes, her hot core connected with his erection, and need raced across her face.

Impatience roared through him, chased by desire, so he lifted Millie off him, laid her on her back and quickly stripped her sexy pyjamas off her lovely body. Taz groaned when he slid his hand between her legs, bathing his fingers with her arousal.

He lifted his eyes and looked into hers, and his heart—dammit—missed a beat. Her gaze was surprisingly fierce. 'I know I'm naked, but I'm not ready to have sex with you.' Her words landed, and he struggled to make sense of them.

Shit... He blinked, trying to slow down and think. 'Okay.'

He immediately removed his hand, and she whimpered, obviously disappointed. 'I know, I'm sorry. I just can't...not yet.' She bit down on her bottom lip and looked away. Her lovely chest rose and fell as she hauled in some air. 'But I don't want to stop either... So can you touch me, Taz? And I-I'—God, even her stutter was adorable—'and I can touch you. If you want that.'

He did. Hell, he'd take anything she could give him right now. He held her eyes and saw the anxiety in them; it seemed she was bracing herself for his anger. He wasn't cross: She had the right to change her mind, to set the boundaries. He lifted his hand to stroke her cheek, needing to banish her worry. There was no place for it between two naked people. 'Okay, let's do this instead.'

He lay on his back and lifted her onto him so that her heat landed on his shaft, her knees on either side of his thighs. Her slick heat enveloped him, and he dug his fingertips into her hips, urging her to ride him. She quickly picked up the rhythm, and soon they were panting, both seeking that exquisite release. A part of Taz couldn't comprehend that he was so turned-on by something that was—if he were being honest—not much more than heavy petting. But he was close, so close...

So was she. The city lights danced on her skin, and in the seductive light he took in her flushed face. But he needed to see all of her so, using his core muscles, he half sat up and latched his mouth on her nipple and pulled it up to the roof of his mouth. She was so hot, so responsive...so into him and what they were doing.

And he, the master of control, someone who knew how to delay gratification, was going to come, hard and very soon. Shoving his good hand between them, he found her clit and told her to wrap her hand around him. She fisted him and rolled her hand to the top and he felt the pressure build at the base of his spine.

'Millie, are you going to come for me?' he growled, not recognising the need and desperation in his voice. A part of him wanted to pull back to regain some much-needed control, but the finish line was just a few seconds away.

As his words hit her lips, she started to shake. Her eyes closed, her mouth fell open, and she screamed her satisfaction. Ridiculously, stunningly turned-on, unable to help himself, he let himself go.

He felt like she'd gripped his soul and squeezed. Taz closed his eyes, trying to get his breathing back under control. Millie moved off him, and he watched through half-closed lids, his heart a loud bass drum in his ears, as she picked up her pyjamas. Then she crossed the lounge and slipped, still naked, into the second and smaller of the two bedrooms.

The snick of her lock was as loud as a pistol shot.

The next morning, after a couple of hours of restless sleep, Millie paced in front of the bedroom window, her bare feet sinking into the plush carpet as she tried to make sense of her too-fast thoughts, her heart thumping at the raunchy memories from last night. She rested her forearm over her eyes, as heat rolled through her and her heart bounced off her ribs.

She couldn't even argue that she'd been seduced or that she'd...*slipped* into the situation. No, she'd tumbled into it, head first, heart racing, with no thought for the consequences. Taz's heated gaze and growled compliments hadn't helped her keep her wits about her. She'd been lost the second she saw the raw appreciation in his eyes—how he watched her, and how he reacted to her touch and her kiss.

Can't think about that now. She *worked* for the man and was *pretending* to be his girlfriend. Millie banged her fist against the window. Her life was veering wildly off-track. She hadn't come here to entangle herself with Formula One's most notorious playboy. She'd joined the De Rossi team to remember Ben and to reconcile who she was with who she wanted to be. But instead of doing some intense self-reflection, instead of figuring out if she could be brave or feel more secure and self-assured, she'd fallen under Taz's seductive spell.

If he was still alive, Ben would argue that kissing Taz— and what followed—had been an act of bravery, a leap far beyond her carefully guarded comfort zone. But that wasn't the kind of courage Millie was searching for. She wanted to change her life, to become someone she respected, not someone who let her control unravel the moment a hot man turned his devastating eyes on her and told her he wanted to take her to bed.

And yet...*last night*. God, she'd wanted to burn. She'd loved his intensity, that laser-focused passion, directed solely at her. And yes, it had been everything she'd imagined and more. A firestorm. A revelation. Hot and sexy and indescribably intense. And it had only been a taster. Taz making love to her might kill her.

She shook her head, before resting her forehead on the window. It couldn't happen again. It *wouldn't* happen again.

Yes, they'd agreed to this ridiculous fake-dating arrangement, but that was as far as it went. They weren't lovers, and they certainly weren't friends with benefits. From this moment forward, they would be professional. Polite. They had to ignore their crackling chemistry.

Because no matter how much her body begged for more, Millie refused to let herself become another Taz De Rossi pit stop. How could she go from dating boring men to being celibate for years to sleeping with the world's sexiest driver? That didn't make any sense, it wasn't a straight line, and she needed to backtrack. Immediately.

She couldn't think of Taz as anything more than her boss, her fake boyfriend. She couldn't forget the hard lessons she'd learned as a child and young adult: the closer people got to her, the more pain they could inflict. Her parents were supposed to love her, but they didn't. She and Ben were supposed to grow old together, but he'd died. It was far easier to distance herself from men, from people, thus avoiding the possibility of being emotionally eviscerated.

But she'd never reacted to a man so quickly or so strongly as she had to Taz, so that meant she had to pull on her emotional running shoes and put a lot of distance between them. Fast.

Decision made, Millie whipped around to find her laptop, to check the schedule. They needed to be at the charity function this afternoon around three and she remembered that Taz wanted to spend some time in the pit with his technical staff. Her next task was scanning the papers and online publications for reactions to his press conference. She was expecting them to be good, but with the press you never knew.

She started a list on her phone and headed for the suite's lounge. She typed as she walked and hit a hard, bare chest. She gasped and slapped her free hand on Taz's muscled pec. It was so hard, so hot, and it was only then that she took in that he was only wearing long loose silk pyjama bottoms.

Taz curled his hand around her neck and covered her lips with his, his tongue sliding past her teeth to tangle with hers. She sighed and sank into the kiss, and it took her a few seconds, maybe a minute, for her brain to remind her that kissing him wasn't something she was supposed to do.

She was being paid to act as his girlfriend, even if it was for Ben's charity, and if she started sleeping with him... what did that make her? No! No! *No!* He'd explained, very directly, that what they did together clothed, naked or at any stage in between—was between them, and wasn't part of their deal. She couldn't start entertaining those denigrating thoughts. It wasn't fair on her. Or on him.

But damn, kissing him, being with him, was such fun. And being on the receiving end of his sexual skill was as addictive as a Class A drug.

It took all Millie's willpower to push away from him. She gripped the bridge of her nose, closed her eyes and tried to get her breathing back under control.

'Morning, Mils.'

His just-woke-up voice was deeper and rougher, sexier. And, no, he shouldn't shorten her name, making it sound sexy and sweet. *Be strong, Millie. He's your boss.*

'*Mr* De Rossi.'

Taz squinted at her and pushed his hand through his messy hair. His jaw was rough with stubble, and the pillow crease on his left cheek made him seem a little less of a bossy billionaire. More approachable and, damn it, lovable.

Get it together, Millie! 'I was just checking your schedule. You've got quite a bit to do before we leave for the polo tournament,' she stated, her tone a little sharp.

His dark-lashed eyelids dropped, and his lips tightened. Right, he wasn't happy with her cool greeting. Well, tough. They'd been out of line last night, and they needed normal this morning. 'No *Good morning, darling, how did you sleep?*'

Oh, the man had a PhD in sarcasm. 'Good morning, Mr De Rossi,' she politely parroted, tipping her head to the side. 'How did you sleep?'

He scowled at her, slapped his hands on his hips and straightened his back. Ah, the warrior pose, designed to intimidate. 'What happened from the time you left until this morning?' he demanded, his normal brusqueness back in his voice. 'Did you not get any sleep?'

She might as well bite the bullet and get them back on a professional footing. 'What happened was that I came to my senses and remembered that we work together and that I am not prepared to be another of your conquests.'

Taz cocked his head to one side, and his gaze bore into her. 'I need a gallon of coffee before we have this conversation,' he stated, gesturing to the coffee machine sitting on the kitchen's Italian marble counter. 'Make me one, will you?'

When she hesitated, he raised a thick black brow. 'You work for me, right? Espresso, double, black.'

He'd manoeuvred her into a corner, leaving her with no option but to play by his rules. It was annoying how easily Taz could trip her up. His fantastic looks, sheer masculinity and raw sexuality meant that she often overlooked how sharp he was and how effortlessly he wielded words like weapons. He was quick, cunning and unaccustomed to anyone refusing to dance to the beat of his drum.

Millie thought fast. She could argue against making him coffee, implying that she thought herself more than his employee, or she could make the coffee, reinforcing the idea that she was nothing more than hired help. Devil, meet deep blue sea.

Damn him for making her question everything. For making her doubt herself.

It was important to stand her ground and reinforce their boundaries. She needed to be smart, to think with her head. She couldn't let her libido hijack her common sense. Last night had been a mistake, a universe-rearranging mistake, and it wasn't one she intended to repeat.

So with gritted teeth, Millie made his double espresso and placed the cup on the coffee table next to him. He didn't say thank you but just smirked at her. He was testing her. *Great*.

Walking into his bedroom, she ignored his huge, messy bed, just managing to stop herself from imagining how amazing it would be to share that with him, and walked into his enormous closet. The hotel staff had unpacked his luggage, and they'd arranged his shirts per colour, his pants and suits too. He had at least fifteen pairs of shoes on the shoe rack. He was in town for ten days: How many pairs of shoes did one man need? Unable to help herself, she picked up his cologne, took a deep breath and sighed.

She was getting distracted and more than a little turned-on. Irritated, she pulled the first T-shirt from a perfectly aligned pile and carried it back through to the lounge, draping it over his shoulder. 'Please get dressed.'

He ignored her and scrolled through his phone. One of these days, she'd brain him with it. Reaching for her iPad on the table, she flipped it open and waited for Taz to pull on his shirt. It lay on his tanned, muscular shoulder, and she knew he was waiting for her to push him to get dressed. She wasn't going to give him the satisfaction.

Summoning her most professional voice, she ran through his schedule for the morning and ignored his surly responses. He didn't like hearing the word *no*. He'd simply have to get used to it. Their sleeping together was not going to happen.

Sex with Taz would blur the lines, make things far too complicated. She was already acting as his girlfriend; she didn't need thorough research to nail the part. As far as she could tell, if she giggled, made the occasional innocuous comment and looked adoringly at Taz, she'd fulfil her end of the bargain.

'Are you going to answer me or not?'

Millie lifted her head, doing a mental rewind. Right, he'd asked her something about what she was wearing to the polo tournament. 'Your stylist sent over a couple of dresses. I'm leaning toward a brown-and-white maxi halter-neck dress...'

He looked thoroughly disinterested. Why ask a question if he wasn't going to listen to the answer?

Millie sighed. Was this her fault? She'd asked him to treat her as one of his staff, and that was what he was doing. She couldn't complain about it now. 'I won't embarrass you, if that's what you're wondering.'

His eyes lifted and slammed into hers. 'I wasn't.'

He was properly pissed. Millie closed her laptop and placed it on the coffee table. They had to spend time together, today and over the next few weeks, and they couldn't snap and snarl at each other. They needed to clear the air. 'Look, Taz, we can't sleep together and work together. I can't be your assistant one minute and your girlfriend the next. It's too confusing.'

And I can't afford to lose track of who I am at any time and let the two bleed into each other. On one hand, she might end up doing a terrible job as his PR person and miss something crucial or, even worse, she might find attraction turning into, God forbid, *like*. Maybe even more. Was she overthinking this? Taz had made it very clear earlier that he wasn't interested in anything more than sex, and she'd grown up witnessing two highly dysfunctional marriages, so long-term wasn't for her. But something held her back. 'This situation is complicated enough without us adding the gasoline of sex to the bonfire.'

His expression remained impassive. 'Fine.'

She threw up her hands, frustrated. 'Is that all you are going to say?'

Turbulent eyes met hers. 'You want to keep things professional, I'm saying okay. What more do you need from me?'

He drained his coffee, pushed the cup in her direction and stood. 'Get rid of that and order a high protein breakfast from room service. I want it delivered in an hour. I'm going to head down to the hotel gym to work out.'

'You have a broken wrist—'

'Not your problem.'

Taz walked away from her, and Millie twisted her lips. Right. Message received. She'd tapped the brakes, and he'd brought the race to a complete stop. She should be pleased. That was what she wanted.

Then, why did she feel so exasperated? And, worse, frustrated?

CHAPTER EIGHT

THE POLO MATCH WAS, essentially, a picnic on steroids—where lemonade was swapped for Moët et Chandon Champagne, PB & J sandwiches for blinis, and jam doughnuts for exquisite patisseries. Designer labels replaced ripped board shorts and battered T-shirts, and inane chatter masqueraded as conversation. Insincere compliments were casually lobbed conversational grenades.

Taz, naturally, was a hit, parrying compliments and questions with effortless charm, utterly polished and charismatic, eliciting sighs and swoons from his captive audience.

Wearing stone-coloured chinos and a navy linen jacket over a crisp white shirt he looked ridiculously good. He hadn't bothered shaving, and the thick stubble suited him far too well. A green-and-blue pocket square peeked out from his jacket, and every so often, the silver bracelets on either side of his Patek Philippe watch caught the sunlight. His taste—or his stylist's taste—was, Millie begrudgingly admitted, impeccable.

She took a sip of champagne and remembered attending a polo match when she was a child. Her mother had insisted on her wearing a white dress and white shoes and got annoyed when both got splattered with mud. She'd been ordered to spend the rest of the afternoon in the car, which suited her fine as she'd stashed her book under the passenger seat. Just another instance of her not being about to live up to their impossibly high expectations. She was constantly set up to fail.

Millie had expected to feel like a fish out of water at this event, but she managed to exchange small talk, side-step questions about Taz and even engage in a conversation about polo. She wasn't half as bored or on edge as she'd thought she'd be. Taz was the centre of attention, and that meant eyes on her too, but she was handling standing in the spotlight better than she'd expected. It wasn't the nightmare she expected it to be. Maybe some of those old insecurities had faded, or maybe she'd simply grown up. Either way, not feeling like she was dancing on the edge of a sharp blade was a pleasant surprise.

Millie jerked when Taz's arm snaked around her waist, pulling her flush against him. She barely had time to blink before he dipped his head, his lips brushing her temple. The warm weight of his kiss lingered as he spoke softly, his words pitched low for her ears alone.

'I'm bored, and this is tedious,' he murmured, sounding irritated. 'How much longer?'

'You *have* to watch the first game and should watch the second,' Millie told him, inhaling his scent.

'Watching and not playing is torture,' he muttered, his grip on her hip tightening.

Taz was a man of action, and she understood his frustration. He wasn't the type to stand on the sidelines. She patted his bicep. 'Hang in there,' she told him. 'Being here benefits you and the charity. It's a win-win scenario. Keep your eye on the prize.'

He pulled back and looked down at her, and her heart stuttered at his expression. 'I'd rather keep my eyes on you.'

An image of her naked on his lap last night flashed behind her eyes, and her cheeks heated. 'Taz...people are look-ing at us,' she murmured, heat in her cheeks.

The corner of his mouth lifted into a sexy smirk. 'I know,' he told her, cupping her face in his hands. His eyes glinted with a curious combination of lust and amusement. 'We want them to look at us, remember?'

Her protest was captured then smothered by his lips. His tongue slipped between her teeth, and the world faded away. He took control of their kiss, and there was nothing she could do but respond. Nothing she *wanted* to do but respond.

Taz abruptly ended the kiss and looked down at her with hooded eyes and a satisfied smile. 'Give it a minute and we'll be all over social media,' he stated. 'The bad boy and the good girl.'

Millie resisted the urge to touch her lips with her finger-tips and worked hard to keep her scowl off her face. He'd kissed her to make a point. Millie sighed. He was punishing her for pulling away this morning, for putting them in oppo-site corners of the ring. He'd been happy to wait for the right moment to retaliate, patient enough to make sure she was on the back foot, sneaky enough to make her feel unstable.

He was unlike anyone she'd met before. Oh, her parents were self-assured, not shy about putting themselves forward, but Taz was so confident, possessing an arrogance and self-belief she'd never encountered before. He knew exactly who he was and what he was doing. If her family was a garden bonfire, then Taz was an out-of-control wildfire. He didn't singe and scorch; he annihilated everything in his path.

Millie felt like she was facing that raging fire holding a watering can.

Taz's low curse had Millie instantly on high alert. She turned to see who'd captured his attention and saw a polo player, dressed in white jodhpurs and a branded shirt, slapping his knee-high riding boot with his leather crop. Hanging onto his hand, like she was the survivor of a shipwreck and he the life ring, was a pale lanky exceptionally pretty redhead.

And Millie knew, with the feminine wisdom she didn't know she possessed up until now, that this woman and Taz had seen each other naked.

Jealously, hot and acid, burned her stomach lining, and she was annoyed at her gut response. She was his employee and fake girlfriend, and while they'd allowed things to get a little out of control last night, she had no right to feel jealous.

Taz murmured a low *Here comes trouble*, and on seeing the polo player's face—hard, defiant and thoroughly annoyed—Millie knew he was right.

'You slept with her, right?' she muttered out of the side of his mouth.

'Yes,' he admitted, unembarrassed. 'She told me they were done. It turned out things weren't as cut and dry as she said they were.'

'Is he going to make trouble?' she whispered.

'Highly possible.'

Damn it, the day had been going well so far. Lots of the attendees had pledged to make donations to the nominated charity—a fund for the victims of natural disasters such as flooding and hurricanes. A fight between the guest of honour and what looked to be the captain of one of the polo teams would be disastrous, especially since Taz was finally, *finally*, generating some decent press.

'De Rossi.'

'Bertolo.'

The two men gripped hands, their fingers turning white with pressure. She caught the redhead's eye and saw her quick wince. Right, she wasn't imagining their death-by-handshake duel.

Millie shoulder-bumped Taz in what she hoped was a playful way and held out her hand for the polo player to shake. He had no choice but to release Taz's hand: a good thing, because she knew how stubborn Taz could be. Without her intervention, they'd stand there for hours. 'I'm Millie, Taz's girlfriend.'

'Brody Bertolo.' He gave her hand a quick shake and placed his hands on his hips. He nodded at Taz's arm. 'It's a pity you're injured, or else I would've suggested you play a chukka with us. If you lasted the seven minutes, I would've made a substantial donation to your charity.'

What a jerk! Millie sent him the sweetest smile she could muster. 'Why don't you make the donation and we skip Taz getting on a horse?' she asked, trying to hide her dislike.

'I could still play, even with a broken hand,' Taz smoothly replied. 'How much are we talking?'

God save her from idiotic men. He had limited use of his fingers, with only his thumb working on his broken hand. How would he control a horse and hold a mallet? It was a stupid comment, and stupidity wasn't something she associated with Taz. Their interaction had drawn a curious crowd, suggesting that Taz and the redhead's affair had been a topic of hot conversation amongst the polo-playing set. And Red was looking a little smug at all the attention.

'A cool half a mil?' Brody asked.

'You'll give the charity five hundred thousand if I last a chukka?' Taz clarified.

'But you have to take part. You can't stay on the sidelines,' Brody countered.

It was a huge donation, and as Taz tipped his head to the side, Millie knew he was considering his suggestion.

He gestured to his clothes. 'I'd need proper clothes.'

Millie's mouth dropped open. Had he lost his mind? Getting on a horse with a broken hand, to take part in one of the most competitive sports in the world, was an absurd idea.

'And if you don't last the chukka, you donate a half million to the charity,' Brody suggested, a half sneer, half smile on his face.

'Deal.'

Millie couldn't keep quiet a minute longer. 'You do know he's an F1 racer, not a polo player, right?'

Everyone laughed, and Millie knew she was the butt of the joke. She swallowed the urge to remind them she was head of Taz's PR and that she knew his sporting history. But she was here as his adoring girlfriend, not his PR representative.

The redhead sent her a pitying smile. 'You're obviously new on the scene, and not part of the polo set.' Millie's nails dug into her skin at her condescending tone. She sounded like her mum and aunt.

'Everyone knows that Taz was one of the most promising polo players in the world when he was in his teens,' Red said, her nose in the air.

Yes, she *knew* that. Millie forced herself to place her open hand above her heart and widen her eyes. 'Oh, I thought he was a scratch golf player and was considering going pro.' She looked at Taz. 'Did I get that wrong, *darling*?'

He shrugged. 'I had options.'

Many options, it seemed. But he chose racing. It was, after all, the family business.

'Are you doing this or not, De Rossi?'

Oh, hell no, he wasn't. Before Taz could agree to this asinine scheme, she'd clocked the *Challenge accepted* in his eyes, slipped her hand into his and smiled. 'I'm sorry, but would you excuse us for a minute?'

'Hold on, Millie,' Taz growled.

She dug her fingernails into the top of his hand. 'I'm sure Mr Bertolo could give us five minutes.'

Irritation rolled off him, but he pulled her out of earshot and put his back to the group congregating around Bertolo and the redhead. His big frame shielded her, so she glared up at him. 'What do you think you are doing?' she hissed. 'You cannot get up on a horse! He's taunting you, Taz.'

'So?'

'So you can walk away.'

'And look like he's got the better of me? That's not happening.'

'What if you fall off?'

'I've been riding since I was three. I don't fall off horses.'

She only had one argument left. 'The press will get wind of this. Everyone's phone cameras are already out, waiting to film you. It will be uploaded online within five minutes of you settling into the saddle, probably less. Whether you win the bet or not, the press will slant their reports to say that you are reckless, that you are risking your recovery to one-up a polo player. They will say your ego can't handle losing, that you aren't taking your recovery seriously, and that if you really wanted to win the championship, you'd never risk it on such a stupid bet! You're a target, so don't give them bullets to shoot at you.'

She could tell he wanted to argue, and Millie waited for his scalpel-sharp response. How would she spin this when it hit the press in the morning, what excuse could she conjure? Whatever she came up with would be weak, because the most logical explanation was that he was an egotistical idiot.

What was it with this man's need to be the best at everything all the time? Why couldn't he back down, step away? Why was he constantly waging battles or engaging in skirmishes? It was almost as if he went out of his way to prove that he was better, stronger, the best of the best. How many people were scratch golfers, ace polo players and Formula One drivers? To be good at one was amazing, to be good at so many things took dedication and hard work and perseverance. Why would he put himself through that? What drove him to excel?

Behind the irritation and the determination was more than a hint of misery. And desperation.

He met her eyes and rubbed his hand over his chin. 'I can't back down, Millie.'

A part of her wanted to roll her eyes and say *Of course you can!* but she knew he didn't want to feel like Bertolo had an edge over him. Why? She didn't know. He was a billionaire owner of a racing team, and Bertolo was a professional polo player. On the wealth and social hierarchy, Bertolo was a bug beneath his shoe.

But if she didn't come up with a solution, she knew Taz would take the bet. So she needed to find one, and pronto. Guess she wasn't only going to earn her million pounds by playing his adoring girlfriend.

She thought fast. 'Be honest. Tell him you can't risk any further injury to your hand, but when the cast comes off, after you win your fourth championship, you are fully prepared to take on his challenge. As a measure of your commitment, you'll donate a half million to the charity now, and you'll bet another half million. I could organise a charity polo day, he can choose a team, you can choose a team, and we'll choose a charity, and your fans can bet on the outcome. You'll both get credit and some good PR.'

He pondered her response before handing her a look saturated with approval. It felt like the warm, early morning sun on her face. How amazing would it be if he could look at her like that for the rest of her life? *Oh, Millie, you're in such deep trouble.*

'I can live with that.' Taz nodded.

Millie released the breath she'd been holding. 'What else can I expect from you? A fencer to challenge you to a sword fight, a swimmer suggesting you swim the English Channel? Is there anything you can't do?' she asked, as he stroked her cheek.

'Apparently, I can't get you back into my bed again.'

She remembered the hint of vulnerability in his eyes, the chink in his armour of arrogance. That smidgen of insecurity made him all the more attractive. It also made her feel more self-confident and braver. He'd told her, clearly, that whatever they did in bed had no connection to her work as his PR officer or as her acting as his girlfriend. She believed him. She couldn't use either as an excuse.

Truth was, she didn't want an excuse. Did she even *need* one? She was a consenting adult who was allowed to have some bedroom-based fun. The fizzy feelings Taz raised in her made her feel powerfully feminine and femininely powerful. When he looked at her like *that*, all thoughts of being less-than and feeling insecure disappeared, and her self-doubt faded away. He made her braver...

And wasn't being brave what she was trying to achieve?

'I think that could be arranged,' she whispered.

Taz smiled, and Millie knew she'd hopped from the frying pan into earth's molten core. Sure, sleeping with him might be a mistake, but if it was, she'd own it. Because, for the first time, she was choosing to be with a man because of her burning attraction, and not because she felt lonely or needed reassurance.

And for her, right now, that was huge.

* * *

Hours later and back in his luxurious South Beach hotel suite, Taz was still curious as to why Millie had changed her mind. He'd tossed out the suggestion of taking her to bed more in hope than in expectation, and her agreement had surprised the hell out of him. And he was a man not easily surprised. His gaze drifted over her lush body, and he hardened instantly. He'd ask her later; right now he wanted to give his full attention to this sexy, stunning woman in his bed.

Millie's skin was so soft, endlessly creamy and lightly fragranced. She was, possibly, the most feminine woman he'd ever met. Taz stroked the back of his knuckles from her neck to her stomach, and her eyes fluttered closed as her back arched to his touch.

She was so responsive, so into him and what he did, in a way few of his lovers had been before. Many had been track bunnies, more interested in bragging rights than sexual pleasure, and others hoped sex was a gateway to accessing his lifestyle. But Millie was fully and utterly present in the moment, lost in how he made her feel.

Her response brought an intensity to sex that had been missing for a long, long time. For far too long it had been a way to blow off steam, a form of escape. Sex with Millie was…more. Taz lowered his mouth to swirl his tongue around her nipple, smiling when her fingers tunnelled into his hair to hold his head to her breast. Surprisingly, Millie wasn't afraid to show him who she was, what she liked and how she felt. He adored her honesty.

More than that, he liked that she was smart and sensible and, albeit temporarily, solidly in his corner. She'd been right earlier: Playing polo would've been a stupid move. Oh, he knew he could've won the bet—that would've been the easy part—but the public reaction would've been swift and brutal. No, as hard as it was to admit, Millie had made the right call and presented him with a solution that enabled him to walk away with his pride intact.

His father's constant comparisons to Alex made him want to be the best at everything, all the time. In his head, he wasn't only competing against Alex but against everyone else. That's what happened when your father considered you as a spare part, as second best, as unimportant. As a teenager, he'd needed to be the best at everything in the vague hope that his father might notice and be impressed. He was better than Alex at every sport, but that didn't matter to his dad. He wasn't Alex.

And why was he thinking about his father when he had this sensational woman in his bed? She'd agreed to sleep with him and wanted to be with him, and he owed her the courtesy of his full attention. But if he allowed himself to deeply dive into her, if he didn't keep some emotional guard-rails up, he might go too deep and not resurface. And if he did, he might come back less…

Detached? Unemotional? More connected?

Taz shook his head, frustrated at the thoughts leaking through his normally impenetrable shields. *Cut it out, De Rossi.* He looked at the tiny triangle of lace that could barely be considered underwear and ran his finger over the fabric, sliding between her legs. Her panties were already soaked, so he sat on his knees and pulled them down her hips, smiling when she lifted her butt cheek to allow him to push them down her legs. He tossed them over his shoulder, thinking that he needed to strip. Sex was more fun when both parties were naked.

But he could look at her for hours: She was pleasure personified. From her messy hair to her freckled chest and lust-soaked eyes, her flushed cheeks and rounded stomach and hips, she was all woman.

And for the moment, all his.

Millie picked up his hand and placed it between her thighs, and he was surprised and turned-on by her boldness. Her silent demand was unexpected. And hot. Was some of his sexual confidence rubbing off on her? He slid his finger over and around her, smiling when she pulled her bottom lip between her teeth. Her fingers went to her breast, and she tugged her nipple, trying to maximise her pleasure. She was being selfish, wanting this moment to be about her and only her…

Good for her. He liked people who knew what they wanted and went for it.

'That's it, Millie. Keep touching yourself,' he encouraged her, moving off the bed. Without undressing, he placed his hands under her thighs and pulled her to the edge of the bed, pushing her knees apart and revealing her, pink and swollen, to his gaze. So, so pretty.

He dropped to his knees and lowered his mouth to her. She arched off the bed, and he placed his hand on her stomach to pin her in place while he worked one finger, then another, into her heat.

He was rock hard, harder than he could ever remember being as he softly sucked her. As his fingers plunged in and out of her, he thought about how he wanted to take her after she came hard on his tongue and fingers. From behind? Her on top? There were so many options but…

What he most wanted was to keep it simple. He wanted to watch her eyes as he entered her, as he brought her to another orgasm, their eyes staying connected. He wanted to see her fall apart, and he'd come as she did. For one blissful moment, one person, the same pleasure. He couldn't remember when last that had happened...or whether it ever had.

Impatient, he pulled back and quickly stripped. Millie thrashed her head on the pillow, and when her hand headed to her core, he pulled it back and firmly commanded her to wait for him. They'd do this together.

After sliding on a condom with more haste than grace, he lowered himself to her. Her legs fell apart, and she moaned when the tip of his cock found her entrance. It took all his willpower not to surge inside her, to bury himself to the hilt.

'Millie, look at me.'

Panting, she tried to arch her hips to pull him in, but he was in charge. They were doing this on his timescale, not hers. He pulled back and her eyes flew open, frustrated. 'Keep your eyes on mine. You close them or you look away, I'll stop.'

As if in challenge, Millie tried to touch herself again. Knowing how close she was, he pulled her hand and clamped it to her side. If he had the use of his other hand, he'd hold her wrists above her head, but his threat of stopping would have to be enough.

'Don't touch yourself, don't look away, and you'll only come when I tell you that you can.'

'*Tazio.*'

Oh, man, the way she said his full name, it was a shot of adrenaline straight into his spine. Unable to wait, he plunged deep inside her, and her heat engulfed him from tip to root. He wanted to make love to her without the barrier of a condom, but despite the thin layer of latex between him, he was consumed by her heat. He knew she was close, and that it wouldn't take much to make her come, but he wanted to draw out this experience, to make it memorable, to stand out from the many sexual encounters he'd had before.

Because this wasn't a mating ritual, this was… God, he didn't know what it was. But he did know he wanted to remember the changing colours in her eyes, the slick of moisture on her lips, the flush in her cheeks and the staggering heat rolling off them.

The room smelled of sex and her perfume, of the calla lilies in the huge vase on the dresser, of clean sheets and sexy woman. A gentle, always-warm Miami sea-breeze blew over their bodies.

'Taz, please, you've got to start moving,' Millie said, tiny pants accompanying her words. 'I *need* you.'

He knew she meant that she needed him right at this moment, needed him to make her feel good and to give her the orgasm he'd promised. But he was, shockingly, entertaining the thought that he needed more from her than just sex.

Why was he going there? Why was he making this more than it was? This could only be the start of a fling, at best, a short-lived affair. They had tonight, but tomorrow they'd say goodbye and would only meet up in Italy for the Grand Prix in Imola in ten days.

He was overthinking…well, everything.

No, this was about sex, pure and simple. So he pumped his hips, stroking her with all the pent-up fury and confusion that had been building since he'd first set eyes on her. He slipped his good hand under her butt, lifted her hips and went a little deeper, a little harder.

But even as her body dissolved around him, as she panted, moaned and screamed through her release, even as he erupted into her, her eyes didn't leave his.

And neither did his.

Taz handed Millie a bottle of water from the hotel's bar fridge before climbing back into bed beside her. He took a long sip from his own, utterly at ease, while her mind remained chaotic and her body hummed.

Bells still rang in her ears, and her skin thrummed with aftershocks from the most intense orgasm of her life. She felt turned inside out, upside down and completely undone. What on earth had happened? That wasn't just good sex. It was earth-shatteringly, soul-stealingly unforgettable.

Taz's hand found her wrist, his touch grounding her. She looked down as he fiddled with the tiny silver racing car dangling from her heavy link, silver bracelet. The charm was subtle, almost unnoticeable, but Taz's sharp eyes had zeroed in on it.

'When did you get this?' he asked, lifting her arm to inspect the charm more closely.

She smiled softly, the memory bittersweet. 'It was Ben's. He used to tie it to the laces of his shoes before every race.'

His hand dropped, resting on her thigh as he leaned back against the headboard, his hand behind his head. The pose was casual, masculine and infuriatingly sexy. 'I remember now,' he said thoughtfully. 'I also remember him losing it once before Silverstone. He was normally so laid-back that the news of him being in a state because he'd lost his lucky charm reached the other drivers. He was, apparently, unbearable until he found it again.'

She chuckled. 'When I was four, I gave him a plastic one from a Christmas cracker. He had a jeweller recreate it in silver.' She ran her fingers over the tiny car, the charm swinging slightly from its link. 'Ben's parents claimed his body after his death, and this charm was on him when he died. I asked his parents for it, and luckily they gave it to me before his will was read or I would never have got it.'

Taz frowned. 'What do you mean?'

'I was Ben's sole heir, and his parents were enraged they

weren't mentioned in his will. Then they heard I was planning to donate all his cash to a charity set up in his name, and they went ballistic. They challenged the will and took me to court.'

Taz raised an eyebrow, his olive-brown skin glowing against the pure white sheets. 'I presume you won?'

'It was a long, hard slog, but I did. Eventually.'' Millie tapped the charm, smiling softly. 'Luckily, I had emails from Ben, where he talked about the up-and-coming drivers he was helping, how he wanted to do more, so I could prove I was acting in accordance with his wishes.'

'How's your relationship with Ben's parents now?' Taz asked.

Millie sighed. 'I haven't spoken to them since the judge ruled in my favour. And because my parents supported my aunt and uncle's bid to contest the will, my relationship with my parents is frosty.'

Taz squeezed her knee, a silent gesture of comfort.

'I liked Ben,' Taz quietly stated. 'And I think he was good for Alex.'

Millie tilted her head, immediately curious. 'What do you mean?'

Taz hesitated, his gaze drifting to the lilies on the dresser. Their sweet scent filled the room, a sharp contrast to the tension that had sprung up between them. 'Ben was grounded. Sensible. Alex needed that.'

It wasn't what she'd expected to hear. 'Alex seemed to be pretty grounded and sensible already,' she said, pressing for more.

Taz shrugged dismissively, his expression turning remote. 'I don't talk about Alex.'

The statement was blunt and final, but she couldn't leave it alone. If he hadn't wanted to talk about his brother, why bring him into the conversation? 'You should. He's your brother.' Her voice softened. 'Losing him like that must've been terrible.'

Taz's jaw tightened, but his silence was as loud as a fog-horn. He'd pulled back, and she couldn't help feeling hurt at his sudden emotional distance. She knew she shouldn't: There was nothing between them but chemistry, a fake relationship and a business deal. Despite knowing that, understanding that, she still desperately wanted him to trust her enough to open up to her. She reached out, brushing her fingers over the back of his hand. 'I'm so sorry, Taz.'

He didn't respond, but his hand tightened briefly over hers before he sat up and drained his water bottle, tossing it neatly into the waste-basket.

'Show-off,' she muttered, trying to lighten the mood.

He smirked, the tension easing slightly. 'I'm multitalented.'

She could attest to that. Millie let her fingers trail over his hand, marvelling at the contrast between its strength and gentleness. These hands had given her so much pleasure— but they were also hands that could steer a car at rocket-like speed over twisty tracks.

'How do you feel about going to Imola?' he asked abruptly. 'Are you going to be okay?'

Her chest tightened at the mention of the track where Ben had died. 'I don't know,' she admitted. 'I thought I'd be fine, but every time I think about it…' She swallowed hard. 'But I have to be there. It's my job. I feel so guilty I didn't see him before he died, but I'm so glad I didn't witness his crash, Taz,' she added.

'Me too, Mils.' Taz ran a hand over her shoulder, soothing and steady. He pulled her close, her cheek resting against his chest. His warmth, his presence, was an unexpected balm to her frayed nerves.

'Families are so complicated,' she murmured, her hand resting on his ridged stomach.

'Aren't they?' he agreed, his hand covering hers.

But his touch, his proximity, stirred something more profound. Slowly, her hand drifted lower, her fingers trailing over the hard ridges of his stomach to his erection. Her fist encircled him, he hardened, and Millie felt, for the first time, powerful at raising such a quick response in such an alpha man. It was such a confidence-booster, but despite her increasing self-assurance, she knew she still had a way to go before she felt wholly at ease in her skin, secure in this world she now moved in.

And that was work she had to do. No man, not Ben and not Tazio De Rossi, could do that for her.

Two things could happen at once… While she worked on herself and learned to stand up straight and be strong, she could enjoy him and enjoy their off-the-charts attraction.

'Whether they're complicated or not,' she said, her voice low, 'this…*isn't*.'

She did not doubt that tomorrow would bring its own problems, but tonight, being with him was all that mattered.

CHAPTER NINE

Imola, Italy

TWELVE DAYS LATER, at the Autodromo Internazionale Enzo e Dino Ferrari, Taz inspected the track with his drivers, debriefed the race engineers and strategists, and held a video conference with his research team in the UK. By mid-afternoon, he'd put in more than a full day's work. Yet his temper simmered as he fielded endless questions from his employees, colleagues and the press about Millie's whereabouts.

Before he'd had a chance to suggest that they meet up in London during the break, Millie told him she'd see him in Italy, and he hadn't seen her since. As she'd done during the Shanghai race, Millie slid into his thoughts far too often and usually at inopportune moments. His thoughts often went to what Millie was doing, thinking, *eating* for God's sake! For the first time in his life, being apart from his lover annoyed him. That he missed her irritated him even more. Exchanging work emails and brief PR-related calls didn't cut it.

For the first time he could remember, the *only* time, work had competition for his attention.

Taz rubbed the back of his neck. Millie'd arrived in Italy six hours ago; she should've been at the track for hours now, but he'd yet to lay eyes on her. Where was she? They might be lovers, but he knew Millie well enough to know that her pride wouldn't let her slack off on the job. And her job meant being at his side or, at the very least, within earshot.

Had some PR disaster occurred he wasn't yet aware of? Was she putting out PR fires? Or was she ill? She'd been working long, long hours in a high stress environment. He was a demanding boss and expected results. Was she finding the work—him—overwhelming?

Taz checked his watch, shook his head and clenched his jaw. He wouldn't find the answers to his questions here. He had a few free hours before the sponsor dinner, enough time to track Millie down and ask her directly. He barked a command at an intern, instructing him to organise a courtesy car to be waiting for him at the turnstiles.

Sliding his aviator shades onto his face, he raked a hand through his hair and strode through the exit. The roar of the gathered fans was deafening, the flashes from cameras cutting through the overcast sky. Hopefully his sunglasses masked his anxiety. He wasn't used to worrying about anyone, ever, and he was exasperated Millie could make him feel this way.

But the world didn't need to know any of that.

As he stepped into the parking lot, his eyebrows rose. Parked a yard away was a sleek, limited-edition Ferrari, a beast of a machine. This was his courtesy car? Nice. Not enough to lift his mood, but nice.

He took the fob the olive-skinned brunette held out to him and ignored her sexy smile.

He slid behind the wheel and ran his hands over the leather steering wheel. The interior was immaculate, the idling engine a low-throated growl as he tapped the start button. He punched the accelerator, the roar of the car rolling over the crowd. His fans bellowed their approval.

Precision and power. He might have to buy one of these for himself.

Ten minutes later, Taz pulled up in front of the boutique hotel where he and Millie were staying while in Italy. Killing the engine, he stepped out and pushed his sunglasses into his hair.

Striding up the stone steps to the small but luxurious lobby, he spotted the hotel manager. With a flick of his wrist, he slapped the key fob into the man's hand.

'Move this for me, will you?'

The man looked from Taz to the Ferrari parked under his portico, his eyes sparkling with appreciation. 'Sì, signore. It will be my pleasure.'

'I understand that Ms James has checked in. Where is she?' he demanded, hooking the arm of his sunglasses into the V of his shirt.

'I believe she is on the back patio.'

Taz nodded. If someone had told him, a few weeks back, that he, the team owner and its principal driver, the most essential component of De Rossi, would be chasing down one of his employees, he would've rolled his eyes. He'd would've snapped terse explanation: he was paying her salary and would demand to know why she wasn't at the racetrack, doing her job.

Work always came first. Vesuvius could erupt, an asteroid could strike, but his team and the De Rossi brand were everyone's number one priority.

But he knew Millie well enough, and trusted her just enough, to know she'd have a damn good reason for not being at the track. Something was wrong. He knew it like he knew his own signature.

Taz stepped onto the back patio, his eyes immediately sweeping over the space. Thick, ancient vines tossed shade over the area, shielding it from the summer sun. It was a peaceful retreat, a world away from the chaos of the race-track. In the far corner sat a low-slung comfortable two-seater couch, paired with a sleek coffee table. Millie was curled up in the corner, her legs tucked beneath her, a lap-top open on her knees.

She was absorbed, her brows drawn together in concen-tration, fingers poised above the keyboard. She was dressed in a pair of form-fitting hot pink tailored shorts and an over-size button-down shirt, sleeves rolled up. Her hair caught the soft light filtering through the vines, and he experienced a punch of lust and a now-familiar hit of need.

He leaned against the door-frame for a moment, watching her, feeling the heat of his anxiety wrestle with something else entirely—a pull he didn't want to acknowledge. He ig-nored the profound whisper of *There she is*. No, this wasn't the time for fanciful bullshit. He needed a reset, immediately. This was about work, and her being AWOL today. When she finally noticed him, Millie would have to justify why she'd skipped work and disappeared when she was most needed.

'Where have you been? And why aren't you answering your phone?'

Millie's head shot up, and her eyes widened. 'Taz...'

He walked over to her, telling himself he had to treat her like he would any other employee. 'Your PR position re-quires you to be trackside, with *me*. I don't recall a clause stating that you can hang out at the hotel!'

Millie looked away and lifted her hand to her forehead, covering her eyes. He frowned. There was no avoiding it: he was definitely missing something. He couldn't remember Millie ever taking a day off and slacking on the job before. She routinely worked long hours and didn't complain. 'Are you sick? Do you have a migraine?'

She shook her head but kept her eyes on her screen, her bottom lip between her teeth. Concern replaced the last vestiges of irritation. 'Millie, look at me,' he softly commanded.

It took her a while to obey his order, and she couldn't meet his eyes, looking at the base of his throat instead. He skimmed his eyes over her face, taking in her red, swollen eyes and her pink nose. She was either having an allergic reaction or...

'Have you been crying?' he asked.

Her small shrug answered that question. Taz silently cursed and rocked on his feet. He didn't engage with people emotionally and rarely had personal conversations. He didn't have the faintest idea how to ask her why she'd cried hard enough to leave traces of tears on her face. Her bottom lip was still wobbling, for God's sake!

'What's wrong? Why the tears?' he demanded, wincing at his too-harsh tone. He prayed she didn't start crying again. He wasn't a fan of emotions and didn't know how to handle a crying woman. Normally he walked away and either left them to get on with it or...

Truthfully, there wasn't an *or*. He never bothered to engage.

Taz looked at the door leading into the hotel and calculated he could be inside in three seconds and back at the car in five, at Imola in fifteen minutes. He knew what he was doing there.

Here?

Not a bit.

But this was Millie, and because she was hurting, the heart he didn't know he possessed ached a little too. Walking away was not an option so he'd have to man up. If he could dice death on a racetrack at three hundred miles per hour, he could do this too.

Maybe.

He rubbed the back of his neck and walked to stand between the coffee table and the couch. Closing her laptop, he pushed it to the side and shoved the table back, making room for his long legs. Sitting on the table he faced her, and up close he could see her road-map red eyes.

'Talk to me, Millie.'

Millie unfolded her legs and rested her forearms on her knees. 'We both know that you'd much rather be anywhere else but here, Taz,' she said with all the charm of a snapping turtle.

She was looking to pick a fight, and he didn't blame her. It was so much easier to be angry than vulnerable. 'Why the tears, Millie?' he quietly asked. 'And I'm not moving until I get an answer.'

'Ben...'

Ben? What about him? Her shoulders slumped, and her head dropped, and she played with the silver charm on her bracelet. The charm that Ben always tied to the shoelaces of his racing boot. The charm Ben had been wearing when he crashed at...

Taz swallowed his harsh curse. Ben had died at Imola. His car had spun out and he was dead before the medics could get to him.

But because he was selfish and self-absorbed, and incredibly busy and highly stressed, he'd forgotten. God, of course Millie would find it difficult to go back to the place where Ben died, to be able to pinpoint the spot where his life ended. Taz rubbed his hands over his face, embarrassed at his lack of awareness. Confused by his need to comfort and protect.

And maybe it was time for him to admit that the real reason he'd left the track, and his responsibilities, was because he needed to be with Millie and was desperate to connect with her. That he'd missed her, and not only in his bed. He'd missed her steadying influence, her wry humour and the way she kept his feet firmly on the ground.

But this wasn't about him and what he needed from her. Faced with visiting the site where Ben had lost his life, the person she'd loved the most, Millie was in a world of hurt. And that was an acid-tipped knife in his soul.

She used the ball of her hand to blot away her tears. 'I thought I'd be fine, but I couldn't make myself go to the track today. I mean, I know I need to, it's my *job*. I also want to lay flowers where he died. But I couldn't muster the courage today.'

He could throw himself into the tightest of corners at three hundred miles an hour and make split-second decisions that risked a car worth several fortunes and the livelihoods of two thousand employees across his racing and technology divisions. But when faced with Millie's tear-streaked cheeks and eyes saturated with pain, Taz felt utterly out of his depth.

She lifted those shattered eyes to his. 'I feel like such a coward, Taz.' Her voice cracked, and he winced. Her raw honesty drilled into him, through him.

His hands itched to comfort her, to stroke her hair, to tuck the damp strands clinging to her face behind her ears. But he held back. There were different kinds of bravery, and Taz knew—deep in the darkest, most hidden part of himself—that hers eclipsed his. He could charm his way into any woman's bed, play polo and golf at near-professional levels and speed-read a contract while dissecting a complicated financial statement.

But showing someone your wounds, revealing the bruises on your soul, took strength he didn't possess. Facing the past, wrestling with its jagged edges instead of locking it away in an unreachable vault, took a fortitude he could only admire from a distance. When it came to emotions, he was broken. Stunted. Incapable of anything more profound than surface-level banter. They said you learned how to love from the environment you grew up in, and while he'd witnessed the love his father bestowed on Alex, there'd been none left over for him. He'd received so little affection and love, he had no concept of how the process worked. To understand meant acknowledging he was unloved, and for most of his life that was too hard to do. He'd fallen into the self-protecting habit of dismissing it as being inconsequential and unneeded. As a result, feelings terrified him, and this woman, with her tears and her unbearable vulnerability, utterly dismantled him.

He tried to form words—words to tell her she was remarkable, that her courage left him in awe—but they stuck in his throat. They were too big, too tangled, too dangerous. They wouldn't come out. So he did the only thing he knew how to do: He retreated. He pulled back, slammed down his emotional shutters and wrapped himself in the cold, impenetrable roll cage that had always protected him. But because he needed to say something, anything, he retreated to where he felt comfortable. 'You should focus on work,' he said, wincing at his too-flat voice. 'You're great at what you do, and it's a good place to...' How to say this without revealing too much? '...lose yourself.'

She tipped her head, her eyes huge in her face. 'Is that what you do, Tazio?'

He couldn't admit that, couldn't widen that crack in his psyche. Not even with her, the woman who'd burrowed deeper under his skin than anyone else. He had to keep some distance, stay emotionally safe. Keep those feelings controlled and contained. 'We have so much to do, and little time to do it in. Let's get back to work.'

When hurt flickered in her eyes, he knew she'd been expecting a hug, some affection, maybe even for him to tell her that he was happy to see her. But he couldn't touch her, not now. If he did, his control would shatter and he'd expose how much he'd missed her, that he wanted her, would show her every inch of his emotional underbelly. Vulnerability was never acceptable.

Disappointment, stark and cutting, slashed through her eyes and across her face, a hot blade through butter.

They said he was an insensitive bastard. Cold. Unfeeling. Selfish. He hated labels and fought against being shoved into a box. But as he stood there, watching the light in her eyes dim, he knew the press, and the world, had him pegged.

CHAPTER TEN

IN THE DE ROSSI conference room at the Imola track, her back to the track, Millie pushed her laptop away and tried to stretch away the stress of the long day. Yesterday and the day before had hurtled past in a blur of chaos—exactly what she'd come to expect from the build-up to race-day. Taz had been busier than normal, his days taken up with race business, his nights with sponsor dinners, and he'd slipped into the bed they shared after she was asleep and quietly left before she was awake.

When they were together on the track, he occasionally wrapped his arm around her waist, dropped a kiss in her hair. But because people were always around when he was being affectionate, she never knew if it was to promote their supposed romance or if he was being genuinely affectionate.

He'd been surprisingly understanding about her absence from the track the other day—she'd expected a harsh scolding because Taz De Rossi did not appreciate his people not doing their jobs to his exacting standards!—and his saying she was doing a great job as his PR person both warmed and floored her. Again, compliments about work performance from him were hard to earn and exceedingly rare.

Millie sighed. They were both exceptionally busy and currently run off their feet and had little time to spend together. Conversations, mainly work-based, were rushed, and while they kept up their fake relationship in public and shared a bed at night, they hadn't connected on a personal level lately. Sure, their days were long and chaotic, but she couldn't help thinking Taz was avoiding her.

Since meeting up again, there had been fleeting moments of…oh, it was so hard to define! A glance. A hesitation. Heat that was quickly banked, a tiny spark of tenderness quickly smothered. He looked, only to her, like a man grappling with something he couldn't control, like he'd pulled the pin on a grenade and now didn't know where to throw it.

Her phone buzzed, and Millie frowned when she saw a message on the De Rossi employees group chat. Taz wanted the entire team to congregate on the track outside the De Rossi pit stop in five minutes. Millie raised her eyebrows. It was the end of the day, and everyone was tired. Why was Taz calling a team meeting now?

Millie made her way down to the track and joined her unusually sombre colleagues, a little confused at the unusual summons.

Taz, dressed in a dark suit with an open-necked white shirt, pushed his way through the crowd to her. He held a massive bouquet of white lilies and roses, which he pushed into her hands. Then, he took her hand in his, linking their fingers. Drivers and crew members from the other teams joined the De Rossi team.

Taz cleared his throat, and the crowd quietened. 'Millie James is Ben Brennan's cousin, and ten years ago, Ben lost his life on this very track.' He looked down at her. 'We are all here to remember Ben, Millie. Let's go, sweetheart,' he softly murmured, his deep voice surprisingly tender.

It took Millie a few beats for her to realise that Taz had arranged a memorial service for Ben, a way for her to commemorate his death and for his colleagues in the racing world to pay their respects to one of their own. And in doing so, he confirmed every instinct she'd had about him: that Taz was far better than the man he pretended to be. Hand in hand, they began a slow, deliberate walk onto the track. Behind them, the crowd followed—drivers, mechanics, managers, and others—moving quietly. The kaleidoscope of uniforms blended, team loyalties forgotten, united in paying tribute to one of their own. A wave of gratitude rolled through her. Taz wasn't just giving her a way to honour Ben, he was honouring her grief, her memories and her love for her cousin in a way that spoke louder than words ever could.

He'd used all his power and influence to create a moment she would carry with her forever. And for the first time in weeks, Millie felt as though she could finally begin to let go. Tears spilt freely down her cheeks. She clung to Taz's hand, his steady grip anchoring her as they walked. After several minutes, he guided her to the side of the track, his hand firm on her waist.

'This is where it happened,' he murmured, his voice low. 'This is where Ben crashed, Millie.'

She nodded, her throat tight with emotion. Dropping to her knees, she placed the bouquet on the edge of the track, her fingers brushing the cool asphalt. Her voice was barely a whisper, but she spoke anyway, hoping that somehow Ben could hear her.

'Ben, I miss you. So much. I wish I'd spent more time with you, that I'd seen you more. I'm sorry.'

On her haunches, she stared at the bouquet, grateful that Taz's big body formed a barrier between her and the crowd behind her. 'I'm trying to be better, Ben, and I'm slowly making sense of my life and my place in the world... I really hope you're proud of me, Ben,' she added, her tears flowing unchecked.

At the same time Taz's big hand came to rest on her shoulder, steadying and grounding her, Ben's voice rolled through her. *There wasn't a day I wasn't, Mils.*

For a fleeting moment, she thought she felt his presence—a breath of wind, his laughter dancing on the air. Then a deep voice rose behind her, singing the first line of 'Amazing Grace'.

Millie's composure shattered. Kneeling on the track with Taz behind her, shielding her, she sobbed for everything she'd lost: for the cousin who'd been like a brother, for the girl she used to be and for the woman she was struggling to become.

Hours later, comprehensively exhausted, Taz stood in the passage outside his hotel suite and rested his hand on the door. It had been a long and tough day in a series of long and tough days, and he was shattered. He was used to working hard, but organising Ben's memorial service had taken more effort than anybody—especially Millie—knew. Getting permission from the stewards to walk the track as a huge group, just a day before the time trials, had taken some persuading—the track was looked after like a newborn baby—and when that was done, he'd contacted the other teams and rallied support for the memorial. He hadn't wanted to raise her hopes in case he couldn't pull it off, so keeping it from Millie had been difficult. Apparently, he no longer liked hiding things from her. His thoughts, emotions, what he was thinking and doing.

And there was the root of his dilemma. He wanted to both protect himself and to deepen his connection to Millie. Wanted to keep his distance yet also know her inside out. While trying to run a multibillion-dollar company, manage his team and promote his charity work, he was consistently battered by conflicting emotions, desires and needs.

God, he was a mess. And he didn't like it. But he didn't—couldn't—regret arranging Ben's memorial service. He had done it partly as an apology for not immediately understanding why she couldn't face being at the track the day she arrived in Italy, and partly because he remembered Millie saying she wanted to visit the place where Ben died. Mostly because he suspected she needed to reconnect, even if it was through death, with her cousin. Bottom line: Millie'd needed it, so he'd stepped up and made it happen.

He couldn't stay out here, so Taz opened the door and stepped into the room. Millie sat on the bed, looking frail and played-out, emotionally whipped. Resisting the urge to scoop her up and cuddle her—he wasn't a cuddler!—he stayed by the door, keeping his restless hands in his trouser pockets.

'You need to eat, Millie,' he stated, his voice rough.

'I can't,' she replied. She lifted her shoulders and let them drop. Her huge, emotion-drenched eyes met his. 'How can I eat when words are bubbling inside me, when I have so much gratitude that needs to be expressed?'

He didn't want her thanks, couldn't handle her gratitude. It was too much. There were too many emotions swirling around, and he felt battered from all sides.

As per normal, he found words and conversation difficult and struggled to find the right response. 'Words aren't what I need, Mils.'

Moving toward him, she placed her hands flat against his chest, stood on her toes and placed her lips on his rough-with-stubble cheek. She stayed there for a long time—a minute or a decade? Who knew?—and when she finally returned to her feet, her eyes slammed into his, and he tumbled into a field of African violets…a lot of blue, hints of purple.

'What do you need, Taz?'

'I need you, Millie,' he whispered. God, he prayed she didn't ask him how or why or to explain that statement any further.

'You do?'

In so many ways he couldn't express. 'Will you stay with me tonight?'

'Yes.'

Millie's arms wrapped around his waist, handing him a hug he didn't know he needed. She was the one who'd cried today, who'd weathered an emotional storm, but now he was the one absorbing her warmth, sucking in her quiet strength. She recharged his batteries and refilled his well. Taz buried his nose in her fragrant hair as panic barrelled through him. What was happening to him and, more importantly, how on earth was he going to find the distance he knew he very badly needed?

After a night spent in Taz's arms—with comfort morphing into blistering sex—Millie woke feeling steadier. Not completely herself, but the grief-tinged panic seemed to have receded. She could go to the track today. Watching the race itself might be too much—she'd already decided she'd retreat to Taz's trailer if necessary—but she'd said her goodbyes to Ben yesterday. Now it was time to do her job.

The Italian sun warmed the hotel patio, and the lush gardens surrounding them buzzed with life. Millie poured fresh coffee into their cups, enjoying the quiet intimacy of the al fresco breakfast. Across the table, Taz looked distracted, his dark brows pulled together. He hummed with energy, and she knew today would be hard for him. For a man who thrived in the heat of competition, who craved control, being sidelined was agonising.

'I don't think you realise how touched I am by what you did yesterday,' she quietly said. 'I'm so grateful, Taz.'

'You thanked me last night, Millie,' he said, reaching for his coffee.

He was so comfortable basking in track victories and in front of cameras and doing deals, but he frowned and shifted in his seat when he was praised for being sweet and sensitive. Millie resisted the urge to say more, hoping Taz knew the depth of her gratitude.

Ben's memorial ceremony, and Taz's role in organising it, had made headline news this morning. Taz had been enjoying some good press for a while now, but this was the kind of story the media loved—a touching blend of tragedy and hope—but Millie knew Taz hadn't done it for the cameras. He'd done it for her.

This man, so tough and impenetrable, could also be tender and infuriatingly thoughtful when he chose to be. He was an enigma wrapped up in a puzzle guarded by layers of computer code. Unhackable.

She bit into a strawberry, watching him. 'Did you have a big funeral for Alex?'

His hand tightened around his fork, his jaw going rigid. Millie winced internally. Wrong question. But she pressed on, hoping for a response. Any response. 'It's so strange and awful that two De Rossi drivers died so young. What was Alex like?'

For a moment, she thought he might answer, but then he replied, his voice colder and unexpectedly clipped. 'Look him up online.'

Her stomach sank. She recognised the tone: His walls

were up, the subject closed. But she couldn't let it go. Not entirely.

'I don't want the internet's version of Alex. I want *your* version, Taz.' She leaned forward, cradling her coffee cup. 'What was he like as your brother? I could tell you a thousand little things about Ben—how he cried during animated movies or hated needles. That he loved shoving asparagus stalks up his nose to make me laugh. It's the stupid things, the little things, that made him *him*.'

'What's with the interrogation, Millie? We're sleeping together, not sharing our deepest secrets.'

His words hit her like a slap, but she didn't flinch. She knew his sharpness masked pain, that he lashed out when he felt cornered. 'I'm trying to have a conversation with you, Tazio, about your brother. This is what people do.'

He tossed his serviette onto the table and released a huff of annoyance. 'I don't,' he snapped.

She should back off, but she had come this far, she might as well see it through. Yesterday had been cathartic for her, and she wanted Taz to feel the same peace. Oh, she still didn't know who exactly she was or where she was going, but she wasn't nearly as lost as she was before.

She felt less emotional, and some of her ghosts had been laid to rest. She wanted Taz to feel of little of the relief she did. Was that so wrong?

'Alex is someone to be proud of, to be celebrated,' Millie gently stated. 'He was a good guy, so why don't you talk about him? He was your big brother and part of your life. And while we're on the subject, why don't you talk about your dad?'

'Millie, I have a busy day ahead of me, and I don't want it to begin with a fight.'

Millie wrinkled her nose. 'I don't want to fight either. I'm trying to have a conversation with you.'

'We can talk about anyone or anything *but* Alex—or my dad,' Taz quickly added.

'Why is everything that matters off-limits with you?' Millie asked, keeping her tone gentle.

Taz's chair scraped against the stone as he stood abruptly, his movements sharp with tension. 'You don't have the first clue about Alex. Or my father. And I don't owe you any explanations.'

She looked up at him, her heart twisting. 'I agree you don't owe me anything, Taz. But holding all this in—it's only hurting you.'

His laugh was humourless, the sound hollow. 'Stay out of my head, Millie.'

And with that, he walked away, leaving her alone on the sunlit patio. As she watched his broad back retreat, she felt something shift between them—a crack widening, impossible to ignore.

When Millie arrived at the Autodromo Internazionale Enzo e Dino Ferrari later that day, she was alone. After storming off, Taz had left the hotel without speaking to her again, forcing her to call an intern to collect her, a humiliation to go along with her shredded nerves.

It was race-day, and her earlier courage had dissolved like water droplets on a hot pavement. Now she was holding herself together with fine, fraying threads of mental superglue. One hour until the race. She glanced at her watch, the ticking hands a constant countdown. Coffee was out, but a cup of chamomile and ginger tea might soothe her jangling nerves, and she'd swallow a few of the homoeopathic anxiety pills she kept tucked in her bag.

Her rational brain told her she was being absurd. What had happened ten years ago was a freak accident and statistically impossible to repeat. But rationalisations didn't quiet her anxiety. It wasn't only the track or the memories, it was the coming together of too many emotions—her deepening feelings for Taz, her lack of sleep and her inability to understand how they could veer from passion to tension to frustration and back again in a matter of minutes.

Millie stepped into the hospitality suite grateful it was empty. The muffled roar of the crowd drifted through the window, and Millie wondered what had caught their attention. Refusing to look out the window, she rubbed her burning eyes.

She missed Ben. He should've been here. Even if he wasn't racing, he'd be at the centre of it all—bantering with the pit crew, trading insults with the mechanics, laughing with the support staff. Ben had been so vibrant, so present. He'd lived in the moment, someone who loved what he did with every fibre of his being.

Millie wanted to be that kind of person. She loved the work she was doing for Taz and was constantly surprised by how good she was at it. Her knack for finding the heart of a problem, for peeling back layers to reveal a story that resonated, had transformed Taz in the eyes of the press. He was no longer just a volatile, selfish hothead—though, admittedly, he still was to some degree. Over the past few weeks, she'd reframed him, and now he was viewed as a burdened team owner and driver, the man who carried the weight of the De Rossi legacy on his shoulders.

And she hadn't spun lies to make it happen. Everything she'd said about Taz was true. He bore the crushing responsibility of his team, his employees, his sponsors' expectations—and his unrelenting ambition. The weight would be staggering for anyone, but for Taz? It seemed to harden his defences, fortifying his sharp edges and impenetrable walls.

His inability to discuss Alex, to allow her to peek behind his emotional walls, was deeply frustrating and a little hurtful. His rejection stung, but she'd noticed the storm raging inside him. There was so much she didn't know—so much he'd never let her see. Unless he chose to let her in, they would never be more than what they were now: unexpected flashes of tenderness, stolen moments in bed, tethered by nothing but desire.

Why did she want more?

Because something in Taz De Rossi called to her. Beneath the arrogance and the fire, she'd glimpsed a man who was deeply lonely, profoundly isolated. And, yes, he could be brutal and demanding, but there was also kindness in him, flashes of goodness that made her chest ache. He was infuriatingly complicated. He was many things at different times, and trying to make sense of Taz De Rossi was like trying to staple mist to a wall.

Her current exhaustion made her feel shaky and weak, and it amplified everything—her hurt, her anger, her impossible attraction to a man who was far too dangerous. When she felt steadier, when she was stronger, she'd untangle her emotions and decide what, if anything, they meant.

But she doubted they'd fade or would shrink to manageable levels, and suspected she was already in too deep. And she didn't think she could swim her way out.

In the hallway, Taz stopped dead as the door to the hospitality suite clicked shut behind Millie, the loud snick reverberating down the empty passage.

He tipped his head back, eyes fixed on the ceiling, looking for a way to ease the storm raging inside him. Today was not going to plan. Not even close. Every cell in his body ached to be on the track, clad in his De Rossi colours, listening to the roar of his car's engine, navigating the track's twists and turns. He knew what he was doing on the track.

He was wasting time and points, hampered and sidelined by his damned cast. Frustration dug its nails into his soul as the ugly combination of rage and helplessness swamped him. And because the universe seemed to delight in screwing with him, he'd taken out his anger on Millie earlier. She hadn't deserved it—but her simple questions about his brother and father had been enough to set him off. It was a topic he'd deflected a thousand times before, so why had it pierced through his shell this time? Why had *she*?

Taz braced a hand against the wall and let his forehead rest against it, his teeth grinding.

Millie was a problem he hadn't anticipated. He'd always compartmentalised his life—emotions in one box, sex in another and racing in a sacred safe all its own. But Millie had smashed some of those boxes, blurring the perfect lines he'd spent years drawing. She was a walking contradiction: infuriating and fascinating, soothing and incendiary. She'd painted his black-and-white world with wild streaks of vibrant colour.

He hated it.

He wanted more.

Taz groaned and banged his cast against the wall, shaking his head to clear it. He'd completed the bulk of the charity events he'd committed to—all with Millie at his side—and only had the ball in Monaco to attend. In three weeks, he'd be racing again, and life would return to being predictable, and he could focus on winning the championship. Proving, once and for all, that he was the best driver in his family, the greatest De Rossi to ever race.

The thought left him hollow.

Instead of relief, he felt…lost.

His jaw tightened. *Enough.* If he was going to survive the next three weeks, he needed to fix the mess he'd made with Millie. Lashing out at her had been cowardly. He hated cowardice; it was wholly unacceptable.

Steeling himself, he slipped into the hospitality suite, locking the door behind him. Millie turned at the sound, her brows arching, her expression cool.

Her outfit was simple—black jeans, a De Rossi team shirt, and high-tops—but Taz's pulse kicked up. Like two thousand other employees, she wore his name, but at seeing his name above her heart, something primal and possessive unfurled in his chest. He shoved the thought down, then stomped on it.

'Millie,' he began, his voice low, careful.

She sipped from her mug, her gaze steady, unwavering. She wasn't going to make this easy for him.

Good. He didn't deserve easy.

'I was out of line this morning,' he said, his words clipped but honest. 'You didn't deserve that. I shouldn't have—'

'Snapped? Stormed off?' she supplied.

'Exactly,' he admitted, forcing himself to meet her eyes. 'Sorry.'

The tension in her shoulders remained. 'Apologies aren't your strong suit, are they, Taz?' she said, her voice softer now but no less firm.

'No,' he confessed. 'But I'm learning.'

Her lips twitched, almost, but she caught herself, the flash of amusement replaced by wariness.

'Why did you snap at me?' she asked, crossing her arms, her vulnerability shielded behind her resolve.

Because you matter too much. Because you see through

the masks I've worn for years, and I don't like it. He didn't say that, of course. Instead he shrugged, his hands slipping into his pockets. She studied him for a moment, her gaze piercing, and Taz realised he was holding his breath.

Finally, she sighed, setting her cup on the counter. 'You're a mess, Taz De Rossi,' she muttered, but there was no heat in her words.

His lips quirked. 'I've been called worse.'

Her mouth softened, and for the first time all day, he felt the knot in his chest loosen. He wasn't out of the woods, not by a long shot, but at least he wasn't wandering in the dark alone.

Tired, he walked over to the fridge, pulled out a bottle of water and cracked the top.

'You're way too nice, Mils,' he said, resting the bottle on his forehead. He rolled it across his forehead, hoping the cool plastic would ease his headache. Words he didn't expect to utter left his mouth. 'Remember I asked you whether Ben had said anything to you about Alex?'

What was he doing? Why was he reopening this door, edging it open a crack? 'We didn't speak about Alex, Taz,' Millie replied. 'Our conversations didn't include a lot of racing talk. What I knew about Alex was what I read online.'

Drivers were normally chatty, sometimes gossipy, guys. Did Ben not talk about Alex because he knew who he really was, and how he spent his free time, when he wasn't with Meredith or out in public? Had Ben known about the drugs and the young girls? If he did, why didn't he say anything?

As soon as the thought formed, he had his answer. Because nobody would've believed him. Alex was the favourite son of the team's owner. If he'd criticised Alex, Ben would've sounded like he was whining or making trouble and it was a case of sour grapes.

There was no universe in which Ben could criticise Alex and come out with his good reputation intact.

He lifted the water bottle, drank half its contents and forced his eyes to meet Millie's. He'd tell her the bare minimum, enough for her to understand. 'I don't talk about Alex because...' Shit, this was hard.

He sighed, swallowed and sighed again. 'Alex wasn't the person everyone thought he was.'

She looked confused, as he knew she would. 'What do you mean?'

'That's all I can say.' There was so much more, but those few words felt like someone had poured acid down his throat.

Millie stood, put her cup on the table and folded her arms.

'Can you give me a little more?' she asked.

Didn't she realise that she'd got more from him than anyone since the night Alex died? That those few halting words needed more courage than barrelling down an endless salt pan in a car made for speed and not safety? Conversations like these were far more dangerous than anything the racing world could throw at him.

Taz dragged his shaking hand over his jaw, his self-assurance in tatters. But instead of probing for answers or demanding more, Millie did something that completely disarmed him. She walked over, placed both hands on his chest and rested her forehead on his sternum. Her arms slipped around his waist in a tight, wordless hug. No ulterior motive. No agenda. Just quiet, undemanding comfort.

Taz froze, utterly blindsided. Like last night, her embrace wasn't sexual or flirtatious—it was *human*. And yet his knees wobbled like he'd walked away from a death-defying crash. He couldn't remember the last time someone had offered him solace without expecting something in return. Before his mother died, perhaps? But those memories were buried under decades of grief and loss, hazy with time.

Millie pulled back, tilting her head to meet his gaze, her eyes were soft with understanding. Her fingertips brushed his jaw in a feather-light caress.

'It must be exhausting always being compared to him,' she said, her voice a low murmur. 'I'm so sorry, Taz.'

Her words pierced his armour and burned his skin. Taz blinked hard, desperate to banish the burning in his eyes. He couldn't lose it, not here, not now. Emotion was self-indulgent and useless, a luxury he'd discarded in his teens. So why was it so damned difficult to push her away? To create the distance he knew he needed?

A knock broke the spell he was under, a welcome distraction. It jolted him back to the present, and when the door-handle rattled, he remembered he'd locked it. Grateful for the interruption, he strode to the door, unlocked it and yanked it open.

The intern standing in the hallway flinched at his scowl. 'Uh… Mr De Rossi, they're waiting for you in the briefing room,' the young man stammered.

Taz nodded curtly, his jaw tight. 'I'll be there in a minute.'

When the intern didn't turn and flee, Taz's scowl deepened. 'Is there something else?'

The kid took a step back. 'Uh… Mr De Rossi…uh…the car is here.'

'The car?'

'You ordered a car to take Ms James back to the hotel, sir. It's waiting for her.'

Right. *That*. He'd forgotten that he wanted Millie away from the race this afternoon. Yesterday's impromptu memorial service had been rough on her, and he suspected she was still dealing with the emotional storm. There were other races she would attend, but there was nothing she needed to do this afternoon. She did not need to watch the race at the track where Ben died.

'Give us a minute,' Taz told the kid and shut the door. Rubbing the back of his neck, he walked over to where Millie stood, clearly confused.

He pushed a long tendril behind her ear and hooked it behind her ear. 'Go home, Millie. You don't need to be here.'

She shook her head, her stubborn chin lifting. 'I can't, Taz. I have work to do.'

No, she didn't. Not today. 'There's nothing that can't wait until tomorrow, and I promise not to cause a PR disaster between now and then.' He cupped her face, and she pushed her soft cheek into his palm. 'I don't want you watching the race. I don't want your imagination working overtime, for you to think about what happened to Ben. Go back to the hotel, swim. Fall asleep in the shade on a lounger by the pool. Think about anything but this race.'

Her stunning eyes filled with tears, and a few ran down her cheek. Her hand covered his and she nodded, her bottom lip trembling. 'Thank you,' she said, sniffing hard. 'I didn't know how to watch the race and not watch the race, if you know what I mean.'

He wrapped his arm around her shoulder and roughly pulled her into him, thinking how well she fit into his much bigger body, like a puzzle piece he never knew was missing. He turned his head to kiss the top of hers. Looking over her shoulder, he caught a glimpse of his watch-face and grimaced at the time. He needed to be down in the pit, at the coalface. 'Mils…'

She pulled back and bobbed her head. 'You need to get going,' she stated, quickly wiping away her tears. 'Of course you do.'

'I'll walk you to the car.' He really shouldn't. He was needed elsewhere, but this was…well, this was Millie.

She sent him a look of reproach, the sting removed by her soft smile. 'And every reporter will wonder why I'm leaving and whether we've fought, whether I'm not feeling well, whether—' she slapped her hands to her face and rolled her eyes '—I'm pregnant! No, let's avoid the drama, and I'll sneak out quietly.'

He didn't like it. 'Are you sure?'

Millie nodded. 'I need a couple of minutes to get my stuff, so you go on.' He didn't move, and Millie released a quick huff. 'I promise you that I'm not going to stay here and work, Taz. I *will* go back to the hotel.'

She was the only person ever who could even remotely read his mind. And because he saw the sincerity in her eyes, he nodded, then swiped his mouth across hers. 'Have a good afternoon.'

She smiled. 'See you later?' she asked.

He nodded. 'I'm not sure when I'll be back.' But he'd be with her as soon as he could. He didn't know where they were going or how they'd pan out, so he intended to spend all the time he could with her.

CHAPTER ELEVEN

Monaco

MILLIE AND TAZ left Italy and arrived in Monaco the day after the race at Imola. Instead of flying, Taz bundled her into what she thought was a Bugatti (her knowledge about cars was abysmal) and they drove from Imola to Monaco. As they entered the heart of Monaco six hours later, Millie made a concerted effort to keep her excitement from showing on her face. It was the week leading up to the Grand Prix, and the city buzzed with anticipation and energy. The bright blue Mediterranean shimmered under the sun, and the luxury yachts in the harbour gleamed.

Locals and tourists alike were caught up in the excitement. Cafés were crowded and lively conversation punctuated the warm air. High heels clicked against the cobblestone streets. The city was a mix of sophistication and chaos, a place where the race was as much a reason for the world's rich and beautiful to gather as it was a sporting spectacle. Monaco gleamed. And preened.

Millie noticed people pointing their phones at them and heard the buzz of excitement when gearheads and Formula One fans recognised Taz. They stopped at a traffic light, and the car was quickly surrounded by fans and paparazzi. Taz was mobbed by requests for selfies and autographs.

Taz leaned across to her, and on the pretence of kissing

her cheek, murmured in her ear. 'I've got to get you and this car off the street, or else we're going to be mobbed.'

Millie nodded her agreement, and when the light turned green Taz revved the engine and inched forward. The crowd parted and they roared away, and a few blocks later reached their hotel.

Because Taz was Taz and a global sensation, they were whisked up to his penthouse suite with a minimum of fuss. The panoramic views of the Mediterranean and the iconic skyline immediately captured Millie's attention. The penthouse was extensive, open and airy, its furnishings sleek and modern. An infinity pool ran the length of the suite, and Millie didn't need to explore to know that it would include a huge bedroom with an oversize bed, a bathroom that could accommodate thirty people and, possibly, a private gym.

Millie stretched, her eyes on the breath-stealing view. It was after two, and since they'd stopped for lunch along the way, they needed to get some work done today. She'd lost time yesterday, and her to-do list was as long as the circuit snaking through the city.

'Are you going to head down to the track?' she asked Taz, who'd walked over to stand next to her. Instead of looking at the view, his eyes were on her face. 'Why are you looking at me like that?' she asked, a little self-conscious at his intense stare. 'Why aren't you admiring the view? It's stunning.'

'Because you are far more interesting,' he told her, his voice becoming a little deeper, a tad richer. Gruffer. 'I have an appointment with the team doctor in an hour, and the stylist is coming here with a selection of dresses for you to wear to the ball tomorrow night.'

It was the last event she'd agreed to attend as his fake girlfriend, and the most high-profile. Millie wrinkled her nose. 'Why can't he choose one? I've got so much to do,' she complained.

'You need to choose.' Taz placed his hand on her hip and pulled her closer. 'But since we both have an hour...'

His lips hit the spot on her neck where she was most sensitive, and she could feel him growing harder against her stomach. She didn't have time for this, she had about a hundred emails she needed to respond to and calls to return. But Taz's lips on her skin felt like heaven, and when he moved his mouth up her neck, across her jaw and onto hers, she sighed. She'd work harder later. Making love to Taz was all that was important right now...

'Millie...'

His mouth claimed hers with unapologetic hunger, bypassing tenderness and heading straight into a kiss that was ferocious, desperate. His tongue invaded, retreated, then plunged back in, a reckless rhythm that left her breathless. He was a fine wine and dark chocolate, a jolt of adrenaline and a dizzying fall. Millie melted into his heat, craving more than his kisses.

She pressed her hips into his, her sigh mingling with his low groan. Yes. More. Of everything he could give her. Work could wait.

But Taz stepped back, his hands the only tether between them as they traced the line of her jaw, his expression fierce yet controlled. 'Why did you stop?' The question slipped out before she realised she'd spoken.

His voice was rough, strained. 'Because I don't want it to be over too fast. I want more for you than fast.'

Her laugh was breathy, laced with need. 'I don't mind fast.'

Taz shook his head, the corner of his mouth quirking into a wicked smile. 'Not this time, Mils.'

His shortening her name softened her. It made her feel claimed and cherished. Dangerous thoughts. This wasn't love—it *couldn't* be. But when he bent and swept her into his arms, carrying her with effortless strength, the lines between what was possible and what was not, between sex and love, blurred.

In the bedroom, decorated in soft sea-greens and whites, he set her down in front of a tall, free-standing mirror. Moving to stand behind her, with a sexy combination of need and simmering restraint, he met her eyes in the glass. His hands came to rest on her shoulders, his touch scorching her skin through the fabric of her shirt.

'Your only job is to watch me,' he commanded softly, his voice like smoke and silk.

With aching slowness, from behind her he undid the buttons of her shirt, revealing her skin inch by inch. His hands traced her collarbone and slid the fabric from her arms, and she shivered as her lace bra came into view. He kissed the curve of her neck, cupped her breasts and kneaded them with reverence and complete focus. Her nipples pebbled under his touch, and her breath caught.

'Look at yourself,' he murmured, voice roughened by desire. 'See how beautiful you are. You're luscious, Millie. Bold and bright.'

'No, I'm just—'

'Just gorgeous, and so sexy you make me dizzy,' he muttered, in his sex-and-sandpaper voice. He shook her lightly. 'Look at yourself. See what I see.'

Her reflection in the mirror shocked her. A sexy woman, one she barely recognised, stared back at her with flushed cheeks and eyes dark with desire. She was luminous and vibrant. Someone who could, and should, be confident in her own skin, in what she could offer the world. In what she could offer *him*. Maybe it was time to start seeing herself differently, to break the habit of putting herself down.

Taz's hands left her breasts to unclasp her bra, the straps falling away like ribbons, baring her completely.

Her breath hitched as he slid a hand beneath the waistband of her shorts, the other hand caressing her spine. 'God, Millie,' he rasped, voice hoarse with need. 'You're stunning. I can't wait to be inside you.'

Swept away with the raw intensity in his voice, her inhibitions dissolved. Millie hastily shed her clothes and stood between him and the mirror, clothed in nothing but heat and hunger. Taz moved to kneel, his shoulders pushing her thighs apart, and she gasped. Too much. Too intimate.

'Trust me,' he whispered.

She did. He kissed her there, where no one but him had kissed her, with such tenderness, such raw intensity. Sparkling sensations rolled over her, pulling her under, scattering her thoughts like wedding confetti. His mouth painted magic over her skin, his fingers teased, and when her climax hit, it was an obliteration, a release that left her trembling and weightless. Transformed.

Taz pulled back, his face flushed, his chest heaving as he gazed at her with reverent satisfaction, pleased by her response, utterly confident in his skill.

He stood, a towering figure of strength and passion, and she held out her hand, lacing her fingers with his. 'Now, Taz,' she whispered. 'Make love to me.'

And when he kissed her again, slow and consuming, Millie wondered if this was love, if Taz was the man she'd hand her heart to. What would he do with it if she did?

Would he cherish it or crush it?

But as long as he kept kissing her like this, she didn't really care.

CHAPTER TWELVE

THE NEXT EVENING, Taz stood by the edge of the infinity pool, the cool night air brushing against his bare chest. With only a towel wrapped around his hips, he scowled at the Mediterranean Sea, its surface unnervingly still.

He should've been enjoying shower sex with Millie, and the taste of her mouth still lingered on his lips, the heat of her body pressed against his. Instead, his jaw was tight, and his hands flexed at his sides as he relived the moment that had shattered their intimacy.

The insistent, strident ringing of his phone.

He'd heard it even through the rush of water in the power shower, but he'd ignored it. Who cared about the rest of the world when Millie was naked in his arms? His soapy hands had been sliding over her curves, her skin slick and warm beneath his touch, when the braying ringing broke the moment.

Reluctantly, he'd stepped out of the shower, water dripping off him as he snatched up the towel and wrapped it around his waist. He'd reached for the phone, already annoyed, and that was when his afternoon rapidly slid downhill.

'What the *hell* do you mean that it's been delayed?'

He checked the knot of his towel and rested his forearms on the railing, taking in his logistics manager's report. Essentially, a large shipment of car parts, including crucial tyres, specialised tools and performance equipment, had been caught up in a blockade by striking truck drivers in France and its arrival would be delayed by several days. Taz gripped the bridge of his nose. The equipment was needed by his mechanical team so they could start fine-tuning the car set-up and getting it ready for the demanding street circuit.

'With the strike still ongoing, no one can tell me when the backlog will begin to move.'

Taz thought fast. They had duplicates of everything they needed at the De Rossi headquarters and research centre in the UK. He gave his manager the go-ahead to hire a cargo plane and ordered him to move heaven and earth to get the parts to Monaco as soon as humanly possible.

Shit. He killed the call and banged the edge of his palm against the railing, frustrated and annoyed.

Dealing with delays wasn't something new, it was part of the logistical circus that came with moving a huge F1 team from one glittering city to another, but tonight Taz felt rattled. The kind of rattled he hadn't felt in years. Control was his oxygen. He thrived on it, needed it, but lately? It was slipping through his fingers, slick and treacherous like oil on a wet track.

Since Shanghai, his life had become an impossible tightrope walk above a thousand-foot chasm without safety ropes. So much changed—and quickly. He'd lost his temper, been sidelined by injury, acquired a fake girlfriend and somehow found a real lover. And yesterday, sitting in his doctor's office, they'd finally cut away the cast on his hand.

'It's been five weeks, and you've healed well. Technically you could race,' his doctor cautiously told him, 'but I wouldn't recommend it.'

But Taz needed to be behind the wheel. Saturday couldn't come fast enough.

He'd kept the news to himself, unable to tell Millie, his race engineers or the team. The Taz he used to be would've already announced his triumphant return to the world he ruled, enjoying the attention and standing in the spotlight. But the man he was today, staring at the late-afternoon sun dipping under the horizon, was different. Over the past few weeks since he'd gotten closer to Millie, he felt like he'd become softer, more vulnerable, like some of his armour had fallen away. He didn't like feeling exposed.

He pushed his hand through his hair, wishing he could blow off the ball, but he was the guest of honour. It was yet another PR circus, designed to soften his image, make him a little more human, a little less controversial. But his idea of having Millie at his side had been a genius one. Sure, a nice girlfriend helped his image but, with her there, he was less impatient, a lot more tolerant, less abrasive. Nicer to be around.

All good things. But what wasn't good was that Millie knew Alex wasn't the saint everyone believed him to be. He'd given her no details, but if he did, he knew she'd understand and empathise. But telling her required an enormous amount of trust, more than he could give. If nobody but him knew of Alex's secret, then it was forever safe. If he told Millie everything about that night, he'd feel utterly vulnerable, exposed and completely dismantled. He'd regret that he'd told her and worry she'd let the information about Alex slip, and those initial niggles of worry would swell to full-blown anxiety.

The sound of soft footsteps pulled him from his thoughts, and Millie's cool hand settled on his bare back.

Her freshly washed hair tumbled over her shoulders in damp waves, catching the fading light. She wore a skimpy vest and a pair of soft cotton shorts, her bare feet silent on the stone tiles.

For a moment, the chaos quieted. The noise in his head dulled.

'Problem?' she asked.

He nodded and explained, enjoying her hand on his bare back. 'It sounds like you found a solution,' she stated. 'Now, what's really worrying you?'

How did she find the crack, the gap, in his carefully constructed emotional fence? When had she developed the ability to blow past his shields and look into the raw, unspoken, unacknowledged parts of him? Goddamn, he hated it.

Taz shrugged, the movement sharp and dismissive. But before he could move away, she gripped his wrist.

'Tazio.' Her using his full name was her way of challenging him, saying that she wasn't going to be brushed off. He wanted to push her away, to keep her at arm's length, but couldn't.

Her eyes met his, as much inquisitive as sympathetic. 'Don't shut me out.'

He planted his feet, his back rigid, his chest tight. 'Why do you have to push?' he demanded.

Her fingers tightened ever so slightly on his arm. 'It was a simple question, Taz. A way for me to remind you that I'm here and ready to listen.'

The words hit him harder than they should have. Because they both knew she wasn't talking about the delayed shipment or him racing on Saturday. She was talking about all of it—the walls, the shields, the secrets buried deep. She was offering him the one thing he'd never allowed anyone: the chance to be seen, truly seen, for everything he was.

Taz opened his mouth, then closed it, unsure what to say. How did he explain that he was beyond fixing?

But he needed to regain lost ground, so he latched on to an easy out.

He raked his hair off his forehead. 'What do you want me to tell you? My standings in the championship are slipping, my lead is eroding. My mechanics are anxious because their parts aren't here, and that's stressful. I also have to make nice at a ball when I should be working on race strategy.'

'Why are you so determined to win a fourth championship? Is it because Alex didn't?'

So sharp. She saw too much, and as a person who'd spent his entire life hiding his emotions, her ability to peek over his walls terrified him.

'Partly.'

'Alex is dead, Taz. Nobody cares,' she stated, confused. He couldn't deny it: The most he'd get when he beat Alex's record would be a brief mention of his achievement by sports journalists. But that wasn't the point. How could he explain it was personal and precious, a way for him to stand in front of the memory of his father, and say that he mattered, he counted, that he was as worthy of space and attention as Alex? That they'd been wrong to ignore and discount him?

'I wish you'd talk to me, Taz.'

Didn't she get it? In just a few weeks, he'd told her more than he'd shared with anyone over the course of his life. 'I rarely talk to anyone, and I never talk to anyone about Alex. Ever.' His voice was harsh and clipped, every word coated with regret. 'I can't trust anyone.'

Her face tightened, and he knew he'd hurt her, saw it in the way she blinked the pain away. But Millie being Millie, she didn't crumble. She held her ground. 'Are you worried I'll say something? Fine. I'll sign an NDA. If anything gets out, sue me for everything I have. I'll repay you the million plus interest.' Her voice was steady, but there was steel in it, a fierce edge that told him she wasn't bluffing. 'But you need to know this. I will *never* betray you.'

The words hit harder than he wanted to admit, slicing through the panic that had been twisting in his gut for what felt like forever. She wasn't the problem. He was. The unfamiliar feelings she raised in him, the feeling of becoming more vulnerable with every moment he spent with her, terrified him.

Panic twisted his gut.

'You're competing with a ghost, Taz.'

He couldn't do this anymore. He dragged his hand over his face, hoping to wipe the tension away. He needed to regain control of himself and the conversation—immediately. Before he could speak, Millie did him a favour and changed the subject. 'So are you going to race on Saturday?'

He looked down at his cast-free hand. 'How did you know?'

She scoffed and rolled her eyes. 'Your cast is off, your lead is slipping, and you want to get back on the track.'

She turned, and he let her go. Watching her walk back into the penthouse, he mused on how he'd once considered their relationship uncomplicated, black-and-white. A fake couple in public, lovers in private.

The one thing he couldn't control—the one thing that threatened everything he thought he knew—was that she might, genuinely, care for him. And that despite his best efforts, he cared for her too. He might even be close to falling for her.

And that was too big a risk.

Because if he let her in, really let her in, she'd be a car he couldn't chase down, a crash he couldn't avoid. Loving her—and losing her, because love never stayed—would tear him apart.

But, God, he wasn't sure that he had enough courage to let her go.

They walked into the ballroom of Le Château du Ciel hotel, and Millie glanced at Taz. He seemed unimpressed by the unfiltered decadence of the best ballroom in the superrich principality. The ceiling was a masterpiece hand-painted with almost-naked gods and goddesses lounging on clouds, laughing down at the mortals beneath them. Impressive, oversize crystal chandeliers dripped from the frescoed ceiling, and the polished Italian marble floors gleamed like glass.

Mirrors on the walls were framed in intricate gold leaf. The floor-to-ceiling arched windows were outlined by velvet drapes in a deep, rich midnight blue. They were, in Millie's view, superfluous because the view of the city and Mediterranean beyond the balcony was incredible.

With her hand lodged in Taz's elbow, Millie looked around and noticed a piano sitting under a spotlight at the far end of the large room. A quartet played, but she couldn't hear any music above the chatter of the rich, famous and infamous. Waiters in white gloves glided through the crowd, offering crystal flutes of champagne and trays of hors d'oeuvres.

Millie caught their reflection in a mirror and cast a critical eye over her appearance. Her dress was deep purple, shot with silver. It hugged her in all the right places, its neckline dipping low enough to make it interesting, cinching at her waist before spilling into a dramatic skirt that showed a hint of her three-inch heels. Her makeup was understated, her hair pulled back into a smooth, sleek tail.

Taz in a tuxedo suited this ballroom like a sword did a scabbard. His classic black suit was exquisitely tailored, the sharp lines highlighting his broad shoulders and athletic build. The crisp white shirt was a stark contrast to his tanned face and neck, and his three-day dark stubble was a reminder to everyone that he was, despite his wealth, a rebel and a bad boy. He looked every inch the charming, untouchable, remote billionaire he was. Oh, his effortless, rakish smile was in place, but she could easily differentiate between Authentic Taz and Pretend Taz. His charm was frequently superficial, his urbanity a cloak he'd pulled on to fool the world.

Since their breakfast discussion in Italy about Alex, he'd been inching away, emotionally distancing himself. Oh, he was still a fantastic lover, devoted to her pleasure, but his conversation was less easy, his responses more measured and never impetuous. It was as if he was afraid to let something important or personal slip.

His retreat hurt more than Millie expected, and hearing the edge in his voice, something he probably wasn't even aware of, stung. His carefully constructed façade had solidified again, she could see it in the set of his jaw, the way his eyes quickly moved from hers when they spoke. His emotional walls were higher than before, and those flashes of vulnerability she'd seen in him were a thing of the past.

Was asking him about his brother such a big sin? Could he not trust that his secrets were safe with her? Her insecurities rushed back, hot and hard, punching and kicking in a relentless ambush. She didn't belong in this opulent ballroom and wasn't good enough to be hanging onto Taz's arm. She wasn't thin enough, pretty enough, vivacious or charming enough.

Recognising her spiralling thoughts, she locked her knees and pushed steel into her spine.

Stop.

Breathe.

Think.

Under her skirts, she stomped her foot, clad in its designer shoe. She loathed her self-doubt and cursed its return. *Remember how far you've come, Millie!* She'd managed to navigate this unfamiliar world, maybe not as effortlessly as her parents and Taz did, but she hadn't embarrassed herself. Nobody, not the press or her colleagues at De Rossi Racing, questioned whether she was good enough to be with Taz. They assumed she was. So why was she doubting herself? Was it Taz's inability or unwillingness to open up and talk to her that made her question herself and wonder if she was sufficiently strong, witty and smart to be his partner, to stand by his side?

It had been his choice not to open up; she'd done nothing wrong. Just like she wasn't defective or substandard because she felt uncomfortable with her parents' pursuit of publicity. Taz and her parents were responsible for their own choices, and she for hers.

While she'd never be a society hostess, she had come a long way, and balls, cocktail parties and red carpets didn't make her quake in her heels anymore. Professionally, in terms of her and Taz's agreement, she'd done her job. She'd rehabilitated his reputation and built it back up in the media after weeks of scandal and bad press. Taz was now seen in a more favourable light, and when he announced he was racing this weekend, the press would go wild. She'd already prepared the press releases, ready to go as soon as he gave her the green light. He'd be fine.

But would she?

Probably, eventually, but she'd have to live with a strange emptiness deep in her soul. She liked her work and enjoyed being good at it, but what she really wanted—what she craved—was simple: to hold Taz's full attention, to be the focus of it. She wanted to be the one person who mattered, apart from and beyond the reputation he was rebuilding or the races he was winning.

Yes, she wanted to stay in his world, but not for the flashing cameras, the extravagant cars or clothes or red carpets. She no longer needed to prove she was worthy, to her parents or to herself. She was, simply because she was Millie. No, her motivation to stick with it was simple: she wanted to be wherever Taz was.

But Taz didn't want what she did; he wasn't looking for anything permanent. He liked the thrill of a lover, but that was where it ended. He couldn't give her what she needed. Her choice was simple: She could either walk away or watch the man she was falling for, the man she loved, leave by degrees.

Either way, she'd end up alone…

'Millie, I asked whether you wanted another drink.'

Taz's annoyance cut through her reverie, and she jerked. 'Uh… I'm fine, thanks.'

Taz plucked her glass from her hand and placed it on the tray of a passing waiter. He raked his hand through his hair and dropped a low-pitched for-her-ears-only F-bomb.

'Problem?' she asked.

He sighed, and a muscle in his jaw ticked. He put his back to the room, and his expression morphed from geniality to annoyance. 'All this?' His gesture encompassed the glittering crowd, the music and the chattering crowd. 'It's a waste of time. I should be at the track, preparing.'

She pulled his jacket sleeve back and squinted at his

Rolex. 'Give it another two hours and you can slip out,' Millie told him. She saw his stubborn face and sighed. 'You agreed to attend, Taz. Your presence and support are *important*.'

His mouth tightened. 'The only thing that matters is what happens on the track. Winning is everything.'

He was so single-minded, and now that he could resume racing, he'd reverted to being selfish about his time. His view had narrowed, and only racing held his interest. Many people, including her, had worked overtime to make this event happen. And the charities were going to get a very healthy injection of funds into their war chest. But all the work they'd done, all the money they'd raised, meant nothing to Taz.

Had he ever seen the real value in aligning himself with the charities, beyond rehabilitating his reputation and winning the championship? Had she fooled herself into thinking he was a better man than he was?

And if he couldn't even value this event, he certainly didn't value her and the work she'd put in on his behalf. Everything, every atom of his being, was focused on and directed at being a four-time championship winner. There was no space in his life for her.

Millie's breath caught in her throat, and her heart wanted to slink out of her chest. She was nothing more than a brief blip in his world of cars and fame and championship glory.

But she was too far in. She'd fallen too hard, too fast and too deep. She hadn't quite hit rock bottom yet, but she knew when she did, it was going to hurt like hell.

Millie walked into Taz's hotel suite ahead of him, his words reverberating through her head. *Winning is everything.*

Winning couldn't be more important than human connections, friendships and relationships. Could it be the only thing that mattered? Surely not.

'You seem distracted,' Taz said, pulling his bowtie loose and shrugging out of his jacket.

Millie kicked off her heels, and the hem of her dress pooled on the floor. She watched him walk over to the credenza holding a variety of spirits. He lifted a crystal decanter. 'Cognac. Do you want one?'

No. What she wanted was to understand this man. To discover what made him tick. She sat on the edge of the couch and rested her forearms on her knees. Taz walked over to the open doors leading to the balcony and infinity pool, leaned against its frame and sipped his drink. Behind him, the lights of the city twinkled with a certain smugness, confident of its place as one of the richest cities in the world.

'Did you mean what you said earlier?' she asked. Tension immediately slid into the muscles of his shoulders and broad back, and his stance widened. He lifted his glass to his lips, but he didn't turn to face her.

'Remind me...' he murmured.

This was the emotional equivalent of being slathered in volcanic-hot wax. 'You said that winning was everything, that nothing else mattered.'

He lifted one shoulder in a casual shrug. She was normally slow to anger, but his small, too-casual dismissal of her question annoyed her. Or was she really angry that, while she'd been falling for him, his priority was winning his fourth championship?

Had she seen what she wanted to see? The thought ratcheted up her temper. 'Do you believe nothing else is important? You've completed your five charity events, Taz, and raised millions for various charities. You've made a discernible difference in people's lives, and that's also worth celebrating,' she protested, desperate for his reassurance.

Was she looking for validation, for him to admit there was more to life than the De Rossi Racing team? Because if he couldn't, then what did that mean for her? It meant she'd made no impact on his life, that she was another fleeting presence, another speed bump hampering his race to victory. She'd felt like that before—too many times to count. Her entire life, she'd battled the fear that she was unworthy of being seen or valued. She wanted to matter to him—not because of what she could do for him but because of who she was. Because she was Millie.

But how much longer could she keep hoping, keep believing that she might be the exception to his ironclad rule, when everything about him screamed that she wasn't?

He turned around slowly and resumed his same stance, his other shoulder pressed into the wall. 'I stand by what I said. Winning my fourth championship is all that matters, the only thing on my mind. Nothing, not my reputation or me playing ambassador for those charities or—' he hesitated, and in her mind she filled in the missing, unspoken word. He'd been about to say *you* and pulled back.

He looked down into his empty glass. 'Winning is everything, Millie. It *has* to be.'

His words were the confirmation of all her fears. Her temper spiked and revved, fast and high. With her parents she normally backed down and away, never able to find the words to hit back, to defend herself. But tonight, the words were searing her tongue, climbing over each other to be released. How dare he dismiss her and what they'd done, her hard work and the time they'd shared? She'd shared her body with him, told him about Ben, cried in his arms.

He was pretending that none of that meant anything. That she didn't mean anything to him. She wouldn't stand for it.

Not today. Not anymore.

'No. There is more to life than winning, Taz,' she announced, pushing herself to her feet, emboldened by the surprise in his eyes and the shock on his face.

'Like what?' he drawled.

'Like making a difference, using your influence and status to shine a light on causes that need to be in the spotlight!'

He released a dismissive scoff. 'Like my brother did? Yes, he was Saint Alex in public and the devil in private.'

She waited for him to say more, and when he didn't she threw up her hands in frustration. 'You can't throw out statements like that and not explain!'

'I can. And don't raise your voice to me.'

His soft command sent her temper rocketing. 'Either explain or stop demeaning your brother.' Still nothing. Millie hauled in a deep breath and her courage. She couldn't back down now. 'Then, you leave me with no choice but to believe you are the insecure younger brother who can never keep up. That's why you act out, right? Because you can't compete.'

God, she ached. She knew that wasn't true, and every bit of her wanted him to let down those shields, to get real, to engage. But his stoic, untouchable force field stayed in place, and she wanted to howl.

But shouting would only cause him to shut down, and she needed to break through. She needed to keep her wits because, after all, she was going to war for his soul. A war she'd probably lose, but she couldn't help herself. She was done staying quiet, hanging back, swallowing her opinions and her feelings.

'We've accomplished something amazing, and I am furious that you can dismiss me and the work we've done together so easily. I've worked long, hard hours to rehab your reputation—'

'I never asked you to do it for free. You did get a million pounds out of the deal.'

How dare he make her feel so cheap. She sucked in a deep breath, then another. 'The world does not revolve around you, Taz. People work really hard, I've worked really hard to—'

'Actually, it does, Millie. I've deliberately created a life and business that does. Racing is my world.'

Her shoulders slumped. He only ever looked at life, at people, in relation to how they affected his ambitions, race standings and the championship he was so desperate to win. He had no desire or intention to make space for her or anything outside of racing. His career and business were all he cared about.

That was his choice. All she could control was her reaction.

And it was time to face reality.

She'd been pushed aside, made to feel like she was insignificant long enough. He might be an in-front-of-the-cameras man and she a behind-the-scenes woman, but she was still consequential, she was important. She had things to do and say and a life to live. His world might revolve around the De Rossi brand, but hers didn't. She wanted something more, something real, a complete man, not someone who would only share a sliver of his life, mind and soul. It wasn't enough.

She had to get out now, while she could. Before she slid back into believing that her place would always be standing in the shadow of someone more brilliant than her.

Millie pushed back her shoulders and gathered the tattered remains of her courage. 'If that's the way you feel, then I guess this is as good a time as any to tell you that I can't do this anymore, Taz.'

His eyes narrowed, trying to make sense of her words, to figure out where she was going with this. 'I'm resigning. I will stay until after the race tomorrow, but on Monday, I will no longer be running your PR or acting as your press officer. Or posing as your girlfriend. If you don't do something asinine, like losing your temper or hooking up with Phoebe again, your reputation should hold steady.'

He jerked at her words and rubbed his hand over his face. 'Look, I admit that we both said some things—'

She held up her hand. 'Don't… This isn't a negotiation, Taz. I'm done. *We're* done.'

'Millie—'

'I'm going to sleep in the bedroom, Taz. You can sleep alone and dream about the race. Maybe you'll consider what I said before, that you are racing against a ghost.' Gathering up her dignity, Millie headed for the bedroom, cradling her battered heart. At the last moment, she stopped and turned back.

'And in case you don't know this…the ghost will always win.'

CHAPTER THIRTEEN

COMPETING WITH A GHOST.

Millie's words roared through his head, and his stomach roiled, filled with anxiety, anger and a healthy dose of self-loathing. The thought of Millie leaving made his blood run hot, then cold, and then stop running entirely. The urge to run down the passage and storm into the bedroom, to gather her to him and rain kisses and apologies on her, was as strong as his urge to win his fourth championship.

He couldn't imagine her not being there and didn't know how he was going to fill the Millie-sized hole in his life. But he also couldn't allow his feelings to get in the way of what he needed to accomplish. He paced the area in front of the open door, his heart rate erratic. He'd given himself a little more leeway because he wasn't racing and had stepped away, just a fraction, but now that his hand was better and he could drive... That meant focusing on what was truly important. And that was racing.

Reaching the pinnacle of this sport, being the very best of the best, being spoken about in the same reverent terms as the greats, required insane levels of selfishness and dedication. Why couldn't Millie understand that he'd allow nothing to come between him and his goals, between him and racing? That if he shifted his focus an inch left or right, he might miss something crucial. And he wasn't only talking about his skills on the track but his management and leadership skills. This industry was filled with bright and ambitious people, men and women who would pounce on his smallest mistake. Being self-absorbed was a strength, not a weakness.

Not having any distractions was another.

He couldn't, wouldn't, let go of his focus on his dream for a woman. Not even for a woman who knew him as well as Millie did. She got him, on levels he never expected, but was she special enough for him to sacrifice his dream? No. Nobody was. Nobody would ever be.

His father never believed in him, so he had to believe in himself. Alex never respected him, so he had to have enough self-respect for both of them. He'd worked hard to get to where he was, battled his father's lack of belief and support and fought for his place in the sun, and he wouldn't surrender the ground he'd gained.

Especially not for something as vague as love. Because love was too indefinable, too much like mist fighting the sun. It couldn't be bottled or contained, anchored or corralled. Love could morph, leave; love could change. He needed ironclad guarantees.

Maybe it was better if Millie faded from his life, both business and personal. If she did, he could go back to being the driven, ambitious, fully focused boss he'd always been. He'd win the championship. It would be a hard battle, but he was the personification of determination—and then he'd settle on a new challenge, a new goal. Something fresh to chase, a mountain—literally or metaphorically—to climb.

A new race to win.

Millie stood in the press room, her thumb flicking against her front teeth as she watched the Monaco race on the big screen TV. Her heart was in her mouth because Taz was having, as the commentators kept repeating, an *inconsis-*

tent race. There were moments of brilliance, followed by him taking a stupid risk, and then him not taking what they called *easy wins*. They were perplexed by his actions and worried he'd slip farther down the field.

Winning the race was impossible. A podium finish the longest of shots.

Her heart ached for him. Millie looked at her laptop bag, mentally reviewing everything she needed to do before exiting Taz's life tomorrow. She had struggled to write the press release stating she and Taz were splitting up, eventually settling on the tried and true *We're parting to concentrate on our careers, but we will remain good friends* hogwash. She had press releases ready to go whether he won, lost or didn't feature in this race—although the last option looked more and more likely.

Whenever she thought of Taz, it felt like her heart was on fire, every beat a struggle. Leaving him felt like she was ripping her soul in half, but what choice did she have? Staying meant questioning every moment with him, his every word, every look. Wondering if she was a priority in his life, and if he could ever love her as much as he loved racing.

And she already knew the answer. He couldn't.

She had to walk because, while she was happy not to stand in the world's spotlight, she needed to stand in his, to have his focus and attention on her. She couldn't be an afterthought. But Taz didn't care enough to make room for her in his life. She'd played her part and restored his reputation which helped his brand. She'd been the perfect fake girlfriend, and they'd enjoyed a mutually satisfying fling.

She'd gotten as much as she could from him. She'd seen a few cracks in his emotional suit of armour, fleeting moments of realness, but they didn't occur often enough, or last long enough, to convince her to stay. There were depths to him she would never know or be able to explore because he'd deliberately shut himself off from her. There was nothing she could say or do to change that.

She loved him. But love wasn't enough. Not when it was one-sided. Not when she was willing to give him her heart, her everything, and he couldn't—or wouldn't—do the same.

Leaving him was the hardest thing she'd ever done, but she had to. Because the only thing worse than walking away was staying and losing herself in the process.

Her phone pinged, and Millie pulled it from her back pocket. She squinted at the screen, seeing that her mum had texted her. That was unusual, as Millie always reached out first. They hadn't had any contact for seven or eight months.

Without opening the message, she instinctively knew what it would say, what they wanted—and that was to bask in the publicity surrounding her and Taz. Her mother didn't disappoint.

Millie, darling. We'll all be joining you in Montreal next week. Book us rooms in the same hotel you are staying with your delicious Taz. Suites preferably. Make a reservation at Vin Mon Lapin, Taz can pay.

Millie didn't hesitate, didn't second-guess herself. Her fingers flew across the keypad as she banged out her short response.

I'm not an idiot, Mum. I know I wouldn't have heard from you had I not been dating Taz De Rossi.

She wasn't anymore, but her mother didn't need to know that.

I'm *not* your ticket to publicity, I'm barely your daughter. Don't come.

Millie saw that her mother was typing a message but decided she wouldn't read it. She wasn't in the mood to be gaslighted today. Millie shoved her phone into the back pocket of her jeans, surprised at how calm she was. Had she finally learned how to emotionally disengage? To let her mum's demands and criticisms roll off her back?

Compared to losing Taz, her family's disapproval barely registered. She'd wasted enough time and energy and was done with trying to please or impress them. She was worthwhile, with or without their approval. She'd found herself, finally saw herself as Ben did. She was smart, capable and interesting, comfortable in her skin and able to walk into ballrooms or boardrooms. She no longer needed their, or anyone's, approval.

Even if Taz couldn't love her, or make space for her in his life, she was *enough*. Excitement in the commentator's voice pulled her attention back to the screen. Instead of focusing on the leader, a driver ranked way below Taz and the other contenders for the championship, the cameras were on Taz's car as he weaved in and out of the pack in the middle of the field. The standings board flashed up on the screen, and Taz had jumped from eleventh to eighth, then to fifth, and now he was in fourth place. He was on the tail of his arch-rival and beating him would give him points in the leadership race.

'If De Rossi keeps driving like this, with verve and confidence, he might take this race. Exceptional driving by an exceptional racer,' said the race analyst.

He certainly had guts, flair and focus. Millie kept her eyes glued to the screen, her heart in her mouth. She'd spend the rest of her life wishing things between them could've been different, that they could've found a way to make it work, but she wanted him to succeed.

She wanted him to win the championship because *he*

wanted it. The crowd roared as Taz overtook his rival, and the commentators and crowd went into hyperdrive. The competitor regained the lead, and his supporters screamed with excitement. The two cars stayed bumper to bumper for the next few laps with Taz fighting for third place. There were a few laps to go, ten, fifteen, and Millie knew this race would go down as one of Taz's greatest.

He'd fought hard, given everything he had to it. She wished he felt the same way about her.

Around one of the longer corners, Taz saw the smallest gap to overtake the driver and gunned his car. His rival closed the gap abruptly, and Taz was between his car and the barrier, his car scraping along the concrete bollard. Taz hung on, trying to keep control of his bullet-fast car, but his rear slid sideways. He spun out, his back clipping his rival's bumper as they headed into the straight. Both cars spun twice, Taz spun again, and the commentators announced the suspension of the race. As both competitors came to a stop, the announcers started discussing who was at fault. Had Taz misjudged the gap he'd tried to squeeze through, and had it been too small? Or had the other driver been too overzealous in trying to squeeze Taz out?

What did it matter? Both men were out of the race, both drivers failed to secure much-needed points. Both would be hot-as-hell furious. Millie, panicking, ran out of the press room and sprinted to the area where his race engineers sat on the pit wall, a structure located against the fence between the pit lane and the main straight. They were in direct communication with Taz, and they would know if he was okay.

Please don't let Taz do anything stupid. Please don't let Taz lose his temper.

Millie, and the world, watched as Taz opened his door and climbed out the window of his car. What was he going to do?

* * *

Taz kept his eyes open as the car spun around, the crowds a blur and the track flipping in and out of his vision.

This, *again*. Once was unlucky, twice was becoming a habit.

As the car slowed down and he could tell he wasn't going to hit anything hard like a concrete bollard, his heart rate dropped and his grip on the wheel loosened. Another day at the office.

When the world stopped spinning, Taz rested his head on his hands on the wheel and thought he was getting a little sick of being a superfast spinning top. This could've ended badly; he could've woken up in the hospital. Or dead. And this time there would've been no Millie in his hospital room. No Millie at all.

He looked around, thinking for the first time that it was just a race, just a place in a championship that no one would care about in a few years. He wouldn't have kids or grandkids to boast about him being an ace driver, all he would have was an empire no one but him cared about.

Empires and money didn't keep you warm at night, couldn't make you laugh, weren't there when you were sick and sad or needed someone to celebrate with.

Empires crumbled. And people who tied themselves to empires did too.

He'd cheated death twice in a car lately, and for what? To prove to himself that he was better than Alex. It was such BS: He *was* better than Alex. He was as good a driver as him, and a better businessman than his dad as he'd grown the De Rossi name into a brand worth billions.

But more than that, he hadn't built it all on a lie. He wasn't one person in public and another in private. He didn't do Class A drugs, and he didn't share them with too-young girls. He respected women. He was a demanding boss, but not overly so. Okay, maybe he was, but his employees were the best paid in the business and received huge perks.

People clamoured to join his team because he had a reputation for excellence. Yes, his reputation had needed work, and Millie had restored some of its lustre. He intended to keep it that way. Oh, he'd never be Alex-in-public perfect, but he didn't need to be.

Two crashes later, and he was done trying to prove that he was better than his brother.

It was time to say goodbye to him, to loosen the hold he and their father had on his thoughts and life. And yeah, it was time to create his legacy and to live his own life. Hopefully with Millie. If she'd forgive him for being a selfish, stubborn, self-absorbed ass.

But first, he needed to exit this car, which was hotter than the seventh circle of hell. Taz pushed his seat back, giving him a few more inches between his torso and the wheel, and pulled a lever to release the steering wheel. After dropping it onto the grass through his open window, he disconnected his harness and hauled his tense body out of the car.

His race engineer's voice cut through the buzz in his head. 'Taz, are you okay?'

He wasn't hurt, but every muscle in his body, thanks to the Gs he'd experienced, ached. 'Bit shaken, but okay.'

He heard Len's sigh of relief. 'Was it your fault or his?' he asked.

Taz considered his question, as he watched Jean-Pierre exit his car and remove his helmet. 'Does it matter? The result is the same.'

Taz looked around. The race had stopped, and the crowd was quiet; it seemed like everyone was holding their breath. He caught Jean-Pierre's wariness and realised the crowd was waiting for his response, to see how he'd deal with this latest track setback.

And because he was Taz De Rossi, he chose a response no one expected. Tucking his helmet under his arm, he walked over to Jean-Pierre and held out his hand. Surprise and shock jumped into his eyes but the man, thank God, clasped his hand.

They didn't speak, neither choosing to claim responsibility, but neither casting blame either. They met as equals, silently agreeing to instil some decency and sportsmanship into the sport and the moment.

The crowd roared its approval, and Taz took the moment to speak into his headset. 'Len, can you get a message to Millie?' he asked, his heart in his throat.

'She's standing right next to me.'

'Give her a headset,' Taz ordered. When he heard Millie's breathy, slightly panicky demand to know if he was hurt, he knew exactly what he should do.

'Mils, I need you at the press conference.'

He thought he heard her sigh of disappointment, but she rallied well and told him she'd manage it all. 'No, you don't get it,' he insisted. 'I need you there. With *me*.'

'Okay,' she replied, and he knew she didn't understand what he was trying to say. But he couldn't talk openly, not when half the crew was listening. He thought fast and said the only thing he could, a phrase nobody but her would understand. 'Mils, you were right. I'm done competing against ghosts.'

Millie stood in front of the window of their hotel suite. It was late, and the sun had long slipped behind the horizon, casting a navy pall over the city, her thoughts spinning.

She'd accompanied Taz to the press conference, but after a quick hug and him squeezing her hand, they hadn't managed to talk, mostly because he'd been besieged. It hadn't been the right time or place to talk, but it was enough for her to know that he wanted her there. Not as his PR person or press officer, but as his lover, his support system.

That was what he meant, *right*? Or had she misunderstood him?

Millie sent a nervous look down the passage of the suite, wondering how long Taz would be in the shower. When he'd led her into his suite, he'd asked her to wait, telling her he needed a little time to decompress and to wash the day away.

She walked over to the bar, lifted a decanter and poured two fingers into a crystal tumbler. The whisky was smooth and sensuous as it slid down her throat. Pausing in front of the window, she rested her hand on the cool glass and wondered what his cryptic message had meant. Could it be that he'd reconsidered her role in his life? Or was she setting herself up for more hurt?

Taz snagged the glass from her hand and lifted it to his lips. His bare feet accounted for his silent approach. Lowering the glass, he lifted his hand and gently, using his index finger, pulled a strand of hair off her cheek and tucked it behind her ear in a tender gesture.

'Let's sit, Mils,' he suggested, taking her hand and leading her over to the couch. She sat facing the view, and Taz sat next to her, his thigh and shoulder pressing against hers. He'd changed into a slouchy navy cotton sweater and straight-legged white cotton pants and hadn't bothered to shave or brush his messy hair. He looked disreputable and hot.

Millie swallowed and took a series of mental snapshots to remember later.

Taz leaned back, his palms on the wide couch behind him. 'It's been a hell of a day,' he said, and she heard the exhaustion in his voice.

'Hell of a day,' she echoed. 'How are you feeling after your crash?'

She felt his shoulder rise and fall. 'My muscles are a bit sore from tensing when I spun out, but I'm fine.'

Should she compliment him on the way he'd handled the crash and avoided a confrontation with his rival? She might as well; it wasn't like he could fire her. Well, he could, but she'd already told him she would be gone in the morning. 'You handled the disappointment well,' she murmured.

'Mmm, but two crashes in a row is ridiculous,' he muttered. 'And before you ask, my hand is fine.'

That was going to have been her next question. Having nothing else to say, she stared at the slumberous sea, conscious of the tension between them. Why was she here? What did he want? But her pride, the little she had left, wouldn't let her ask. He'd either tell her or he wouldn't. She was done begging people to let her in.

'My dad wasn't interested in me,' Taz said, his voice soft. 'I was my mum's kid, and I rarely saw him, and he and Alex were a tight unit. When my mum died when I was six, I was... *forgotten* is a good word. Ignored too. I was the third wheel.'

Millie turned to face him, blindsided by his out-of-the-blue-statement and openness. She lifted her thigh onto the couch. 'Why are you telling me this now, Taz?'

He pushed his fingers into his damp hair. 'Because you're the only one I *can* tell, Mils.'

Okay, but she was leaving in the morning. Why now?

She waited for him to speak, her eyes on his face. He looked uncomfortable but also determined, like he had a rotten tooth poisoning his system.

'Alex wasn't the charming, jovial, great guy everyone thought he was.' His words left his mouth in a rush as if he couldn't get them out fast enough. He shoved his hand into his hair and tugged the expertly cut strands. 'He was difficult, rude and often obnoxious. Entitled.'

Misery skittered across Taz's face. 'But in my father's eyes, he could do no wrong. His behaviour was excused because of his extraordinary talent at throwing cars around the track.'

It was so strange to hear about this other side of the sports hero. Knowing how hard it was for him to open up, to share this with her, Millie placed her hand on his knee and squeezed. She was still processing his words when Taz spoke again. 'I wanted to go to the same driving academy Alex attended, but my father refused to pay. I continued to beg, he continued to say no. I think he got a kick out of my desperation because, more than anything, I wanted to race.' Taz rubbed the back of his neck. 'I begged, pleaded, ranted, raged, and he eventually gave in. I think he was desperate to get me to shut up.'

He'd been desperate to go to such lengths to push his father into giving him the same opportunity he had Alex. He must've felt so lonely, battered by being consistently rejected. Her heart ached for the boy he'd been.

'My father caved. I started in F3, then was given a chance with another team at F1 level. I only moved to the De Rossi team because Ben died, and the press gave my father a hard time about not employing his other talented son.' She heard the bitterness in his voice and understood it. She'd be bitter too.

Taz fiddled with the strap of his expensive watch and twisted his leather and silver bracelet around his wrist. He looked nervous, his knee was bouncing up and down, and Millie laid her hand on his arm.

This was hard for him, and he was worried about saying too much. 'I'm still happy to sign that NDA,' she murmured, nuclear-strike serious.

'I wouldn't tell you this if I didn't trust you completely, Millie,' he replied. He held her eyes, and Millie felt like she was taking possession of his heart and soul. She tried to dislodge the tight ball in her throat by swallowing. Something was happening between them, but she wasn't sure what.

'I need to tell you about the night he died.'

She shook her head. Discussing Alex was painful, and he'd endured enough. 'You don't, Taz, because everyone knows that he slipped and hit his head.'

He released a half laugh, half snort and slid his fingers between hers, his grip tight. 'That was the end result, Millie. Nobody but my father's very expensive attorney and I know what happened before that. I want to tell you. Alex flew to New York for the weekend. His fiancée was away. He did that often. He called it Alex Time. Alex dropping off the grid was commonplace, and everyone figured he spent the weekend on his own, decompressing.' Taz dropped his head and stared at the floor. 'That weekend in New York, he didn't know my dad was staying in the Upper West Side house, that he was upstairs.'

Millie bit her lip. What was he about to tell her?

'My father heard a scream, came downstairs and saw a teenager standing in the kitchen. She was young, half-undressed and stoned. There were coke lines on the table, and they'd been drinking. She was crying. He asked where Alex was, and she pointed to him. He was on the floor. She told him he'd run to answer his phone, slipped and cracked his head open on the edge of the marble counter.' He rubbed his hand over his face. 'My dad held him while he died.'

Millie wiped away a tear. The pain in his voice made her heart ache.

In a monotone, Taz went on to explain that his dad had called his lawyer instead of 911. The attorney took him upstairs and when he allowed Matteo downstairs later, there was no sign of the drugs, alcohol or the girl. The first responders and Alex's body were gone, and the house had been cleaned. People had been paid off.

Matteo's simple explanation—that he came downstairs and found Alex on the floor with a cracked head—was accepted. It was the truth, but not the *whole* truth. After Matteo suffered his first stroke that night, somebody had been required to make decisions, to run the De Rossi empire, and he'd stepped up. When Matteo had died, Taz became the keeper of his and Alex's secrets.

Millie wrapped her arms as far as they could go around Taz's shoulders and hugged him. He buried his face in her neck for less than a minute before pulling back. 'Don't cry for someone you didn't know, Mils. It breaks my heart.'

Millie swiped her hand over her face. 'I'm crying for *you*! Nobody should have to go through that.'

He cradled her face in his hands and wiped away her tears with his thumbs. 'Do you know why I told you my biggest secret, Millie?'

She looked into his eyes, so tender, so sincere, his expression so wide open, and shook her head. 'No, I have no idea,' she whispered.

'Partly because I want you to know everything about me, both good and bad. I've never wanted that before, have always put a wall up between myself and everyone else, shown them what I wanted them to see. But it's also because I trust you, Millie. You're the first person I've told, and you'll be the last.' He smiled and kissed her nose. 'I don't want us to have any secrets going forward.'

'Going forward?' She sounded like a parrot but couldn't help it. She was struggling to catch up.

He stroked her cheek. 'You're the only one for me, Millie. You're my championship, my ultimate win. Nothing compares to having you in my life.'

She stared at him, unblinking. What was happening right now?

'Life isn't about winning races or championships or fame and fortune. Life is seeing your lovely face every morning, being able to look at you when my temper spikes but you smile and all the frustration fades away. It's about making love with you and maybe, one day, making the family neither of us had.'

Millie held his wrists, unable to believe what he was saying. She lifted an eyebrow. 'Want to run that by me again?' She needed him to keep explaining until it made sense.

His open smile liquified her knees. 'I want to be better than the man I was before, Mils. Since meeting you, I've had to up my game, and that's been the best gift anyone could've given me. I want to be a better friend, boss, partner and lover.' He sent her a look so full of admiration, love and sincerity that her knees would have buckled if she'd been standing. 'You're real and lovely and kind, occasionally feisty, and so damn patient.'

'You forgot *good in bed*.' She had to joke because if she didn't, she'd start to cry again.

His eyes turned to liquid silver. 'You're amazing in bed.' He lifted her hand and kissed the back of her knuckles. 'And when you look at me like that, your eyes a little purple, a lot hot, I can't think about anything but getting you naked.'

She reached for him, but he shook his head and scooted down the couch, out of her reach. He held his hands up, palms facing her. 'I've still got things to say.'

There was *more*?

Taz rubbed the back of his neck. 'In my safe in my apartment in London is my mum's engagement ring. She loved it, and I want to give it to you.'

She slapped her hand on her heart. 'Oh, that's—' Wait, *what*? Why did he want to give her his mum's ring?

Taz moved off the couch and went down on one knee. What was he doing? He looked nervous, unsure. He was putting himself out there....*way* out there. Tears burned her eyes. It was so unlike Taz.

He swallowed, his cheeks pink beneath his olive skin. 'Millie, I love you. Will you be my wife?'

She cocked her head, happiness bubbling inside her. 'Pretend wife, or real wife?' she asked, a part of her needing to make sure he wasn't joking.

'My very-real, stay-with-me-forever and keep-me-out-of-trouble wife.' He looked down at the hard floor and lifted an eyebrow. 'This is the most uncomfortable position known to man, so a quick answer would be appreciated.'

She leaned forward and flung her arms around his neck. She was loved, and she'd found herself and her place. Best of all, she'd found herself before she'd found her man. She knew who she was, and that was everything.

'Yes, I'll marry you, Taz.'

Taz rested his forehead against hers. 'Thank God,' he murmured, his lips claiming hers. After a tender kiss, he pulled back and cradled the side of her face in his palm. 'You, this...it's everything. Nothing will top this moment, Millie.'

'Not even winning a fourth championship?'

Taz smiled at her. 'Not even close, sweetheart.' His voice cracked with emotion as the last of his shields disintegrated and his emotional walls collapsed. 'You're...you're my every breath, my future, the mother of my children, my best friend. God, you're *everything*.'

She was someone's—no, Taz's *everything*. And for the first time, Millie's world, and life, made complete sense.

EPILOGUE

Abu Dhabi

MILLIE STOOD IN the centre of the De Rossi Racing crew, oblivious to the celebrations happening around her. Droplets of sprayed champagne landed on her face and mingled with her tears. It was the last race of the season, and Taz, despite racing his heart out, had ended the year with the same number of points as his closest rival. But because Jean-Pierre won more races over the season, he'd snatched the world championship title from Taz at the very last moment.

De Rossi Racing winning the Constructors' Championship was great news, and Taz would be happy with that, but she'd wanted the fourth championship for him. Biting her lip, Millie watched Taz pose for photographs on the podium, looking festive and happy, his smile wide. But her fiancé was exceptionally good at hiding his real feelings from everyone but her, and she knew there was pain behind his charming grin.

Because, despite telling her he was done competing with his brother, she knew a part of him still wanted to beat Alex's record. She stamped her foot, wishing she could loudly announce that Taz De Rossi was ten times the man his brother was…in every way that counted.

But she'd promised Taz she'd keep his secrets, so she

would. She wouldn't do anything, ever, to jeopardise their happiness.

Taz jumped off the stage and pushed through the people swarming him to stand in front of her. His hair was wet from the champagne, his grey eyes sparkling. He clasped her face in his hands and swiped his mouth across hers, feeding her a kiss full of love and heat…

Bending his head he spoke above the roaring crowd. 'You are looking a bit militant, my darling. What's up?'

She shook her head and wrapped her fingers around his wrist. 'I wanted you to win. You worked so hard, and you *deserved* to win.'

He shook his head, wrapped his arms around her and boosted her up. Her legs locked around his hips, and they were nose to nose, their focus on each other, both ignoring the cameras pointed in their direction.

'Are you thinking about what happened in New York?' he asked, his voice pitched just loud enough for her to hear.

She nodded and Taz shook his head. 'I'm done competing with him, Mils. I have been for months. I care about racing and the team, but it's not my reason for living anymore. You are, sweetheart.' He lifted his hand to drag his thumb over her cheekbone, to let it rest in the middle of her bottom lip. His eyes radiated sincerity, and Millie knew that he was well and truly done with competing with Alex. That their relationship, their amazing life, was all that mattered and was his highest priority.

She brushed her nose against his. Millie had no doubt how much she was loved, but because occasionally she needed a little additional assurance, in a teasing tone she said, 'Prove it.'

His eyes remained locked on hers, intensely determined, very Taz. 'I swear I will. Every day, for the rest of my life,

Mils. I also promise to love you more tomorrow than I did today, more the next day than I will tomorrow…you get the picture.'

That was a *lot* of love. Her eyes burned with unshed happy tears, and Millie pulled him closer. The world around them faded. The cameras, the noise, all of it disappeared as his mouth claimed hers, sealing his promises with a kiss that tasted like forever.

* * * * *

Did Fast-Track Dating Deception *leave you enthralled?*
Then don't miss Joss Wood's other dazzling stories!

The Nights She Spent with the CEO
The Baby Behind Their Marriage Merger
Hired for the Billionaire's Secret Son
A Nine-Month Deal with Her Husband
The Tycoon's Diamond Demand

Available now!

MILLS & BOON®

Coming next month

ENEMIES UNTIL AFTER HOURS
Natalie Anderson

Mia drew on a defensive smile and headed into Sante's office—leaving his door wide open behind her.

Trying to steady her heartbeat. The appalling thing was that increasingly her body responded with chaos to his proximity. It didn't seem to care that he was a heartless jerk who'd betrayed her brother, her body just wanted his near. So, she was ignoring her body. Controlling it.

'You've screwed up my scheduling.' He glared at her.

'Where?'

He jabbed a finger at the screen, and she was forced to round his desk to study it. Big mistake. There was nowhere near enough of a barrier between them and she desperately needed to calm her overexcited response.

'You've blocked out a significant portion of my day tomorrow.'

She leaned closer and he turned his head toward her, meaning his mouth was only inches from hers. It was *searingly* intimate. It would take nothing to lower hers and—

What the hell was she thinking? Why had the idea to kiss him popped into her head? She stared into his brown eyes for three seconds too long.

Continue reading

ENEMIES UNTIL AFTER HOURS
Natalie Anderson

Available next month
millsandboon.co.uk

COMING SOON!

We really hope you enjoyed reading this book.
If you're looking for more romance
be sure to head to the shops when
new books are available on

Thursday 26th February

To see which titles are coming soon, please visit
millsandboon.co.uk/nextmonth

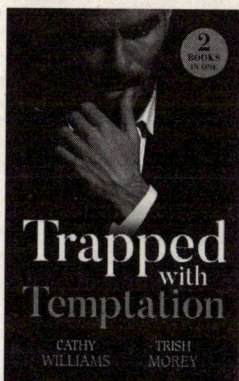

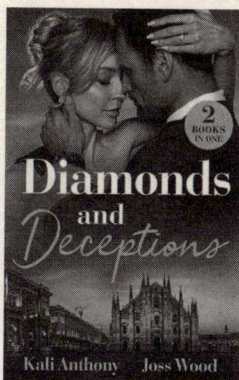

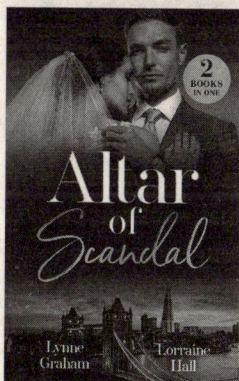

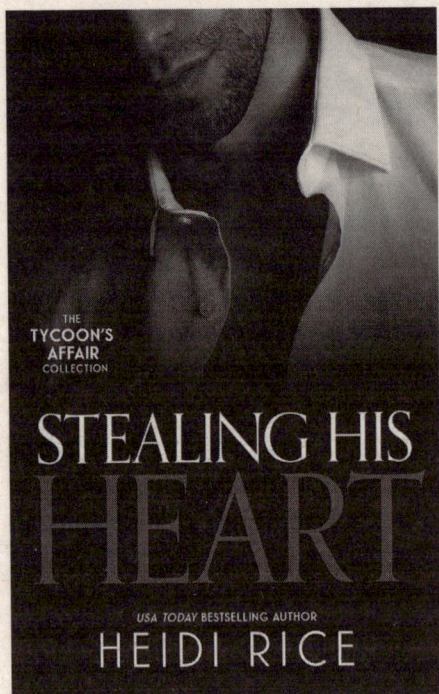

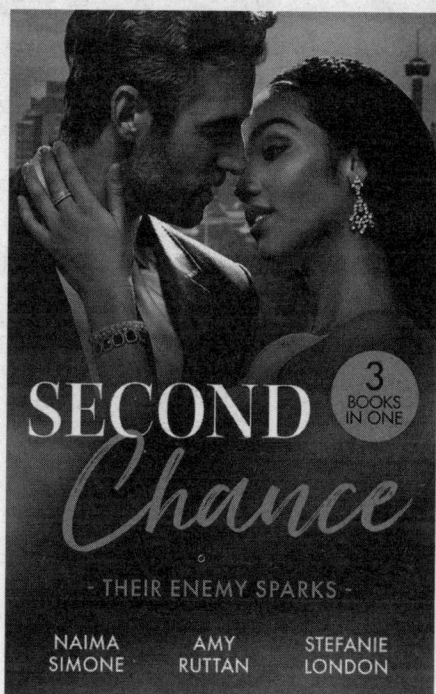

LET'S TALK

Romance

For exclusive extracts, competitions and special offers, find us online:

- **f** MillsandBoon
- **X** @MillsandBoon
- **⊙** @MillsandBoonUK
- **♪** @MillsandBoonUK

Get in touch on 01413 063 232